MICHAEL ARDITTI

Unity

MICHAEL ARDITTI

Unity

Reflections
on the personalities and politics behind
Wolfram Meier's legendary lost film

Published in 2005 by
The Maia Press Limited
82 Forest Road
London E8 3BH
www.maiapress.com

ISBN 1 904559 12 3

A CIP catalogue record for this book is available
from the British Library

Printed and bound in Great Britain by Thanet Press

For Luke Dent

(21.2.1955–15.4.2001)

'And have no fellowship with the unfruitful works of darkness, but rather reprove them. For it is a shame even to speak of those things which are done of them in secret.'

St Paul

'He who fights with monsters might take care lest he thereby becomes a monster. And if you gaze for long into an abyss, the abyss gazes also into you.'

Kierkegaard

'If you don't love the character, then you can't play him.'

Laurence Olivier

'Whenever I hear the word culture, I reach for my pistol.'

Hermann Göring (attrib.)

Unity

CAST

Unity Mitford	Felicity Benthall
Diana Guinnesss	Geraldine Mortimer
Jessica Mitford	Carole Medhurst
Lord Redesdale	Gerald Mortimer
Lady Redesdale	Dora Manners
Sir Oswald Mosley	Liam Finch
Sir David St Clair Gainer	Hallam Bamforth
Brian Howard	Luke Dent
Adolf Hitler	Ralf Heyn / Wolfram Meier
Joseph Goebbels	Manfred Stückl
Magda Goebbels	Liesl Martins
Hermann Göring	Henry Faber
Emmy Göring	Renate Fischer
Julius Streicher	Dieter Reiss
Ernst Hanfstaengl	Helmuth Wissmann
Heinrich Hoffmann	Conrad Seitz
Erich Wielderman	Erich Leitner
Eva Braun	Luise Hermann
Eva Maria Baum	Hannelore Kessel
Elderly Jew	Per Lindau

Director	Wolfram Meier
Producer	Werner Kempe
Screenplay	Luke Dent
	(from his own play)
Executive Producer	Thomas Bücher
Director of Photography	Gerhard Korn
Music	Kurt Stolle
Production Designer	Heike von Stripp
Make-up Artist	Beate Pauli

Filmed on location in England and Germany, and at Bavaria Studios, Munich (August–October 1977)

Contents

Introduction

For a writer to have gone to university with an international terrorist is a mixed blessing. On the one hand, he feels pressure from both his publishers and himself to provide his unique slant on the story, on the other, a reluctance to reopen old wounds. So much nonsense has been printed about Felicity Benthall that I would dearly like to set the record straight. And yet a fear of what my investigations might uncover has so far restrained me. What if a chain of complicity reaches back to the chance remark of a college contemporary's – or, worse, of mine? What if an old acquaintance reveals Cambridge to have been as fertile a breeding-ground of fanaticism in the 1970s as it had been forty years before? I am caught between conflicting abstractions. Commitment to the truth contends with the determination to spare my friends – and, indeed, my whole generation – from further attacks.

The facts of the matter are plain. In October 1977, Felicity Benthall, a twenty-three-year-old English actress, attempted to blow up the diplomatic representatives of most of the United Nations at a service to commemorate the eleven Israeli athletes murdered at the Munich Olympics five years before. She succeeded only in killing herself, her uncle the British Ambassador, his deputy, two secret servicemen and the Polish chargé d'affaires. Immediately after her death, a statement was issued in Beirut by the Popular Front for the Liberation of Palestine claiming her as a martyr to its cause. Meanwhile, in Stuttgart, the Red Army Faction (otherwise known as the Baader-Meinhof group), the small band of revolutionary Marxists whose campaign of terror over the previous decade had plunged West Germany into its greatest political crisis since the end of the Second World War, also claimed that she was acting on its behalf.

Nowhere was the shock of the atrocity more deeply felt than among those who had known – or who thought that they had known – Felicity best. Try as we might, it was impossible to square the cynic who had drawled that all ideology was a bore with the fanatic who died for a principle that was, in every sense, foreign to her. Like any other observer – but with an added sense of frustration – we were left to wonder whether her behaviour had been driven by idealism or nihilism: whether she had been malevolent or mad. Moreover, by a coincidence which I decline to call an irony, she had been playing the role of Unity Mitford, the English aristocrat whose extremist views led her to fall in love with Hitler. The film, by Germany's foremost post-war director, Wolfram Meier, was then abandoned. Like Sternberg's *I Claudius* and Welles's *Don Quixote*, Meier's *Unity* has become one of cinema's most celebrated might-have-beens. The untimely deaths of many of the leading players have contributed to its legendary status, creating the cinematic equivalent of the curse of *Macbeth*.

That was clearly the opinion of the film's writer, Luke Dent, who, in the immediate aftermath of the attack, declared: 'I know now that a writer must take full responsibility for his ideas, like a scientist with the H-bomb. There is certain research that is too dangerous to publish. It should be left in the study or the lab.'[1] My own reluctance to engage too closely with Felicity's story stemmed from a similar unease. But, with the discovery of Geraldine Mortimer's diaries and Luke's subsequent – or, indeed, consequent – suicide, it became a task that I could no longer shirk. To which end, I have gathered together the varying – and often conflicting – records of events surrounding the film, in the hope of casting light on both Felicity's actions and the social, political and metaphysical issues that these raise.

---

[1]   Letter to the Author, 6 November 1977; page 157.

i. *Credo*

I should say from the start that I have never believed in evil. I take an innocent until proven guilty attitude to the human race. Even in guilt, there are mitigating factors. At prep school, I was taught that 'evil is good gone wrong'. And, although I soon came to realise that that left much unanswered, the loss of credulity did not lead to a loss of faith. I have been sustained all my life by the figure of Christ and the knowledge that God's love was embodied in a man – and, by extension, in every man. This, together with my fervent conviction, often held in the face of all the evidence, that people are fundamentally decent led me, first instinctively, and then intellectually, to reject the concept of Original Sin. Later, Marx and Freud, two philosophers who in both appearance and stature came to resemble the prophets they had displaced, added secular authority to my belief that what was commonly called evil was simply the behaviour of people in the grip of social and psychological forces that they could not control.

'What? Even Hitler?' is the automatic response of my critics. Hitler is, after all, a byword for evil (and a not inconsiderable presence in the account that follows). 'Yes, even Hitler,' is my reply. The nature of the forces that shaped him may be open to dispute – and was, indeed, the subject of several on the set of *Unity* – but that is hardly surprising when it is impossible to reach agreement on something as uncontroversial as his favourite film.[2] I am convinced, however, that such an interpretation is possible (in my amateur way, I made the attempt at Cambridge). Explanation is extenuation. After all, what is the alternative? Are we going to make him such a symbol of evil that he moves beyond the realm of human responsibility? In demonising Hitler, we are employing the same imagery that he did of the Jews.

---

[2] Historians have proposed *Snow White, Cavalcade, The Lives of a Bengal Lancer, King Kong* and Fritz Lang's *The Nibelung*.

A comparable danger awaits those who try to draw parallels between Unity and Felicity. I admit that the idea has its attractions. They were both young Englishwomen (Unity was twenty when she first met Hitler; Felicity twenty-one when she first met Wolfram Meier), who sprang from a similar upper-class background. Both loved to shock: Unity took her pet snake to deb dances and gave the Nazi salute at the British Embassy; Felicity played a record of *Spirit in the Sky* from the belfry of her college chapel and claimed that her family motto was 'Spit, don't swallow'. Both were seduced by a cause of which they knew only the trappings. But there the comparisons end. To suggest that history was repeating itself is almost as crass as to suggest that Unity's spirit had entered Felicity. There is no store of primal evil working itself out down the generations, nor was Felicity the victim of diabolic possession.

Such lurid speculation[3] was much in evidence in the months following Felicity's death. Talk of the over-identification of actor and role has become a staple of newspaper arts pages, fostered by actors themselves in an attempt to authenticate their performances by reference to their psychic pain. But, unless we are to believe that the profession is made up of intrinsically unstable people – a view which, admittedly, the ensuing pages do little to refute – we would do well to search for our explanations elsewhere. Or is every Othello a potential wife-murderer, Faust a necromancer and Dr No a menace to the world?

My resistance to writing about Felicity stemmed from practical as well as psychological causes. I am a novelist, not a journalist or a historian, and yet any attempt to fictionalise her story would be bound to provoke accusations that, far from trying to establish the

---

[3] Blonde Bombshells, *Daily Mail*, 2 November 1977; The Deadly Debutantes, *Sunday Times*, 13 November 1977; Britain's Bloodline, *Vanity Fair*, March 1978, etc.

truth, I had something to hide. Added to which, the more I reflected on events, the more I grew convinced that it was in the sheer incompatibility of the different interpretations that the truth lay. This distinction would be lost if I tried to tell the story in my own voice. Moreover, I myself was present only at the beginning of *Unity*'s life and, although I was the recipient of a first-hand account, my experience of the filming was one of distance, which I cannot believe is of interest to anyone other than myself.

Gradually, my doubts were whittled away. After completing my third novel, I resolved to take a break from fiction. Instead of giving interviews, I would conduct them. By tracking down the remaining participants, I would make up for my own absence from the set. I am grateful to Thomas Bücher, Liesl Martins, Manfred Stückl and Carole Medhurst for submitting so graciously to my questions. My thanks are due to the trustees of the British Film Institute and to the executors of the late Lady Mortimer for allowing me to reproduce Geraldine Mortimer's Munich diaries.[4] It was Lady Mortimer's bequest of her husband's and step-daughter's papers to the BFI that sparked off this inquiry, and I am obliged to my friend, Ralph Waller, for alerting me to the material. I am likewise indebted to Renate Fischer for allowing me to quote from her monograph on Wolfram Meier, which, for reasons that will be touched on later, has yet to find a publisher in her native land.

My literary priorities have changed to a greater degree than my writing practice. I may not have invented the narrative but I am still shaping it, not least in the arrangement of the various contributions. There is no reason for my placing Luke Dent's letters before Geraldine Mortimer's diary other than my desire to give them pre-eminence: to make them the template for all that

---

[4] A cursory reading of the Hollywood, London and Paris diaries suggests that future historians will find comparable riches.

follows. They were my own introduction to the story. Those who prefer to read the book in the order in which it came into being should read Geraldine Mortimer's account first. Those who prefer to read it in chronological order should read Renate Fischer's. Before reading any of the others, however, I hope that they will read mine.

ii. *Cambridge*

Although it later became a cause of contention and now seems a dubious honour, I still claim credit for conceiving the *Unity* play. Its genesis was at Cambridge, which Felicity, Luke and I all attended between 1973 and 1976. It was a golden age. When I was asked at a recent reading to define the purpose of a university education, my instant reply was 'the pursuit of knowledge in the company of friends'. The students looked blank. Their overriding purpose was the pursuit of qualifications with a view to a job. There could be no clearer indication of the passage of time. Twenty-five years ago, we had invested all our efforts in college entrance . . . it would not be too fanciful to see our passion for the 1920s as a reflection of our own sense of miraculous survival and licence to have fun. In any case, we gave no thought to the future. We had passed the test (which was something far subtler than the examination). We waltzed through the portals of privilege with our destinies assured.

After a first term still imbued with the ethos of school, I focused more on friends than on knowledge. The two who came rapidly to dominate my life – indeed, to define it – were Felicity and Luke. We met at an audition and our subsequent relationship was, in varying measure, tinged with the theatrical. I was the only one to be cast, which immediately set me apart. The real distinction, however, came later that evening when Felicity stayed in Luke's room. 'Placing Girton so far out of town, what do they expect?' she asked, in defiance of the college's founders who believed that distance would be a safeguard of virtue. I met them for lunch the next day. I had not yet alerted them to my sexual preferences (I had not yet articulated them to myself), but Felicity's casual assumption conveyed instant approval, while Luke's grammar school background left him with no residue of guilt for which to atone.

Such a tight-knit trio inevitably gave rise to gossip, but our relationship was far more conventional than it appeared. Felicity slept with Luke and I slept with no one. When Felicity joked that I should be called a homosexless, I laughed because I thought it was funny. At least I think that I did. Felicity and I slept together once – with Luke's bruised blessing – but it was more of a biology lesson than a romantic tryst. At the time, my heart was still set on acting. Stanislavski was king and Felicity insisted that I required a heterosexual experience to store in my emotional memory. Needless to say, I never slept with Luke. I sunbathed with him in Naxos, showered with him in Scotland and rubbed make-up on his back in ancient Rome. But I never slept with him. I am, however, the one who wrote the inscription on his grave.

The attractions of the arrangement for Felicity and myself were clear. I was able to cast my adulthood in the mould of my childhood, while she was able to swathe herself in an aura of mystery as thick as the fug produced by her trademark *Black Russian* cigarettes. Too fastidious for orgies and too indolent to sleep around, she looked to us to save her from the bourgeois (the dirtiest word in her dictionary). We brought a touch of Truffaut into a world of E. M. Forster, even if the triangle were less elegantly balanced than that of *Jules et Jim*. Above all, she feared commitment. Just as her chronic procrastination derived less from inefficiency than from a sense that something more exciting must be about to happen elsewhere, so she loathed being tied down. A third person provided the prospect of release even if, in my case, it was more symbolic than real.

For Luke, the attractions were both less obvious and the subject of constant speculation on my part, as I attempted to reassure myself of his commitment to the trio. I was convinced – wrongly, as it turned out – that any rupture would be brought about by him. My self-lacerating conclusion was that Luke was a liberal who saw me as a potential cause. He pictured himself defending me from the repercussions of a scandal, waiving private distaste for the sake of a general principle. At times of greater self-confidence, I cast myself as his soul-mate . . . the friend for whom he used to yearn when he was growing up in Africa and forbidden to mix with the local boys: the friend for whom he used to yearn when he returned to England and found that all the significant allegiances had already been formed. His primary motivation, however, was the desire to please Felicity, his first proper girl-friend, to whose personal volatility was added all the enigma of her sex.

iii. *Felicity Benthall & Luke Dent*

Contrary to my method with fiction, I find myself needing to describe Felicity and Luke. In no other area is a novelist so despotic as in his allocation of physical traits. Conscious of my power to dye a brunette blonde, make a hook-nose snub and pluck beetle brows at the stroke of a pen, I prefer to leave such details to the reader's imagination and concentrate, instead, on my characters' inner lives. In this case, however, the protagonists exist not only in my mind but in my memory. My task is not so much to make them well-rounded as to make sure that they are clearly defined.

Felicity was a large girl – nothing in comparison with Unity, who was six foot with enormous hands and feet – but tall and big-boned. Height was neither an encumbrance nor an embarrassment and she had long since dispatched her mother's attempts at camouflage to the Oxfam Shop. Her hair was the colour of Harvest Festivals. Her pale eyes stared straight from an Arthur Rackham edition of an Arthurian romance, while her creamy complexion evoked a world of cowslips and Cornwall and antique lace.

Luke matched her in both stature and presence. He was broad-shouldered and so lean that, when he sat down, his skin did not even crease. He had a mass of sandy curls with surprisingly dark roots that, when Felicity and I ganged together, we would suggest were in need of attention (his utter lack of vanity prevented his taking offence). His long lashes gave him a hint of ambivalence, but his expression was far too guileless to be gay. His high cheek-bones were prone to flush at the first sign of either a compliment or a rebuke. His smile would make sense of suicide pacts.

A unique blend of good looks and good nature made him as attractive to men as to women. His own warmth was reflected in a universal welcome which, Felicity and I were agreed, gave him an unrealistically rosy view of the world. He had a childlike open-ness which, according to circumstance, I regarded either as admirable or naive. A perfect example occurred when he inter-preted his German supervisor's departure on 'a busman's holiday' to Greece as a coded confession of a taste for rough trade. He expressed his support with a theory, largely culled from me, that gay men needed differences of caste to make up for their sameness of sex, only to face the full fury of a closeted don who was leaving for a United Nations conference on developing literacy. It is fair to say that even Luke's hyperactive cheekbones had never flushed so fast.

They could not have come from more dissimilar backgrounds. Felicity was the granddaughter of a baronet – and the daughter of a younger brother, as her mother never let her father forget. They lived in the dower-house on her uncle's estate. As a young man, her father had raced cars, now, he drank. Her mother bred roses –

her daughter maintained that she preferred not to think of anything higher up the reproductive chain than a flower. She had a brother in the city and two sisters 'at stud'. She was the youngest by ten years ('not so much an afterthought as a reproach'). For all the obvious precedents, her affair with Luke was not meant as an act of rebellion, since one of the banes of her life – and, I feel sure, a primary cause of the disaster that ended it – was that she had nothing against which to rebel. Her father showed himself a democrat in that he spread his contempt evenly across society. Her mother showed herself an aristocrat in that she modified her morality to suit her own needs. Far from wishing to shock her parents, she had long ceased trying to attract their attention. I have no doubt that, within the limitations of her egoism, she genuinely loved Luke.

In its very different way, Luke's upbringing seemed to exude the same glamour as Felicity's – at least from my privet-hedged perspective. His father's post-war disillusion prompted him to leave England for the Sudan where he worked in the embryonic oil industry. He met Luke's mother, a nurse, when she flew out on a year's contract. Luke and his brothers grew up in one of the most volatile regions of Africa. As children, they picked bullets out of the sofas at the airport after it had been used by a firing squad. On another occasion, the violence edged even closer when a gang of rebels murdered a security guard in the European compound. The following day, his colleagues randomly rounded up a group of Africans, chopping them into pieces which they then placed, as a warning, on the compound walls. When the eight-year-old Luke cried at the sight, his father told him to be a man.

In the late sixties, the family lost everything, having been forced to flee the country overnight after Luke's father found himself on the wrong side of a coup. They moved to Hastings, from where his father sold encyclopaedias for an old army friend. His parents never addressed a further word to each other from the moment that they boarded the plane. Luke dated his interest in theatre to that day.

It is unnecessary to say anything about myself. I am merely the Prologue. It falls to me to set the scene for the action that follows. I have published three novels and a collection of stories. Anyone interested can look up the biographical details in a stack of interviews, although I would not vouch for their unalloyed truth. As regards my appearance, I shall no doubt succumb to the traditional authorial vanity of a photograph on the cover. I trust that more dispassionate observers will not share my difficulty in chipping out the fresh-faced undergraduate from the granite-faced middle-aged man.

iv. Unity *in Cambridge*

Unity was born out of pique. In spite of her startling performances at several Smokers[5] (I still chuckle at her impersonation of a suburban matron whose 'husband has never been a handful in the underwear department'), Felicity failed to be cast in the annual Footlights revue. She fell victim to internal politics – specifically, one of her rivals bedding the professional director first. Her fury erupted in a flurry of sanctimonious slurs. All her dreams of glory – and, more pressingly, an answer to the question of what to do come June – had collapsed. Luke, in a valiant attempt at consolation, offered to write her a play that we would put on ourselves. It was pointless her tackling Millament or the Shrew ('or Cleopatra,' Felicity interjected), who would simply be drowned out in the usual classical clamour but, if we could choose the right – that is, controversial – theme, the Footlights would be put in the shade.

---

[5]   Informal concerts presented by the Footlights, a Cambridge club that has nurtured the careers of many of Britain's most popular comic talents.

The primary requirement was a peach of a part for Felicity . . . 'One that will showcase all your many facets', I fawned. 'Not possible!' she retorted. My rudimentary knowledge of marketing – I was on the theatre-hiring committee – combined with Luke's literary tastes to favour the historical. Our collective self-image narrowed the field to the 20s and 30s. The choice fell on Nancy Cunard, the tempestuous heiress whose drift from Belgravia to Bohemia seemed to be the perfect fit for Felicity, but we found ourselves unable to do justice to her advocacy of black power from the ranks of our Cambridge friends. It was then that I – or, possibly, Luke (as in so many relationships, paternity only became an issue after the split) – hit on Unity.

The timing was perfect. A brilliant account of her life had appeared the previous year.[6] The Mitfords were beginning to establish a hold on the national consciousness as a madcap sorority who stood, as one of the Edinburgh reviewers neatly put it, midway between the Brontes and the Beverleys.[7] Moreover, the subject tapped deep into Luke's rich and hitherto unexposed vein of social unease. This stretched all the way from Felicity's Leicestershire home where, he confessed, confusion over the phrase 'gun-broken' had caused him more anxiety than the knottiest French or German translation, to Cambridge itself. I had failed to grasp how alien he felt from the dominant undergraduate ethos: the effortless assumption of superiority with which I, ever the chameleon, contrived to blend. It was as if he identified, in the gilded immaturity, a moral vacuum that could so easily be filled, like Unity's, with salutes to the 'divine Storms!'[8]

---

6   *Unity Mitford, A Quest* by David Pryce-Jones, Weidenfeld & Nicolson 1976.
7   A musical trio popular in the 50s and 60s who made the classic progression from schmaltz to camp when they were taken up, twenty years later, by gay men.
8   Her pet name for the Nazi Storm Troopers.

v. *Unity Mitford*

Unity, the fourth of Lord and Lady Redesdale's seven children, was born in 1914, having been conceived when her parents were prospecting for gold at a place called Swastika in Canada, thereby providing conclusive evidence for those who view geography as fate. After an unconventional upbringing, overtly fictionalised in her older sister Nancy's novels and covertly fictionalised in her younger sister Jessica's memoirs, she attended finishing school in Munich in 1934, where she honed her fascist sympathies. A year later, she attained the pinnacle of her desire when Hitler summoned her to join him in the restaurant where she sat, day after day, hoping to catch a stray glance. During the four years that followed, she was to enjoy a further one hundred and forty such meetings, mainly for lunch and tea and mainly in Munich, although he also invited her to his mountain-retreat at Berchtesgaden and to the Chancery in Berlin.

So close was their friendship that, on one occasion, Lord Redesdale was obliged to place an announcement in the *Sunday Pictorial* denying that they had plans to marry. It was a friendship that exposed her to equal suspicion from both British diplomats and the Führer's own staff, many of whom were convinced that she must be a spy. Her political influence was nil, although she may have confirmed Hitler in his belief that England saw Germany as a kindred spirit and would not oppose its territorial ambitions. After the *Anschluss*, he declared: 'They said England would be there to stop me but the only English person I saw was on my side.' That person was Unity, who had rushed to Vienna in order to hail her hero at his moment of triumph.

At the outbreak of war, Unity shot herself – in another geographical quirk, the place that she chose was Munich's English Garden. The bullet lodged in her head and she was taken to a nearby hospital, where Hitler visited her for the last time. As soon as she had sufficiently recovered, he arranged for her to be transported to Switzerland, where she was collected by her mother and brought back to England. She lived on until 1948, incapacitated and incontinent and, according to her nephew, with a mental age of around eleven.[9]

Felicity's portrait of Unity was based on sibling rivalry. Strongly influenced by a supervisor who had achieved broadsheet fame with her monograph, *Shakespeare on the Couch*, she saw the key to Unity's malaise as 'middle child syndrome', exacerbated by membership of such a competitive family. She was a bundle of negatives: neither as witty as Nancy, as beautiful as Diana, as clever as Jessica nor as cosseted as Deborah. She was a romantic without a cause – until she found one in Hitler. Her intellectual flirtation with Mosley had been compromised by his marriage to Diana. Through her friendship with Hitler she became, for the first time, the dominant sister, putting Diana's parochial conquest to shame.

To Hitler, Unity's attraction seems to have been that she was the one person who spoke to him freely. The same lack of imagination that rendered her insensitive to the horrors of Nazism blinded her to the character of its leader. To some extent, we were guilty of a similar misjudgement. For all our awareness of the Holocaust, our approach remained studiedly superficial. Not only did we fail to look seriously at Unity's politics, we cited her as proof that we did not need to take politics itself seriously. In our hands, extremism became eccentricity: glamour conquered all. Now, I see her as the perfect representative of a nation that prefers its fascists dressed in frou-frou and tulle than in greatcoats and jackboots. At the time, I saw her as the heroine of a real-life *Beauty and the Beast*. The fact that Luke later wrote me such a detailed account of his months in Munich attested, I believe, to

9   Jonathan Guinness, *The House of Mitford*, Hutchinson 1984, page 437.

his own desire to redress the balance. Unity was not the only one deserving of blame.

vi. *The Author as Hitler*

I played Hitler, although I trust it is superfluous to state that, unlike Felicity, I was not typecast. Physically, I was hardly ideal, although it is surprising how much can be achieved with a well-judged moustache. My claim to the role was assured when I not only gave up the part of Cyrano de Bergerac, but persuaded Cambridge's leading director, Brian Sterkin,[10] to scrap his whole production and take on ours. As one whose school syllabus stopped short at the Glorious Revolution, I date my interest in twentieth century history to that summer. Had I put the same effort into reading my set texts as I had into researching my character, I might have emerged with a better degree.

It is my deep conviction, reinforced by thirty-five years of theatre-going, that no actor can play pure evil. I call it the Edmund syndrome, in which Shakespeare's most gratuitously malevolent character is endowed with a boyish swagger or a winningly self-aware smile. An actor needs a motive as much as he needs an audience. So Richard III is driven by his disability, Macbeth by his lack of an heir and Edmund by the stigma of illegitimacy. Indeed, I suspect the reason that actors in previous eras were excluded from society (all those dead-of-night burials that fired my childhood imagination) lay less in their sexual laxity than in the fact that their artistic practice refuted the simple pieties of the Church.

I was no exception, my dramatic instincts and philosophical insights leading me to the same place. I played Hitler as a frus-

---

10 Currently Head of Drama at the University of Santa Fé.

trated painter, the key to whose character could be found in his failure to be accepted into the Vienna Art Academy and his subsequent discovery that four out of the seven members of the Jury who rejected him were Jews. He wrote a letter to the Director which ended with the threat 'For this, the Jews will pay.' And, if nothing else, he proved true to his word. I still stand by the basic interpretation. As Chancellor, Hitler liked to surround himself with artists and, indeed, to be regarded as one himself. When Eva Braun pointed out that he was whistling an operatic air out of tune, he replied 'I am not out of tune; the composer made a mistake here.' He took an active role in the infamous 1937 Exhibition of German Art. Even holed up in the bunker, when Allied bombers were effecting his squalid Götterdämmerung, he sat for hours staring at a model for the rebuilding of his home town of Linz.

This was the aspect of the man with which I found it easy to identify. I too was fired with the desire to become an artist: an actor, working in the one medium that would perfectly combine my need for self-expression with the ineluctable fact that I had nothing to say. Since my schooldays, I had spent every spare hour projecting myself into the personae of people more passionate, articulate, clear-cut and, paradoxically, more alive than myself. But I was increasingly aware that a serviceable talent was too flimsy a foundation on which to build a career. As I sat, in mid-performance, listening to the voices of actors who effortlessly scaled the heights up which I sweated and strained, the name *green room* took on a new meaning. With my dreams of a world in which every theatre would be closed down by a regime more rigorous than the Puritans, I was able to relate to the whole 'Is Paris Burning?' side of Hitler: the impulse to destroy, which no one but a thwarted artist can fully comprehend.

vi. Unity *in Edinburgh*

Even as I was coming to terms with my lack of talent, Luke had
revealed a new one. His play, originally a token of love from a
latter-day troubadour, rapidly took on a life of its own. The result
was a sell-out success. We added a special midnight matinee for
which, at Felicity's insistence, the audience was required to wear
evening dress. Among them – by the sort of twist that makes a
family tree resemble the London tube map – was one of her
distant cousins, who offered to underwrite our appearance on the
Edinburgh Fringe. Fears of not finding a suitable space turned out
to be unfounded when we sublet a building from a group of
Texans, who were performing the *Agamemnon* in Greek. Despite
its being only two doors down from the Film Festival, we expected
little passing trade. In the seventies, cultural demarcation-lines
were heavily policed. And we observed them as slavishly as
anyone. Although we had tracked down the smallest one-man
show at the most way-out venue, we had no idea what films were
being shown a hundred yards away until Luke, idly flicking
through the programme, discovered a Wolfram Meier retrospec-
tive.

Meier was an exception to the theatre-cinema divide. He had
started in the theatre, and his films, while totally cinematic,
employed a host of stage devices and non-naturalistic effects. No
other contemporary director had a vision so framed by the prosce-
nium arch. What's more, he broke the cardinal *Cahiers du
Cinéma* rule and gave as much weight to words as to pictures. It
was an emphasis of which I heartily approved, even though the
long voice-overs and trademark 'chapter headings' put a severe
strain on my subtitle-weary eyes when Luke introduced me to a
late-night season of his work. In spite of Felicity's carping at the
Teutonic lack of humour (her preference was Coward with everything), I was immensely moved by *The Passion of Albrecht Dürer*,

its historical intensity the equal of Bergman's *Seventh Seal*. At the same time, I relished the ironies in his portrayal of Rosa Luxemburg as a gutsy Hollywood heroine, as determined to nab her revolution as Joan Crawford her man.

Insisting that it would be the perfect antidote to three years of Cambridge German (and lying to Felicity about its length), Luke bought tickets for the British premiere of Meier's *Faust* which was, fortuitously, playing on the one night that we weren't. This was a sumptuously irreverent version in which Faust was tempted not by Mephisto but by Christ; Helen of Troy was replaced by the Virgin Mary; and Gretchen's love proved to be the greatest snare of all. It came as no surprise to learn that it had offended both literary purists and the Catholic Church.

When he took to the stage at the end, Meier turned out to be an identikit iconoclast in a leather cap and waistcoat, soiled white T-shirt, jeans and boots. The one anomaly was the pair of spectacles dangling oldmaidishly around his neck. It was, however, his speech that struck me most. Although it was filtered through an interpreter, it had the same squeezebox stridency that I had noted in recordings of Hitler. He deflected praise with a show of modesty and dissent with a play of failing to understand the question. To the interpreter's mounting irritation, 'It is not so in German,' became the constant refrain. As I recall, his single forthright reply came when he was urged to explain the rationale behind his approach. 'You English,' he declared, a presumption that drew an audible hiss, 'can produce faithful versions of the classics, with your Oxford accents and your "Britons never will be slaves". But how can we, when we see where they lead?'

Two nights later, Meier repaid our compliment by attending a performance of *Unity*. Even now, it seems barely credible that a world-famous film director should have visited a student company – although no less so, I suppose, than that a twenty-year-old

Englishwoman should have penetrated the Nazi elite. One of the cast said that he had come because he was planning a film on Hitler. If so, he could have chosen any of the half-dozen versions of his life which were playing that – as every – year on the Fringe. Another said that it was because he was dodging a persistent journalist; yet another that he was sheltering from the rain. Brian Sterkin claimed that, having spotted Luke at the screening, he had been so smitten that he had dispatched an aide to seek him out. If that is the explanation I favour, it is because, like my 'frustrated artist' theory of Hitler, it is the one to which I can most easily relate.

At the end of the show, he appeared, unheralded, in the communal dressing-room, cast a lazy eye over a couple of half-dressed SS men and congratulated us on our performance in broken English which, I later learnt from Luke, was a weapon he wielded like broken glass. Then, with a shrug of apology, he declared that the language barrier made it impossible for him to talk to more than two people at once, and promptly invited Felicity and Luke to dinner. Sterkin and I were so chilled by our exclusion that we went straight back to our digs and, to our mutual disgust, slept together for the first and last time. The next day, Luke and Felicity burst in with the news that Meier wanted to film *Unity*. I tried to attribute my scepticism more to bitter experience than to sour grapes. Either way, it proved to be unwarranted, since further conversations with members of Meier's entourage, the precise nature of whose functions remained as obscure to Luke as they did to me, resulted in a contract for him to fly out to Munich to work on the script.

Meier, whose impulsiveness struck Felicity as the mark of a true artist, confided, at that first dinner, that he planned to use both English and German actors. She immediately extracted a promise from Luke to make her casting a non-negotiable part of the deal.

Nervous of his bargaining-power, he tentatively intimated that he might have more success with one of the supporting sisters: a proposal that she dismissed out of hand. I knew full well that I would hardly be in line to play Hitler and, to my eternal chagrin, I lacked Felicity's hold over Luke. Nevertheless, I felt that my contribution to the script – both in conception and performance – might be acknowledged in the offer of some lesser role: an attendant aristocrat or fascist. So I was quite nonplussed by the violence of Felicity's response when I suggested it.

'Can't you just be glad for Luke? It's always the same with success: all the little people crawling out of the woodwork, claiming to be the brains behind *Eleanor Rigby* or *Citizen Kane*.'

Two days later, we left for London on separate trains. With no asset but my degree, I made my way to the Gabbitas Thring agency[11] and to a job in a prep school so minor that they employed me on the strength of a single phone call and the promise to be with them by the end of the week. My classroom responsibilities covered the entire curriculum, with the exception of Latin and Scripture, which were entrusted to more seasoned hands. My extra-curricular duties ranged from Wolf Cubs to chiropody. At first, I was as disorientated by my change in status as a priest who swaps titles with his father, but I swiftly negotiated the transition from surname to Sir. My world was reduced to a few crusty bachelors and a matron whose moustache made a mockery of her maternal role. No hungry boy looked more keenly to parcels from home to sustain him than I looked to letters from abroad.

Reading them again over twenty years later, I can't but wonder whether, had Meier been sufficiently impressed – that is to say, attracted – by my performance to invite me to Munich, I might have exerted some influence on the course of events. Would my

---

[11] A long-established English educational agency, satirised as 'Church and Gargoyle' by Evelyn Waugh in *Decline and Fall*.

presence have acted as a restraint on Felicity: another voice to counter the chorus of the fanatics? Or would I have been too awed by the actors, too dismissive of the radicals and, as ever, too bound up with Luke?

1

Luke Dent's Letters

My career as a teacher lasted for six years, although in a bid to remind myself that the position was only temporary, I avoided the more authoritative schoolmaster. While, to my surprise, I enjoyed considerable popularity with the boys, I never felt a comparable welcome from my colleagues. In retrospect, I admit that the fault may have been mine. My drive to succeed must have rankled with men for whom the school gates marked the boundaries of their ambition. As I gazed around the common room, my greatest fear was that I too would succumb to the fatal lure of the valedictory dinner.

Luke's letters offered me a glimpse of a world from which I felt that I must remain forever excluded. Having basked in his reflected glamour at Cambridge, I now did so at one remove, demanding location reports 'for the boys' like an ageing pop fan requesting an autograph 'for his daughter'. He responded with characteristic generosity, the very length of his letters attesting to the depth of my need. Re-reading them for the first time in years, I am struck by their exuberance, their candour, their delight in words. He failed to keep my replies, which, I suspect, is a sign of the relative weight that we attached to our friendship – although it may simply denote my greater commitment to preserving the past.

Needless to say, Felicity was not such an assiduous correspondent. I received a single postcard from her during the entire shoot. Depicting a group of bronzed Berliners performing handstands by a lake, it presented more of a challenge than a greeting. The letter which, according to Luke she had promised me in Cannes, never arrived. Even so, as soon as her casting was assured, our Edinburgh estrangement was set aside. In the autumn of 1976, when

Luke was away in Munich, she rang me regularly at the school, although her ever more unlikely guises (my sister, my mother, Barbara Castle, Margot Fonteyn) tried the authorities' already limited patience. On one memorable occasion she drove down for a visit, boosting my credibility with the boys while exhausting my credit with the Headmaster.

The truth was that she had lost interest in me. Returning to school, in whatever capacity, offended her never-look-back ethos. At Cambridge, I had been puzzled by her failure to maintain contact with a single one of her Benenden[12] contemporaries. I long presumed that her schooldays must have been miserable until, much later, one of her classmates informed me that, on the contrary, she had been among the most popular girls in her year. A clean slate was essential to the pursuit of fresh experience, for which she possessed a voracious appetite. In any case, I was no longer of use to her. At university, I provided a necessary balance – even ballast – in her relationship with Luke. Once she met Wolfram Meier, she preferred to cast that role elsewhere.

Reading Luke's letters alongside Geraldine Mortimer's journal, I am conscious of a marked difference in perspective. What is less clear is how much this is a function of their individual tempera-ments and how much of a genuine ambiguity in the incidents that they record. Luke, as he freely concedes, had little time for politics whereas Geraldine was not just a political animal but a political predator – hence the far greater space that she devotes to the hostage crisis engulfing Germany. Felicity's own interest in that crisis is self-evident. What remains at issue is whether she was driven by a genuine commitment or whether it was simply her latest – and, in the event, last – pose.

To my mind, an equally vexed issue is what could have led her to abandon Luke, although I am aware that my concern cannot be

12 Leading girls' boarding school, whose alumni include the Princess Royal.

divorced from the Derby and Derby fantasies to which, against all logic, I continue to cling. To have jilted Luke, once the pinnacle of my desire, now the lost hope of my youth, strikes me as doubly perverse. Nothing in his letters pains – or, indeed, shames – me more than his assumption that I will share his disgust at her attempt to thrust him on Meier, unless it is his related assumption that I shared his outrage at her attempt to thrust him on me. It is one of the greatest ironies in a narrative crammed with them that, while Unity pimped boys for her friend Brian Howard, forty years on it was the actor playing Brian whom the actress playing Unity pimped for her friend.

In the absence of any direct testimony, we can only speculate on Felicity's feelings for Wolfram Meier. Luke's report of her declaration of love for him is at odds with Geraldine Mortimer's picture of professional gratitude. It is telling that Luke should have placed less emphasis than Geraldine on Felicity's relationship with Ahmet Samif, whose heterosexuality would seem to make him a more dangerous rival. But then he may have subscribed to my own belief that Felicity would regard Meier's homosexuality as a goad rather than a deterrent. Such a relationship would hold particular appeal for a woman whose reading of 'The course of true love never did run smooth' had left her with a preference for the bumpy. My personal opinion, which I offer as an addendum to those printed below, is that, contrary to usual practice, her sexuality was the product of her bohemianism rather than the other way round. She displayed an exaggerated respect for artists not because of an aesthetic sensibility but because art supplied the one alternative to her parents' world that they could not dismiss out of hand. Nevertheless, in another irony, the first casualty of her action was the film.

*

41

I have reproduced Luke's ten letters in their entirety, retaining all personal allusions (several of which still elude me), private jokes and, on occasion even, errors, altering only punctuation and, where absolutely necessary, grammar. My criterion for the use of footnotes, here as elsewhere, has been comprehension rather than consistency. The letters were extremely long and, in some cases, legibility deteriorates with length. For such a resolute man, his handwriting was surprisingly formless. From the letter of 23 September 1977 onwards, when he bowed to my request that he should type, clarity was assured.

8 München 40,
Giselastrasse 23,
West Germany.

14th Oct 1976

Lieber!

Well, when in Rome . . . After three weeks, I'm beginning to find my feet – no easy task in a city so overrun with bicycles. The cyclists must be the direct descendants of Rommel's Panzer-Division. Sorry, cheap joke.

I swear there are more bicycles per head than in any other city in the world, including Cambridge. Perhaps you could do a comparative survey with your geography class? I'm living near the university. One girl with whom I had a near miss told me that her bike was as much a part of her as her shoes. The analogy was lost on me. Do you see your shoes as a part of you? Well, perhaps those whiffy old brogues . . . Only kidding. I can picture your pained expression already. The district is called Schwabing. It's supposed to be the Munich Left Bank (as in J-P. S. and S. de B.), awash with poets, artists and bohemians various. All I ever come across are tight-lipped old ladies walking their dogs. And no, no dachshunds. Before you ask, I haven't seen a single one since I arrived in Germany . . . but then I've never seen a British bulldog either.

I'm sorry not to have written before but I've been busy finding my feet . . . see footnote.[13] The address at the top is the one where all letters should be sent (hint!) not to mention spontaneous, unsolicited gifts such as Fortnum's hampers. Aren't they the traditional remedy for homesick Englishmen? Joking apart, should you ever find yourself near a jar of Marmite . . . I know that you

---

[13] There was no footnote. Luke evidently thought that the pun could stand alone.

consider it an abomination on a par with Birmingham but it's the one thing (present correspondent excepted) that I miss. Anyway a jar sent to me here, care of von Hirsten (very *Almanach de Gotha*) will guarantee you a friend for life.

Almost directly in front of us is the house where Thomas Mann wrote *Buddenbrooks*. It may not mean a lot to you with your Shakespeare über alles prejudices, but that was the novel that made me want to study German. I waltz down the road, to the consternation of afore-mentioned old ladies, like Freddy Eynsford-Hill singing *On the Street Where You Live*.

The house – ours not his – is the perfect illustration that a German man's home is his bank: solid, impenetrable with a hint of hidden opulence in the classical frieze on the facade. Wolfram gave me a quick who's who but, frankly, when you've seen one languishing maiden, you've seen them all. I can't even remember whether it's art deco or art nouveau. But, before you choke on your collected Aubrey Beardsley, just remember where I grew up.

I have never lived anywhere with so much space: two bedrooms (so, should you need a refuge from Dotheboys Hall[14] . . .); a drawing-room (which, in deference to the Mitford[15] connection, not to mention Fliss, I shall never again call a lounge); a panelled hall which cries out for a buxom maid with a feather duster (the tenant wouldn't say no either); an old-fashioned bathroom straight out of a murder mystery. The corridors are hung with prints of Old Masters. My favourites are a Filippo Lippi Annunci-ation with a peacock-plumed Gabriel; a Rembrandt bathing-beauty Bathsheba; and the most incongruously serene Holy Family by Il Sodoma. Fliss said that it makes her think of you – for the serenity, of course.

[14] The school at which the eponymous hero of Dickens's *Nicholas Nickleby* was employed. The headmaster was Wackford Squeers (see references below).
[15] Nancy Mitford's *U and Non-U* banished lounges, along with fish knives, notepaper and mantelpieces to a lexicographical lumber-room.

We had the best time when she was out here last week. She seems so much more relaxed now she's finished with Cambridge. Anonymity suits her – not necessarily the most reassuring thing to say about someone preparing to star in a film. She's jealous of my prior involvement. I told her that it'd be the other way round come June. Like one of those night-shift marriages, I'll be finishing work just as she starts. She promised to ring you when she got back to London. Did she? Is it allowed? I envisage Old Wackford (I hope I've got that right. The trouble with being away from home is that you can't cite with confidence) standing over you with a stopwatch. 'We're not running a charity, Mr Arditti. You must be sure to make up the time.' On second thoughts, I'll stick to the post.

You were right to tell me to hold out for my own flat. No, don't worry: no 'number threes'. I can't decide whether to feel flattered that you believe that everyone is after my body or humiliated that you consider me incapable of looking after myself. No means nein in anyone's language. The truth is that Wolfram's place is such a sty that I'd have been driven mad within the hour. I know; I know. I'm sure that you and Fliss are right and it says something deeply sinister about my character (though I still don't see why arranging my LPs alphabetically is such a crime), but I need order. Perhaps it's because I'm an artist. Maybe the more reckless you are in your imagination, the more regular you have to be in your routines?

Well, that's my theory and I'm sticking to it. Though I admit it falls apart with Wolfram. He has a vast, five-storey house (also in the bunker/banker style). Lord knows how he can afford it. He appears to be on his uppers – financially as well as pharmaceutically (I'll dish the dirt later). When they bought it ten years ago, the group was, at least nominally, a commune. According to Dorit, one of the founders (do you remember that advert where a woman metamorphosed into a tiger? Think Dorit), it was the sort of commune that the French aristocracy lived in at Versailles. No prizes for guessing who played Louis. He still holds court today, although to a largely new selection of favourites. Marriage, betrayal and exile have taken their toll. The current *maîtresse en titre* is Mohammed, whose antagonism towards me seems to stem from a suspicion that I have designs on the king. I want to tell him to lighten up. My intentions are entirely literary. But, when I talked it over with Renate, she told me not to waste my breath. All Arabs believe that all Englishmen are gay. Do you suppose it's a hangover from T. E. Lawrence?

You must have met Renate in Edinburgh, the evening we all went for drinks at the Caledonian. She certainly remembers a very charming, good-looking Englishman (I rest my case) . . . although it's true that her description could equally fit Brian. She lives at the top of the house, in a former maid's room, where she nurses a hopeless passion for Wolfram. That's not just my opinion. She admits it freely to everyone. I expect she did to you – that is if it was you and not Brian. I tried to commiserate (fatal!), but Fliss was fierce. For one terrifying moment she turned into her mother as she compared Renate to a housemaid hauling up her skirts to show you her scars. Ouch! Renate, convinced that she has found a sympathetic audience, treats me to a description of all the humiliations she has endured in order to raise cash for Wolfram. It's so insulting. Does she suppose me incapable of spotting a fantasist? Her most pathetic fantasy is that Wolfram means to marry her. They slept together a few times (it seems that he plays for both City and United). Ever since, she has stalked him like a character in a French tragedy . . . one of those spurned mistresses who burst in on the action without ever having to knock on a door.

Other residents include Dieter, whom I like a lot, a quiet, sensitive actor who is, understandably, preoccupied since he's playing Hans Castorp in *The Magic Mountain*, and Kurt, who has composed the music for all of Wolfram's films, apart from *The*

Great Beast, which was made at a time when they were deadly rivals in lust. Deadly is the word, since, according to Renate – admittedly, not always the most impartial of witnesses – Kurt took out a contract on Wolfram's life. Fortunately, she found out about it and was able to warn Wolfram who, after confronting his would-be assassin, cast him as a bandit in the film. He also – amazingly – recovered his respect for Kurt . . . Do you know of any technical term – perhaps coined by a Hollywood analyst – for filmmakers who are unable to distinguish between the world on and off the screen?

Somehow – don't ask me how – the films get made. Deals are done, not always in the best of faith. Werner, one of the producers, told me that he had sold 150% of the distribution rights to *The Magic Mountain*. I only hope that *Unity* is more legit. I foresee the reels gathering dust in a vault while lawyers wrangle and I am robbed of the chance to deliver my Oscar-acceptance speech. OK. I confess I do have a few words up my sleeve. But, be honest now, wouldn't you? Let me paint the scene. As my name is announced, the commentator's rayon tones – synthetic silk, geddit? – rise above the roar of applause that indicates the near – no, let's not mince words here, totally – unanimous approval of the hall. Exuding an air of bemused detachment (patented in Stratford), I make my way to the podium, pausing only to shake hands with Marlon and Jack, and fall straight into Sophia's arms (or whatever). Then, before an audience of billions, I pay tribute to my best friend, Michael. Our minds are so in sync that we can't even remember which one of us thought of telling the Mitford story first. 'Here's to you, Michael', I say as I hold up the statuette. Cue music; an adoring Sophia; more applause.

I digress . . . I dream . . . I digress. The Serpent's Nest – that's what they call the house, but it's a bluff on so many levels that it might as well be Chez Nous – is a throwback to an age when art was a collective endeavour. It reminds me of one of those

Renaissance studios, the schools of Raphael and Titian whose paintings fill Felicity's uncle's house, or else one of those medieval workshops that her father wants to revive. Not being in love with his daughter, you may have escaped his lecture on the last hope for England's salvation. From what I can make out, it lies in a return to a pre-industrial society, complete with Lords of the Manor and maypoles, master-craftsmen and guilds. Although I found a lot of it distinctly dubious, and a lot more, incoherent (an occupational hazard when dealing with Papa), the part about restoring the dignity of labour made a good deal of sense.

Dignity is not the first word that springs to mind when you think of Wolfram – especially after watching him throw a tantrum (and I'm talking the full carpet-chewing works) the moment his will is crossed. To an outsider it's deeply disconcerting, but to his friends it's almost routine. There's no doubt that it's being surrounded by a team he can trust that has enabled him to be so prolific. Why, this month alone he's doing publicity for *The Judge*, which is about to open in Berlin (guess who'll be squeezing into a rented tux for the premiere!), shooting *The Magic Mountain* twelve hours a day and then working on *Unity* every evening with me. After which – wait for it – he storyboards the next day's scenes. When does he sleep? You may well ask. Remember what I said about pharmaceuticals. It's not just the set that's covered in snow. He keeps going on a lorry-load of coke. In case any customs officer opens this letter or Mr Squeers is reading it over your shoulder, I should like to make it clear that I'm talking about the drink that makes the whole world sing and not the drug that makes it sniff.

The Mann should be stunning. The entire action takes place in the Alps ('No, really?' I hear you say, 'and I thought it would be under water.'). Heike, the designer, has covered the set in a white tarpaulin, which, close-up, looks as tatty as anything we ever hung at the ADC,[16] but, under the lights, truly glows. The film is a co-production with German television, which surprised me since Wolfram recently described TV (there's nothing like biting the hand that's interviewing you) as a medium that 'tells lies twenty-fives times a second'. He gave the questioner the waggy-tail look of one who has brought off a successful allusion, but she failed to respond.[17] I find it strange that he should have embarked on a literary adaptation at all given his professed aversion to reading. He asks (rhetorically) who has the time to read these days and dismisses it as though it were a solitary vice, akin to masturbation – and equally damaging to the eyes.

Talking of which, can you confirm the rumour about Charlie Thynne? Fliss said that he'd gone to work for the Tories. Can this be true? Don't they vet their employees? Did no one ask why someone tone-deaf should be so passionate about English choral music? Find out more.[18]

I've been given my own (tiny) office. It doesn't have my name on the door – this is *Bavaria* not MGM – but I'm thinking of smuggling in the letters and gluing them on, one by one, until Herr Dent becomes a permanent fixture. Do you have a study? I imagine it as oak-panelled, hung with yellowing Punch cartoons, and dwarfed by an ancient roll-top desk besides which a sprat of a boy stands quaking (see Charlie Thynne above).[19] Mine is all glass

16 The Cambridge student theatre in which we performed.

17 The allusion is to Jean-Luc Godard's dictum that photography is the truth and film is the truth twenty-four times a second. Meier is not merely inverting Godard but adding an extra lie to reflect TV's extra image.

18 Thynne did, indeed, work for Conservative Central Office and then, at the 1983 election, was duly returned as an MP. Following the scandal that ended his Parliamentary career, he converted to Roman Catholicism and is now a leading advocate for the restoration of the Tridentine Mass.

19 In this, as in so much else, Luke was mistaken. I didn't have a study, merely a shared space in a common room where the chairs were allocated according to length of service (mine had no arms).

and chrome with a huge (locked) filing cabinet, which I'm convinced must be crammed with unmade scripts by untried Englishmen, a bright orange carpet, and a life-sized poster of Liza Minnelli in *Cabaret* (did you know that it was shot here?). Although it could never sell itself on its view (it looks out on a row of sound-stages), it boasts the most amazing acoustic. It's directly above the cutting-rooms and, with the windows open, I can hear the editors at work on post-production. Every day, I'm greeted by a weird cacophony: snatches of music and dialogue, bursts of storms and gunfire and traffic, played at, alternately, Brand's Hatch and State Funeral speed.

The studios are about twenty minutes away from home by car and forty by tram (it's not all chauffeurs and champagne). Every time I walk through the gates, I hear the blast of a fanfare in my head.[20] I stroll to my office by way of one of the sound-stages, drinking in the romance of the dismantled, Dresden-like sets. After a morning at my desk, I try to escape into the surrounding woods for lunch (with no Fliss to complain, I can freely indulge my 'fetish for fresh air'), although it's become something of a running gag since I fell for Wolfram's line that it was the Black Forest. Now everyone – right down to the security guards – thinks that they have carte blanche to suggest a different type of black food for my picnic. And, believe me, there's a depressingly large choice. I'm subjected to constant digs along the lines of Renate's 'You can say it till you're black in the face' (their black is our blue). My glazed smile is wearing thin. It's not true that the Germans lack a sense of humour. What's missing is a sense of proportion. The moment that they find a joke, they bludgeon it to death.

Still, I wouldn't want you to think that I sit here, planning meals and speculating on cultural differences, every so often

---

[20] Luke's handwriting here betrays his fatigue. It is unclear whether he has written 'fanfare' or 'funfair'.

offering a sop to work as I substitute 'cut' for 'curtain'. Wolfram wants hundreds of changes. And the more I research, the more I realise how lucky we were to get away with as much as we did. The angels who fear to tread must have been watching over us . . . I've spent hours in the screening-room looking at newsreels of Hitler. Count yourself lucky that you just had to listen to the tapes. The problem is that, in an age that values subtlety over sweat, I find it hard to take him seriously. It's like the Forbes-Robertson Hamlet.[21] I keep reminding myself that performance styles have changed and his original audiences wouldn't have seen him as such a ham. And did you know that he also made home-movies (I mean, would you Adolf and Eva it?)? I don't know which are the more sickening, his displays in public or in private. Seeing his bashful smiles and exaggerated chivalry towards his women guests, I am more convinced than ever by the feminist equation of courtesy and contempt.

Wolfram wants so many changes that I sometimes wonder why he didn't simply hire someone new to provide a fresh perspective. As you know better than anyone, I'm not one of those writers who is as wounded by cuts as a haemophiliac. But I still bruise. I'm beginning to suspect that some of those callous things you said about his motives may have been true. Don't get me wrong. I'm not blaming you. I'm sure I'd have said them myself in similar circumstances. I'd like to think that I wouldn't, but I expect that I would. When challenged, he claimed to find me indispensable. It was my story – my soul. He then went on to locate said soul squarely in the Home Counties, as he launched into his vision of an opening scene set at a hunt. It was the perfect image of blood-lust: a galumphing girl galloping after the fox, surrounded by a pack of snarling hounds.

21 Luke and I had both been hugely disappointed by a National Film Theatre screening of archive footage of Sir Johnston Forbes-Robertson's 1913 performance.

This immediately posed several questions:

a) Do we know that Unity ever hunted? There's no mention of it in Pryce-Jones or any of the memoirs. We don't want to give the keep-to-the-facts brigade a stick to beat us with in the very first scene.

b) Does he suppose that all Englishmen are born in the saddle? I've never been anywhere near a hunt. Nor do I intend to. Thank goodness Fliss was around to explain 'blooded'. She'll have to feed me appropriate dialogue. I can fake it as long as we're working on the outline. But the only hunting term I know is Tally-ho!

c) There was a c) but I've forgotten it. If it comes back to me, I'll add a p.s.

I'm learning to keep my own counsel. He picks up on the most casual remark. Last week, I happened to let slip that Unity's second name was Valkyrie. At two in the morning, he rang with instructions to write a dream sequence in which the six Mitford sisters dressed as Valkyries (don't ask), soar through the night sky and hover over the Nuremberg Rally. A few days later, that was, thankfully, forgotten when he became even more excited by my mentioning that Hitler's favourite film was *Snow White*. Suddenly he began planning an animated sequence in which Snow Unity is rescued by Prince Hitler from the clutches of an as yet unidentified Wicked Stepmother, the principal candidates being Neville Chamberlain and Queen Mary.

On which note I'd better end. If Wolfram is right and no one has time to read any more, then I expect you feel intimidated by anything longer than a postcard. Besides, we're off on a works outing to the *Oktoberfest* – that's Munich's annual beer festival. Did you know that half the world's breweries were based in Germany? Perhaps that could be another project for your geography class? Or perhaps not. Do they have 'moral turpitude' in prep schools? It's a mixture of circus acts (human and flea), fairground attractions, ox-roasting and beer halls. What's more, it's been taking place every year since the early nineteenth century. How often do I have the chance to get smashed in the name of culture?

If I die of alcohol poisoning, I bequeath you my second-best bed (the first, naturally, goes to Fliss). If I survive, I promise to write again soon.

Yours, till the beer freezes over,

Luke.

8 München 40,
Giselastrasse 23,
West Germany

22nd Nov 1976

Wertester Herr Studienrat!

Many thanks for yours of the 8th. I loved the story of the Head-master walking in when you were tied to the desk during your Robin Hood rehearsal. I quoted it to Wolfram, who was willfully obtuse. 'What is a sheriff doing in England? Why are the homeless men happy?' It was doubly welcome after a letter from my mother, who doles out news the way that she doles out food, on the basis of what's good for you rather than what's tasty. So I was treated to half a page on the plans for a new road to Battle and two lines on Tim and Sheila's separation. Of course, she didn't say a word about my father. It's as if they're living on either side of the Berlin Wall. Fliss is convinced that it's part of some kinky role-play: they pretend to be strangers in order to spice up their sex life. Yuck! I asked her to explain how being strangers could make sex more exciting. But she acted dumb, giving me one of those forehead kisses which always make me feel small, and singing the first line of her Footlights song: 'Variety's the spice of life, but my heart belongs to Basil.'

My heart belongs to her so completely that I sometimes wonder if it's mine at all. Perhaps I was operated on in my sleep by Christian Barnard? Last week she paid me another flying visit, during most of which I was tied up (sorry!) at the studio. I can't understand why she won't stay longer. There's nothing to keep her in London . . . at least, nothing she's told me. But then she's so secretive about the way she spends her time. I accused her of confusing mystery with mystique. 'Do I demand an account of every minute of your day?' she asked. 'I wouldn't mind,' I said and proceeded to give her one, unbidden. The only thing I can think of is that she's scared that, if Wolfram sees too much of her, he'll see through her and cast someone else. Which is crap. She is Unity! But she's so insecure. Do you think you might investigate (discreetly)? And swear – on pain of death – not to mention me. I know it's asking a lot, but she trusts you. She talks to you. I'll admit that there've been times when, seeing the two of you together, I've felt decidedly spare. It's weird. All the women in the novels I read are looking for the one man who will love and understand them, and yet all the women I know seem to be happiest with men who are gay. So is it the writers who are getting it wrong, or is it me?

It all boils down – doesn't everything? – to sex. Fliss likes sex. Well, I don't need to tell you. I still blush when I think of Naxos. From now on, when I book a hotel, the first thing I shall check is the thickness of the walls. On the other hand, she can be so coy, like that awful phrase she uses, 'number threes', as if it were a form of excretion. . . . I've just had a thought: do you think she may have overcome her armpit aversion and joined one of those women's groups in London: the sort that tar us all with the same brush? She's become so much less responsive (if this embarrasses you, skip to the end of the paragraph or, possibly, the page). It's as though making love were a gift for her to bestow on me rather than something for us to share. She said, knowing full well that she was being unjust, that it was the only reason I wanted her to come to Munich. I explained that, without her, I felt like a child away from home. You and I (that's 'you' Michael, not 'you' Fliss) can keep up our relationship on paper. We can swap ideas and impressions, although it takes an extra effort – and costs a fortune in stamps! But, with her, I need something more tangible. Of course, she totally misunderstood and said that I wanted her for her body and you for your mind. Thank God, I ditched the analogy of Wolfram and his cocaine.

To make matters worse, she was having her period. Count yourself lucky that all you have to worry about is a stubbly cheek. Now I know why my mother's 'headaches' were so violent. Fliss's are even worse. After three years, I'm an expert. The pattern's always the same. The first day, she grows listless and lumpish as if there were a great weight bearing down on her. She withdraws further and further into herself. Then, when the bleeding starts, she becomes wildly exhilarated, as if she'd defeated Nature for another month – and so successfully that she needs no one else. Suffice it to say, sex is not on the cards. When I told her that I wasn't squeamish, she looked at me as though I'd stepped out of the Stone Age. Perhaps you're doing the same now. Stupid, isn't it, to let your happiness be so dependent on another person? If that's not one of Nature's design faults, I don't know what is. At Cambridge, Fliss and I used to feel sorry for you, forever the odd one out – don't take offence, it was compassion not pity. Now, I think that it ought to be the other way round. You're the lucky one. Your life isn't at the mercy of someone else's nervous system. But then there are compensations. Did you know that, when she's aroused, her labia form a perfect heart?

'Back to *Unity*, please!' I hear you implore. I wonder if that's the first time the word 'labia' has penetrated your sacred halls. Or is it also the Latin for tongue? Are generations of boys desperately trying to commit it to memory with no idea of the pleasures that lie in store? '*Unity*! *Unity*!' Very well. Everything is proceeding according to plan. I've handed in the outline and the producers have been formulating budgets. You'll be pleased to hear that the hunt has been called off. The cost of thirty stunt extras would have been prohibitive. I thought that Wolfram would hit the roof, but he remained unusually calm. Having inserted a scene where Unity goes to a dance with her pet snake draped around her neck (I haven't dared break the news to Fliss), he has decided to begin with one where she traps mice and feeds them to it live.

I'm currently working on a rough draft, which has to be in by

Christmas. Then, after more script-conferences (i.e. more rewrites), I've a deadline of the first of April for the master draft which we take to Cannes, where (great excitement) *The Magic Mountain* has been chosen for the main competition. There, we hawk the script to actors as well as trying to raise any extra finance and land foreign distribution deals. And yes, you did read that right. It is 'we'. Yours truly is no humble hack chained to his desk but a fully accredited member of the production team. Then it's back to Munich for a final fine-tuning (at least in theory), leaving us with a shooting script by June. All things being equal, the cameras should be ready to roll at the end of July.

The plan is for a ten to twelve week shoot, including a fortnight or so in England, although most of the English interiors will be recreated here in the studio, where labour costs are cheaper (I sound like my mother). For the rest, Wolfram aims to use as many of the actual locations as possible. This is partly to ensure authenticity but also to test a rather Gothic belief that every building retains a unique energy (I'd have thought that there were some which it would be wiser not to tap into, but never mind). In Munich, this is easier than you might have supposed. While much of the city centre was destroyed during the War, it was rebuilt along its original lines. Besides, as luck would have it, many of the principal Unity sites remain intact. Almost every day, I walk down the Ludwigstrasse, which is where she had her pension and Diana her flat. Having escaped both the bombers and the developers, its blandly symmetrical architecture stretches for miles without a trace of individuality or caprice. Even the four ancient philosophers guarding the library, known for reasons I have yet to fathom as the Three Wise Men, appear to have railway-timetable minds.

The Osteria Bavaria has survived, thinly disguised as the Osteria Italiana. Last week, Wolfram took me there for dinner. I felt a strange mixture of excitement and unease to think that I was standing in the room in which Unity first met Hitler. It was here that their story – and, in a sense therefore, ours – began. My discomfort increased as he pointed to the corner where Hitler had his permanent table. There, he would sit among his fawning followers and painstakingly study the menu before ordering the inevitable ravioli, accompanied by some equally predictable by-play with the waitresses about his expanding girth. I remember how, at Cambridge, you insisted that, unless we made Hitler human, we would absolve the audience of responsibility. But, surely, this was a trait too far? It begins with pasta and ends with the Hitler Cookbook. I no longer felt comfortable about eating there . . . and, fortunately, I didn't have to, since as soon as the owner learnt of Wolfram's presence, he stormed out of the kitchen and ordered us to leave. It seems that one of the early films, *Stadtguerillas* (it was never released in England), featured the restaurant in a less than favourable light. Despite Wolfram's show of outrage, I think he was secretly flattered. Energy or not, that is one set that will have to be built.

Authentic Third Reich architecture poses a different problem, namely, that there is so little of it left. Knowing your aversion to schlock, I don't suppose that you've seen *The Eagle Has Landed*.[22] Wolfram and Heike are scathing about the opening scene set in a Berlin building with very English sash windows. That grates on German sensibilities the way that Hollywood's treatment of British history ('Crusades, crusades, crusades, that's all you ever think about, Dickie Plantagenet!'[23]) does on ours. The illusion should be easier to sustain given Wolfram's decision to film in

[22] The 1976 film, directed by John Sturges from Jack Higgins's best-selling novel, about a group of Nazis who parachute into England on a mission to capture Winston Churchill.

[23] The actual remark 'War, war, that's all you ever think about, Dick Planta-genet!' was made by Virginia Mayo to Rex Harrison in the 1954 film, *King Richard and the Crusaders*.

black and white ('my two favourite colours'). His aim is both to establish a Thirties style and to prevent the audience from identifying too closely with the characters. 'This is the story of Germany and England not a romantic melodrama.'

All is not lost – or bombed or demolished. In Munich, there are two existing buildings which are perfect for our purposes: the *Haus der Kunst*, now the Museum of Modern Art (I was about to say too modern until I remembered that that was also Hitler's attitude) and the *Führerbau*, the administrative headquarters where he signed Chamberlain's 'piece of paper' and which is now a music and drama school. In Berlin, the Nazi sites are less accessible. If only the Wall had been erected a mile or so to the right (I'm sure it's a deliberate Commie plot to thwart us!), we could have used the Propaganda Ministry and Göring's Air Ministry. As it is, we must pin our hopes on a couple of embassies (I think they're the Spanish and Italian). Meanwhile, there's the Olympic Stadium, complete with Speer's original street-lamps, which is run-down but serviceable. Incidentally, the nearby toilets are very popular with men of your persuasion. See, I may be hundreds of miles away, but I still have your interests at heart.[24]

I had the chance to explore Berlin for myself when we drove up last week for the premiere of *The Judge*. When I envisaged a future of bright lights and glamorous galas, this was not quite what I had in mind. Let's just say that it caused a bit of a stink (literally!). I don't know whether the furore made the English papers, but it was front-page news here. It contained the perfect ingredients: politics and sex; a mixture as inflammatory to the Germans as religion and sex is to us. The film tells the story of a Judge (the title, at least, is straightforward) who is spearheading the fight against

---

[24] This remark reflects a native prejudice that Luke could never quite throw off. Having denounced the excretory associations of Felicity's sexual terminology, he shows no qualms in adopting a similar line with me.

terrorism. While ostensibly leading an exemplary private life, he is locked in a seedy sado-masochistic relationship with his valet. One evening, when his wife and cook are out (the ease with which Wolfram clears the house made me look more kindly on my own contrivances), he summons the valet for a session which hinges on an exchange of identities. When the doorbell rings, the valet, whose new role is only robe-deep, hurries to answer it. He is shot by two terrorists avenging their imprisoned comrades. As the Judge tries frantically to reclaim his clothes, his neighbours, drawn by the gunfire, discover him. In the ensuing scandal, he is forced to resign. His wife leaves him and his children disown him. Meanwhile, the terrorists are split between those who view the valet as a capitalist lackey fully deserving his fate and those who mourn him as an innocent dupe of the ruling class.

The film similarly polarises its audience. For weeks, journalists have been fabricating a controversy. They weren't to be disappointed. In spite of a heavy police presence, a group of protestors infiltrated the hall. One found her way to the projection-box and, overpowering the projectionist, disrupted the film with a series of slides which denounced both it and its director as, by turn, trivial, corrupt, reactionary and bourgeois (remind you of anyone?). Meanwhile, her friends had let off a string of stink-bombs (a choice of weapon which betrays their cast of mind). Fearing that this was a dummy run for something lethal, the audience fled. I tried to commiserate with Wolfram, only to find him looking jubilant (which I initially attributed to drugs). 'The film is strong,' he explained, 'and, now, it will reach many more people.' Which does, indeed, seem to be the case. Last week, the cinema owners, in between wrangling with the distributors over the bill for additional security, ordered thirty new prints. When it opened yesterday in Munich there were queues stretching right around the block.

We missed a trick when we were publicising *Unity*. We should have hired protest groups to accuse us of whitewashing Hitler. I say 'trick' because it has become increasingly difficult to dismiss Renate's claim that Wolfram engineered the whole brouhaha himself. I wouldn't put it past him. Besides which, connections between the actors and the Red Army Faction go back a long way, to the communes and anti-war movement of the Sixties. Wolfram may have loudly – though not persuasively – dissociated himself from the terrorists, but it wouldn't be hard for him to mobilise their support.

I find it strange to be among people of such strong convictions. Most of my Cambridge friends thought politics were for our parents. Most of my Munich ones think that politics are about their parents. No wonder Wolfram said that the English liked their governments as tepid as their tea. Maybe I'm doing you an injustice and you've been a closet activist for years . . . The nearest I came was when I canvassed for Wilson at the '74 election. I still cringe at the memory of visiting one council estate. The archetypal little old lady opened the door and I went into my spiel about the need to vote Labour. 'I'd like to, my dear,' she said, 'but, you know, I'm doing so much better under Mr Heath.' (I think he'd put a few pence on the pension.) 'That's all very well,' I said, 'but what about the country as a whole?' I can't recall her reply, but I'm ashamed to think that it was polite.

Do you ever feel so full of self-disgust that you want to slash yourself? Of course not. You lead such a worthwhile life. I can picture you now, shepherding a group of well-scrubbed boys on a nature walk or a trip to the county museum: opening their minds; moulding their characters; forging the citizens of tomorrow. And perhaps I shall achieve something similar through my writing. Do you remember Brewer, lecturing on Lawrence, pounding his fist like a latter-day John Knox? 'People who do not read are people

unable to base their moral judgements on imaginative engage-
ment with others.' Maybe the same holds true of people who don't
watch films.

Or is that the ultimate writer's fantasy: the fantasist's final
delusion? Which question, oh keeper of the conscience, I pass to
you.

> Ever your devoted pal,
>
> Luke.

Hotel Majestic,
14 blvd de la Croisette,
06400 Cannes,
Côte d'Azur,
France

20th May 1977

Mon cher Professeur,

Look carefully at the notepaper (Ouch! Nancy, that hurts!). No, I didn't steal it. Nor am I Fliss bribing a footman to sneak a stack out of Kensington Palace. It's provided for the use of guests. Yes, the boy from Khartoum is in Room 212, rubbing shoulders with the great and the good at the Festival. Shall I tell you about candlelit dinners with Jane Fonda? Well, no, because she isn't here. But I did stand three fans away from Robert Altman. I was congratulated on my performance in two movies I'd never heard of – one of which I couldn't pronounce! I've even glimpsed a starlet in her natural habitat: topless on the Croisette – no, that isn't something that the French eat with butter and jam, but the mile or so of prime real estate that we big shots stroll up and down (it's not who you see but who you're seen with). To be honest, my view was obscured by the stampede of photographers. I don't know why they make such a big deal. This is Breast City. If the women were any more décolleté, they'd be appearing at the Windmill Theatre.[25]

What's more, as well as the legitimate actors, there's a large contingent of porn stars. Just writing that sentence makes me realise how easily language can be debased: the traditional distinc-

[25] The Windmill, famous for being the only London theatre to remain open throughout the Blitz, featured a repertoire of fan-dancers, comedians and, most famously, near-naked women.

tion was between the legitimate stage and Variety. It beats me why the authorities allow them to gather here – at any rate during May. They cheapen what the rest of us do. That said, I know better than to voice my opinion in certain quarters. The moment you suggest that something – anything – should be banned, Wolfram leaps in with charges of 'Nazi tendencies'. How did we arrive at a position where anyone who dissents from a laissez-faire, let-it-all-hang-out ethos can be routinely branded a fascist? I keep reminding myself that provocation is his stock in trade. Nevertheless, I find it hard to respect anyone – let alone, an artist – who dismisses fiction and extols pornography.

What's the difference (this is Wolfram-speak) between actors who simulate sex in a haze of synthetic sweat and porn stars who use their entire bodies? Why is the fake admired and the truth reviled? The reply that immediately sprang to mind was 'Art', but I knew that he would dismiss it with some 'eye of the beholder' claptrap. So, weighing my words, I said that it might be that pornography was too real. It's the same reason that we value a painting more than a photograph – and a formal study more than a holiday snap. Art is about selection; about leaving gaps; about engaging in a dialogue with the public, whereas pornography permits a dialogue only with itself and, from what I've heard (I'm not being coy here; I've never seen a porn film – have you?), it is largely restricted to grunts. I quoted your phrase (watch out for the boomerang!) about the distinction between erotica and pornography being that pornography aims straight for the groin without stopping at the imagination along the way. Art, I concluded, lay in what was held back. 'Yes,' he replied pointedly, 'holding back is what the English do best.'

Do write and let me know what you think – although don't address anything here. We fly back to Munich at the end of the week. I wish you could fix a trip. Why not pretend to come down with scarlet fever or something equally noxious to growing boys?

(I still remember your scrofula in *Troilus*). It would be an act of compassion. I can't tell you how starved I am of intelligent conversation . . . well, I could, but it would make your head swell. When I rang last month, I was greeted so brusquely – I presume by your shot-putting matron – that I vowed never to risk it again. It's not that people here aren't friendly, but there's no one with whom I can kick around ideas. Let's hear it for those after-hours sessions in your room in Christ's! Fliss is, as ever, my salvation, but she appears to have inherited her mother's belief that ideas are best contemplated in private, like bank-balances and bowels. You ought to have been there last Christmas when Um (that's a phonetic representation of my confusion over what to call her) pounced on my mere mention of castratos. 'A eunuch is not a fit subject for the dinner table,' she decreed. I had to do a quick check to ensure that my own balls were still in place.

Speaking of bowels, you ought to be very grateful that you weren't cast as Hitler, given the aspect of his psyche that Wolfram intends to stress. If you're not familiar with *coprophilia*, look it up in the school dictionary as soon as the boys are safely tucked up in bed. On the other hand, you may find the pages so well thumbed that they open of their own accord the way that mine did at *orgasm*. 'A climax of venereal excitement': even now the words carry an electric charge but, then, they were so seductive that I almost confirmed the definition on the spot. I very much doubt that the same will apply to you. A sick-bag may be more in order. Nevertheless, it should be instructive. Don't ask me how he plans to shoot it; I'm only the writer. And, as if to prove that writers don't enjoy the same cachet in Cannes that they do in Cambridge, Fliss came out with a joke that was doing the rounds in the Carlton Bar. It concerned an actress so dumb that she slept with the writer. Wolfram guffawed; Mahmoud sniggered; I smiled politely. I was surprised that she should show so little self-awareness. When you think about it, the joke's on her.

If you can't place Mahmoud, substitute Mohammed. After all, that's what I've been doing for the past six months. No wonder he's been giving me such filthy looks. Why didn't he say something? If I'd been mangling your name, wouldn't you have set me straight? But, no, not a whisper. I wouldn't have felt so bad if it had been anyone else: if I'd been Wolfganging Wolfram or Renéeing Renate. Mohammed makes me sound like my father addressing every black man as 'Boy'. I was so convinced that it was an epithet unique to Africans that, when a teacher in Hastings yelled 'Boy!' at me, I was appalled. 'You can't say that,' I piped indignantly. 'I'm English.'

Mahmoud . . . Mahmoud . . . Mahmoud: it's ingrained on my mind and on my conscience. Wolfram took him to the Festival Ball. I thought it very brave of them to go as partners, but Fliss maintained that Mahmoud's gender was less of an issue than his race. His Arab blood inspires a level of prurience that would be lacking if he came from Tunbridge Wells. I admit (to you, and you alone) that I too have indulged in the odd speculation. Even so, it ill behoves Fliss to rail against national stereotypes while dealing them up herself. Not content with Germans who eat frankfurters, French who chew garlic, and English who are *rosbifs*, she has produced an adult version. The Germans believe that you can do whatever you like so long as you're locked in a cellar; the French that, whatever you do, you must be home in time to dine; the English that, no matter what you do, you'll have to pay for it in the end.

Enough of this dodgy shag story and back to the Festival. *The Magic Mountain* was a triumph. The film is said to be a hot tip for the Palme d'Or (although Wolfram holds out little hope after his run-in with Rossellini[26]) and Dieter Reiss to be favourite for Best

---

[26] Roberto Rossellini, the Italian film director and President of the 1977 Festival Jury.

Actor. I worried that, if he wins, he might pass on playing Julius Streicher which is, after all, a minor role. Wolfram, however, was confident of his loyalty. The group works like an old-fashioned rep. One week, you're playing the Countess and the next, the maid . . . unless you happen to be Renate, in which case you're always the maid. She's here too, of course, although, according to Fliss, she had to buy her own ticket. She would have been reduced to sleeping on the beach, had Kurt – the composer – not lent her his bath. Wolfram was furious, damning him for a traitor. Then, the following day, he took out a wad of notes (we're talking Godfather-thick) and told Renate to buy herself a dress for the premiere . . . Sometimes, I yearn for the clear-cut animosities of the ADC.

The film's success was especially welcome, given the problems of financing *Unity*. Wolfram depends on official subsidy, but the board unexpectedly turned him down. Werner says that this is partly the result of the continuing controversy over *The Judge*, but also of fears about the subject. The Germans, understandably, have stringent laws about representing Hitler. (I should have liked to ask Wolfram how that squares with his anything-goes philosophy. Are they manifesting Nazi attitudes in banning depictions of Nazism? But, as always, my *esprit d'escalier* was stuck on the bottom step.) Wolfram claims that the reason for the board's fighting shy is a mixture of a budget which is far higher than for his previous films (news that fills me with a perverse pride) and his decision to shoot in English. Fortunately, he has found a backer in Thomas Bücher, an independent producer whose work is unknown to me – to judge by the titles, they're the kind of flimsy romantic comedy that would sink in mid-Channel. He has had a chequered career, including a spell in a concentration camp, a fact that made me intensely apprehensive about meeting him. Feeble I know, but I felt so callow in the face of his experience. I was sure that I would say the wrong thing (It's your fault with all your digs about foot-in-mouth disease!). What's more, I was filled with an overwhelming dread that, the moment he sat down, he would roll up his sleeve. I needn't have worried. His cuffs were as perfectly aligned as the rest of him. He is a sixty-year-old man of great dignity: poker-backed, silver-haired, with haunted, hooded eyes like the Buñuel actor, Fernando Rey.[27] With his impeccable clothes and grooming, he looks as if he were permanently setting out for the opera.

At the end of *The Magic Mountain* press conference, Wolfram announced his plans to film *Unity*. He then summoned Fliss and me on to the platform (WITH NO WARNING!). I was horrified to hear him say that *Unity* had won the Best Play award in Edinburgh and that I was under commission to both the RSC (or, as he put it, the Royal Stratford Company) and the National Theatre. Do you think they collect cuttings? Will I be writer *non grata* for life? As we faced the photographic firing squad, I broke out in a muck sweat. Fliss, on the other hand, was coolness personified. In contrast to the starlets, she played the English rose, fresh and demure but with prickles – a *Dorothy Perkins* crossed with Dorothy Parker. Her mother would have been proud. The journalists went wild for her family tree. You'd think she were a member of the Royal Family rather than a remote connection. Some of their reports even elevated her to Lady Felicity (strangely enough, the German press did the same to Unity). Still, it seems to have worked. When it comes to column inches: Breeding Five, Breasts One.

When not meeting the press, we've been meeting actors. Since we start shooting in less than three months, you may think that it's cutting it a little fine (and you wouldn't be far wrong), but it's Wolfram's way. He likes to bring me along, ostensibly to help with the English but, as he already has an interpreter, I just sit there

---

[27] The Spanish actor, best known for his roles in Buñuel's *Tristana*, *Viridiana* and *Le Charme Discret de la Bourgeoisie*, who beat Dieter Reiss to win the 1977 Prix d'Interprétation Masculine at Cannes.

sending out positive vibes. Sometimes he even forgets to introduce me, which is fine except when I'm taken for his boyfriend, as happened with Sir Hallam Bamforth or, worse, when I'm left to entertain a boyfriend as happened with Kris Bryant (all I can tell you is that the legendary muscles of steel stop short of his wrists!). Said boyfriend's entire conversation consisted of gym routines and health food ('I've checked out every grocery store in town. And you know what? No wheat germ!'). I felt like Mrs Carter, forced to watch a display of folk-dancing while her husband and President Brezhnev determined the fate of the world.

Sir Hallam, by the way, is ninety percent committed. 'My memory's too poor for the stage and my hooter's too big for the box, so it's the flicks or the workhouse,' he said, with a disarming smile. Wolfram has asked him to play the British Consul, which may surprise you, but the part has been beefed up for the film. He has one great scene (though I say so myself), where he makes an impassioned plea to Goebbels to abandon the whole Nazi programme. Signing him would be such a coup. There can be no finer representative of civilised values, nor one who inspires more affection across the globe. It makes no sense: fifty years of triumphs in the classics and he's best-known for playing a purser in a disaster movie opposite an actor (and I quote) 'whose phenomenal gross – though discerning viewers might prefer to transpose the epithet – has made him the toast of Hollywood.'

Knowing that he was once your idol, I took pains to remember everything he said in order to report back. I expect that you've long since reordered your pantheon in favour of Thomas Arnold or A. S. Neill[28] but, on the assumption that you still have a niche for old heroes, I offer this account. As with Bücher, I was terrified about meeting him – although for different reasons. Again, I was

[28] Arnold was the headmaster of Rugby School in the 1830s and Neill the founder of Summerhill School in 1927.

instantly put at my ease. As soon as we'd cleared up the confusion over my status (he was mortified), we had an excellent talk. He has the modesty that accompanies true greatness (I've always thought that a cliché until now), expressing his profound gratitude that young people should take an interest in him, since they – we – are what keep him fresh. Fliss gave his words a sinister slant, alleging that he's rapaciously queer, but then she says that about everyone she admires yet doesn't fancy. He strikes me as utterly asexual – as though he'd spent so many years reciting Shakespeare that his veins flow with blank verse rather than blood.

We met in the hotel bar, where Fliss seems to have taken up permanent residence. She claims to be studying how the rich spend their money (she's so acquisitive[29]). When I suggested that she look a little closer to home, she did her usual trick of describing the dower house as a tied cottage. Meanwhile, I pass the time by playing celebrity-I-spy. That evening, the first that I spotted was Sir Hallam. Unlike an American star with his phalanx of publicists, he was sitting alone. Charged by Fliss, I invited him to join us. To my surprise, he accepted. He was embarrassingly flattering about the script . . . although Fliss later told me to discount his praise since he's infamous for only ever reading his own role (which explains his appearance in *The Academy* among all those debauched Athenians). He informed us that he had met Unity backstage at the Old Vic. We pumped him for memories. 'I think it was Diana Wynward who brought her. Now there was an actress. Did you see her Beatrice? No, of course not. You're far too young. . . . The only thing I recall about her is that she barely spoke. But then very few people do in a dressing-room. Especially when you're playing a king. And I've played so

---

[29] Given the impossibility of determining from either handwriting or context whether this should read 'acquisitive' or 'inquisitive', I have opted for the former as the truer assessment of Felicity's character.

many. It says in one of the books that I was a heartthrob of hers. Oh dear! One does attract some very strange people.'

As if on cue, an American matron with a magnifying glass dangling on an already voluminous bosom descended on us and asked 'Sir Bamforth' if he would sign an autograph for her granddaughter. The slighted knight graciously obliged.

Just as Wolfram relates everything to the cinema, so Sir Hallam does to the theatre. Mention any world event of the past fifty years and he'll tell you what he was appearing in at the time. As soon as I brought up the Munich crisis, he told me that he had been 'at the Haymarket in *Rosmersholm* with darling Hattie. It was terribly bad for business. The audience stayed away in droves.' He himself made an extensive tour of Germany in 1936 ('the summer between *Quality Street* and the *Dream*'), which he described, rather archly, as his sauerkraut days. It started with a mission to Berlin to persuade Christopher Isherwood, whose verse plays with Auden had enjoyed a modest success,[30] to write a piece for him. 'Of course, it came to nothing. I think they regarded me as too West End.'

He is endearingly indiscreet. Talking of 'darling Hattie', he remarked that her autumnal success was 'conclusive proof of the adage that old age is the revenge of ugly women.' George V, who slept through a command performance of *Henry IV*, was 'a man so lowbrow he thought highbrow was spelt eyebrow.' Churchill, who watched productions of Shakespeare with the text propped on his knee, 'used to collect his thoughts so slowly that he appeared to be anthologising them.' On learning that Geraldine Mortimer was being mooted to play Diana, he described her as 'a woman who has never been able to live down to her reputation', adding that 'most actresses are wanting to be discovered; she was discovered

---

[30] Bamforth must be mistaken about the date, since Isherwood and his lover, Heinz, left Germany in 1934.

to be wanting.' Fliss, ever the cynic, claimed that the line sounded so rehearsed that he must have used it before.[31] He is adamant that, if Geraldine is cast, he will have a clause written into his contract banning her from talking politics on set.

I, on the other hand, will be more than happy to sit through his entire repertoire of anecdotes. And there'll be ample opportunity. This is one writer who won't be restricted to a courtesy tour of the studio, taking care not to trip over the stars. At first, Wolfram asked me to stay on as dialogue coach (oh yes, like I'm going to tell Sir Hallam Bamforth how to speak his lines!). Now, however, he has decided to cast me as Brian Howard.[32] There's no need to rack your brains; Howard is another post-Edinburgh addition. It's not a large part so I don't expect my Oscar to gain a twin, but it should be fun. I only wish that I hadn't agreed to write a rather steamy scene between Howard and one of the boys that Unity pimped for him at the Munich *Fasching*.[33] Wolfram's purpose – and it's an honourable one – is to highlight Unity's double standards in indulging her friends while, at the same time, her beloved Storms were dragging sex offenders to jail. If I suggest toning it down, he'll accuse me of exhibiting double standards myself. I suppose I'll just have to grin and bare it – and hope that my mother nips out for an ice cream.[34]

There are some things that I won't bear, and some people that I won't bare them for, at any rate in private. Not everything in Cannes has been stardust and glass slippers. Three nights ago, I

[31] Felicity was right. See Gillian Denny's biography of Bamforth, *Every Inch A King*, Sinclair Stevenson 1991, page 216.

[32] English writer and aesthete, reputedly the wittiest man of his generation. See Marie-Hélène Lancaster, *Brian Howard, Portrait of a Failure*, Anthony Blond 1968.

[33] This has nothing to do with fascism but is, rather, the annual Lent carnival.

[34] Luke's fears were misplaced. When I recently viewed the salvaged footage of *Unity* at the Meier Foundation, this scene was particularly powerful.

had a nasty run-in with Wolfram, which I was convinced would put paid to my whole film career. I should make it clear that there was no damage, apart from the permanent dent in my trust. But it shook me. We'd come back from the Warner Brothers party. Fliss accompanied some actors for a drink in the bar and Wolfram followed me upstairs, saying that he had something to discuss. I don't know whether he was buoyed by the reception of his film or high on drugs or simply in holiday spirits, but he pounced on me, right here, in this room, on the bed where I'm writing this letter. I'll spare you a full account, except to say that, for someone so skinny, he was remarkably strong. I was so taken aback that I was afraid he'd mistake my shock for acquiescence. I decided that the best bet was to treat it as a game: a bout of locker-room horseplay. 'I give in,' I yelled. 'You're the winner!' But he was having none of it and grappled with me like a man possessed. I had no recourse but to hit back, which I did, punching him hard in the chest. I winded him and broke free. I expected him to slink away. But not a bit of it. He accused me of provoking him, of giving off signals, of not knowing my own mind, oh, of all sorts of rubbish. I'd accuse him of attempted rape if the word weren't so loaded (although I now know that it is no more restricted to women than Boy is to blacks).

What is it with the stalky business of sex? How could he have shown such a lack of respect for my feelings, not to mention his own dignity? I'm not naive (no, really, you and Fliss played that card far longer than was warranted); I'm aware that he's attracted to me. But so what? I'm attracted to his films, and yet I don't try to steal his camera. I decided right from the start that the most sensible tactic was to make light of his interest and root our relationship in play. Anything else threatened to turn me into the stuffed shirt of his allegations. So I studiously ignored his leaning against me in lifts and rubbing his leg against me at dinner and giving me neck massages which left me far tenser than when I was hunched over the keys. My reserve merely confirmed his view of the cold, passionless English: a confusion of temperature and temperament with which, to avoid embarrassment, I was willing to comply.

Please don't be offended, but can you explain to me why gay men assume that anyone who doesn't respond to their advances must be repressed? I know that it's a generalisation and there will always be exceptions (I'm writing to one now), but you only have to think back to Brian and Crispin solemnly asserting that all queer-bashers are secretly queer in order to appreciate the truth. They're as bad as the people who claim that Hitler was anti-Semitic because he feared that he might have Jewish blood: a view which is not merely flawed but dangerous. It's as if self-hatred were the only hatred that can be understood and – what's more insidious – that can be justified.

I'm sorry to dump all this on you, but I thought that you'd want to know. Fliss, on the other hand, showed a lack of concern that was almost hurtful (although that may have been my fault for fudging the details). Even so, I'd have been murderous if he'd tried anything similar with her. Like Judge Out-Of-Touch castigating a victim for wearing a mini-skirt, she managed to make out that I was the one in the wrong. She accused me of over-reacting (her exact phrase was 'being a drama queen', which struck me as particularly inapt). Sex was such a trivial thing (this, remember, was my girlfriend speaking!); it would cost me so little and please him so much. I should think of it as cabbage (I presume in the sense of swallowing something unpleasant). She dismissed my disgust as a morbid fear of penetration. Which is nonsense. If it's anything, it's a healthy fear of pain. Besides, as she knows better than anyone, it goes way beyond the physical. I'm not gay. The closest I've ever come was when I was playing Patroclus. And you may recall how slippery I found him. What you don't know – but then this seems to be the moment for revelations – is how hard I worked at his sexuality. Stumped by his attraction to Achilles, I decided to improvise. I locked the door, stood naked between the wardrobe mirrors, stared at my bottom and wanked. It didn't help.

My fears about having to face Wolfram turned out to be groundless, since he acted as though nothing untoward had occurred. I was determined to prevent any further misunderstanding so I told him what I'd told Fliss, namely that I was in love with her and could never contemplate sleeping with another woman, let alone a man. Neither of them responded in the way that I'd hoped. Fliss, ignoring my avowal, tempted me with Brigitte Bardot. I explained that it would make no difference if the woman on offer were Brigitte Bardot or Hermione Gingold; it still wouldn't be her. Wolfram patted my cheek (a sure sign that I was back in favour) and called me his incurable romantic – 'mein unheilbarer Romantiker' – which, needless to say, was not a compliment. In his view, believing in love in the age of Freud is as anachronistic as ironing a shirt in the age of nylon or reading a book in the age of film. 'Romantic love is dead. *Madame Bovary* and *Anna Karenina* will be as obscure in the future as the bible stories that inspired our grandfathers are to us.'

I have to stop now, which is probably just as well since I'm sure you have your fill of tortured sexuality at school. Fliss has come back from the Menachem Golem party. See what I give up for you! She wants me to tell you that she thinks you're a star for ploughing through all this (Gee, thanks for the vote of confidence!) and that she promises to write you a letter soon. She also wants me to tell you . . . what . . .? I can't quite make out above the water, but I think it's that 'just because I can't be bothered doesn't mean that I don't care'.

Must dash. The room is filling up with a delightful scent of lavender and I'm being summoned to scrub the most gorgeous back in Cannes.

Ever your devoted pal,
Luke.

8 München 40,
Giselastrasse 23,
West Germany

11th Sept 1977

Wertester Freund,

Thanks so much for the Oxo cubes. You've saved my life. I won't pretend that they can ever replace Marmite, but they're easily the next best thing. And, until the manufacturers (what a miserable word for the geniuses behind Marmite) come up with an airmail version, the jars would be ruinous to post. You've made an old Marmiteholic very happy. So, once again, many thanks.

Now, please, please, please, can we drop the guilt-trip? So what if your letters are shorter than mine? In the immortal words of Fliss's yoga teacher, 'it's not a competition'. Besides, an Oxo cube is worth a thousand words. No, but seriously, if anyone should apologise, it's me for rambling on. I put it down to growing up in the Sudan. Every month, my grandmother used to send us one of those niggardly pre-paid air-letters, which felt as if every phrase had been carefully costed. She wasn't going to pay for any excess verbiage! An analyst would probably say that was what drove me to the other extreme ('It is quite clear, Herr Dent, that your hostility towards your grandmother springs from a repressed desire to sleep with her'). So, if you have a problem, blame it on my childhood. I always do.

I also owe you an apology for having waited so long to reply, but Munich has been manic. At least now we've survived the first week of shooting, we can take the odd moment to relax. The schedule here is even tighter than in England. You must have grasped the pressures we were under when you visited us on loca-tion (Now that really was too short!). I'm only sorry that you chose such a dreary day. If you'd wanted to watch a chauffeur park a Rolls Royce ten times, you could have taken the tube to Bond

Street. In fact, that was all too familiar a pattern. Unbeknownst to anyone (apart from Fliss and her entire family, who thought it not worth a mention), Schloss Benthall is in the direct flight-path of an American airbase. As the five-hundredth plane roared past, we started to suspect that they were under secret instructions from Hollywood to fly as often and as low as possible. Even so, I hope that you picked up enough tips to impress the boys – if only with your inside knowledge of the factors that can disrupt filming. I'm sorry if I failed you on the 'dish-the-dirt' front. I know what an old gossip you are! When I'm summoned to MGM, I promise to give you the exclusive story of my love-nest with the stars. Speaking of which, Fliss sends her love.

Meanwhile, why the sudden attack of reticence? Of course I'd be happy to jot down a few observations of life on set for your English class. What's more to the point is whether you'll be prepared to shoulder the additional guilt such a letter is bound to inspire (I know that's below the belt, but you deserve it). There's no point in my trying to squeeze into Size 4 shoes, so I'll just have to hope that the boys are interested in the same things I am (which, if you believe Fliss, is more than likely). I give you full permission to discard or embellish whatever you wish.

I think that my overriding impression is one of muddle, although I don't suppose that that's very helpful ('Clarity of thought, Dent minor. That's what's kept the upper classes up!'). Wherever you look, there are people busy with their allotted tasks. The grips are laying cables from the generator vans and tracks for the cameras. The electricians are installing lighting rigs. The sound engineers are checking . . . well, I leave you to guess. The actors are being ferried between wardrobe and make-up, while their stand-ins seize a solitary moment of glory in front of the focus puller's tape. And yet out of all the mayhem, the crash of equipment and egos, there somehow emerges a film.

My second impression is harder to convey. It has to do with

vulnerability. As with the planes, we're forever at the mercy of forces beyond our control. Take last Monday. We were filming at the Führerbau, the former Nazi reception building. (For all Wolfram's talk of psychic resonance, I find it spooky. Lord knows how the drama students cope. Cambridge ghosts were oppressive enough and few of them were mass murderers.[35]) The scene in question was one where Unity and Diana take Lord and Lady Redesdale to tea with Hitler. Although it could hardly have been simpler – an establishing shot of Martin Bormann greeting the group on the steps and ushering them indoors – tension was heightened on account of its being the two Geralds' (Geraldine's and her father's) first day on set in Munich. Apart from the hanging of two giant eagles above the doors, the building itself required remarkably little transformation, but Gerhard (the Director of Photography) spent hours adjusting the lighting. Wolfram's trademark 'Seid Ihr fertig?' became ever more pointed, but Gerhard refused to be rushed. Then, the moment he declared himself satisfied, the heavens opened. So we all trooped inside to a mock-up of Hitler's office, which had been prepared as a contingency, only to find that the sky had turned so overcast that it too had to be relit.

Dora – that's Dora Manners in case you're wondering (although I think I introduced her to you in England[36]) – who's playing Muv,[37] put it best when she compared it to queuing for bread in Russia. As soon as it's your turn, they run out of supplies. In our

[35] Luke was particularly sensitive on this point, having been harassed by Irish nationalists during his third year at Sidney Sussex, when he lived in Oliver Cromwell's old room.

[36] Luke is mistaken. All the actors, apart from Felicity, were busy during the day I spent on set, but I was warmly welcomed by the make-up assistants and runners.

[37] Muv and Farve were the names by which the Mitford sisters knew their parents.

case, it's Gerhard who's cast as the villain. Every shot, however short, requires its own lighting. First we do the master shot. Then it's relit. Then we do a close-up. Then it's relit. Then we do a reverse shot. Then it's relit. And, each time, the actors are left to kick their heels. Do emphasise to any budding Bogarts or Bogardes in the form how essential it is that they develop a liking for crosswords. I shall never again sneer at film stars who complain of exhaustion (all that 'working on a trawler is nothing compared to the trauma of filming *The Cruel Sea*'). In a twelve – and sometimes fourteen hour – day, they face the camera for a matter of minutes and yet they have to remain in a constant state of alertness. On reflection, it's less like waiting for bread than waiting for a bomb.

Talking of Dora (or should that be thinking of Dora? See, I can read you like a book), let me tell you that she's amazing. I swear that, given half an hour, you'd be crazy about her and I don't mean in that gay man/icon kind of way. She's exactly what you'd expect from all those Ealing films. It's almost a shock to see her in colour. The husky voice is every bit as seductive off-screen as on.[38] The champagne curls and retroussé nose are every bit as charming. Far from damaging her looks, the laugh lines (her actual laugh is deliciously dirty) add authenticity. Lord knows how old she is. Fliss, who hasn't taken to her (do you detect a whiff of the hen coop?), says that she starred in her first film before the War, so she has to be knocking sixty. You'd never guess. I made the mistake of suggesting that it must be because she's small-boned. Ouch! She certainly makes no concessions to age and has been openly flirting with younger actors. One of them, Liam Finch (a.k.a. Oswald Mosley), actually asked her how old she was. 'It all depends where you measure from,' she purred. 'How about birth?' he replied.

---

[38] Kenneth Tynan, in a characteristically barbed review of her 1963 performance in *The Second Mrs Tanqueray*, wrote that she 'tended the frog in her throat as lovingly as if it were about to turn into a prince'.

She even tried it on with me – not in so many words, I admit, but, hey, I'm a writer; my middle name is Subtext. I was explaining how I'd been going out with Fliss for nearly four years. 'I know,' she said. Though I can't imagine how, since I'm sure Fliss didn't tell her. What's more, she made me promise not to tell any of the Germans in case they regarded us as freaks. 'But as a distinguished conductor once asked me,' Dora said, '"Are you mono or stereo?"' 'Mono, I'm afraid,' I mumbled. 'I'm an old-fashioned guy.'

After that diversion, I had better take you back to the set, although I'm not quite sure to which part. I'd like to say something about Wolfram's techniques, but I must stress (as should you) that they are highly idiosyncratic. He never plans his shots in advance. Indeed, he rarely visits the location at all before the shoot. He storyboards (in lay terms, sketches the camera angles) the previous night or early in the morning or, sometimes even, while they are setting up (it's not just in private that he likes to live on the edge). But – and this is crucial – he has spent weeks prior to the filming talking to Heike and Gerhard and the rest of the team about how he intends everything to look. He trusts them enough to leave them to take care of the details. Which is one of the reasons that they work for him time and again. The other is their absolute respect for his vision. They insist that, appearances to the contrary, 'he knows exactly what he wants'. To them, that is the pinnacle of praise.

He grants similar licence to his actors but it is not always so welcome. He encourages them to rehearse for far longer than most directors – and directs them far less. Then, barring accidents (see above), he likes to shoot in a single take, which, as you can imagine, places the entire unit under tremendous strain. He claims to be less interested in technical perfection ('Fuck perfection. Life isn't perfect.') than in spontaneity. His watchwords are the three 'a's: *Ablauf; Aktion; Atmosphäre* (or, in English, the two 'a's and a 'p': action, atmosphere and pace). His critics allege – not without some justification – that he has made an aesthetic out of his own impatience. But even the harshest of them cannot deny its success.

While his regular actors are accustomed to his methods, outsiders can find them daunting. On set, this creates a gulf between the English and German factions that would be more appropriate to a war film than a story of international friendship. With the notable exception of Ralf Heyn, whom Wolfram cast after seeing him play Hitler in a Berliner Schaubühne piece about the 20th July plot,[39] the Germans have all been working for him since the Bettlertheater days. Indeed, some critics might allege – not, of course, that I would be among them – that he has made an aesthetic out of their inadequacy. They are a tight-knit group who exude the same hostility towards newcomers that I encountered when I started school in Hastings. For all their show of friendliness, they are permanently on their guard against any potential prize-winner or Teacher's Pet.

Meanwhile, in the English camp . . . sorry, trailer, discontent is rumbling. I speak on the authority of Luke the actor, who has access to areas from which Luke the writer would be barred. So far, I've been spared any conflict of interest. Although, from the way that Wolfram quizzed me yesterday, I began to suspect that he had cast me primarily for my abilities as a spy (that's one element that you mustn't omit from your location report: paranoia). I exempt Fliss from the ranks of the dissenters since spontaneity is her strongest suit. For all her exceptional qualities, she lacks the experience to reproduce an emotion over a succession of takes. What she does have is an extraordinary vitality and freshness, which, from the footage I've watched, Wolfram has perfectly caught. I

39 The failed coup against Hitler on 20 July 1944, after which hundreds of suspected conspirators were executed.

know that you'll think me partial but wait till you see for yourself (at a private screening, of course). You won't believe that it's the same girl with whom you acted at the ADC. What's more, she has made a quantum leap in confidence. Having read that some famous actress (is it Glenda Jackson?) considers it the root of self-consciousness, she refuses to look at herself in the rushes. She has, however, received enough positive feedback, especially from Wolfram, to feel happy with what she has done. Her entire outlook has lightened. I realise now that the hiccup in our relationship last spring (hiccup – I felt as though I were choking!) sprang directly from her fears about the film. Part of her was convinced that it would never happen (a latter-day Lana Turner would be trapped in the drug-store for life) and the other part that, if it did, she would make herself a laughing-stock. I feel such a heel for having been so heartless: for focusing so intently on the script that I was blind to her needs. After all, it's only my words on the screen (and, in some cases, not many of those!), it's her soul.

Of all our compatriots, the two who find it hardest to adapt to Wolfram's approach are Geraldine and Gerald. When we finally shot the office scene on Monday afternoon, she inquired plaintively about a second take. Having grown up in a city where nips and tucks are as commonplace on-screen as off, she expected her performance to be spliced together in the cutting-room. When Wolfram told her that they would be printing the first, she looked desolate. But, in a rare show of sensitivity, he took her aside and soothed her nerves (I wasn't snooping; the interpreter's voice was deliberately pitched at a wider audience). He explained that the most important person on any film was the casting director and, on his films, that was him. She could be absolutely sure that she was the best actress for the part with a unique quality that would bring Diana alive.

I think that, of everyone involved in the film, I find her the most intimidating. It's the usual actor/fan thing coupled with a return to childhood (at six, I even had a copy of *The Swiss Family Robinson* with her picture on the front). In her company, I feel as if my teddy bears had come alive and taken me on their picnic. Besides which, I am awe-struck by her beauty. While her politics make her the least likely casting for Diana, her looks are the perfect match. And yet she seems to disparage them, making a determined effort to appear as plain as possible. The paradox is that it works in reverse, the way that Dora's fondness for trousers emphasises her femininity. Moreover, she is so cold – the polar opposite of her on-screen persona. Do you suppose that some people have a warmth that is only captured on camera the way that others have an attraction? There again, it may be armour. It can't be easy to have been a star at eight, a has-been at eighteen and, now, to be making her first film in over ten years – to say nothing of having been relentlessly pilloried in the press. I'd like to ask her about her opinions but such is the strength of the caricature that it's hard to sound sincere. The jury is still out on whether she's a genuine idealist or a disingenuous fanatic. But then confusion is only to be expected when Alice walks into Wonderland and comes back as Madame Mao.

Having Gerald Mortimer for her father muddies the waters still further. And, by the way, what egoism . . . I'm surprised that the vicar didn't raise a protest at the font. Given that his fights for King and Country, not to mention Queen and Empire, have made him a true blue hero wherever the celluloid flag is flown, her politics can be read as a direct attack on him. That's certainly the impression he has fostered in a series of ever more caustic interviews in which he blames her for his waning career. In the latest, he expressed the hope that she would marry and change her name or else he might have to change his by deed poll (playing all those hidebound Victorians must have addled his brain!). There was, however, no sign of acrimony when Geraldine (and what seemed like half of Germany's press corps) drove out to the airport to welcome him. There was something strangely poignant about seeing a man who had fought his way so memorably through the Malay jungle, standing arm in arm thirty years later with a Japanese wife. At least there was for me. I can't speak for his daughter. As she hugged her father and pecked her new step-mother on the cheek, Geraldine's face was a blank.

Unlike his daughter, Gerald seems to have stepped – or rather jumped – straight out of one of his movies. Indeed, he bounded from the plane as if he were about to lead his troops into battle. There can be no doubt that he has worn well. In contrast to Sir Hallam, he has retained a full head of hair, although the white is tinged with the yellow of a smoker's moustache. As with so many small men (think Jim and that actor at Pembroke[40]), he seems to be constantly seeking the advantage. Even the way he stands, leaning forward with the weight on the balls of his feet, feels like a threat. His press conference showed that he may be in civvies, but he remains as combative as ever. One journalist (from a British paper, natch) asked him if he felt comfortable playing an aristocrat, given that he was one of Nature's NCOs. 'Listen lad,' he bellowed across the airport, 'I was cocking my little finger when you were fingering your little cock.' Somehow, I don't see that featuring prominently in the *Daily Mail*. So far, he has addressed barely a word to me – no more than he did in England. Whether he is keeping in character as Lord Redesdale and views all writers as 'sewers' or whether he is being true to his Hollywood training and regards us as expendable, I can't say. Either way, I expect I'll survive. Ho hum!

---

[40] This appears to be an allusion to Anthony Dupont who went on to achieve fame in the ITV sitcom, *Jack and the Beanpole*.

I am intrigued by his relationship with Sir Hallam. They clearly have some kind of history . . . no, don't get excited: not that kind of history! We're talking Hollywood Bath Spa not *Hollywood Babylon*. When Sir Hallam arrived on Wednesday, Gerald was waiting for him in the lobby and insisted on accompanying him to his suite. 'What's the betting,' Dora asked, 'that Gerald will have moved before the morning's out?' Later, when I asked her how she'd known, she said that it was easy. 'No estate agent has a keener eye for the measure of rooms than a veteran actor.' It's a joy to listen to them spar. First, Gerald treats Sir Hallam to an exaggerated show of deference: 'A chair for the premier knight of the British theatre! A drink for our eminent Shakespearean!' Then, Sir Hallam betters him without even raising his voice. 'These begging letters are very tiresome, Gerald. Ever since I won the Oscar, people think I must be dreadfully rich. But then I don't need to tell you. You must have gone through exactly the same.' What he knows full well is that, for all his seventy-odd credits, Gerald has never once been nominated.

That Sir Hallam should have beaten him at his own game is particularly galling to Gerald, whose natural tendency to turn the whole of life into a virility contest is accentuated when it comes to the contrast between cinema and theatre. And yet, the more I see of filming, the more I am persuaded that, in spite of the widespread conviction that real men don't wear tights, it's on stage that actors live up to their name. On screen, they are merely fragments of a director's vision. Sir Hallam expressed it with his customary discernment when he said 'On stage, I am a person; on screen, I am a prop.' Then he walked on set, chanting 'prop, prop, prop,' as if it were a mantra. When I challenged him, he replied 'Oh yes. Something beautifully polished and highly prized, like a Sheraton chair, but a prop all the same.'

Sir Hallam (Hallam . . .? Hal . . .?) has already become a firm favourite with the crew. He joins them for breakfast at seven even when he's not called, although Gerald, with predictable malice, claims that it's simply a way to save on his per diems. He refuses to stand on his dignity – sometimes literally. Yesterday, when the rest of the cast were driven to the set, he rode pillion with one of the grips. Gerald excepted, the one person whom he has failed to win over is yours truly, ever since he sent in some amendments to his dialogue, along with a covering note pointing out phrases that 'an English gentleman would not use'. Wolfram handed it to me with the exultant look of someone sniffing out an impostor. But I've never pretended to be anything other than Tradesman's Entrance. I come from a world of people who circle their 'i's and loop their 't's. Besides, he is hardly a scion of the ancient family of Von Meiers.

By the way, do you know how you pronounce 'scion'? It's a word that I've only ever seen on the page. I shall make it my mission to revive it. From now on, you won't hear the sons for the scions.

Even Wolfram is in awe of Sir Hallam, which he manifests by refusing to speak to him except via the interpreter. This plunges the knight into agonies of self-doubt. He yearns for firm direction. At the first rehearsal, he confided that 'All my little tricks, you must knock them out of me, Wolfram, dear fellow. Just beat them out as hard as you like.' Which, to my surprise, was rendered as '*Prügeln Sie das aus mir heraus*', making it sound as though he wanted to be whipped. Having been criticised throughout his career for being too theatrical for the camera, he was particularly perturbed when Wolfram told him to play the scene 'Exactly as in the theatre.' Thinking that something must have been lost in translation, he appealed to me to intercede. The reply, however, was the same. I explained that, from my understanding, Wolfram's principal demand of an actor was that he make no attempt to disguise the person that he was off-screen. His brief was to adapt the character to his personality rather than the other way round.

The rationale for this is that we all spend our lives acting. We have no authentic selves. I am not a friend writing this letter; I'm playing the part of a friend writing this letter. And so forth. It's a depressingly cynical view of humanity, but it makes for undeniably powerful movies. Wolfram's one general note at the read-through made a similar point (I'm translating freely). 'You are not to play the characters but the characters' idea of themselves. I don't want any of that Stanislavski shit. I don't want identification and angst. But I don't want the Berliner Ensemble[41] either. I don't want Ralf's comment on Hitler or Felicity's on Unity; I want Hitler's comment on Hitler and Unity's on Unity.' Suddenly, the whole basis of his casting made sense. It didn't matter that he had one of the greatest actors in the world alongside a girl who'd just left Cambridge Their own talents were simply a reflection of their characters' abilities across a range of roles.

I hope that this is along the lines that you were expecting. As I said at the start, feel free to use as much or as little as you wish – although you'd better go easy on the Gerald stuff. It would be just my luck if some snotty-nosed kid in the back row turned out to be the son – scion? – of his agent.

Meanwhile, this comes with the very best wishes of one who is definitely not acting when he signs himself,

Ever your devoted pal,

Luke.

---

41 The influential theatre company founded by Bertold Brecht with a performance style based on the *Verfremdungseffekt*, which is commonly (and crudely) translated as the 'alienation effect'.

8 München 40
Giselastrasse 23,
West Germany

20th Sept 1977

Dear Michael,

I'm afraid this isn't a Greetings from Merry Munich letter. In fact, I suggest you save it until you're feeling strong. I've been confronting the reality of Nazism. And, with all due respect to the poster in my office, it wasn't Sally Bowles singing while the Reichstag burned. Life isn't a cabaret, old chum. Or if it is, it's set in an operating theatre and performed by a cast of amputees. I'm not naive (no, the time for jokes is truly over). Having grown up in the Sudan, I'm under no illusions about mankind's capacity for violence. But that was tribal. It was nasty people doing nasty things to each other. TO EACH OTHER! It was the same lust for power that has driven every tyrant from Genghis Khan to Stalin. It was a perversion of humanity but it was humanity all the same. The Holocaust, however, was different. The Holocaust was hate in the abstract: hate by decree. It was inhumanity on such a scale that the human race can never recover. The most it can hope for is to make amends.

The Holocaust . . . Nazis . . . the words are muffled by figures. The litany of the dead drowning out the roll-call of the damned. I think that's the problem. I can't get my head around the figures. Perhaps I've been asking for explanations from the wrong people. I should look to mathematicians rather than historians. Six million murdered . . . six million! It's the 'million' that's the killer. As a kid, I imagined a million to be another word for infinity. It was the crock of gold at the end of the rainbow. Now it's the dust that lines a mass grave.

There again, perhaps the problem is the words. Look at how quickly they lose their meaning. Take conscience. You've read

Hamlet. It's what makes cowards of us all. But you've also read the glossary. In Shakespeare's day, it meant consciousness – what Hamlet had too much of – not the guilt feelings that forced Claudius to his knees. I'm no etymologist (now there's a good word, clear-cut, one which could never refer to anything else), but I long to know at what point in the last four hundred years the meaning changed. Who was it that decided Hamlet out, Claudius in? The question is, admittedly, in every sense academic, since Hitler rejected the very concept of conscience – or rather he took the Claudius sense of the word and placed it in the Hamlet sentence. He derided conscience as a Jewish invention. He didn't merely destroy their humanity; he destroyed his own.

Conscience is a big word (although, in German, it's slightly shorter[42]). What about a smaller one, such as Jew? 'What do you call that thing standing in front of you, Fritzi?' (I'm sorry, but this is one instance when stereotypes strike me as justified). 'It's a man, Papi.' 'Take a closer look.' 'It's a man like the sky, Papi, with a star on his coat.' 'No, it's a rat – a Jew rat.' 'But he doesn't have a tail. Don't rats have tails, Papi?' 'They chop them off, Fritzi. When baby Jews are born, they're taken to a rabbi – that's a special Jewish butcher – to have their tails cut off. They may look like you and me but they're rats. And what do we do with rats, Fritzi?' 'We put down poison for them, Papi.' 'That's right, Fritzi.' 'And what do we do with Jews?' 'We put down poison for them, Papi?' 'Good boy, Fritzi. You'll make the Führer proud.'

And that, O Best Beloved, is how the Jew lost his meaning.

But wait, because there are more words – and more lost meanings. As you've probably guessed by now, I've been to Dachau. I shall try to put down my thoughts about it – no, I shall have to put down my thoughts about it – later. The Nazis went to extraordinary lengths to deny their victims' humanity, stripping them of

---

42 The eight-letter *Gewissen*.

clothes, of colour, of hair, of flesh, so that killing them came to seem more like refuse collection than murder (the fact that they needed to go to such lengths was, of course, a testament to the very humanity they were determined to deny). They also stripped them of language. Inmates of concentration camps were forbidden to use words such as casualty or corpse; they were ordered to describe the living as *pieces* and the dead as *rags*. They were non-people suffering a non-death. This went way beyond the necessary disposal of bodies. It went way beyond the common negation of truth. It was so patently untrue that it became an elaborate game. For the first time, I felt some sympathy with those philosophers who claim that nothing has value any more, who place a tea-bag and a Monet side by side and insist that they amount to the same.

I also understand why Simon Lister circulated his petition round Cambridge demanding that the Oxford English Dictionary remove one of its definitions of *Jew*. I can't remember the exact phrase but I know that it was something offensive about being a usurer or a miser. It's still there so you can look it up for yourself. Perhaps you signed. To my shame, I refused. I argued that the meaning should stand (secondary and obsolete, of course) as a way of understanding the past (along with *fig* and *dug* and all those other remaindered idioms). But, having understood the past in Munich, I've changed my mind. Such bigotry should go. It has no place in a living work of reference. Do you remember the talk after the *Faust* screening in Edinburgh when Wolfram linked British integrity with Oxford accents? Huh!

I'd hate to touch a nerve, but do you feel as strongly about words like *pouf* and *queer*[43]? I've never realised until now how similar

---

[43] Had Luke been writing twenty years later, he would have seen *queer* become a term of choice for young gay men and women. They have rehabilitated the word at the expense of many older people's pasts.

the process of denigration is. You put your feet on a pouf; you turn a Jew into a lampshade. They're part of the same linguistic scheme.

On the heels of the words come the jokes. Manfred, who's playing Goebbels, has done some research – the sort that I should have done before tossing off a May Week entertainment – and found that Goebbels was partial to Jewish humour. Do you suppose that was humour about Jews, as in 'how many Jews does it take to plug a gas leak?', or humour by Jews, as in 'died a death at Dachau'? Of course, the best joke of all was the one told by that prince of comedians, Adolf Hitler. But then he was the Führer, so he had a duty to excel. As we know, our Adolf didn't have much time for God, or for his son. I expect he didn't care for the competition. But he couldn't risk alienating the millions of pious Germans. So, to absolve them of any taint of *Rassenschande*, he declared that, according to strict Nazi classification, Jesus wasn't a Jew, since, by virtue of the Virgin Birth, he only had two Jewish grandparents. Boom boom!

Well, it had them rolling in the aisles at Nuremberg.

But how many of them? That's what's bothering me. I've been questioning some of the German actors who say that the hardest thing for them to accept when growing up was that everyone they knew had been an anti-fascist. They were left baffled as to how the Nazis had ever gained power. I know that there were six million victims, but how large was the number of the perpetrators? I search for an answer in the face of anyone over fifty I see on the street. Fliss accuses me of boorishness, but it's a moral quest. Last week, after filming, I took a stroll down Murderer's Lane. Did you realise that Hitler's flat – the one in which he lived with his niece Geli – is still standing? As I gazed up at the windows trying to guess which had been his, this elegant elderly lady, with hair like crystallised ginger, emerged from the door. 'What do you want?' she asked. 'Can I help you?' But, of course, she knew full well what I wanted. It was another game. 'Never mind what I want. How much did you know?' was what I longed to reply. But of course, I didn't. I'm an Englishman. Putting someone on the spot just isn't playing the game. So I smiled and, saying that I was a student of architecture, admired her gables.

I find the women hard to pin down. Whereas I can dress the men in makeshift uniforms, 'What did you do in the War, Mutti?' evokes a more equivocal response. Beate, the make-up supervisor, told me about her mother who works as a cleaner for the widow of a Nazi general. Since military pensions are based on rank, she is very well off, whereas Beate's mother, whose husband was in the Resistance, receives nothing. Her mother has heard her employer agitating on the phone about the Jewish menace and knows that she funds neo-Nazi youths (then, when they're sent to jail, she bakes them cakes). Beate has begged her to report her to the authorities, but she refuses. She says that she is happy in the job; the woman is kind to her. And, besides, didn't Beate's father bring enough trouble on them?

It might almost be the plot of one of Wolfram's films.

Do you think that 'Don't ask me; I'm only the cleaning lady,' may have been the prevalent attitude forty years ago? The evidence points two different ways. On the one hand, you read that the boycott of Jewish shops, which Hitler instituted after coming to power, gained so little support that it was quietly dropped and that, the day that Jews were made to wear the Yellow Star, Berliners averted their eyes to avoid embarrassing them. On the other, I discovered at Dachau that there were 10,000 – you said that you've been finding my letters difficult to decipher, so I'll write that again and, this time, in words, ten thousand – concentration camps. I'd assumed that there were just a handful: the infamous names that are trotted out repeatedly as a shortcut to shame. But 10,000 . . . how could people not have known?

In the Sixties, parts of China were infested with sparrows. The government decreed that citizens should drive them away by clapping their hands. This they did in true revolutionary spirit and, because they had nowhere to land, the birds were quickly eliminated. Do you think that the Germans may have taken a similar line in the Third Reich, believing that, if they clapped their hands (or closed their eyes), the Jews would all disappear?

We went to Dachau last Sunday, much as Munichers on a trip to London might visit Hampton Court – that's to say, it's about the same distance from the city centre, although there the resemblance ends. When we left (I'm sorry but I have to tell the story in reverse), I felt so bad that I wanted to go to church. No, I haven't suddenly found religion. Indeed, if anything were guaranteed to turn my wishy-washy 'don't know' into a hard-and-fast 'don't believe', it was what I'd just seen. I went, not to look for God, but to remind myself of the many generations who had trusted in him and trusted that all they had to do was to put a cross on the roof of a building and he would be there. But as we sat, surrounded by that unique ecclesiastical dampness which my mother and her friends take for sanctity, we heard the unmistakable roar of a passing train. Fliss and I looked at each other with a thought too obvious to put into words. Unless the organist had been a dedicated party member who pulled out the stops at the first distant rumble, there was no way that that congregation could plead ignorance. Nor, if he exists, could God.

Wolfram arranged with Thomas, our backer (I think I may have mentioned that he'd been sent to Auschwitz), for us to be given a guided tour. I assured him that we wouldn't be going as tourists. 'On the contrary,' he replied, 'I hope that's just how you will go.' To my dismay, he called up an acquaintance who'd been a prisoner there. Fliss dismissed my qualms, saying that I hadn't objected when Lord Montagu showed us personally round Beaulieu. It struck me as hardly the same.

Josef, the guide, was as gnarled as a woodcut of Winter. He'd been brought to Dachau in 1943, which was itself something of an anomaly since it wasn't designed to take Jews (in fact, many of the prisoners were priests). He owed his survival to his skills as a carpenter (although he never again picked up his tools after leaving the camp). One of the fruits of his handiwork, the whipping-block, is prominently displayed in the museum. 'I saw my friends and fellow-inmates beaten and tortured on this,' he said. Then, very softly, he began to wail – except that he wasn't wailing but reciting a list of names. 'Why don't you ask the question that's lying on your tongue?' he said. 'How many lashes were they given?' I asked. 'No, the question that you really want to ask,' he said with a hint of scorn. 'Do you feel guilty?' I asked, projecting my own feelings on to him. 'Thank you,' he said, 'the moment people begin to lie again in Dachau, it should be razed to the ground.' Then he took both our hands. 'Touch it,' he said, in defiance of the notice. We tentatively rubbed the wood. 'You see. After more than thirty years, it's still smooth. I made sure that, however butchered their backs, not a single splinter would pierce their chests. Does that answer your question?' 'Yes,' I said, even though it didn't. 'Thank you,' I added, praying that he wouldn't ask me again.

He took us to the main gate with its infamous *Arbeit Macht Frei* fretwork, which appeared even more sinister when read from behind. You know about that, of course, but what you may not have known (I certainly didn't) is that it was a cynical allusion to the Great Depression and the success of the Nazi employment programme. Another day, another irony . . . and another abuse of language, although this one served a dual purpose. Work might not make the inmates free but nor, the authorities were determined, would anything else. Which was why they reacted so furiously when anyone committed suicide. You might have thought that they'd have been pleased. After all, it was one prisoner less to worry about. But it struck right to the heart of their self-image. What was the point of playing God if they were denied the power of life and death?

He took us into the central square where he spoke of standing for hours during evening roll call, watching the sun setting over the Alps. When I suggested that such beauty must have given him hope, he said that, on the contrary, it was more chilling than any of the guards. I was relieved to escape into the barracks. But further horrors lay in store as he described the significance of the bunks with all the composure of Lord Montagu discussing a bed that had been slept in by royalty. They were constructed on three tiers and the life expectancy of their occupants was similarly graded. He stressed that there were no rules but, on average, the men at the top could hope to last for two to three months; the men in the middle for a week; while, at the bottom, they would be lucky to live through the night. When Fliss asked why, he pointed to the gaps in the slats through which excreta dripped down from sick and squashed prisoners, turning the bunk into a cess pit.

It was as if, having survived for four years as a courier in the trenches where the majority of his fellows died within a week, Hitler had asked his henchmen to construct the one place on earth where the survival rate would be even shorter.

As we emerged into the open to find a party of Japanese tourists photographing one another by the crematorium, Josef said that they may have been able to recreate the buildings, but the one thing that they could never recreate was the silence. Dachau had been so achingly quiet. No one had the energy to waste on talk.

He took us to the museum cinema where we watched a short documentary on the world of the camps. Once again, the grainy, Giacometti-like figures flickered into life. Images that had been blunted by reproduction seemed to regain their edge by dint of the setting. Dachau housed only men, but, as the focus shifted else-where, I felt a slither of shame at the memory of my classmates poring over photographs of Auschwitz victims. It was perversion from necessity rather than choice. They were the first naked breasts that they had seen. Painting and sculpture were canvas and marble, but flesh, however shrivelled, was real. And I felt a rare moment of gratitude that I had been brought up in Africa. As the film ended amid scenes of the camp's liberation complete with fleeting shots of harrowed Americans, I judged that the true tragedy of Dachau lies less in its revelation of our inhumanity than in its exposure of our humanity. It shows us that we are nothing but those bony, breakable bodies with their indistinguishable screams.

When we left the cinema, it wasn't just our eyes that were unaccustomed to the light. I asked Josef the question that had been gnawing at me throughout our visit, namely how could he bear to go back there, and not only once but day after day. He replied that he'd made a pledge, before explaining how, during his incarceration, he'd seen hundreds of men transported to the death camps. Each time, he'd known that, if his work no longer satisfied or if the Commandant took against him, he might be selected himself. Then on one such occasion – which was outwardly no different from any other – he'd been overwhelmed by despair. Existence seemed to be futile. Even if he should one day be released – and, by this stage of the War, rumours of the Allied advance had reached as far as Dachau – how could he continue to live in a world inhabited by people? So he climbed up into the wagon – not heroically, not in order to take somebody else's place, but the way that a free man throws himself from a bridge. And one of the prisoners, although too weak to stand, somehow found the strength to kick him out. With fitful eloquence, he persuaded him that private pain was no longer valid: that, if he gave up, he wouldn't merely be destroying himself but conniving in mass extinction. He had to remain alive in order to tell their story to the world.

Have you noticed how our lives are bound by stories: the 'tell my story' of the dying man balancing the 'tell me a story' of the child?

That obligation was the reason that he'd joined the Dachau Memorial Committee. I asked him whether he considered a visible monument to be a necessary safeguard against fascism. He replied that, in his view, the danger of any resurgence was remote. He believed – and, here, I'm paraphrasing wildly – that the Holocaust had been a unique combination of national character and historical circumstance. In the future, we might see another such unjust system but never such systematic injustice. Nonetheless, it was essential to bear witness: firstly, in order to honour the dead, a precept which stood at the heart of his tradition; secondly, to act as a mirror. I was startled by the usage. I should make it clear that, for Fliss's benefit, he'd been speaking English (almost flawlessly) all afternoon, but I presumed that he'd been misled by the German *Reflektor*, which can be both *mirror* and *remembrance*. 'You mean a reminder?' I suggested. 'No,' he confirmed, 'a mirror.' And I would swear that, as he spoke, his beard glinted in the sun.

21st Sept

If I'm not careful, this will look as though it were written by a six-year-old, with a different-coloured ink for every line. Fliss must have walked off with the pen I was using yesterday. She's gone to watch a newsreel of the *Anschluss* with Diana and Hitler in his private cinema. I think I can safely give that a miss. Besides, the Dachau visit had a sequel which I want to share with you. I left the camp resolved to discover more about what had happened. I decided that my best bet would be to ask if any of the Germans would be willing to talk to me about their experience of fascism. This wasn't as confrontational as it might sound since, with the exception of Henry Faber who has flown out from London to play Göring and of some pre-war star who's been cast as Fräulein Baum,[44] they're all too young to be held to account. The oldest is Conrad, our Heinrich Hoffmann,[45] who, at forty-six, is a former member of the *Flieger Hitler Jugend* (although making model gliders is the closest that he ever came to piloting a plane). As well as helping me to understand the Nazis, I hoped that they might be able to shed some light on their own generation and, in particular, on why so many of them were prepared to use violence in pursuit of their beliefs. I don't know if much about the latest incident has made it into the English press (in any case, I'm wise to your trick of skipping straight from the Front Page to the Arts), but it has dominated everything here. Some group with links to the Baader-Meinhof (but then the terrorist network appears to be as inter-twined as the British aristocracy) has kidnapped a leading industrialist called Schleyer. They're threatening to kill him unless the government releases Baader and his comrades from jail.[46] So far no deal. A frenzy of interest has swept the country and even penetrated our set. Fliss is fascinated (calling on me to translate a dozen stories every day). I wouldn't mind but I know that she's only doing it to impress Geraldine Mortimer, with whom she's become very thick. If you ask me, there's a bit too much of the 'biting the silver spoon that feeds them' – though, for Heaven's sake, don't repeat that to Fliss.

My own view is that the whole business is a storm in a tea-cup or, as the Germans, who don't share our national obsession, put it, *ein Sturm im Wasserglass*. We're making a film about a far more dangerous group of fanatics and we run the risk of being

---

[44] Unity Mitford's friend and governess at the finishing school, whom she later turned against and denounced, on slender evidence, as a Jew.

[45] Hitler's official photographer and close confidant.

[46] Andreas Baader, his girlfriend Gudrun Ensslin, Irmgard Moller and Jan-Carl Raspe were imprisoned in Stammheim.

distracted. It's only fair to say that there are those who associate the two, claiming that it's the enduring legacy of the Third Reich that is precisely the terrorists' target (just how enduring becomes clear when you learn that the Allies were forced to abandon their attempt to de-nazify the country for fear that there would be no one left to run it). Even more alarming is the view that the violence from the left will inevitably provoke a reaction from the right. This begs the question that has been at the back of my mind from the start: is fascism a specific historical movement or something endemic to the German character? I say *German* because, in spite of Mussolini and Peron; in spite of Mosley and Unity; in spite of the man on the tube who once asked me whether the headline 'Nun executed in village square' referred to England or abroad; it was only here that the full barbarism took root.

Wasting no time, I began my quest at Wolfram's Sunday evening party. I saw no point in being coy and I'm hopeless at being devious, so I went straight to the point. I was heartened by the response. Far from being offended, most people were only too glad of the chance to talk. After all, it's a question that they've been asking themselves for years. I've found it hard enough to make sense of my father and mother and all they've done is not speak to each other for a decade. I realise that I've had it easy. According to someone – I forget who it was but, since they are all strangers to you, we'll call him Actor on the Right: 'It's as though everyone's parents have a secret and it isn't just that they've cooked the books or slept with their secretary. It's that they knew.'

Everyone had a story to tell. Dieter's father had been a member of the SS. He was imprisoned after the War, narrowly escaping being hanged. He was released when his son was six but, far from disowning his former methods, he adapted them to the domestic sphere. 'He beat me for every trivial offence. It was as if he made our home into his own little camp. I was his Jew.' Perhaps even more disturbing were the stories of people who'd thought that they had no story. Erich Leitner who plays Erich Wieldeman[47] (and is a vast improvement on Patrick!), recounted his. It was instructive that he had to couch it in the second person. 'Your father wasn't an SS man or a part of the Nazi machine. He was a businessman and you can breath easy because his involvement was merely economic. Then one day, when you're in your late teens, you learn that the company he worked for employed men from the camps, and the clothes you wear and the chairs you sit in were paid for by slave labour. And your parents wonder why you'll only wear jeans and sit on bean-bags. The worst thing is that, however hard you try, you can't hate your father; you can only hate yourself for loving him.'

Then there is Luise Hermann who is playing Eva Braun (you may remember her as Gretchen). She sat there nodding her head. 'It was the same for me. My mother used to say that we had nothing to be ashamed of. If anyone challenged us, we could hold our heads up high. Then, when I was twelve, I did a local history project on the Jews in Cologne. No one ever spoke about them. They were something you were aware of but knew you should never talk about to the grown-ups. A bit like sex. The one time I'd asked my mother, she'd said that they all emigrated to America before the War and became millionaires. They hadn't been bombed. They hadn't been invaded. As usual, they'd landed on their feet. When I started to do my research, of course I found out the truth. But there was worse to come. In the city archives, I discovered some documents regarding our house. Far from having belonged to my grandfather as I'd been told, it had been sequestered from a family who'd been sent to Auschwitz. My parents moved in the very next day.'

There were other equally revealing stories but, if this letter gets much longer, it'll be cheaper for me to fly home and hand it to you

---

[47] Unity's long-term Munich boyfriend, a photographer.

in person! So, I'll stick to the one told by Helmuth Wissmann who's playing Putzi Hanfstaengl.[48] He said that, if I wanted to see the real residue of Nazism, I'd come to the right man. And, to my surprise, he arranged to take me the following evening to visit his father in a nursing home. Even more to my surprise, Fliss, who is usually so tired at the end of the day that she wants to do nothing but fall into bed, insisted on coming too . . . By the way, if you're finding it hard to credit my new-found interest in politics, I expect that you find it well nigh impossible to credit Fliss's. You remember how she originally insisted that we play down 'that side of things', with all the distaste of her mother faced with a pregnant maid? You'll just have to take my word for how much she has changed now that she's seen the truth at first hand.

The nursing home is on the outskirts of Regensburg, about an hour's drive from Munich. It is housed in a former convent, traces of which remain in both the staff and the decoration, notably a life-size portrait of the penitent Magdalene graciously baring her breasts for the benefit of the as yet unredeemed. One of the nuns escorted us to Helmuth's father, a gaunt man in a pince-nez who, displaying no visible sign of illness, sat rapt in a book. He was so overjoyed to see Helmuth that I felt a tinge of unease, but it disappeared as soon as he began to speak. Contrary to my expectations, he was perfectly happy to talk about his past, not, as you might suppose, in a spirit of atonement but, rather, of defiance. His crime was that, for two years, he had worked as the interpreter for a death squad in Poland. 'And this is the man who taught me language,' Helmuth declared.

As he offered his account, it was clear that he had failed to profit from the example of the clinic's patron saint. He apologised, but for the excesses of the system rather than the system itself. His

[48] Ernst (Putzi) Hanfstaengl, Hitler's foreign press secretary and an intimate of both Hitler and Unity.

repeated references to 'the people with the Star of David' goaded Helmuth. 'Come on, father,' he snapped, 'you can say *Jew*. It won't kill you.' The old man (both Fliss and I put him at close to eighty) stood on his wounded dignity. 'If I believe that there's a threat to Western civilisation and that the people . . . the Jews constitute that threat, then I have a duty to eradicate them. I have a moral imperative to use means that I would otherwise deplore. You may question my judgement but you've no right to impugn my integrity.' He even managed to charge the victims with responsibility for their fate, claiming, first, that the Nuremberg Laws had simply instituted the segregation that orthodox Jews desired and, second, that the meekness with which the Jews went to their deaths was proof of their inferiority.

He maintained that, had the Germans won the War, the Jews would have been reduced to a footnote. Clearly, morality as well as history is written by the victors. He looked back on the Third Reich with marked affection. 'We took pride in ourselves then. Now, when my son goes abroad, he speaks English. If someone asks where he comes from, he says Denmark.' He felt at a loss to understand why Helmuth's generation was so intent on raking up the past. 'If they're ashamed of what happened, why can't they put it behind them? It's as if our suffering isn't enough; they have to pile it on themselves.' 'Your suffering!' Helmuth cried. 'Millions of people died. You just spent ten years in prison.' For the first time, the old man's composure cracked. 'We lost everything, don't you understand? Not just the War. Not just our homes. Not just our friends and our families. But our most sacred beliefs. We couldn't change them overnight like having a car re-sprayed.'

It was clear that his loss of control embarrassed him far more than his war record. He insisted that Helmuth did not believe what he said but was simply looking for a means to attack him, in the way that his brother spent every summer working in an Israeli 'camp' (I was sure that he chose the word deliberately). 'He has a first-class degree in engineering and he picks oranges. Why? For the same reason that this one brought a Jewish girl to the house. They want to punish me.' Helmuth, provoked beyond endurance, pointed to us. 'No, other people want to punish their parents. Her mother refused to let her wear make-up . . . his father wouldn't let him drive his car. But you were attached to a squad that killed thousands of Jews.'

As if on cue, a nun slid in and said that she was sure we wouldn't wish to tire Herr Wissmannn. Helmuth shrugged, as though his father's condition were of no consequence. We exchanged a perfunctory farewell, leaving the old man so crumpled that, in spite of myself, I felt a surge of sympathy. And . . . well you know me: just an ordinary semi-sensitive bloke. What I fail to understand is how, if I felt compassion for him, a guilty old man, he could have felt none for the hundreds of innocent people, old and young, men and women, whom he'd seen tortured and shot and bludgeoned to death. More than just a loss – even a collective loss – of humanity, this must have been a deliberate rejection. Everything I've seen in the course of an admittedly short life has convinced me that people have a natural sympathy – a human sympathy – for one another, independent of personal considerations like friendship or love. At worst, it springs from the fear of what we might suffer in another's place. At best, it constitutes an innate moral code.

You even find it, however warped, in Hitler. Many people are perplexed by his love of animals. Here was a man who passed a law on the most humane way to cook a lobster[49] at the same time as he prepared for the annihilation of an entire race. I, however, find it understandable . . . almost inevitable. Human beings are

[49] On 14 January 1936, a regulation was issued that 'crabs, lobsters and other crustaceans are to be killed by throwing them into rapidly boiling water. When feasible, this should be done individually.'

not built to hate. Anyone who hates others as fervently as Hitler did, must find a commensurate source of love. So let's hear a woof for Wolf.[50]

As for morality being written by the victors, we must guard against that at any cost or we'll all find ourselves living by the gospel of Coca Cola. I'm convinced that the only viable morality in a world that is shrinking and a universe that's expanding is one that is based on the sacredness . . . or, if that sounds too pompous, the inviolability of every human life.

Please let me know what you think, or I shall be reduced to sitting in the *Marienplatz* talking to myself. I tried to discuss it with Fliss but she took an extraordinarily hard line and said that what I called sympathy was mere sentimentality, whereas true sympathy was based on an understanding of class oppression . . . She never ceases either to amaze or to worry me. Do you suppose that I should warn her against her friendship with Geraldine? I thought that it was a female solidarity thing, not a revolutionary cell.

It's time for me to stop. I've tried your patience long enough. Besides, I have another letter to write. Do I hear the words 'glutton for punishment'? Believe me, it's quite the reverse. I'm dreading putting pen to paper. It's to my father – and not one of those jolly *liebfraumilch* and *lederhosen* letters that are passed wordlessly across the breakfast table, but a declaration of intent. I'm sure that you must have been bored rigid by all my complaints of how rarely he touched – let alone, kissed – me (or Tim or Derek) when we were kids. I used to blame it on the English taboo against all physical contact between men unless there's a ball in play. But, just before I came here, my mother, in a rare acknowledgement of my father's existence, told me that 'his trouble' (it's

[50] Hitler's pet dog in the 1920s.

always 'his trouble') sprang from his having been one of the first soldiers to enter Bergen-Belsen. It seared him for life.[51]

He wouldn't speak about it to anyone, not even to her – especially not to her, since it would have brought it too close to home, and domesticity was his one remaining ideal. Nor would he have dreamt of seeking professional help (they didn't have therapy where he came from; they had beer). So he locked it inside himself and carried on with his life. As soon as he had the chance, he left England for what he trusted would be a cleaner, less corrupt world. But he couldn't leave the memories . . . the memories that have been brought alive for me by the horror branded on those fresh-faced American soldiers, suddenly forced to accept that no, they weren't in Kansas any more. He married, only to grow estranged from his wife; he had three sons to whom he failed to relate; and his new world proved to be just as corrupt as the old. His only comfort was his collection of rare insects, so lovingly assembled and preserved . . . and painfully abandoned when we fled. I don't know what it is that's welling up in me: whether it's sympathy or sentimentality or something more personal, but I do know that I have to write to him. I need to tell him that I understand what it must have been like for a young man, not much older than I am now, to have lifted the stone on that verminous world. I want him to know that there is finally someone he can talk to. Me.

In the meantime, I send you all my most potent wishes,

Ever your devoted pal,

Luke.

---

[51] I choose the more striking 'seared', although Luke's writing leaves it unclear whether he intends 'scarred' or even 'scared'.

Goldener Anker Hotel,
8580 Bayreuth,
Opernstrasse 6,
West Germany

23rd Sept 1977

Dear Michael,

Bowing to popular demand, I'm typing this letter!

Thank you for yours etc. It was great to hear your news and views. You're so right about all the Americans searching for their roots in Ireland being driven by 'nostalgie de la peat'. I may borrow the phrase if you don't mind. Beware of writers bearing notebooks! What a coincidence that you should have seen Dora at Chichester this summer. I'd have thought her a tad too <u>mature</u> (admit it; I'm learning!) for the part. Didn't the original Marguerite die in her twenties?[52] I was intrigued that you thought her a little too buttoned up 'both literally and metaphorically' to play a prostitute (I have no trouble with your writing. Ouch!). To my mind, she's more broderie anglaise than French knickers. But then she herself defined a star as someone who didn't have to take off her clothes even when she was playing a stripper.

Without doubt, she's my favourite actress in the cast – always excepting Fliss, of course. It's to do with the dry wit and the willingness to laugh at herself. She told me the other day – she always talks so unguardedly – that, for a woman who's no longer twenty-nine, she doesn't do too badly for men. 'You must have inner beauty,' I replied, knowing, the moment I'd opened my mouth, that I'd said the wrong thing. 'No, dear,' she countered sharply, 'not even inner niceness.' She's been married twice: the first time to a novelist and the second to a playwright, which she claims has

[52] Marie Duplessis, the model for Alexandre Dumas's *La Dame aux Camélias*, died at the age of twenty-three.

given her an unwarranted reputation as an intellectual. The first husband was a monster who used to hit her. The second was a sweetie who – and I quote – 'never raised a hand to me. Sadly, he never raised anything else either.'[53] Do you think that's true or just a good line? She's been in so many well-made plays that she talks in dialogue. And there's more. On husband number one: 'I divorced him twenty years ago but I still carry round the papers. Whenever I feel depressed, I take them out to read.' She remains married to husband number two – 'although not in the eyes of the Pope' (a joke that's lost on me). She claims that there's no point in an official separation because her astrologer has told her that someone close to her is about to die and she assumes that it must be him.

There's no love lost between her and Geraldine. They loathed each other on sight when they appeared as mother and daughter in *The Nesting-box*, during one of Dora's rare excursions to Hollywood. 'I came back to London and played Medea – with a vengeance.'[54] She finds no virtue in anything that Geraldine does from her espousal of politics to her rejection of publicity. 'The moment I hear an actress talk about the need to respect her privacy, I know that she must have something to hide.' She professes, somewhat implausibly, to be shocked by the scale of Geraldine's sex life. 'I'm no slouch, but she makes me feel like a bookshop next door to a public library.' I relayed this to Fliss (big mistake), who retorted 'In that case, it must be an antiquarian bookshop where the merchandise is mouldy and there hasn't been a customer for years.'

[53] The line is a paraphrase of one from *The Glass Widow*, the play written by Harris Weston for Dora Manners, which she performed with great success in London in 1965/6. As the play was widely assumed to be based on their marriage, it is unclear who has borrowed from whom.
[54] There is no record of *Medea*, or indeed of any Greek drama, among Dora Manners's credits.

I should have known better than to say anything that might be construed as a slur on her precious Geraldine. They've become as thick as – not thieves – student anarchists in Tsarist Russia. Fliss has even been reading some essays on revolutionary theory that Geraldine gave her. Fliss . . . the woman who used to maintain that theories were for people with spots! She admitted that she was finding them heavy-going but dismissed my suggestion that that was a deliberate ploy by writers anxious to conceal their lack of ideas. So I hit below the belt (can you do that to a woman, or is the foul conveyed in the punch itself?), saying that it could hardly help her portrayal of Unity for her to devote herself to opinions at the opposite end of the political scale. 'When Geraldine played Heidi,' she snapped, 'she didn't spend the evenings in Beverly Hills tending her goats.'

Gramsci one; Stanislavski nil.

Filming must be taking its toll. I know how we used to scoff whenever we read a story of another tortured star.[55] But seeing it at first-hand has made me circumspect. It's not the money or the glamour or the adulation that sets actors apart from the rest of us; it's all the time that they have for introspection. A few intense moments in front of the camera are followed by hours of enforced inactivity. Take yesterday. We came to Bayreuth to shoot one of the most populous scenes in the film. Fliss, Geraldine, Sir Hallam and practically the entire English community in Munich (including Brian Howard) were rubbing epaulettes with the Nazi top brass at the Festival. By eight o'clock in the morning, hordes of extras were milling around in evening dress. The stars were all made up with nowhere to go but their trailer, where they waited for the next twelve hours. At the end of which, with the light

---

[55] It was when reading of Elizabeth Taylor's marital problems that Luke commented with unwonted sharpness, 'She must be the first person to travel down the road to Calvary in a chauffeur-driven limo.'

already fading, they drove in a convoy up the Green Hill, temporarily reverted to its Third Reich name of Adolf-Hitler-strasse, and climbed the opera house steps.

Watching them put back the clock was at once fascinating and alarming. All the usual problems of dressing an outside set were exacerbated by the German law forbidding displays of Nazi insignia. But the official permits were duly presented and the crew worked through the night, removing and masking telephone wires, lamp-posts and parking meters. The local fire brigade was on hand to provide rain (so much for my EXT: BAYREUTH. SUNSHINE). At six o'clock when I arrived, the cameraman on the crane had turned blue and was having to be revived with regular nips of brandy. In spite of the cold and the hour, a large crowd had gathered. Prominent among them was a group of local lads who proceeded to play a very noisy game of football. Apparently, this was a ploy and one to which the unit manager was wise. He carried a supply of petty cash solely for the purpose of bribes. The boys, however, grumbled that we gave them far less than the Americans who had shot a documentary here in June.

What I didn't find out until later was that they were promised a bonus at the end of the day to keep the bystanders quiet and away from the filming. But, after a succession of complaints from outraged members of the public who had been punched while waiting patiently for autographs and a doctor who had been knocked to the ground while walking his dog, the boys were paid off. I can't have been the only one who made a connection with the SS guards walking aimlessly nearby.

Swastikas flew from flag-poles and armed soldiers lined the street for the first time since the War. I longed to know what memories they brought back for our most eminent spectator, Winifred Wagner. Was she recalling how she had allowed the Festival to be commandeered by Hitler? Did she regret having been on the wrong side or simply on the losing one? Did she disown her former connections or was she another Diana Mosley, holding court in her Paris pavilion extolling Hitler's wit and charm? It was Winifred who, on Hitler's instructions, nursed Unity when she contracted pneumonia at Bayreuth. Her patient described her as 'such a nice motherly person', a tribute that was not reciprocated ('she wasn't interesting enough to me'). She stood all day silently watching. When one of the grips offered her a chair, she waved him away. She was the English friend of the Führer who had survived.[56] And, when I was finally introduced to her – having sworn to say nothing contentious – and felt her cold Tudor eyes on my face, I understood why.

Question: Why are writers like policemen?

Answer: Because they are compromised by the company they keep.

The transformation proved to be too real for one observer who crept up on an SS guard – in reality, a Munich drama student. He declared himself elated by what had been done to the town. He had never thought he would live to see Bayreuth restored to its former glory. It was clear that there was still hope for Germany while it produced such outstanding young men. At first, the student was too shocked to reply, but he rapidly recovered and thrust aside the proffered hand. At this, the man appeared to wake up to what he had said and slipped away into the crowd. I didn't see him but I understand that he was both well-dressed and well-spoken, prompting speculation that he was either a banker, a lawyer or, quite preposterously, the Mayor. The student tore off his jacket and nothing (not even the cold) would induce him to put it back on. One of the opera-goers was conscripted to take his place in the line.

Fliss looked ravishing, albeit freezing, in a silver evening dress. She wore the lightest make-up in deference to Hitler's disdain for

---

56 Winifred Wagner, born Winifred Williams, was, in fact, Welsh.

cosmetics (the one – the only – matter on which I agree with him). I'm enclosing three photographs which I've filched from the Unit Photographer so that you can see what a great blonde she makes. But, when I told her so myself, she took it quite the wrong way and accused me of being 'pathetic and predictable'. I tried to explain that I was paying her a compliment not expressing a preference. She remained unappeased.

The extended delay allowed the two of us the chance to explore the theatre, although we were prevented from entering the auditorium by an attendant so officious that I felt sure he must have been a relic of the ancien regime. As we gazed at photographs of past productions, we drifted into a discussion on the nature of art. Standing in what must be the greatest of all monuments to an artist's sense – or should that be delusion? – of grandeur, it would have been hard to avoid a momentary consideration of artistic responsibility, even without an awareness of the forces massing outside. After all, Wagner created not only supreme works of art but the supreme image of the artist. It is commonplace to question his work – how much it was distorted by Nazi philosophy and how much it was the source of it – but it is equally germane to examine the nature of the man himself. It was he, far more than Nietzsche or anyone else, who introduced Hitler to the concept of the dictatorship of genius: the great man – ostensibly an artist but, as you brought out so brilliantly in your performance, he interpreted the word *artist* very loosely – who was entitled to ride roughshod over all personal and social obligations in pursuit of his vision.

Do you remember Brian, whose knowledge of theology far exceeds mine and, I suspect, yours, supplying an eloquent explanation of why artists should not be judged by conventional moral standards? Orthodox belief states that, at the Last Judgement – the only one that truly counts – we will be assessed not by our actions but by the consequences of those actions after our deaths. So

Tolstoy, Shelley, Byron (I think he also included J.M.Barrie, but that was just swank) and the rest may have behaved like pigs to their wives and families, but that was outweighed by the insight, joy, even grace that they have subsequently brought to millions of readers. Them I grant, but what of Wagner? He provided both the inspiration and the imagery of fascism. To talk of his work in purely musical terms is disingenuous. Look at the difference between Wagner's version of the Grail myth and Mallory's. Mallory extols the purity of his hero's character; Wagner the purity of his race. His is an exclusively Aryan redemption. He purged the Grail of any taint of Semitic origin fifty years before Hitler. Israel is right to have banned the performance of his work.[57]

Whereas I see unbridled individualism as the danger – perhaps the gravest – facing any artist, Fliss sees the opposite. To her, single-mindedness is the essence of any true artist from Wagner to Wolfram (Don't make too much of the coupling; I'm sure she did it purposely to annoy me). She claims that, if I'm so intent on social improvement, I should write odes to tractors in the Ukraine (it's noticeable that her new-found sympathies are all for the revolutionary elite and stop short of the toiling masses). It may be because of my Cambridge training – I should say 'our Cambridge training' since I know you feel the same – that I lay so much emphasis on the moral value of art.[58] The word *moral* rings immediate alarm bells for Fliss, who maintains that I sound like Mrs Doasyouwouldbedoneby embroidering homilies on a sampler,

[57] Wagner's music was never officially banned in Israel, but there was an unassailable cultural consensus against its performance which began after Kristallnacht in 1938, when the Palestine Symphony Orchestra declared that it would no longer play his works, and which lasted, despite the endeavours of Zubin Mehta, Daniel Barenboim and others, until October 2000, when the Rishon Lezion Symphony Orchestra performed the Siegfried Idyll.

[58] Luke is referring to the influence of F. R. Leavis, which was still strong during our time at Cambridge.

but you know very well – as does she, though she won't admit it – that I'm talking not of dispensing moralistic precepts but rather of extending human sympathies. Religion is divisive, and, moreover, its premise is increasingly tenuous. Art, especially in the public arena, is now the only place where we can come to celebrate our common bond. I understand that the art-humanity equation may cause problems for Wolfram and his friends who grew up in a country that produced Heydrich.[59] But their history is not ours. They have Wagner; we have Shakespeare.

Besides, I feel that Wolfram is simply rationalising his own instincts. He holds that people are fundamentally selfish (remember the line that he gave to Mephisto: 'altruism is just egotism in Lent'?) and that it is impossible for them to make any genuine connections. Whereas the whole reason I'm here – I'm talking Germany, but we might equally be talking life – can be found in my conviction that the shortest distance between any two people is art.

Fliss attacked me on that front too. She claimed that my work will never compare with Wolfram's because he 'embraces his demons' (don't ask!). He struggles to find the beauty in ugliness. But, given that there is so much beauty in beauty, doesn't that strike you as perverse? She insisted that I wouldn't amount to anything unless I dared more. Artists had to experience everything. Yes, I replied, in their imaginations not in their lives. We then resorted to name-dropping. I cited Trollope in his post office, Kafka in his insurance company, Eliot in his bank. She cited Cellini, Ben Jonson and Burroughs, all murderers, Verlaine shooting Rimbaud, and various drug-taking Romantics. She called me a minnow, which she later amended to squid because I . . . No, let's try another riddle.

---

[59] Reinhard Heydrich, the deputy-chief of the Gestapo, was a talented musician.

Question: Why is a writer like a squid?

Answer: Because he sends out clouds of ink to defend himself.

Feel free to use it on the boys.

It turns out that, when she talks about my need to experience everything, what she is actually talking about is my need to experience Wolfram. Maybe you won't find it bizarre – I'm sorry; I know you and I should know better – but she has taken it on herself to plead his cause. The truth is that the incident in Cannes wasn't the end of the matter. I've spared you a protracted report of his sexual manoeuvres, partly because they're squalid and tedious, but mainly because I don't take them seriously, any more I suspect than he does. It's as though it's a ritual we're bound to observe. He makes a move. I deflect it. Both our honours are satisfied. Fliss, on the other hand, supposes him to be in earnest. She says that the film is suffering on account of his obsession with me and that I make myself ridiculous by resisting. After all, women constantly have to sleep with undesirable men.

What makes it worse is that she claims I've encouraged him: that I've been flirting with him ever since Edinburgh. When I told her that she was talking balls (as you'll appreciate, my patience had run out), she declared peremptorily that I was at the mercy of my unconscious. She compared me to her niece who, at six years old, sits on her father's lap, making sheep's-eyes and stroking his thinning hair. Gee thanks! Don't worry, she said, I'm not suggesting that she wants to have sex with him, rather that she's aware of his sexuality and instinctively plays on it. The net result of her remarks has been to make me so wary of Wolfram that, this morning, he asked me why I was in a perpetual sulk.

Why does she say such things when she knows they hurt me? Of course she admires Wolfram; of course she's grateful to him, but she has an odd way of showing it. I think the answer is that she's not at all the sexual sophisticate she would like to appear. Do you remember that time in Greece when she suggested that you and I should share a bed and 'consummate' our friendship – as if friendship followed the same course as love? The idea was appalling. I could see that you felt as insulted as I did, although, with characteristic tact, you chose not to embarrass her. I've even begun to wonder if women might fantasise about two men together the way that men do about two women. At least that this man does. But a fantasy is a fantasy. I wouldn't expect anyone – especially not Fliss – to make it real. So I asked her point-blank if the thought of Wolfram in bed with me turned her on. 'You're disgusting,' she said in a voice curdled with scorn. 'I don't know what he sees in you.' 'What do you see in me?' I countered, immediately regretting the question. 'You may well ask,' she said and walked away.

I've talked it over with Dora. I left out some of the details, but she seems intuitively to understand. Not the way you do, of course. I miss you awfully. Fliss says the same. It's one of the few things on which we still agree. At least you'll be out here for half-term, by which time it should all be over bar the shouting. Normal service will be resumed.

In the meantime, I send you my very best wishes,

Confused of Munich.

8 München 40,
Giselastrasse 23,
West Germany

2nd Oct 1977

Dear Michael,

Our letters must have crossed. Perhaps we should institute a system whereby we each write every second Thursday. That way we ought to keep in synch. At the risk of repeating myself, please don't worry about not replying at length. I know you're under a lot of pressures. So am I. But the one that I can escape is time. I hope you won't consider this self-aggrandising, but would you keep these letters from now on? It's not that I'm planning a collected edition of my correspondence; I'd just like to preserve a record. You're the only person to whom I'm writing regularly . . . the only one to whom I could begin to say the things I'm going to say today. Perhaps one day, I'll write an account of the filming and the letters will jog my memory. Or perhaps one day, I'll look back from happier times in order to refine my definition of *sad*.

I've reflected a lot on your remarks about the cruelty of schoolboys in relation to my visit to Dachau. The incident with the glue and the horsehair made me squirm. I know that the link has been made before. Wasn't it Auden who claimed that he was fully attuned to the horrors of fascism having attended an English public school?[60] When I first read that, I dismissed it as the typical hyperbole of his class and, if you'll forgive me, orientation, but I'm no longer so sure. Perhaps horsehair is the piano-wire of the pre-pubescent. And, inside every schoolboy, there's a Gestapo officer waiting to grow up.

---

[60] 'The best reason I have for opposing fascism is that at school I lived in a Fascist state.' From Auden's essay on Gresham's in *The Old School*, edited by Graham Greene, Jonathan Cape 1934.

My father would certainly endorse that. The same post that brought me your letter brought me his. I've told you that he was one of the first British soldiers to reach Bergen-Belsen. I felt impelled to write to him after Dachau to express – what? solidarity . . . sympathy . . . I'm not sure. He replied with a very formal letter, written in a deceptively neat hand, insisting that he could not allow me to labour under a misapprehension. His experience of the camp had, indeed, been hellish, far more so than I could ever suspect from the newsreels. Sight had not been the only outraged sense. But the real horror – if I were determined to use such emotive words – was what had occurred afterwards, when he was among a group of soldiers who were so inflamed by what they had seen that they took revenge on a German woman who was hiding in a nearby farm, forcing her to have sex with a horse. 'So you see,' he concluded, 'there's a little Eichmann in every man and he lurks between your legs. Ever your affectionate father.'

Meanwhile, life on the home front has been equally desperate. You remember how Fliss and I always said that we'd make you the godfather to our first child? Well, I shouldn't choose a christening mug yet. I wasn't sure that I'd tell you until I began this paragraph (and I'm still not sure that I'll post the letter), but we've split up. Kaput! Finito! I suppose I should try to save face and claim it as a joint decision . . . best thing for both of us, etc, etc. But, if the truth were known, I was simply the first to be told. It seems that we've grown stale; we've been together too long; we need to branch out on our own, meet new people (you get the picture). To quote dear Geraldine – and she does: 'Making love to one man, you learn about him, his likes and dislikes, how to be a couple. Making love to different men, you learn about you, your likes and dislikes, how to be yourself.'

So there it is. No 'let's try to talk things through'. No 'there must be a way forward after all these years'. No 'you're as much a part of me as my own body'. No acknowledgement that, as I write this, every nerve feels as though it has fallen down five flights of stairs. You know us. We're a pair. We belong together. We're 'Felicity and Luke'. It's always 'Hi, Felicity, where's Luke?' or 'Luke, where's Felicity?' We used to joke that we were the Pushmi-Pullyu of Cambridge. Well now, we'll be pulling in different directions. It's so cruel – and immature – and selfish. If it weren't for me, she wouldn't even be in Munich . . . there wouldn't be a *Unity*. I'm not asking her to stay with me from a sense of obligation, but common decency demands that she postpone any decision until the end of the shoot (by which time it will be superfluous because she'll be able to think straight again). And yet, when I said as much, she asked if I were trying to destroy her confidence. Did I believe she wasn't up to the part? Was it too much to hope that we might stay friends?

She demeans friendship by her subterfuge. What you and I are is friends. Friendship isn't love with the passion taken out like non-alcoholic wine.

I'm convinced that she's having an affair with Mahmoud's brother, Ahmet. Have I told you about him? I'm so confused. I remember reading an article about Dieter in which he claimed that he always had to check he was wearing clothes before he went out and thinking 'What a poseur!'. I humbly beg his pardon. In the 'losing the plot' stakes, I win by a length. So, to be on the safe side, I'll assume that I haven't mentioned Ahmet before. He arrived from Lebanon on a family visit. Not that Mahmoud seems particularly pleased, although, in his case, a curt nod probably counts as the acme of pleasure. Fliss told me – at a time when she was still telling me things – that Ahmet belongs to some offshoot of the PLO, only more extreme (her word was 'committed'). He and Geraldine have known each other for years. They bump into each other at conferences (the Old Lefties Network). If you ask me, they share far more than a taste for Trotsky. But, according to Fliss, they are simply comrades in arms. He thinks of her as a sister. I presume that she means in the Borgia sense.

Given that he's on holiday, you would have thought that he'd want to take a break from politics, but this interminable kidnapping seems to have given him carte blanche to spout all kinds of hackneyed slogans about Western decadence and capitalist corruption (oops, sorry! I forgot that they're the same thing). Fliss hangs on his every word or, at any rate, pretends to. I even overheard her telling him how she narrowly escaped being sent down for throwing a bucket of paint at Eysenck[61] when he came to deliver his Senate House lecture. When I pointed out that this was a lie – the heroine of the hour was Susie Philbeach[62] – she was unrepentant. 'I'm an actress,' she said. 'That's what actresses do. They appropriate bits from other people in order to build up a character.' 'But that's when they're playing a role,' I said, 'not when they're being themselves.'

Ahmet, needless to say, was smitten. He must be the sexual equivalent of a champagne socialist. Or does he rationalise his affairs as penetration behind enemy lines? I make no excuses for the pun. I make no excuses for anything. I'm not the one with anything to excuse. I can picture you reading this and thinking 'Poor Luke, he's paranoid.' I don't blame you. I'd probably feel the same if our positions were reversed. But, by my definition – and I don't have a dictionary to hand – paranoia is an excessive, unjustified fear. Whereas anyone who saw Fliss and Ahmet together – constantly sharing jokes and whispering secrets – would confirm that my fears were fully justified. And, while I admit that Geraldine usually makes up a third, you of all people should know that Fliss has always preferred to conduct her romances in company.

---

61 Hans Eysenck (1916–97), German-born British psychologist who attracted controversy for his views on racial differences in intelligence, as propounded in *Race, Intelligence and Education*, Gower 1971.

62 Now Head of Current Affairs for BBC television.

The person who seems to be happiest about what has happened is Wolfram. I'll return to him later, but then you're so quick, I expect that you've already guessed what's coming. Given his relationship to Ahmet, it's as if he's able to keep everything in the family: that extended – no, convoluted – family that he has built up around himself. He has long wanted to separate Fliss and me: to make us singly and jointly dependent on him. Now, through his boyfriend's brother, he has. What's more, he and Fliss will be collaborating more closely than ever since he has taken over as Hitler: a role to which, according to some of the company (no names, no leaks to the press), he is ideally suited. Having burdened you with all my domestic woes – almost as one-sided as sending you a Wedding List – I'm somewhat reluctant to add an account of the on-set battles, but I'm afraid that disasters don't arrive neatly spaced out, one per letter, with a cheery piece of trivia at the close, like the nine o'clock news.

The big bust-up actually took place about ten days ago – although precise dates have been obscured by the intervening drama. Wolfram and Ralf had a tremendous row about the treatment of Hitler. You have to understand that Ralf is an intensely serious actor who has devoted his career to the kind of socially aware stage work that Geraldine would tackle if her commitment were sincere. He'd become increasingly miserable about the way that Wolfram was asking him to play the part. The problem was more than one of interpretation: it was one of ownership. Everyone has his personal take on Hitler. He's one of those figures, like Christ or Hamlet, who can be shoehorned into any number of theories. My own reading, for what it's worth, is that he was the archetypal outsider, who never felt at home anywhere, in his family or class or country (look at how hard he tried to reinvent himself as a German). The only place that he was able to achieve any sense of belonging was in the army during the Great

War – and that had ended in humiliation. So, convinced of his own uniqueness and yet desperate for acceptance, he set about moulding an entire nation to his will.

Ralf, however, disagreed. People might have their own Hamlet, but their own Hitler was a luxury they could not afford. He insisted that his characterisation was based on strict historical analysis. He saw Hitler as the supreme opportunist, who had an uncanny ability to ride the waves of what was happening in Germany in the Twenties: the disillusion of defeat; the curse of unemployment; the misery of inflation; while, as a former corporal, he was perfectly placed to appeal to the bands of disaffected ex-soldiers who were roaming the streets. In Ralf's view, the emphasis that Wolfram wished to lay on Hitler's pathology was both titillating and distracting. A focus on psychology as fate could only lead to fatalism. 'So Hitler's father used to beat him . . . so Hitler endured the horrors of war . . . so Hitler had shameful sexual desires: so what can any of us do?'

I'd have thought that we could start by making sure that fathers don't beat their children . . . that men aren't sent to war . . . that people are taught not to be ashamed of their desires. But the question wasn't addressed to me.

It was addressed directly to Wolfram, who ignored it. He is unwavering in his conviction that the key to Hitler lies in his sexuality. He sees the same rejection of the Judaeo-Christian code in his private as in his public life. According to Wolfram, sex is where Hitler, like the rest of us, played out his innermost conflicts. In his case, these centred on the deep sense of uncleanness that sprang from his fear that he had Jewish blood. Whether or not it was warranted is not the issue. The merest suspicion was enough to defile him. His only relief lay in being shat on. This both confirmed his sense of uncleanness (by giving it a definite object) and purged it. The one person with whom he could satisfy his craving was his niece, Geli, who was of his blood and therefore implicated, and of his circle and therefore discreet.[63] But when she died – either by her own hand or another's – that outlet was removed. He had no way to deal with his sense of uncleanness except to deflect it – and on a massive scale. To put it crudely, he shat on an entire race.

Whatever the merits of this as a psychological profile – and, to my mind, it says as much about Wolfram as about Hitler, it has considerable drawbacks as the basis of a film. For a start, Geli was long dead by the time that Unity arrived in Munich (and, with all due respect to Fliss, *Blithe Spirit*[64] it ain't). Moreover, while it's perfectly easy to write 'Geli shits on Hitler' (I've done so myself, albeit under protest), it's far harder to shoot it and to shoot it in such a way that the audience is alive to the meaning and not just to the disgust. Wolfram's solution is to show Hitler alone in his flat, unlocking the room that he has kept, Queen Victoria-like, as a shrine to his dead love. He picks up his sketchbook and leafs through the drawings of Geli squatting over his face. At which point, the screen dissolves into a re-enactment.

Ralf refused point-blank to play the scene. Wolfram retorted that he had thereby broken his contract. Neither of them backed down. The end result is that Ralf has been fired and Wolfram has taken over the role. This, according to several of his friends, is

---

[63] Neither Geli nor Hitler himself were, however, discreet enough. Otto Strasser, one of the founders of the Nazi party, claimed to have received a tearful confession from Geli in which she described her uncle forcing her to urinate on him. Putzi Hanfstaengl asserted that Hitler was subject to a blackmail attempt in 1930 on account of depraved, pornographic drawings he had made of Geli. The coprophiliac elements in Hitler's sexuality have been identified by writers ranging from the German historian, Konrad Heiden, to the American psychologist, Walter C. Langer.

[64] In Noel Coward's 1941 comedy, a writer and his second wife are haunted by the ghost of his first.

precisely the outcome that he had always intended. Why else, they ask – I merely record – did he cast an outsider? Why else, after three weeks of filming in Munich, has he shot so few of Ralf's scenes, and most of them in close-up? (Werner calculates that the entire reshoot will take no more than four or five days). And yet even I wouldn't accuse him of going to such lengths in order to indulge his love of intrigue. The truth is that, in spite of his considerable experience as an actor, it would have been far harder to finance the project if he had proposed to appear on both sides of the camera. This way he has left the backers no choice. They either go ahead with him or lose an already substantial invest-ment. So he has had his way with the minimum of pain to all concerned – except Ralf.

The shit stays. And I fear that it may grow worse. The other day, he expressed a fascination with the treatment of the 20th July conspirators. In the course of being hanged – strung up, in Hitler's own phrase, 'like carcasses of meat' – their trousers were pulled down to expose their erections. 'I can't shake that image from my head,' he confessed. I reminded him that the executions didn't take place until the last year of the War and that, besides, there was no proof that Hitler himself had ever watched the film that was made. 'Pity,' he said. 'I'd have liked to have incorporated it in the script.'

Assuming a worldly-wise air, he assured me that no one would ever understand life – let alone Hitler – who failed to understand the universal human need to inflict pain. I wondered (aloud) whether it were universal and not uniquely German, considering that even their folk-dances require them to deal each other hearty slaps.[65] Dieter, who makes no secret of his inclinations, claimed that, if there were any national influence, it was religious rather than racial. 'Sado-masochism,' he declared, 'is the supreme

---

65 A reference to the Bavarian folk dance, the *Schuhplattler*.

Protestant ethic, embodying the belief that pleasure can only be achieved through pain.'

I suspected that their outlook might have more to do with their sexuality: that gay men (yes, I know: I except you and Socrates and Michelangelo) live without rules, free to explore their dark sides like mercenaries at a massacre. I remembered your saying that the reason so many of them were attracted to sado-masochism was that they had no children on whom to vent their aggression.[66] So I told Wolfram that it was he, in fact, who failed to understand the universal human need for tenderness. But, when I added that my own preferences could be summed up in the phrase 'making love', he replied with scorn 'And I expect you only eat the breast-meat of chicken.'

There's more. I intend to tell you everything because you're an integral part of it, in spite of not being here . . . although, if you were, I'm sure that none of this mess would have happened. What you must bear in mind is how low I was feeling after the break-up with Fliss. She'd gone to stay at the Four Seasons and I was alone in the flat. I'd been on set for fourteen hours. I could hardly keep my eyes open and yet the last thing that I wanted was to go to bed. I said 'no' to dinner with Dora since I couldn't bear to face anyone, least of all myself. Then the door-bell rang and my mind was made up for me. Wolfram and Dieter announced that they had come to take me to a club. Even though the only dance that I felt up to was the limbo, I agreed to go.

Wolfram promised me that the club catered for both men and women. What he neglected to say was that the women were exclusively lesbians. Still, if nothing else, it appealed to my self-disgust.

---

66 Although I have allowed the reference to stand, I cannot believe that, even at the age of twenty, I would have said anything so crass. What I may have said is that gay men take up sadomasochism because they had no outlet for their aggression as children or, even, because they had so much aggression taken out on them as children.

There were two brightly lit podia. On one, a lip-synching drag queen was proving that imitation may be the sincerest form of flattery but it's the most bogus form of art. On the other, a waif-like boy was gyrating, as though under hypnosis, dressed in nothing but his underpants and a coil of barbed wire.

After a few minutes, even disgust failed to sustain me and I wanted to leave. At which point Wolfram handed me some LSD. You see, it's not just on screen that he replays *Faust* . . . No, that's too easy. I'm a free agent; there's no one to blame but myself. 'This will take you into a whole new dimension,' he swore. (If you scratch off the Tipp-Ex, you'll find *dementia*. I should have let it stand.) 'It peels off the layers of consciousness. With one leap, you'll attain a level of transcendence that would take the most devout Buddhist years.' Fired by his words and the belief that a single tab couldn't harm me when he must already have swallowed a fistful, I gulped it down. I felt nothing apart from a smarting beneath my eyelids. Then I suddenly turned to catch sight of Neptune, ten foot tall and crowned with seaweed, acknowledging the obeisance of the crowd. What was strange was that he didn't frighten or even inhibit me but, rather, encouraged me to dance on . . . to dance faster . . . to do nothing but dance.

My skin grew slick with sweat so, at Wolfram's suggestion, I tore off my shirt. My strip was greeted by a chorus of wolf-whistles. I had no idea whether they were genuine or ironic. Nor did I care.

All at once the room darkened, and I was gripped by a sensation of burning coldness, as if I were buried in snow. I found myself facing a bearded biker, his jacket open to the waist. I watched in horror as a golden eagle swooped down from the rafters and pecked at his chest. But, instead of writhing in agony, he stood grinning widely and raised his mug to salute me. I realised that he was high on drugs – and not just him but the entire club. I alone had sufficient self-possession to see. I tried to shout a warning but

I couldn't formulate the words, so I ran towards him waving my arms. When the bird failed to take flight, I made a grab for it. My main concern was to prevent it reaching his heart.

The next thing I knew was that the smarting in my eyes had grown worse and my face was dripping with beer. All around me were shouts and scuffles as people rushed to part us, but the only sound that I registered was the malignant wheeze of Wolfram's laugh. I fell back as Neptune raised his trident over my head. Then he disappeared and I disintegrated. Wolfram laughed louder, while the room spun into a blank.

The following day, I was plunged into the most searing despair when Wolfram explained to me that the eagle had been tattooed on the man's chest. I should have listened to Sir Hallam when he maintained that the most important lesson he'd learnt in nearly fifty years in the business was never to trust a director who sniffed.

Your sadder but wiser (a lot sadder and a little wiser) pal,

Luke.

8 München 40,
Giselastrasse 23,
West Germany

14th Oct 1977

Dear Michael,

At the risk of sounding like Sir Hallam, there was a legendary production of *Dr Faustus* where, in the scene where Faustus conjures up devils, an extra one appeared unbidden on stage. Now you may argue that the actor was a little the worse for sack or that one of the company was playing a trick on him, but what if it actually happened?[67] Given the common belief that we can invoke the forces of good (I'm choosing my abstractions carefully) when we pray, why shouldn't we do the same with the forces of evil? Suppose that Wolfram is right about the energy preserved in buildings and that, by restoring the Nazi leaders to their original settings, we are somehow unleashing their spirits?

And no, Mr Liberal Humanist, I haven't flipped – nor have I taken any more of Wolfram's acid. If drugs, in the words of my would-be pusher, are art for the people ('now everyone can compose symphonies in their heads; now everyone can fly around the Sistine chapel'), then I am an unabashed elitist. I'm merely trying to account for the sense of total enervation that permeates the set, as though we were stranded at Gatwick Airport. Faces are tense and tempers frayed. Even Sir Hallam, hitherto the soul of courtesy, berated one of the assistants because his tea was cold. Meanwhile, it's paranoia city, as rumour and gossip run rife and no one is spared. For my own part, I'm convinced that Wolfram is

---

[67] The only reference to this that I have been able to find, in Richard Huggett's *The Curse of Macbeth and other theatrical superstitions*, Picton 1981, records that the audience ran out screaming and the leading actor died of a heart attack.

shunning me. Perverse as it sounds, I'm beginning to hanker for the days of gropes and innuendoes. It's as though he lost interest in me the moment he found that I could be seduced (by the drugs, I mean).

To make matters worse, there appears to be no end to this kidnapping crisis. The whole country is in a state of siege. I've tried to black it from my mind (my personal version of Callaghan's cancelled trip[68]), but it has even intruded on set. Wolfram's radical sympathies are well-known (or, at any rate, they're taken for granted), nevertheless it came as a shock when last week, in the middle of shooting a scene at the Munich *Fasching*, he was hauled off for questioning by the police. It seems that *Bild*[69] has accused him of supplying money to various terrorist groups and he is now some sort of suspect. Of course, he could reveal nothing about Schleyer's whereabouts, but the investigation has left him vulnerable. Having received death threats, he is now demanding protection from the very police force he was recently reviling. Meanwhile, he has hired two bodyguards whom – you have to hand it to him – he has kitted out as SS officers and roped in as extras.

He has the luck of the Devil. Despite all the upheaval, Ralf's departure turns out to have been a blessing. In contrast to Wolfram and the other cheque-book socialists, Ralf has been harbouring a suspected terrorist in his house – although, given the current hysteria, the term could refer to any girl who danced with Baader at a disco ten years ago. I must confess to feeling torn. On the one hand, an actor's job is to give life to people, not to blow them up. On the other, Ralf is at least prepared to stand by his

---

68 On 9 September 1977, at the start of the Schleyer crisis, Prime Minister Callaghan postponed a visit to Chancellor Schmidt in Bonn.
69 *Die Bild Zeitung*, Germany's most notorious tabloid and the thinly disguised target of Heinrich Böll's *Die verlorene Ehre der Katharina Blum* (1974).

beliefs, however misguided – in contrast not just to Wolfram, but to a certain Geraldine Mortimer, who felt that her wearing a white headband[70] to a Hollywood premiere was a scorching protest against the American presence in Vietnam. The moment they heard the news of Ralf's arrest, both Geraldine and Felicity tried to mobilise the cast in an attempt to put pressure on the government. Oh yes, I thought, and perhaps they should march on Bonn in their uniforms to make a point.

Still, who would have thought it of Ralf? It just goes to show that you can never be sure of anyone, not even your best friend.

Meanwhile, the authorities are clearly determined to make Wolfram squirm. Yesterday, after two more visits to the set, they returned to search his house. Although they must have found enough drugs to warrant several charges, their sole concern was the gun that was hidden in Ahmet's room. Conclusions were reached – not to say jumped to (remember, we're talking Palestinian here) – only to be refuted by Felicity, who admitted, first, to sharing the room (so much for the Four Seasons!) and, then, to having pinched the gun from the set. While her story was easily verified – it was precisely the type of 1930s pistol that had been issued to various Nazis – her logic took longer to explain. And, no, it wasn't to protect herself from Ahmet's unwelcome advances (the last remaining straw slipped from my grasp), but rather to spice up their sex life. Freud would have a field day! I only have it at second-hand but, when the officers pressed her to elucidate, she reputedly declared that there was 'nothing so thrilling as to force a man to make love to you at gunpoint.'

That's news to me. She never suggested anything of the sort during the four years we were together. Which is just as well, because she knows what I would have replied! It's sick. And, what's more, it isn't Fliss. She can't have changed that much in a

---

[70] Worn by the Vietnamese as a symbol of mourning for the dead.

single week. Am I the only person who still wants to make love normally, that is, as Nature intended, with nothing between us but skin?

Ever since the search, Felicity has been looking insufferably smug, as if she has yet again demonstrated her superiority over 'the little people'. I want to warn her that the German police aren't as easily fooled as the Girton porters. I don't trust Ahmet. I'm afraid that he may be playing a very dangerous game and the one who really has a gun to her head is Fliss. But I can't say anything. I have no basis for my suspicions other than his being a Palestinian – a word with such negative associations that it is almost taboo. So how should I proceed? Have a quiet word in the ear of a German inspector? 'On what do you base your accusations, Mr Dent?' 'Only stereotypes, I'm afraid.' 'Stereotypes, splendid. Pull up a chair. Have a glass of schnapps. You're a man after my own heart.'

Whatever else may be blinding Felicity to Ahmet's intentions, it isn't love. She admitted to me, 'now that we can talk to one another openly and freely' (at least she had the grace to refrain from 'rationally'), that it's Wolfram on whom she has set her heart. Yes, you did read that correctly. Despite every provocation, my hand is steady on the keys. She professes to have been smitten with him from the first evening in Edinburgh but to have told herself that it was hero-worship, born of her deep admiration for his films (Who is she trying to kid? Doesn't she remember 'like Thomas Mann but without the jokes'?). She quickly realised, however, that her feelings were genuine. It was only because (wait for it) she had never known such passion that she had been suspicious of it. At first, she had felt doubly miserable, seeing Wolfram living with Mahmoud and pining for me but, as time went by, her perspective changed. She came to realise that she was privileged just to be near him, to work alongside him, to know that there was a man like that in the . . . in her world.

Besides, she hasn't given up hope of their becoming lovers. 'But Wolfram's queer!' I exclaimed. I'm sorry, but there are times when you can't mince words – perhaps the Germans put it best with their *warmer Bruder*. 'Bisexual,' she replied, flooding me with the full force of her contempt. She seizes on his occasional lapses like a schoolboy wading through *Lady Chatterley's Lover* for the glimpse of a *fuck*. 'Look at Renate!' she said. Whereupon I'm afraid that I laughed. I was amazed that she could take heart from a woman who is known to have ruined herself paying for his male prostitutes. She added that she considered Wolfram's gayness to be a pose (so, at least, she has some insight into his character), on a par with his workman's clothes and irregular washing ('refusing to uphold society's hypocritical standards of hygiene' was her precise phrase). It was his ultimate 'fuck you' to the world. 'Only he's not,' I said. 'Not what?' she asked. 'Fucking you.'

She claimed to have Unity to thank for teaching her that a woman can be blissfully happy even when there is no possibility of consummating her love. And, the moment she said that, I understood her relationship with Ahmet. Just as Unity slept with his adjutants in order to consolidate her position with Hitler, so Fliss is doing the same.[71] While it may seem perverse to sleep with the brother of her gay friend's boyfriend (I'm not even sure if I've got the relationships right), it's clear that, when it comes to logic, there's good sense, there's nonsense, and then there's Felicity. You were wise to that from the start. I remember when, after our first lunch at the Eros (you've no idea how I long for moussaka and chips for three), you told me how much you liked her but

[71] This is, to say the least, contentious. Although there is some evidence to suggest that Unity slept with several Nazis including, on her own confession, Stabschef Viktor Lutze, the leader of the SA after the murder of Röhm, there are equally authoritative reports that she died a virgin. Luke's certainty on a matter about which he would usually express caution is an indication of his pain.

cautioned me against becoming too involved. She said that . . .
well let's just say that she cast aspersions on your motives. Now I
know which one of you had my best interests at heart.

Enough reminiscences! I'm neglecting my duties as location
correspondent which, on the evidence of your letters, is my forte.
I'm not the only one to have been swept up in an off-set drama.
So, if you're tired of my *nouvelle vague* weepie (although, to do it
full justice, the Anglo-German dialogue would need to be dubbed
into French), I can offer you several alternatives: Sir Hallam
Bamforth and Gerald Mortimer in a black comedy; Geraldine
Mortimer in a political thriller; Henry Faber in a historical epic.

I don't suppose that I've said much – if anything – about Henry.
He's the quintessential character actor: efficient on set; unas-
suming off it. All of which made his outburst the other day doubly
disturbing. We were shooting a scene between Göring and Unity
in which he expresses his allegiance to the Nazi cause, using what
must be the most chilling words in the entire script (an authentic
phrase for which I can claim no credit): 'I have no conscience. My
conscience is Adolf Hitler.' To Wolfram's mounting impatience,
the usually word-perfect Henry was floundering. Tension was
heightened by their use of the interpreter, a blatant absurdity given
that Henry's pretence to understand no German is as transparent
as Wolfram's to speak no English. Finally, Wolfram strode on to
the set, grabbed Henry by the shoulder and hissed the line in his
ear. Henry flung him aside and, white with fury, told him never
again to address him like that – not when he was wearing those
clothes. Wolfram looked at himself. We all looked at Wolfram.
Suddenly, the problem was clear. Ever since he took over from
Ralf, Wolfram has been directing the film in full Führer costume
and make-up. What, for the rest of us, has been a curious anomaly
(especially when he trails on his hands and knees in the wake of
the camera) has, for Henry, been an agonising reminder.

What followed revealed Wolfram at his best, as he tore off his moustache and hair-piece and hugged Henry. He asked him if he wanted to take a break. 'Not at all,' Henry replied, as though ashamed of having surrendered to his emotions. Then, in a silence that was unusually intense, he gave a faultless rendition of the scene. Meanwhile, my attention was gripped by Thomas (the backer), who sat in the shadows, watching Henry's outburst as though it had been scripted. He has a singular detachment which makes him seem an outsider, not just from the film-crew, but from humanity itself. Showing none of Henry's misgivings, he is happy to lunch with a fully made-up Wolfram as if they were in the Osteria Bavaria rather than the *Bavaria* canteen. Do you suppose the difference may be that, having survived Auschwitz, Thomas has been purged of the horror whereas, for Henry, it remains unresolved?

In case you think I am being fanciful, there are grounds for such speculation. After the take, we went back to the communal trailer (which, for all Geraldine's grumbles, does generate intimacy). I learnt more about Henry in the next hour than I had in the preceding three weeks. What I hadn't realised was that this was his first visit to Germany since he left in 1935. He had been an up-and-coming actor in Berlin when the rise of the Nazis prevented him from obtaining work. 'But I wasn't surprised. If Bruno Walter was forbidden to give concerts: if Otto Klemperer was forced to retire, what hope could there be for me?' Nevertheless, like so many of his coreligionists, he'd been prepared to sweat it out until, one day, he woke up to the fact that his position had become untenable. 'A law was passed banning Jewish doctors not just from treating any but Jewish patients, but from dissecting any but Jewish corpses. When I discovered that we could even corrupt the dead, I knew that there was no longer any place here for me.

'The truth wasn't that the Germans – not only those that I knew as friends but the ones that I saw around me – actually believed that the Jews were responsible for all the ills that afflicted the country, but that they elected to believe it. It offered them an escape clause. Sometimes, it's easier to forgive Hitler than the ordinary Germans in the street. He was, at least, convinced by the filth that he spouted. They chose cynically to endorse it.'

He tried, without success, to persuade the rest of his family to accompany him. Like so many others, they had been lulled into a state of false confidence. Some Jews thought that they were safe because they had been assimilated into a wider society – the Germans had, after all, granted them greater liberty than any other European nation. Some thought that they were safe because either they or their fathers had fought in the Great War, alongside a certain Austrian corporal who had been awarded the military cross. His father, however, thought that he was safe because of God. 'He believed that the Lord would watch over us in spite of his not very encouraging record.' I was surprised to see Dora cross herself and wondered whether it were childhood or faith.

Henry was the sole survivor, not just of his immediate or even of his extended family, but of his whole community. 'The only Bible story that I ever read to my daughters was Noah's Ark.' He came to England where he was free, at least until the outbreak of war when he was arrested as an enemy alien and interned. To all practical purposes, the camp was controlled by militant Nazis who treated the Jews with the same savagery as their comrades had on the Continent. The authorities showed little concern for the domestic quarrels of a group of Germans. It was only by considerable subterfuge that he was able to smuggle out a message to a writer with whom he had worked at the BBC. He, in turn, put pressure on the Home Office to secure Henry's release. For the rest of the War, he enjoyed a schizophrenic existence, broadcasting anti-Nazi propaganda on the radio and playing German officers in films.

The latter have been the staple of his subsequent career. He is acutely aware of the irony in his having derived a substantial income from playing the very people who slaughtered his family. He has had a particularly close association with Göring, to whom he bears a startling resemblance. If nothing else, this similarity (which proved to be near-fatal on one occasion during the Blitz), holds the lie to Nazi theories of physiognomy. The reason that he accepted the part in *Unity* was not for the challenge of playing his fifth Göring but because, after more than forty years, he felt that it was time for him to return to Germany. But the moment that he stepped off the plane, he realised that it was too soon. The hardest thing for him to accept was the sound of the language all around him. 'Speaking in English – and thinking in English – was what helped me to forget. I want to thank you for your language. For forty years, German was simply the coin in which I was paid.'

Henry's tale had an unexpected postscript. The following evening, he was sitting in the hotel bar, along with his wife Mathilda, Gerald and his wife Haroko, Geraldine, Sir Hallam, Dora and me, when a frail old man with a shock of ginger hair shuffled hesitantly towards us ('If he has to dye it,' Dora said to me later, 'he might at least have offered a sop to Nature.'). He had the wide-eyed, plump-cheeked artlessness characteristic of certain monks – I except Fray Luis Antonio de Mijas.[72] He stood straight in front of us, shifting his glance back and forth between Henry and Sir Hallam. The latter, adopting a tactical blindness, con-

---

[72] The Spanish monk and poet whom Luke had invited to read at the Milton Society in Cambridge. Having put him up in a Sidney Sussex guest room, he awoke in the night to discover that, whatever vows Fray Luis may have observed, chastity was not among them.

tinued with his story – I forget what it was about, but you can be sure that Hattie or Johnny or Larry featured prominently. Mathilda, whose protective instincts had been honed by Henry's recent outburst, challenged the intruder. He appeared reluctant to speak, as if expecting that either Henry – or, more improbably, Sir Hallam – would recognise him. When both looked blank, he resigned himself to explaining. His name was Per. He had been a dresser at the *Deutsches Theater* in the Thirties, when Henry was a member of the company. Moreover, he had met Sir Hallam on his visit to Berlin and was plainly hurt by his lack of recollection. 'You must remember Rolf!' he kept insisting: a demand which appeared even more unreasonable when it turned out that Rolf was a dog.

Henry, however, leapt up and clasped him in his arms (he later confessed that it was the past that he was embracing, since he had only the dimmest memory of the man). Sir Hallam, equally gracious but more restrained, stood and held out his hand. As Per took it, a collective shudder ran around the table, which Sir Hallam, to his credit, ignored. Per shyly apologised. He had lost three of his fingers in Sachsenhausen . . . 'Enough of this doom and gloom!' I hear you cry. 'Take me to the *Oktoberfest*, where I can join all the middle-aged Germans in drowning my memories. Tell me about the trials of strength and the mock executions:[73] anything to keep away from the camps.' I'm sorry, but no can do. You have to know the truth and not only in your role as keeper of the conscience. Per's fate has a particular significance for you.

We made space both for Per and his story, which he told with remarkably little fuss. He had been arrested by a policeman posing

---

[73] Luke is referring to the Schichtl magic and vaudeville show, a popular *Okto-berfest* attraction since the early nineteenth century, which traditionally climaxed in a gruesome execution, with barkers announcing the 'beheading of a live human being on an open and well-lit stage'.

as a hustler in the Tiergarten.[74] He was sent without trial to the camp, where he was forced to sleep with his hands on top of the blanket to prevent his succumbing to the solitary vice to which all such 'libidinal felons' were prone. The temperature in the hut was several degrees below zero and he caught frost-bite but, even so, he didn't dare to break the rule. He had seen the punishment meted out to a man found trying to warm his hands against his thighs. Four guards had dragged him from his bed and on to the parade-ground where they doused him with buckets of water. In the morning, he was discovered frozen stiff, covered in a sheet of ice as though he had been gift-wrapped in cellophane.

Per had been put to work in the quarries, carting rubble dug up by Jews who were harnessed to each other like horses. When it was learnt that he spoke three languages (his English was demonstrably perfect), he was transferred to the registry. It saved his life. It did not, however, save him from degradation, such as having to empty the swilling latrine buckets towards which, as a homosexual, he was supposed to feel an affinity. Nor did it save him from being brutally assaulted by the guards who, while publicly denouncing sodomy, were privately prepared to make exceptions. They were worthy students of the Berlin masters who had framed the law on race defilement to exclude rape.

As he spoke, I kept thinking of you: what I could have done to help; how little I would have been able to do.

Then, in 1943, Himmler issued a new directive. The German war machine needed men, even men with pink triangles. Anyone who agreed to be castrated would be released from the camps. Per volunteered and spent the rest of the War in a munitions factory outside Frankfurt. He spoke of it all so casually – as if he had merely had his gallstones removed – that it took me a while to

---

74 The public park in the centre of Berlin. It has remained a busy gay cruising-ground.

register the truth. The moment I did, Fliss's mother's diktat that 'A eunuch is not a fit subject for the dinner table' echoed through my head, and I yearned to scratch his story on her polite conversational veneer. But first, I had to hear its conclusion. At the end of the War, he returned to his mother. Not once, in the remaining twenty-five years of her life, did they exchange a single word about what had happened. 'I felt ashamed for myself, that it was my sexuality that had led to my arrest and humiliated her before all her neighbours. I felt ashamed for her that she hadn't raised a finger in protest but, rather, connived at a system that allowed such things to take place. And I felt ashamed for us both that we never found the courage to mention it. More had been taken away from me than the use of my hand.'

'Did you at least have the chance to discuss it with friends?' I asked, in a question designed more to assert a semblance of normality than to elicit a response. 'No' was the simple answer. His friends had all been sent to the camps. There was no newfound country waiting for them. One of the few who survived (at this, he raised his mutilated hand, although whether as a figure or a metaphor I couldn't say) had been liberated from Buchenwald. He was informed by the commanding officer that, under American law, he had committed a crime and one that was uniquely heinous. Since he had served only five years of his eight-year sentence, he was to be kept in jail. Per corresponded with him until his death from typhus eighteen months later. 'At least he had the comfort of knowing that he died to protect our saviours.'

It was only now, he added with a wry smile, that people were beginning to show an interest in his ordeal: the researchers and historians who saw him less as a person than as a chapter in a best-selling book.

His visit had an unexpected consequence when Wolfram heard about it, the way that Wolfram hears about everything, and offered him a part in the film. He is to play an elderly Jew whose flat is requisitioned and earmarked by Hitler for Unity (in reality, it belonged to a young married couple). Showing a callousness remarkable even for her, Unity sized up the rooms, measuring curtains and trying out colour schemes, while the owners looked on. Although he has a mere half-dozen lines, for Per it is the fulfilment of a lifelong ambition. He describes himself as the Grandma Moses of the acting world.

Meanwhile, please don't laugh – although you deserve the chance to; we all do after what we've been through – but I'm having an affair . . . though it's hardly so formal: a romance . . . though I don't feel romantic: sleeping with . . . but then she's such a light sleeper that, when we've done the business, she likes me to leave: a fling . . . I'll try anything to avoid having to finish the sentence and reveal her name. It's Dora. Yes, I know: Dora of the 'let's just say I'm at an age when anyone asking the time is likely to be making a perfectly innocent request'. But haven't you heard about the attractions of the older woman? And it's not just a question of experience. Her body is really, well, young. If you put her head in a bag – no, that sounds dreadful: she has the most beautiful face. Not that I need to tell you. It's only a couple of months since you saw her on stage. But she looks equally good on the pillow. Everything about her is so soft and powdery. And, whatever anyone may say, she is a natural blonde. There's something enormously refreshing about making love to a woman you're not in love with. It has to do with a lightness: an emphasis on pleasure: an acceptance of boundaries. Everything is so deliciously of the moment. There's no history because there's no future – or should that be the other way round?

Felicity is flattering herself if she expects me to sit at home and pine. There are plenty more fish in the sea/pebbles on the beach etc etc. But promise me you won't put my liaison (that's the most accurate word) with Dora down to some sort of tit for tat. I'm not the one who plays games with people. Dora is a wonderful person.

I may not be in love with her but I am tremendously fond of her. She gives so much and asks for so little in return. 'Use me,' she said. 'Use me in any way you wish.' And, without going into details, she has shown me ways that you wouldn't think possible. Suffice to say that I shall never regard *armpit* as an insult again. Sex is such fun! And I mean to have a lot of it. But flesh on flesh sex. Nothing involving drugs, or guns, or defecation. Did you know that in the American state of Arkansas laughing *in flagrante* used to be a crime? Dora told me that at the same moment as she was inciting me to be a multiple offender.

By the way, many thanks for elucidating the papal reference. My only comment on husband number two is that he can't have known what he was missing. Oh, I'm so glad that I've told you everything. As always, even by proxy, you've done me a power of good.

Your grateful pal,

Luke.

8 München 40,
Giselastrasse 23,
West Germany

29th Oct 1977

Dear Michael,

I don't suppose that you've been poring over reports of our hostage crisis. No doubt 'Small kidnap in Cologne' ranks pretty high on the Skip to the Arts Page scale. Even so, you must have read that at long last it has ended. Schleyer, not the finest advertisement for Western democracy, was found dead in France. The passengers were freed from the hijacked Boeing. Baader and his cohorts have committed suicide. And life here is slowly returning to normal. The overwhelming feeling, even on the Left, is one of relief, especially that the plane was stormed without any further casualties. Did you know that eleven of the eighty-six passengers were beauty queens? Imagine: one day, they're parading in swimwear and evening-dress, professing their hopes and ambitions; the next, they're sweltering on the tarmac at Mogadishu at the mercy of a madman. In common with half the male population of Germany, I was ready to volunteer for the rescue operation myself! Soldiers apart, the hero of the hour is Chancellor Schmidt, who has seen his softly-softly approach vindicated. Had it failed, there were plenty of people eager to offer hard-line alternatives. What I find so incomprehensible is that if I (and I'm sure you) can see that violence is counter-productive, why can't the terrorists? Are they so in love with their own legend? Carole Medhurst[75] claims that it's a calculated strategy: to force the State to become increasingly repressive and so inspire people to rise up against it. Well, it certainly hasn't worked that way in the past. This is

---

[75] Luke appears to be unaware that he has not previously mentioned Medhurst, the actress playing Jessica Mitford.

Germany, home of the Reichstag Burning, and yet the Red Army Faction perpetrates arson attacks on department stores. In every sense, it's playing with fire.

At least we should be able to concentrate on our work with no further interruptions. Dora swears that she has never known a film like it. As a rule, sets are a world unto themselves. It's what happens off them that becomes 'unreal'. This one has been quite the opposite. At every corner, SS guards and Nazi officials can be found in furious debate about the merits of their spiritual successors. What with the reshooting around Wolfram and the technical cock-up over the Diana/Mosley wedding, we are now two weeks behind schedule. We need to devote all our energies to the matter at hand.

Someone who won't be able to profit from this peace dividend is Sir Hallam who, after suffering a stroke, has had to be flown back to England. It's such a humiliating fate, and particularly for one who prided himself on his vitality. I can still hear him lamenting 'old age that creeps up on you in carpet slippers only to lash out with its stick', and yet doing so in a voice supremely confident of warding off the blows. Last week, he collapsed under their weight. What happened is open to dispute but, as a guest in the adjoining suite, I can speak with more authority than most. I was spending the evening with Dora. She had just rung down for a bottle of champagne – not to drink: at least, not primarily. She likes me to dip my prick in it before we make love. At first, I resisted (I've hardly ever drunk the stuff, let alone anything else), but she told me not to be so boring (do you detect a pattern? I'll give you a hint: it's in the first syllable). She declared that it was the perfect combination of her two favourite tastes. Such pleasures, however, had to be deferred, since the expected knock wasn't room service, but rather Dieter, in a muck sweat and dressed in a Nazi uniform, frantically beckoning us next door.

There, in a heap on the bedroom floor, his clothing rumpled, his skin puckered and clammy, was Sir Hallam. And yet the felled actor still glowed with the lustre of a lifetime's roles. His last appearance on stage was as John of Gaunt, a man who both extolled and exemplified England's virtues. Much the same could be said of Sir Hallam, who played so many kings: who played before so many kings, and was now lying in a pool of his own urine. An hour or so later, once the ambulance had arrived and Dora had accompanied him to hospital (I wonder if her veto on my going sprang more from the wish to spare me pain or a mistrust of German authority), I spoke to Dieter and pieced together what had occurred. As the entire unit knows, he has been having problems with Streicher. Who can blame him? It can't be easy playing a man whom even Himmler deemed to be excessively anti-Semitic, a man who horsewhipped his enemies and forced elderly Jews to eat grass. Sir Hallam had offered to coach him (hence the uniform), but the violence of the part overwhelmed him and induced a stroke (Does that make me in some way responsible? Was it my lines that delivered the *coup de grace*?). At first, Dieter assumed that he must have fainted. He loosened his shirt and slapped his face (a little severely, I'd have said, to judge by its colour). Then, when that had no effect, he tore off his shirt and massaged his heart.

The poor chap was distraught. I assured him that no one could have done more. Shortly afterwards, Dora rang with the news that Sir Hallam was out of danger. His long-term prospects, however, were not encouraging. He had suffered a severe haemorrhage. His left side was paralysed and his speech seriously impaired.[76]

---

[76] Bamforth never recovered sufficiently to act on stage again. He did, however, make a number of cameo appearances in films, most notably in the 1982 version of Sir Walter Scott's *The Black Dwarf* (US title, *The Man of the Moors*), for which his voice was dubbed by Marius Goring.

I visited him in the hospital which, although it had been largely rebuilt after the War, was the same one where Unity was treated following her suicide bid. I took him a new biography of Vivien Leigh that I found in the English bookshop and, in an attempt to rouse him from his torpor, pointed out his name in the Index. To my acute discomfort, his only response was 'Potty!', which he repeated with all the passion he had once invested in Lear's 'Howl'. I presumed that he was alluding to her well-known mental problems and that his brusqueness was simply the result of the stroke. 'No! Potty!' he said, dismissing my gentle chiding. He grew so agitated that I feared that I must have misunderstood and asked if he wanted me to call a nurse. 'Potty, potty!' he cried. So I frantically scanned the room and, sure enough, on the top shelf, concealed by a towel, was a chamberpot. Not knowing – and, to be frank, not caring to know – how he planned to use it, I took it down, only to watch him fling it aside with a great wail. 'Oh the potty of it!', he exclaimed. And, with tears welling in my eyes, I was forced to agree.

This letter comes stamped with a capital D.[77] I know you're as silent as the proverbial but, please, don't repeat a word of it to a soul. Sir Hallam needs the chance to recuperate without being hounded by the press. Even Gerald has been relatively solicitous – although his explanation for what caused the stroke was beyond gross. The man has missed his vocation: he should have written for *Der Stürmer*.[78] Perhaps the saddest moment of all came yesterday, when Sir Hallam was due to be flown home. The only person who could be found to collect him was his agent. He has a legion of admirers but not a single available relative or friend. 'Oh the potty of it!' indeed.

[77] A reference to the D-notice sent to newspapers, asking them to withhold certain information in the interests of national security.
[78] Streicher's newspaper, founded in 1923 and much loved by Hitler, notorious for its quasi-pornographic stories about Jews.

After so much high drama, I think you'd agree that we were entitled to a few days of calm, a few days with nothing to do but to sit in the trailer, complaining about the script (!) and the director and the interminable waiting. But no, that would have been too much like a normal film. For *Unity* read crisis, and this time the culprit was Felicity – or rather, Felicity and Geraldine together. As I mentioned before, when they heard about the failure of the hijack, Baader and two of his comrades committed suicide (a fourth was rescued). You'd have supposed that it was an open-and-shut case, but not for Geraldine Conspiracy-Theory Mortimer or Ahmet Smash-Imperialzionism Samif. Not content with blaming the government for every other injustice, they now blame it for the deaths which, in their view, were assassinations. But surely, even if the authorities were that devious, they wouldn't be that stupid, when they know every disaffected activist will be on to them, crying 'Foul!'?

To listen to Geraldine – and you don't often have much choice – you'd take Baader for another Che Guevara. Felicity, as always, echoes her sentiments as though they were Holy Writ. Then, on Thursday, without a word to anyone – including, if you can believe it, Ahmet – they took the train to Stuttgart, where the three terrorists were to be buried. Can you credit such irresponsibility? We were forced to jettison a whole day's shooting. Wolfram's rage was awesome, not least because he was dressed and made-up as Hitler. Even so, it was the sight of the usually imperturbable Thomas tearing pages out of the script that brought home to me just how serious the disappearance was. All day long, a hundred people sat kicking their heels, with nothing to do but think up increasingly bizarre explanations for what had happened. The only one who seemed to be enjoying himself was Gerald, unexpectedly cast in the role of anxious father. He immediately held a press conference at which he maintained that, in spite of her having issued a statement condemning the abduction of Schleyer, his daughter remained a target for neo-Nazis. He had scarcely finished speaking when the studio received the first of a spate of calls from men who claimed to be holding both actresses under duress.

Eager to escape the Jeremiahs, I returned to the hotel with Dora. As we sat waiting for news, I idly flicked on the television, only to catch an outside broadcast from Stuttgart. I instantly – instinctively – knew that that was where the two women had gone. And I wasn't alone in my intuition. At the very moment that the camera zoomed in on the pair, each wearing regulation dark glasses and carrying a single rose, the telephone rang. It was Wolfram who, not pausing to draw breath, subjected me to a ten-minute diatribe on my failure to control my 'girlfriend'.

I'm ashamed to say that I lost my rag. I shouted back that she was no longer my girlfriend. He had seen to that. I poured out my resentment about the way he had treated us both and swore that my experience on this film had soured me so much that I would never go near another. Abandoning all restraint, I ran through my repertoire of insults, ending with the charge that he was typecast as Hitler. Dora looked on amazed: convinced, as she told me later, that the rift was irreversible. But, to the surprise of us both, he waited until I wore myself out and then asked me to meet him in the hotel bar at six.

I duly presented myself along with Dora, who had insisted on my need for a witness, only to find him slouched over a beer. As he swivelled towards us, looking more febrile and emaciated than ever, I was struck by the fear that he would die before the end of shooting. I tried to suppress it as he patted my cheek – both cheeks, to be more precise (all four, to be graphic) – and handed me a box containing a heavy gold bracelet. 'For my English Robespierre,' he declared: an allusion that left me almost as confused as the gift. I could never wear it (I'd feel like Ronnie Biggs!), but I felt strangely touched. Here was a sign that, whatever Dora's misgivings, our relationship might still be repaired.

Don't put up the bunting yet, but I have hopes that a further repair job may be possible. Felicity and Geraldine returned to face the wrath of the entire unit. What's more, Felicity was given an official dressing-down by the Embassy. For weeks, the papers have run stories about her relationship to the Ambassador. They have now taken an unwelcome twist. Her uncle is due in Munich this weekend to attend a commemoration service for the eleven Israeli athletes who were murdered at the '72 Olympics. It was originally scheduled for six weeks ago but, along with everything else in the country, it had to be put on hold during the hunt for Schleyer. Dignitaries and politicians, including Cyrus Vance and half the Israeli cabinet, are flying in from around the globe. Felicity is supposed to be accompanying her uncle. So it must be the source of some embarrassment, to say the least, to HMG that she was photographed at the funeral of three people who, if not actively engaged in it, remain popularly associated with the Palestinian cause.

True to form, Felicity expressed no contrition, but nor did she show any of her usual naughtiest-girl-in-the-school defiance. She endured the rebukes with an air of martyrdom, claiming to be astounded that no one – not even Wolfram – had applauded her stand. Then, citing exhaustion and an early call the next morning, she went up to her room. I waited for a few moments before following, half-afraid that she would leave me outside the door. To my relief, she seemed pleased to see me, but the presence of Geraldine and Ahmet put paid to any intimate chat. Geraldine then launched into a blow-by-blow account of the aftermath of the funeral, when the police set up road-blocks and harassed the departing mourners, arresting anyone who protested, including her. She was hauled off to a police station where she was strip-searched by two (male) officers. I found this as improbable as Baader's murder, but I knew better than to press the point. When I advised her to file a complaint, she snarled that this wasn't 'an episode of Dixon of Stuttgart Green'.[79] So I proposed, instead, that she appeal to the British Consul – there must be some benefits to friendship with the Ambassador's niece – only to be harangued on the various smears that the British government had used against her. At which point, I resolved to keep my suggestions – and doubts – to myself.

I was unnerved by her naked hostility. It's hard enough being a scapegoat for the crimes of my race and nation without adding those of my sex. Ahmet even insinuated that it was only a lack of uniform that prevented me from behaving as brutally as the officers – a strange accusation from one who takes guns to bed. Fliss, on the other hand, was friendlier than she had been for weeks. Paying little attention to Geraldine and Ahmet's departure, she perched on my chair and said that she wanted to talk about me. I should have known that what she meant was my attitude to Geraldine. I offered to patch up relations with a grudging 'for your sake', at which she charged me with being a typical Englishman who still swallowed his medicine 'for mummy'. Then she sounded a note of the old Fliss and said that one of the things she had always loved about me (check out that adverb!) was my desire to see the best in everything. On occasion, however, that became culpably naive. The world wasn't as simple as a Boy's Own Story. Sometimes the only honest response was to blow it up and start again. But by then I'd stopped listening for, while the words were recycled Geraldine, the tone was authentic Fliss. And, sure enough, a moment later we were in each other's arms and she was

---

[79] *Dixon of Dock Green*, a long-running BBC television series, presented a benign, if outdated, portrait of the genial and incorruptible British 'bobby'.

telling me that she loved me: she always had and she always would.

The words are resounding in my head even as I write and, although I don't think that they can ever again carry the simple charge that they did before we came to Munich, they fill me with hope. I was wrong to condemn her for going to the funeral. My guess is that she had some sort of revelation at the graveside: a recognition of the fragility of life which persuaded her that what the two of us share is far too precious to throw away. So, strange as it may sound, I owe Baader a debt of gratitude. What's more, it's time for me to acknowledge my own role in the split. You wouldn't believe that anyone, let alone a writer, could have been so insensitive. Here's Fliss, in her screen debut, worrying that the entire burden of the film rests on her shoulders. And here's me, a veteran of the dailies, assuming that she's as enchanted by her performance as everyone else. So, do I reassure her? Do I give her confidence the much-needed boost? No. I leave her to flounder in her insecurities.

Yesterday was devoted to mending fences. Uncle Ambassador rapped Fliss over the knuckles but he still wants her to accompany him to the service. His hand was weakened by the illness of his wife (familially known as the Diplomatic Bag). Fliss made her usual profession of indifference but I could see how desperate she was to go. Whatever she may say to her po-faced friends, you and I both know that there is a side of her that hankers after status. I suspect that it's in an attempt to keep it under wraps that she has made me promise to stay away from the stadium. Not that she has any need to worry. Given its size and our respective places in the VIP stand and the terraces (don't worry; I shan't labour the symbolism), it would be a miracle if we managed to spot one another in the crowd. Nevertheless, I've no intention of arguing. I only applied for my ticket at her request. I shall be glad of a quiet

Sunday. Besides, I may need to recover my strength. The best news of all is that she has agreed to spend tonight at the flat.

I don't want to tempt fate, but I feel in my bones that we'll be back together before too long.

Question: what's incurable yet in the best of health?

Answer: a romantic.

Well, it works for me.

And, to think, you'll be out here yourself in a fortnight. I doubt I'll have a chance to write to you before then, so please don't forget to send me all the details of your arrival. Unless I'm wanted on set, which, given that Brian has only one remaining scene seems unlikely, I'll be holding up my Welcome sign at the airport.

Ever your devoted pal,

Luke.

8 München 40,
Giselastrasse 23,
West Germany

6th Nov 1977

Dear Michael,

You're very kind. I have heard the phone ring, but you must forgive me if I didn't answer it. I'm beset by journalists. They, at least, are paid for their prurience, unlike my so-called friends who mask their curiosity as concern. Dora sent around a crate of champagne, although whether it was out of sympathy or lust I couldn't say . . . Thank you so much for the Marmite. You're very kind. And airmail too. I hope it didn't bankrupt you. I shall save it until I've been able to work out whether nothing tastes of anything or everything tastes the same.

Fliss loved you, you know, however much she used to tease you. She was the one who insisted that we include you in all our plans. To be honest, there were times when I found the constant presence of a third party oppressive. You seemed to be so sensitive to everything except for our need to be alone. Fliss forbade me to mention it for fear of hurting you. But then she didn't feel the same way. To her, three could never be a crowd. The universe was built on threes: from the three persons of the Trinity to the three particles of the atom to the three acts of *Private Lives*. Triptychs and trilogies and trios. Besides, in a triangle, she could stand at the apex. In a couple, she would always be on one side.

Did you see the photographs? The German press showed no restraint. All that slaughter splattered across the front pages: the perfect complement to their breakfast sausages. We slept together the night before. After such a gap, it felt like a repeat of the first time but without the nerves or, rather, with only good ones. I say *slept* but, in truth, we barely dozed. We made love and we talked. And we were so at one with each other that we completed our sentences twenty kisses later. We devised schemes for our life back in England. Was that the mark of someone who was proposing to plant a bomb the next day? Was the whole night a charade? No, absolutely not. What no one understands is that I knew Fliss. I would have known if she had intended to play truant for an afternoon, let alone plot a murder. And you'll back me up. You knew her too. In a world full of closed minds, we shall hold out for the truth.

All those bits. Eight hours earlier, she had been lying in my arms. She was a whole. We were a whole. Then, suddenly, all those bits . . .

Nothing makes sense. Fliss believed in irony, not commitment. She would no more have thrown a bomb than I would have . . . I can't think of anything sufficiently improbable. They say that she carried it in her hat, a great black-and-white affair that she asked the wardrobe department to run up for her. And they were happy to help in spite of working at full stretch. Is that the sign of a seasoned terrorist? I wish that you could have seen her as she left for the hotel. Think Catherine Deneuve in *Belle de Jour*. She looked so beautiful: so dignified: so serene. What's more, she held her head up high. Do they seriously believe that she had a bomb wedged on top of it? So what if it was only three inches wide? So what if it weighed less than a pound? She still had to set it off. We're talking Fliss: the only actress in Cambridge who could make 'I am glad to say that I have never seen a spade'[80] ring with conviction. Instead of conducting their forensic tests, they should study some basic psychology. But no, they prefer to cling to their delusions.

Let's accept – purely for the sake of argument – that the experts are right and Fliss was carrying a bomb. What was she proposing

[80] Felicity's Gwendolen in an open-air production of *The Importance of Being Earnest* was a highlight of the 1974 May Week celebrations.

to do? Take off her hat, place it under the seat and then excuse herself in the middle of the service? She would have had ten seconds, at most, to escape from the blast. Or do they suppose that she intended to sit quietly through the prayers and the eulogies and wait for her head to explode? Fliss despised suicide (you remember Ronan Bristow?[81]). She loved life. She loved me. That night, she even talked about having a baby. That's right. The woman who commended Susie Philbeach for smoking during pregnancy and claimed that, if the foetus were stunted, it would make for an easier birth, wanted to have lots of children. They would naturally all be boys, and I had to promise to name the eldest Wolfram.[82] Is that the remark of a woman who was planning to kill herself the next day? The police aren't interested. They call it an enquiry, but they merely wish to confirm their preconceptions. I've given up trying to convince them. What does it matter what the rest of the world thinks so long as the people who knew her remember her as she was? But I can see nothing but bits: all those bits. It's as if I have to push my pen over them to reach the page.

Fliss's bomb – by which I mean the bomb that killed her – was a sophisticated weapon. But you don't have to be Einstein, or even Ulrike Meinhof, to make one yourself. All you need are a few basic components: sulphur and phosphorous; potassium chlorate, which you can buy at any chemist's as an antiseptic; ditto charcoal (for indigestion). Put them together with the insides of a lighter and an alarm clock and Bob's your uncle . . . or, in

---

[81] A St John's historian who drowned himself when he failed his Finals. On hearing the news, Felicity remarked: 'You're supposed to speak only good of the dead. He's dead: good.'

[82] Although I said nothing to Luke, I wondered whether she might have been influenced by Unity, who had declared after the War that she intended to have six sons, the eldest to be called Adolf and all the rest John. Pryce-Jones page 254.

Fliss's case, your uncle's dead. It's kid's stuff. Any schoolboy with a grudge could construct one. So be sure to keep the science labs locked up at night. Precise instructions are set out in a manual called something like – and I kid you not – Teach Yourself How To Be An Urban Guerrilla.[83] The police claim to have found a copy in Fliss's room. I suspect a frame-up. Nevertheless, when they asked me how she might have come by it, I had no hesitation in naming Geraldine, who'd had a box of Leftist books sent out from England. But, according to her – and to the receipt – they were classic texts by Trotsky, Gramsci and Marcuse.

Geraldine issued a statement deploring the loss of life and admitting a degree of responsibility. But don't hold your breath. That responsibility only stretched to persuading Fliss to accompany her to the Baader-Ensslin funerals, where they witnessed the full brutality of the German state unleashed on the mourners. At the subsequent press conference, she apparently rolled up her sleeves to reveal the livid bruises left by the police who assaulted her. And, suddenly, to her undisguised delight, everything has become about her.

The police called me in for three interviews, although I have to say that I didn't encounter any brutality – quite the reverse. The only antagonism came from the Embassy official who escorted me which, given the circumstances, was understandable. I confided the full extent of my suspicions about Ahmet and berated myself for having said nothing until then. And, before you accuse me of settling old scores, take a look at the evidence. Why else would a Palestinian – a self-declared militant – come to Germany in the middle of a hostage crisis? It certainly wasn't in order to visit his brother. Who else out of Fliss's acquaintance had expressed a murderous hatred of the Jews? Fliss wasn't remotely anti-Semitic.

---

[83] This was almost certainly Carlos Marighella's *The Mini-handbook of the Brazilian Urban Guerrilla*, the bible of the Seventies terrorist.

On the contrary, her favourite cousin had married a Rothschild. And it's no use telling me that one of Unity's uncles had married a German Jewess.[84] The position is not the same. If all that isn't enough to implicate Ahmet, what about his disappearance on the very afternoon of the explosion? No one has heard a whisper from him since then. Moreover, how did he manage to travel so easily when he had no passport, just some sort of Syrian laissez-passer?

I'm compiling a dossier on the ways in which terrorists prey on gullible women that, when published, will clear Fliss's name. What's more, I shall save other women – innocent, trusting women – from falling into the same trap. Take the case of the two English girls who, in 1972, were befriended by a pair of Arab students in Rome. The girls were flying on to Tel Aviv where the Arabs promised to join them, giving them a transistor radio as a pledge of good faith. The bomb that was hidden inside detonated in mid-air although, miraculously, it failed to destroy the plane or injure the passengers. The girls had been duped just like Fliss. Only she wasn't so lucky. She ended up in . . . bits. All I can see are the bits. They say that they were scattered for yards.[85]

---

[84] Unity's Uncle Jack was briefly married to Marie-Anne von Friedländer-Fuld, whose father was officially rated as the richest man in Berlin. After the passing of the Nuremberg Laws, she wore a Star of David made of yellow diamonds. Pryce-Jones pages 15–16.

[85] Luke might also have mentioned the Dutch and Peruvian women who, in separate but similar incidents, were found with bombs as they boarded planes from Rome to Tel Aviv in 1971. What he could not have known was that, on 17 April 1986, the Jordanian Nezar Newaf Mansur Hindawi would bid adieu to his fiancée, a thirty-two-year-old chambermaid, Anne Marion Murphy, as she took a flight from Heathrow to Tel Aviv, where they were to meet a few days later. He had given her a bag packed with 'surprise gifts' to open when they landed. The biggest surprise was that it contained a bomb which, had it not been discovered, would have destroyed her, their unborn child, and all the other passengers aboard the El Al jet. As she was led away for questioning, Murphy kept repeating, 'I loved him. I loved him. I loved him.'

Do you think that Hitler's vegetarianism was born of a genuine concern for animals or a revulsion from the carnage that he saw in the trenches? All those bloody flanks. All that exposed offal. All the dead comrades gazing up at him from every plate of cold cuts.

The film has been abandoned. It could survive Ralf's defection: it could survive Sir Hallam's departure; but it couldn't survive Fliss's death. There were too many key scenes still to be shot. The financial loss will be covered. The one advantage of such a public catastrophe is that the insurers cannot deny liability. The emotional loss will be harder to compensate. Everything feels so incomplete. There was no wrap party, which Dora declared to be as essential to mark the end of a film as a funeral to mark the death of a friend. Then she turned pale and tried to change the subject. She and Gerald and Carole and the rest have returned to England, while the Germans have dispersed around Munich to await Wolfram's call. In time, I too will have a future – I'm too ordinary not to have one – although I've no idea what it will be. The only thing I do know is that it won't be on celluloid.

I've made several attempts to see Wolfram. I never realised how much some of his old associates resented me until I saw the pleasure that they took in conveying his rebuffs. The one exception is Dieter, who not only came to the flat but brought me a bunch of flowers. He disclosed that Wolfram hadn't slept for a week but survived on a diet of cocaine. To increase his intake, he had sworn to both Dieter and Renate that each was the only one arranging the supply. Meanwhile, whether it's from a drug-induced high or a genuine excitement, he is buzzing with ideas for a new film – an 'anti-film', which will intersperse scenes from *Unity* with footage from the stadium, interviews with the public and hard-core pornography. For the moment, he is concentrating on the last.[86]

---

[86] No trace of this project has survived.

So he has no need of a writer. Which is all to the good. Writers have far too much power. Over breakfast, I can decide to send a character to war or to jail or to Hell. Over lunch, I can dispatch another to blow up churches or governments or God. And, provided that it rings true, provided that it is part of a coherent vision (and always provided that it doesn't cost too much), my blueprint will be followed. Truth, however, is no justification. I know now that a writer must take full responsibility for his ideas, like a scientist with the H-bomb. There is certain research that is too dangerous to publish. It should be left in the study or the lab. I was the one who brought *Unity* to life, even if it required others to bring it to fruition, so I am the one who must shoulder the blame.

You ask when I'll be coming home. It's hard to say. I've put myself at the disposal of Fliss's parents for as long as they remain here. In any case, I wouldn't dream of returning until the Germans release the body. I couldn't leave her here alone. Body? What body? How can they be certain that all the bits will be hers? You remember how fastidious she was. She even hated sharing a bathroom. It's unthinkable that she might be jumbled up with strangers. At a pinch she might tolerate her uncle, but not the bodyguards and the Pole. I shall insist that they respect her integrity. It's the least I can do.

I plan to settle in Hastings for a while. It's the one place where I can be sure of being left alone. But I promise that we'll meet up very soon.

In your previous letter – I'm sorry I never replied but I know you'll make allowances – you mentioned that you'd been asked to produce the school play. I beg you not to accept. Take the boys for model-making, stamp-collecting and country walks, but keep them away from acting. One of them might be hooked.

Luke.

I visited Luke several times on his return, although we failed to resurrect our former intimacy. My friendship with Felicity, from which he had once claimed to draw comfort, now made him wary of me. The horror of Munich had taken its toll. In an attempt to find a meaning – or in despair of ever finding one – he joined a fundamentalist Baptist church and, within months of coming home, moved to Sunderland, where he worked in a series of dead-end jobs and devoted himself to the Gospel.

We kept in desultory contact, although the obvious means was ruled out by his church's taboo on celebrating Christmas. He wrote letters of carefully weighed praise on the publication of my first two novels. His amusement at our changed status was the sole remnant of the old Luke. It was the new Luke, however, who took it upon himself to condemn my sexuality (and, in particular, its public expression in my third novel, Easter*). He sent a long letter (one habit that he never abandoned), castigating the 'abomination' and warning that, unless I repented, I was heading for Hell.*

He backed up his injunction with a battery of Biblical texts but, although deeply wounded, I resolved to avoid conflict, citing instead the case of my prep school master (he of the Boys' Own *definition of evil) who had informed us that 'the Bible isn't perfect in every particular. There are several commas that are misplaced.' He hit back, Bible-first, with 'The fool hath said in his heart: There is no God.' While prepared to admit the epithet, I utterly refuted the charge and brought the correspondence to an end.*

Luke never married nor, as far as I can make out, did he enjoy any other close relationship. For over twenty years his life, weekday as well as Sunday, centred on his faith. Then, in April 2001, three months after I sent him a copy of Geraldine Mortimer's diary, he denounced the church and all its works from the pulpit, returned to his lodgings and hanged himself. At his funeral, I sat alongside his two brothers and their wives, from whom he had also grown estranged. There were no mourners from the church. With his brothers' blessing, I undertook to provide a headstone. For weeks I agonised over a suitable, non-scriptural inscription, finally settling on the simplest.

'May he know eternal felicity.'

2

Renate Fischer's Memoir

Just as it would be futile to produce a portrait of Unity Mitford without including one of Hitler, so it is futile to attempt an analysis of Felicity Benthall without including one of Wolfram Meier. From a reading of Luke's letters, it appears that the key to Felicity's conduct and to the transformation she underwent in Munich lay in her relationship with Meier. My own deep hostility to Meier inclines me towards a similar conclusion. I find it hard to forgive a man who revealed his indifference to me on sight and who, while occupying my consciousness for years, instantly banished me from his. I find it hard to forgive a man who drove a wedge between my friends and myself. I find it hard to forgive a man whose manipulation of those friends left me with a profound mistrust of commitment, the effects of which lie outside the scope of this book.

On the other hand, it was Meier's intervention that saved me from life as a mediocre actor and led me to hone my talents as a writer. During the desiccated years, first as a teacher and then as a copy-writer, my need for a means of self-expression prompted me to transfer my allegiance from the stage to the study and embark on the arduous apprenticeship which, after a decade of false starts, discarded drafts and rejected typescripts, resulted in the publication of my first novel.

Of the various accounts of Wolfram Meier that I have read – intimate memoirs, critical studies and Joachim Bürger's full-scale biography – by far the most illuminating is that by Renate Fischer. Her book consists of a general introduction, followed by chapters devoted to each of Meier's stage and screen productions (the incomplete Unity *is excluded). I am extremely grateful to Fischer for making the typescript available to me and for allowing me to* extract the introduction (*I also wish to acknowledge the assistance of Hilda Meister in preparing the translation*). For many reasons, some of which will be evident from the text and others which will be touched upon later, it remains unpublished. Nevertheless, I trust that readers will share my estimate of its worth.

Earlier, I cast scorn on the notion that Unity's spirit was working through Felicity. It is, however, indisputable that Felicity's abject devotion to Meier resembled Unity's enslavement to Hitler. Moreover, the coincidence of Meier's playing Hitler is too convenient to ignore. Even before his assumption of the role, his treatment of his colleagues had been likened to Hitler's subjugation of his henchmen. In the final paragraph of this extract, Fischer draws a direct parallel between the ruthless exercise of their wills.

In the absence of Felicity's own testimony, I am left clutching at analogies. Fischer's memoir is particularly helpful for, although it mentions her only in passing, the intensity of the writer's obsession with Meier mirrors Felicity's. Both women effaced their own needs in order to pimp for him – although, if Liesl Martins is to be believed, Fischer went on to bed him herself. Her contention that Felicity took up arms on behalf of Meier receives little support elsewhere. Luke's description of the furore surrounding The Judge suggests that Meier's politics were, at best, ambiguous (*critics, including Fischer herself, might prefer the word* opportunistic). Felicity was surely sharp enough to recognise that his politics were subservient to his art – if not that his art was subservient to his egotism.

Parenthood apart, a degree of egotism is essential for all human achievement. An excess of it, however, is responsible for all human vice. Indeed, many of my objections to the concept of evil would be met by the simple substitution of egotism. Gone would be the associations of Hieronymus Bosch and the Spanish Inquisition: gone would be the shades of a humanity steeped in sin and doomed to hell; and in their place would stand the callous *disregard for the rights of others which, in my view, united Felicity and Meier. Meier was an artist: a licensed egotist. To adapt his own aphorism, if altruism is egotism in Lent, then art is egotism at Christmas. Felicity, however, lacked such an outlet. Her egotism left her permanently dissatisfied. She was one of life's table-hoppers, renouncing the chance of present happiness for the illusion of excitement elsewhere.*

My mother, who never took to Felicity even as a prospective daughter-in-law (a role for which she was prepared to overlook any manner of fault) judged her to be flighty. It can be no accident that, in the Biblical myth of the Fall, what incites mankind to evil is curiosity. With Felicity in mind, I prefer to approach it from another angle and to identify Adam's sin less as the lust for knowledge than as the dread of being bored.

Wolfram Meier died on 17 June 1984. The doctor pronounced a verdict of natural causes. He had abused his body for so long that it collapsed. His chest was as thin as a communion wafer. His skin was as tacky as fly-paper. His heart was hugely enlarged. Some writers might mine that for a symbol, but Wolfram abhorred such sentimentality. Whenever he encountered it on stage or screen, he would flap his arms and quack in mockery of Ibsen's *Wild Duck*.

He left behind him an extraordinary body of work. Along with Rainer Werner Fassbinder, Werner Herzog and Wim Wenders, he had laid the foundations of what became known as New German Cinema, of which he was, arguably, the brightest light. His twenty-six films, from *The Ratcatcher* in 1968 to *The Holy Family* released posthumously in 1984, constitute a unique testament, at once an extended cinematic autobiography and an exhaustive portrait of post-war German social and cultural life. His output was prodigious and, in retrospect, it is tempting to suggest that he had received a premonition of early death. Moreover, whatever the personal tragedy for his circle of friends, there is reason to believe that his best work already lay behind him. His last two films betray signs of negligence. The economic climate that had facilitated the funding of his films had turned cold. The sexual well from which he had drunk so deep was poisoned.

Wolfram was born on 16 October 1944 although, in interviews, he would always cite a date a year later. This was neither a conventional nor a commonplace vanity but, by ascribing his birth to 7 May 1945, the day of Germany's surrender to the Allies, he aimed to portray himself as a phoenix rising from the ashes of war (there were some who maintained that the ashes were those of Hitler's bunker). He was therefore able to forge a parallel between his own development and that of his country. The process of self-definition had begun.

The inability to know the truth about a fellow human being was a recurring theme of Wolfram's work and one that he exemplified in his life. He lied not only about his age but about his background. When he arrived at the Bettlertheater, he claimed that he had been born in the GDR. He confided in each of us individually – and supposedly uniquely – that he was the illegitimate son of a top-ranking politician, even hinting that it was Ulbricht[87] himself. He warned of the danger of our being seen in public with someone who was under constant surveillance by the *Stasi*. Such was the paranoia and, I am forced to admit, the chemical consumption of the day that we believed him.

Wolfram's alleged father had met his alleged mother while she was plying her trade on the *Linienstrasse* during the War. He was subsequently brought up in a brothel, the details of which brought tears to our eyes until we discovered that they had been taken straight from a biography of Edith Piaf (in whose life-story Wolfram long hoped to film the author of this memoir[88]). The truth is at once more mundane and more moving. His father was killed on the Russian front. His widowed mother scavenged and scrounged to provide for her three-year-old daughter and six-month-old son. The ravages of peacetime took their toll and the little girl died – officially of typhus, in reality of malnutrition. For the rest of her life, Wolfram's mother blamed herself for neglecting her daughter in favour of her son. Wolfram, on the other hand, never uttered a word of regret for his dead sister. On the contrary, his solitary survival confirmed his sense of destiny.

[87] Walter Ulbricht (1893–1973), Secretary-General of the East German Communist Party.

[88] It would have had to be a very free recreation. On the face of it, few actresses could have been less suited to playing the 'Little Sparrow' than the hefty, big-boned Fischer.

That sense was reinforced by his guilt-ridden mother and the household of doting female relatives who lived with them. Kristel Meier spoke many times of how, from his earliest years, Wolfram's behaviour marked him out as exceptional. When asked by his teacher to name his favourite smell, in place of his class-mates' hot chocolate or sizzling sausages, he answered 'American soldiers'. When that same teacher found him digging assiduously in the school sandpit, she inquired if he were making a castle. 'No,' the eight-year-old replied, 'I'm digging your grave.' He was transferred to a new school shortly afterwards. When challenged about the incident years later on a chat-show, he declared that his strongest reason for wanting to kill his teacher had been the 365 Day calendar on her desk. Every morning she ripped off a page at Registration as if time were just so much waste paper.

Time for Wolfram was a precious resource. Childhood was fast disappearing. When he was ten, his mother married again. Her new husband was a butcher (a profession vilified throughout Wolfram's work). Stepfather and son made no secret of their mutual loathing. Wolfram also turned against his mother, pouring particular scorn on her explanation that she had only accepted the proposal in order to provide him with an adequate diet. A year into her marriage, she became pregnant. When she went into labour, she left Wolfram in the care of his stepfather. On the first night that they were alone, the two slept together. Wolfram told the story with glee, relishing the horror on our post-adolescent faces. He denied that he had been in any way harmed by the encounter, insisting that, on the contrary, he had been its insti-gator, feeling the simultaneous thrill of consummation and of power. He claimed that every boy of that age had sexual feelings and would welcome such an opportunity: a view that never proved to be more contentious than when he voiced it in the presence of the Hollywood actress, Geraldine Mortimer, who physically attacked him.[89] His mother's and stepfather's baby was stillborn.

After his wife's empty-handed return from hospital, Wolfram's stepfather treated him even more perversely, alternating brutal beltings with lachrymose pleas for love (Wolfram relished both as proof of his dominance). To preserve the peace, Kristel connived to keep the pair as far apart as possible. The simplest means was to send Wolfram to the cinema. He went every day after school and, increasingly, instead of it. So began the great love affair of his life. He himself takes up the tale, courtesy of Andy Warhol's *Interview*: 'I was Christopher Columbus: I discovered America. Smokey bars. Sunlit prairies. Rita Hayworth. Spencer Tracey. The Manhattan skyline. The mob. Teenagers . . . A world of vast landscapes and minuscule gestures. A world where everything was fluid yet everyone had a place. And for that I have to thank my mother. If she hadn't married again, I might never have known.'

Cinema was Wolfram's life and it therefore stands at the heart of this memoir in the form of a detailed interpretation of each of his films by the author, the person best qualified to bring Wolfram's work to a wider audience. I was not merely his closest professional associate – the only actor to have appeared in every single one of his films – but his wife. One might suppose, given Wolfram's very public proclivities, that our marriage was a mockery but, on the contrary, it attests to the deep devotion he felt for me that, despite the absence of desire, he wanted the union. Nevertheless – and unlike some of my less privileged former colleagues – I retain the right to exercise my critical faculties. I am under no illusions about his failings – at least not now, a decade after his death.[90] While he lived, I was in total thrall to

[89] It is curious that there is no mention of any such incident in Geraldine Mortimer's journal.

[90] Renate Fischer's memoir was written in 1995.

him. It was a madness that I never understood until we worked together on the unfinished *Unity* and I learnt about loyalty to a dictator.[91]

I first met Wolfram Meier at the Bettlertheater in Munich in the mid 1960s (dates from that period are particularly hazy). His cousin, a stagehand, had sneaked him into a performance which impressed him so much that he returned again and again. He never applied formally to join us (he would never have revealed such vulnerability), but he used to sit and drink with the actors late into the night, becoming one of the group by stealth. He did not hold back on his criticism of performances that he considered inadequate. Some of those under attack were incensed that this upstart – this yob – should give them notes, but it was an article of our faith that everyone be allowed his say. Goethe's view of *Faust* was of no more consequence than that of the woman who sold the ice-cream in the foyer.

At first Wolfram was employed backstage but, when an actor in Büchner's *Leonce and Lena* fell ill in mid-rehearsal, he offered to take over the role. His ambitions did not stop there, but stretched to taking over the company. Conditions worked in his favour. Although Klaus Bernheim and Manfred Stückl were nominally in charge, we were a collective. We decided to put our principles into practice by doing away with a director and taking all decisions (artistic as well as administrative) by vote. The democratic ideal soon proved to be unworkable. Anarchy prevailed until Wolfram, trading on the fact that as the most recent recruit he was the one least subject to personal allegiances, took control. He brought in some friends to build the set. He worked with his cousin on the lighting. He instructed the actors on the staging. The play opened on time.

[91] It is unclear whether Fischer is referring to dictatorship in the film or on the set or, indeed, if the ambiguity is intentional.

His intentions were initially obscure. It was not so much that he imposed himself on us as that he made himself the only means whereby we could achieve our goals. He persuaded us to present *The Ratcatcher*, only now there would be no lip-service paid to democracy. Not only did he write and direct it himself but he supervised every aspect of the production. He took particular care over the posters, which read 'Wolfram Meier and his Bettlertheater present . . .' We were horrified. Since when had the theatre become his? And yet we said nothing, not from cowardice but from embarrassment. We were unwilling to draw attention to such overweening ego.

He played on that embarrassment along with the faint unease that each of us felt in his presence since, while we were expressing solidarity with the proletariat, he was the real thing. He had grown up among prostitutes, pimps and pushers. The experience had marked him – literally, in the livid scar on his frequently exposed chest. He was the representative of the class that our parents had oppressed. Our sense that they had exploited him left him free to exploit us. It was time to make amends.

His cause was aided by his intense physical allure. Everyone fell for him. The author just fell the furthest. He exuded sex with his shock of white hair and his rake-thinness, his appealingly pock-marked face and his feral smile. He used to say that hack actors had to be beautiful to be loved, but that he could make audiences love him in spite of his looks. He wore the same ragged clothes every day and rarely bathed: a practice he maintained throughout his life and one that became progressively less acceptable. At first, however, it seemed like a return to the natural man: an authentic whiff of the streets: two fingers raised to the deodorised department-store world. Besides, it was 1967: the theatre was thick with incense.

He consolidated his position by seducing Liesl Martins, the third member of the company's original triumvirate and the source of much of its finance. Their subsequent affair, played out largely in public, placed her boyfriend, Manfred, in an acute dilemma. According to his own code – not to mention his agreement with Liesl – he had no right to be proprietorial. And yet his amour propre had been pierced. When the relationship became too heated for him to ignore, he engineered a showdown with Wolfram, who responded by seducing him too. For one who was by nature a cynic, he held an incongruously romantic view that sex would secure a person's loyalty. Which, by and large, it did. When it became clear that he had both of them hooked, he ditched them unceremoniously while continuing to live in their house, conducting his tortuous liaisons under their very noses.

With Wolfram at the helm, the Bettlertheater became Munich's most fashionable venue. The cream of the city's radical youth flocked to our exposés of the older generation's sins. As has been well-documented, among their number was Andreas Baader. He regularly attended performances with members of his set – I hesitate to call it a group since I doubt that, at that stage, it had become so organised. It was, rather, a crowd of like-minded friends who gathered around a mesmeric figure the way that we gravitated towards Wolfram. They made an enthusiastic but critical audience who would jump to their feet and harangue the actors when they judged our analysis to be wrong. Sometimes they provoked stand-up fights in the auditorium as the worlds of art and activism clashed. Soon, more conservative theatregoers were booking seats in the hope of witnessing a confrontation. They felt cheated if a play proceeded uninterrupted to its close. Some of the company were outraged, but not Wolfram, who recognised the value of a scandal. At the time I accused him of opportunism, but I realise now that his commitment ran deeper. He and Baader shared an agenda, embracing disruption both on and off the stage.

The Baader connection dogs the surviving members of the company to this day (the author of this memoir can never embark on any project without the Red Army Faction being invoked). It proved to be most damaging during the abortive film *Unity*, when the young English actress in the title role attempted to blow up the Munich Olympic Stadium. Many explanations have been put forward for her action but, in the view of the author, who was present throughout the shooting, Felicity Benthall had become infatuated with Wolfram. She appeared convinced both that he was being unjustly vilified for his tenuous link with Baader and that, by planting her bomb, she would be acting as his surrogate, helping to realise his political dreams. In this, she not only totally misread the director, but caused him to forfeit his most ambitious and deeply felt film.

A catch-phrase of the Sixties held that the personal was political. For Wolfram, the political was personal. He used public life as a subject for melodrama. Once, on location in London at a time of industrial strife, he likened the rubbish piled in the streets to the parcels of excrement that the young Salvador Dali had secreted in drawers to shock the maids. Far from endorsing the dustmen's struggle, he compared it to the prank of a precocious Surrealist. Even more indicative of his lack of political acumen is the fact that, when dealing with the most notorious leader of modern times, he should have conceived of him exclusively in terms of his sexuality: Hitler's impotence; his coprophilia; his homosexuality; even his lack of a second testicle. While the Führer saw himself as a Wagnerian hero: Rienzi, Siegfried or Lohengrin, Wolfram saw him as the cursed Klingsor in *Parsifal*, suffering from a genital wound.

In the spring of 1968, the theatre burnt down. The cause was never officially established although, unofficially, few of us harboured any doubt. Baader and his friends had grown disenchanted. They had become part of the very performance they had wanted to disrupt. It was Feydeau-Baader that audiences were queuing to see. He felt emasculated so he destroyed the theatre, thereby creating the pattern for the rest of his life. The group was devastated, with the exception of Wolfram. It was as if he knew that it was time to move on. His last big success had been Schiller's *Don Carlos*, with the Spanish court transposed to Hollywood (I would use that as a symbol, but I hear him quacking even as I write). Baader also moved on. A few weeks later, he burnt down Schneider's department store in Frankfurt. Suddenly, subtly, Germany was at war. It was the most devastating fire since that of the Reichstag. It seemed that no one had learnt anything in the intervening forty years. People simply stood and watched as history went up in flames.

Unknown to any of us, even Liesl, Wolfram had insured the building only weeks before the attack. Some praised his prescience; others took a more sceptical view. But even the most painstaking investigation by the insurers failed to uncover a link. With the proceeds, Wolfram bought a camera and equipment and made his first film. The fact that the money belonged to the collective never appeared to cross his mind. He laid claim to it on the grounds that he would put it to the best use. Which was, of course, true. Those who took issue with him were ruthlessly purged: an event that the survivors subsequently dubbed the Night of the Long Knives. The failure of the rebels in their future careers was to be a lesson to us all.

Even shoe-string films are costly. When the insurance money ran out, Wolfram shaved his head and, making the most of his Albino looks, appealed to various foundations to fund the film, on the grounds that he was dying from cancer. When their contributions left a shortfall, he exhorted some of the actresses to walk the streets. His success bore witness not only to his powers of persuasion but to the spirit of the age. It was typical of Wolfram that he should have drafted feminist ideology into the service of his masculine ego, claiming that all women prostituted themselves:

most did so to their husbands, trading sex for security; we, at least, enjoyed the distinction of doing it for art.

Wolfram entertained few scruples about the source of his funding. The majority of his films were financed through co-production deals with television. At times, however, the controversial subject matter caused the money-men to shy away. A case in point was *Unity*, where they were worried by the emphasis on the Führer's private life (no doubt they would have been mollified by a few establishing shots of Dachau). So Werner Kempe, the producer of all Wolfram's films from *Rosa Luxemburg* until their rupture on *The Holy Family*, approached Thomas Bücher, Germany's most successful pornographer, who was later to gain notoriety when a model died during the making of one of his films.

Bücher saw the film as a solid investment, but he also secured Wolfram's promise to direct a feature for his own studio. He had been courting him for years, no doubt to provide some private measure of respectability. All Wolfram's friends advised against his making any such commitment. Pornography had not then penetrated the mainstream to the extent that it has done today, when its former stars can be found in Hollywood films, on Paris cat-walks and in the Italian Senate. Reputation and reality were united in confining it to the back streets. Wolfram, however, saw it differently, passing off his private addiction as an artistic credo. The actors in pornography espoused the rawness that constituted his ideal. They did not hide behind bourgeois notions of character: they did not hide behind anything at all. They were themselves, naked and unashamed. As he declared to a stunned Berlin Festival: 'Just as all art is said to aspire to the condition of music, so all film should aspire to the condition of pornography.'

The Ratcatcher was acclaimed at festivals throughout Europe. At home, it won a state prize. Wolfram's career was launched and, from then on, it rarely faltered. Although lazy critics questioned his work-rate, the quality of the work never suffered (which is more than can be said for that of his private life). He showed extraordinary loyalty to his original Bettlertheater actors, tailoring parts to our particular talents with the result that we became known far beyond Munich. Fame, however, came at a price. 'Caligula made his horse a consul,' he said to Dieter. 'I can make you a star.' Every time that he claimed that anyone could act, the public presumed that we couldn't. He was the alpha and omega of his films. We were as much a part of the aesthetic as the lighting and costumes. We had no reputation outside his: no roles apart from his. You could no more cast us in another director's film than you could recycle one of his sets.

We were stars for an age without illusions and a public that knew how films were made. This was a public that watched sex scenes not to derive vicarious pleasure, but to enjoy the humiliation. They knew that, however lavish the setting, we were performing in front of indifferent cameramen and prurient make-up artists on a set cold enough to make the biggest stud shrink and give the greatest goddess goose-flesh.

Wolfram made no attempt to temper his ruthlessness. The fascist streak inherent in all directors was especially pronounced in him. He pressed his natural tendency to sado-masochism into service, alternately coaxing and bullying the cast and crew. I was never able to work out whether he tortured us so that he could make a better film, or made the film in order to torture us better. He claimed that he was fulfilling our secret desires. In his view, the greatest pleasure in most peoples' lives was subordination. It was, therefore, understandable that we harboured ambivalent feelings towards him. We wanted to hate him because we were subservient to him, but we couldn't because our subservience brought us satisfaction – which, in turn, confirmed our hatred of ourselves.

Like every dictator throughout history, he both demanded our dependence and despised us for it. Even at his most autocratic, however, he retained a degree of insight. I myself was present during the filming of *Unity*, when he explained to the actor playing Hitler how easy it was to become a megalomaniac when surrounded by sycophants. Then he laughed, as though he realised the significance of what he had said. In the early days of the Bettlertheater, we lived as a commune – as much for pragmatic as for idealistic reasons, given the tangle of relationships involved. Later, we became his vassals. He was determined to be the principal lover in all our lives. So, when Liesl Martins announced that she was pregnant, he immediately offered her the title role in *Margarite* (a part that had been originally earmarked for the author). The shooting schedule, however, would require her to have an abortion. One evening, at his regular weekend party, he put her publicly on the spot in a truth game designed to winkle out which she wanted most: a baby or the mammoth leading role. Two days later, she entered a clinic. In spite of her decision, Wolfram never allowed either Liesl or her husband Manfred to come as close to him again.[92]

Wolfram was drawn to violence. He delighted in provoking his partners. Like the heroine of a cheap thriller, he believed that the intensity of the blows attested to the strength of the love. He adopted similar tactics with his colleagues, deliberately riling them in the hope that they would lash out with either fists or words. Like Hitler, he believed in the principles of divide and rule and survival of the fittest. The one watched Himmler, Göring and Goebbels jockeying for power, the other Manfred, Dieter and Kurt. The author was not the only person to whom the Nazi analogy had occurred. On one occasion when we were all gathered in a

92 Martins and Stückl later adopted two Vietnamese orphans, Anh Dung and Tuyen.

café, someone read out a newspaper article about life at Hitler's Berchtesgaden retreat. Erich Leitner, who had listened to the behaviour but not to the names, exclaimed in fury that it was libellous of *Bild* to print such a story about Wolfram and the Serpent's Nest. The error caused deep embarrassment to all but one of those present. He merely flashed an inscrutable smile.

Like a child, Wolfram acknowledged no boundaries between the world and his desires, only challenges. As his fame grew, he abandoned any kind of self-control (at the same time, his control over his films grew ever tighter). He failed to realise that the ability to gratify his desires was not freedom as long as he remained a slave to those desires. He aped the behaviour of a rock star, once ordering a bottle of champagne in a restaurant not to quench his thirst but because he wanted to cool his feet in the ice-bucket. He left a trail of trashed hotel rooms, the managers sending incriminatory photographs to the Studios, who paid handsomely to have the negatives destroyed. He lived on a cocktail of drugs that stimulated his output but ruined his health. At the end of every crisis, he would give his solemn word to Werner that he would clean up his behaviour. Meanwhile, he had found the perfect way to feed his habit in public. With a patent-worthy perversity, he doctored a nasal inhaler so that, when pressed, it released a line of cocaine.

Wolfram's sexual habits were equally extreme. He was predominantly homosexual, although he evinced a deep-rooted contempt for the aunties and old queens.[93] In every relationship, he was the aggressor, and he preferred to work out his aggression on straight men: black men: working-class men – and, on occasions, women. While emotionally he always remained at a distance, physically he reached ever deeper, substituting penetration for intimacy. He made no apologies for his inclinations. Far from regarding them as

[93] This is an approximate translation of two pejorative German terms: *Tunten* and *Schwuchteln*.

unnatural, he felt that, by sleeping with a man, he was reaching to the heart of Nature, embracing it in all its dark impersonality rather than dressing it in the sentimentality of a bourgeois code.

The constant craving for novelty that served him so well in his work ensured that, by the end of his life, sex had become scatology. He wanted to sanctify wastes: the bodily fluids and, sometimes, solids of which we had been taught to be most ashamed. He felt that, if we made love to someone, then we should do so at the moment of our greatest vulnerability. By then, he admitted no distinction between public and private lives. He drew his insights from the bunker and the board room and adapted them to the bedroom. People were animals and so that was how he made them behave between the sheets. He took the history of the past fifty years and repeated it, not as tragedy or farce, but as pornography.[94]

His character was not so much a mystery as a paradox. Just as it was the commercial success of his films that allowed him the freedom to denounce capitalist values, so he coupled his critique of American culture with films that mimicked the style, structure and, sometimes, even the plots of Hollywood melodramas. He was steeped in the Studio system, relating every dilemma facing himself or his associates to one resolved by Glenn Ford or Barbara Stanwyck. Indeed, his main reason for wishing to turn his actors into stars was that Hollywood was his Valhalla.

He dominated us without effort. The author herself was his abject slave. It was as if the word *no* had been excised from my vocabulary or else that I had renounced it voluntarily, like *dwarf*. He cast me as a lesbian, a murderess and a tramp. I look at pictures of myself taken twenty years ago and I see a beautiful woman, but he made me feel so undesirable that I could justify

---

94 It is instructive to note the difference between Meier's view and that of Dieter Reiss, as recorded by Geraldine Mortimer on page 292. Whereas Meier wanted the bedroom to reflect the world, Reiss wanted it to redeem it.

my existence only when reflected through his lens. The one remotely glamorous role in which he cast me was the Virgin Mary in *Faust* and, even then, the choice was not innocent, since he knew that nothing would more outrage my father, a Lutheran pastor, than the scene in which I offered the hero my nipple and the screen was flooded with milk.

My longing for him came at the expense of all self-respect. The familiar story that I paid for his whores is, I regret, true. What is less well-known is how I did so. It was not with money stolen from my father's collection-box, however much that might have appealed to his taste for sacrilege, but rather with my body. I prostituted myself in order to provide him with prostitutes. My degradation was the price of his pleasure.

Whether as a reward or a punishment, he married me. It was at once the happiest and the most desperate day of my life. On the steps of the town hall, he began to flirt with one of the secretaries. He skipped the wedding meal for an assignation with her. It had to be a *her*: a *him* would have been both too easy a challenge for Wolfram, and too small a humiliation for me. He later claimed in an interview that he had married so that he could be like any other German husband and abuse his wife. I alone could unpeel the layers of irony behind that remark. There is one way in which he continues to act as a warning. The further that we move from the Nazi era, the stranger it seems that so many ordinary, decent people should have surrendered their will to a single man. But anyone struggling to make sense of that headlong stampede into insanity need only speak to Dieter Reiss or Dorit Huber, to Liesl Martins or Manfred Stückl, to Luise Hermann or Helmuth Wissmann, or, for the most authoritative account of all, to me.

3

Liesl Martins & Manfred Stükl

in conversation

Renate Fischer's generosity in placing her memoir at my disposal was offset by a refusal to meet me face to face. My attempts to make contact with other of Meier's associates drew a similar blank. Following the director's death, the close-knit group had unravelled and long-standing friendships dissolved in acrimony. Dieter Reiss alone responded to my request, summoning me to his hospital bed in Munich, but the ravages of illness made sustained questioning impossible. So I was especially glad to meet Liesl Martins when she visited London in September 2001 to launch a season of Meier's work at the National Film Theatre. Meier's films had fallen from favour in the 1990s, their density of thought and texture out of place in a culture of sensationalism. Their renewed popularity is due in part to the change in climate and in part to the tireless promotion of the Meier Foundation, which Martins heads.

We had in fact met once before, when Meier was on location in England. Then, despite our both being visitors to the set, she had barely deigned to acknowledge me – a slight which, in my depressed state, I had taken as my due. I now felt able to address her on an equal footing – although her open indifference to fiction threatened to sap my confidence. While wary of any rehash of the Unity *debacle, she soon appreciated the seriousness of my approach and promised me every assistance. In March 2002, I flew to Munich for a private screening of the surviving* Unity *footage which, owing to protracted legal disputes, is kept locked in the vaults. On the evening of 2 March, I visited Martins and her husband, Manfred Stückl, in their house on the outskirts of the city. Conversation was subject to various distractions (not least the excellent dinner) and became at times hard to follow. While their memory of events that took place twenty-five years earlier*

remained excellent, their grasp of English was erratic. Nevertheless, I trust that this transcript does justice to their views while
giving further insight into Felicity's motives.

Martins and Stückl provided an unexpected perspective on the
filming. In common with other contributors, they showed so little
interest in Luke that I was forced to query my own belief that it
was breaking up with him that had upset the balance of Felicity's
mind. In contrast to Fischer, they downplayed the role of Felicity's
passion for Meier (what will not be apparent from the transcript is
the derisory laughter that greeted my mere mention of the
subject). They chose to concentrate instead on England in both
their account of the film and their analysis of Felicity's behaviour.
At first, I attributed this to a misguided sense of patriotism but
then I realised that, given my own emphasis on psychological
influences, I would be wrong to portray Felicity as though she had
sprung up fully formed in Munich – or even in Cambridge – but
needed to follow her back to her childhood home.

Felicity liked to portray herself as having made a heroic attempt
to escape the clutches of her family – and my own brief acquaintance with them led me to endorse her resolve. The Benthalls
combined the worst characteristics both of their tribe and their
nation. Their arrogance and insularity would have made the Haps-
burgs blush. Stückl expressed surprise at the housekeeper who had
visited London only once. Her employers may have been more
seasoned travellers, but their horizons were equally circum-
scribed. A few years ago, I found myself opposite Frieda Benthall at
a wedding. She affected not to know me, but the tactic was transparent. I determined to be conciliatory and curb my lingering
resentment that neither I nor any of her friends had been invited
to Felicity's funeral. 'What are you doing now?' she asked. 'Writing
novels,' I said. 'Oh, I never read novels,' she replied, 'they're too
full of ideas and none of them are one's own.' It's no wonder that

Felicity disowned her, although the damage may already have been done.

The switch in focus to England marked a shift in my investigation from Felicity herself to the forces she represented. When Luke, in a rare mention of the Schleyer kidnap, wrote that he feared a resurgence of fascism, he identified it exclusively with the Right. In strict historical terms he may have been correct, but my concern is with the broader fascist temperament – that total conviction in the supremacy of one's cause and the legitimate use of violence to promote it, which unites extremists at both ends of the political scale.

In Felicity's case, I trace the rot to the heart of her family. Meier employed the Benthalls' house to serve for the Mitfords', but he missed his chance by failing to employ its occupants. With his carefully cultivated eccentricities, Peregrine Benthall would have been perfect casting as Lord Redesdale, although his opinions on the Jews – or rather 'the Chosen People' – were far more pernicious than any attributed to Unity's father. Besides, while I would never equate social exclusion with mass murder, the existence of societies such as the White Knights of Britain, to which Felicity's neighbour belonged, bears witness to the deep strain of anti-Semitism that runs through English national life. Felicity may have been right to identify an element of role-play in the group (although the same might be said of the SS), but her readiness to dismiss them as harmless buffoons suggests that she retained a dangerous affection for the world of her childhood. The degree to which that world informed her views is open to question, but it can be no coincidence that, for all their ideological polarity, the Far Right in the 1930s and the Far Left in the 1970s both chose to target the Jews.

Meier, according to Martins, judged British integrity to be an illusion and, on the evidence set down here, it would be hard to disagree. Hitler, who was nothing if not an astute politician, regarded Britain and Germany as natural allies. His interest in Unity Mitford was triggered not merely by her Aryan looks and aristocratic background but by her descent from the first Lord Redesdale, whose preface to Houston Chamberlain's The Foundations of the Nineteenth Century,[95] *one of the bibles of Nazism, identified him – and her – as a friend to the fascist cause. It is surely not fanciful to detect a similar identification of British and German interests in Felicity's activities in Munich forty years on.*

---

[95] Chamberlain further ensured his place in the Nazi pantheon by his marriage to Wagner's daughter, Eva.

I'd like to start by asking you to summarise your first impressions of Wolfram Meier.

M.S.   Young.

L.M.   Sexy.

M.S.   Dirty.

L.M.   Confident.

M.S.   Thin.

L.M.   Thin.

M.S.   Mean.

You can use more than one word if you like. This isn't a psychological test.

L.M.   That is the problem. With Wolfram, it must either be one word or a whole book. We met him in the summer of 1965.

M.S.   Since then so much water has flown down the Rhine. We were rehearsing for the *King Ubu*. There was already a big scandal about the pigs.

L.M.   People thought we would have an orgy: actors and pigs.

Really?

L.M.   We said 'Where is the problem? For you, we are all pigs anyway.'

M.S.   Liesl was to ride on one naked.

L.M.   My God, I was young!

And you?

L.M.   Manfred kept his – how do you say in English? – his sceptre wrapped in.[96]

M.S.   Before we opened, we sold all of the seats.

L.M.   Most of them to the police.

M.S.   We started the group half a year before. Liesl, Klaus and I. Klaus Bernheim. Now he is a Green MP in Strasbourg.

L.M.   He changed colours quicker than a traffic light.

[96] It is unclear whether this is a reference to Père Ubu's royal status or a pun on the lines of 'crown jewels'.

M.S.   Liesl . . .

L.M.   We found an unused pub. We took chairs from an old church. One girl of our group, her father was a pastor.

Would that be Renate Fischer?

L.M.   You know Renate?

She's mentioned in Luke's letters.

L.M.   She is a sad case. We will not speak of her.

M.S.   We put on our plays. We found our audience. We fulfilled our dream of theatre. And then we learnt that, under Hitler, the building where we played was used as a prison. We thought we were safe from history. We thought we knew what roads we must not walk down – what buildings we must not walk into. But we were wrong. We laughed where they screamed. We had a meeting.

L.M.   We had always meetings.

M.S.   Then suddenly no more meetings. The building burned down.

Was that when you met Wolfram Meier?

M.S.   Not at all. We are losing the line. He came when we rehearsed the *King Ubu*. With the pigs.

L.M.   And the smell. There was such a smell. Some of our group said 'No more!' Renate, Little Miss Pastor's Daughter.

She walked away?

L.M.   But she walked back.

M.S.   Then one day Freddi, who did our lighting, brought Wolfram. He was, as we say, a cousin around a thousand corners.[97] And, while everyone else protested about the smell, he loved it. He said that it was the smell of art.

L.M.   He looked so strange with his white hairs and his pickle-face.[98] And he was very thin. Still his shirts were too small.

---

[97] i.e. distant.

[98] i.e. acne-scarred.

There was always a button burst and a patch – like a diamond – of skin. It made every woman want to be a mother to him.

M.S. That was not the word you used at the time. You said eat him.

L.M. Eat? Mother? It is the same.

M.S. We gave him the job of looking after the pigs. He was so good that we believed he grew up on a farm. But we were wrong. He hated the country. Many years later, when we were in England and filmed in the house of your friend, we sniffed the air. The rich air. The rich man's air. One day, we found Wolfram behind the generators, sniffing the fumes. *'Was machst du?'* I asked. 'I cannot breathe,' he said. 'I must have the city to survive.'

Was he serious or was he simply out to shock?

M.S. With Wolfram, it was the similar thing.

L.M. *King Ubu* went. The pigs went. Wolfram stayed.

M.S. No one spoke of it. But at the next meeting –

L.M. We had always meetings.

M.S. He was there and held up his hands with the rest of us. From then he was a part of us. At first, he helped behind the stage. And, later, he began to play.

L.M. His playing was like no one else. He had no shame.

M.S. He lived with us – in the house of Liesl – for two years.

L.M. Many people did it. I had the house. They had to sleep. It was normal.

M.S. Wolfram was different. Remember that it was 1966 . . . 1967. Everyone said goodbye to private property; Wolfram believed it. Even the beds. You came home in the middle of the night and found him asleep in your bed. Sometimes alone. Sometimes with other persons.

L.M. Sometimes with you.

M.S. And the smell. It was clear why he was happy with the pigs.

L.M.   And it wasn't Manfred who washed his dirty clothes.

M.S.   But it was Manfred who pulled them from his back. He cried out like a little child: 'But I like my smell.'

In a way, there's something admirable about that. We're all so hung up on hygiene. At times I think that I'd feel less uncomfortable leaving the house naked than leaving it without a deodorant.

M.S.   I gave him his first chance to direct. Sometimes I think this will be all that remains from me.

L.M.   Nonsense, darling. You made so many films. Now you help other people to make films.

M.S.   Yes, but none of them gives me goose-skin. I sit in my office all day and meet with directors. And, every time, I hope to find a new Wolfram: someone who makes me see the world with fresh eyes.

What was this play that he directed?

M.S.   He said that it was written by a friend, a young man who just came out of prison. It was full of drugs and violence and sex and criminals. It was like jazz.

L.M.   But there was no music.

M.S.   Some of the group did not want it. They said that it was romantic and distracting. But I disagreed. I called a meeting for when I knew that these persons were out of the town.

L.M.   We have a phrase: when the cat's away, the mice will dance on the table.

M.S.   And we won enough voices. I was excited. I saw the truth of the writing. I say this against me but also in admiration of Wolfram because, as you perhaps guess, the play was written by him. And, two years later, it was the model for his first film, *Der Rattenfänger*.

L.M.   Which we just released in a new copy that was shown world-wide.

And how did the film come about? Was there a prototype Manfred Stückl doling out money to young film directors in the late sixties?

M.S.   What happened was most extraordinary –

L.M.   Let me tell it, darling. You make it too mysterious. It was really very simple. We told you that the theatre burned down. Thanks to good luck –

M.S.   And to Liesl.

L.M.   We had an insurance. We could have put the money into another theatre but we decided that after three terrifying years.

M.S.   I think you mean terrific.

L.M.   Terrific, naturally. You must excuse my English. After three terrific years, it was time to move forwards. Wolfram asked us to put the money into his film. We did it. And, from then on, everybody knows the story.

Is it quite that straightforward? I hope that you won't take offence but, as I'm sure you're aware, Renate Fischer tells it rather differently.

L.M.   Renate Fischer is a liar! What do you really want? You tell us that you must find out the truth about your friend. You send us your books and say that you are an author. But you are not. You are a journalist!

Forgive me. I only meant to suggest that different people remember the same events very differently.

L.M.   Yes, some people remember the Nazis as heroes and others as monsters. Does that mean that both views have equal worth? Renate is a sad woman. She is a sick woman. She is a successless woman. She has nothing in her life but the past. So she – how do you say in English? – colours it in. She makes all these reports about Wolfram as another Hitler. But look at us. Look at Manfred. Look at me. Do we look so weak?

No, of course not.

L.M.   Renate believes that, because she was Wolfram's wife, she should also be his widow. Wolfram married her in 1978. It was his worst time. *Unity* was in boxes instead of on the screens. Mahmoud, his boyfriend, went back to his home in Beirut. Right now after he returned, he was killed by a bomb. And Wolfram married Renate. It was a joke. One evening, we were all together – no, sorry, Manfred and I were not with them but Dieter and Kurt explained about it to us. Wolfram wanted to go out and Renate started to fight with him. He lost his patience and told to her, 'Why don't you shut your mouth and open your legs?' So she stood up like clockwork and pulled down her skirt. Wolfram, to save her the shame, took her upstairs to bed. Still I am furious that I was not there. Two weeks later, he married her.

M.S.   He was always a masochist and to marry Renate was the most masochist thing that he could do.[99]

L.M.   Poor Renate thought that she now had rights over Wolfram and over all of us. But he made fun of her when he lived and, again, when he died. He left to his mother all his money and all his films. He left to Renate some rubbish.

It's the second-best bed syndrome.

M.S.   Excuse me?

When Shakespeare died, he left his widow, Anne Hathaway, his second-best bed. For centuries, people have speculated on why it wasn't his first.

M.S.   You English and your Shakespeare – excuse me, your Royal Shakespeare! Do you ever speak about anyone else?

L.M.   Wolfram's mother set up the Meier Foundation. For the first five years, she was the leader. Then, when she grew tired, she asked me to take her place. Me, the friend, and not the widow. Renate wrote a book – a book that is full of

99 The German word *masochist* can refer to someone who is simply self-destructive. Given the overwhelming evidence of Meier's tastes, I presume that Stückl is using it in this, rather than in any sexual, sense.

lies – about Wolfram. She is bitter at me and the board because we did not give her the rights to use the letters or the scripts or the pictures. I am sorry, but when we work very hard to keep the films healthy, we do not allow Renate to pour acid on the prints.

M.S. Of course Wolfram had his failures. He could be rude. He could be cruel. He could make you pull out your hairs. *(With a laugh.)* When I had my hairs. But he could also be the most exciting, the most fascinating man who ever lived (and, yes, I include your Shakespeare). Sometimes, still, I dream about him. I never tell this even to Liesl. I am in hospital. I have pains. I look across the room and all my dearest friends are lying there. Some have no arms and no legs. Some have terrible cancer. Then, right now, Wolfram comes through the door followed by a camera. And, after a few moments, we are well: we are whole; and we dance. He turns the ward – he turns the world – into a Hollywood musical and we are all the stars.

L.M. When Geraldine Mortimer spoke about growing up in Hollywood, Wolfram said 'I too.'

M.S. He was a boy when the safest thing for a German was to be an American. Later, he started to hate America but he never lost his love for Hollywood. He said always that Hollywood wasn't America. Hollywood was the world.

L.M. He had the most extraordinary fantasy. All those stories, all those people coming from the head of one man. There was no surprise that he was so thin. He was like a mother who hungers to feed the childrens.

M.S. He gave us such chances. He made us known world-wide. When we went to New York or Tokyo or Australia, they asked how is Dieter or Luise or Dorit. No need for family names.

L.M. We were a family. We were Wolfram's family.

M.S. Some persons said that he put us in chains. He did not allow us to work for another director. But what did that matter when we made such a good work for him? He gave us one, two, sometimes three films a year. And he found a role for everyone.

L.M. We were so excited when he told us of a new project. If it came from a book, we all ran to buy it. Who was the heroine? Was it Luise or Irma or me? And sometimes there was pain. But, for every Mayor's wife or schoolmistress, next time it was Rosa or Margarite.

I think that Rosa Luxemburg *is my favourite of all his films.*

M.S. We never complained when he cast someone else from the group. It is true there was sometimes silence – and sometimes worse. But not for long. It was when he looked outside, there were the problems. There were the problems for him and there were the problems for us. The new persons, they did not understand how he worked. Naturally, they wanted to be in a Wolfram Meier film but they did not see that it meant more than just learning a Wolfram Meier script.

L.M. What he could never win was the market. It is a cruel joke – no? – that, in his films, he shows so strongly how the market eats up people. And, in the end, the market eats up him. He becomes successful, so people want more of him. They want him in bigger cinemas on bigger screens so he has to make bigger films with bigger stars.

M.S. In a bigger language.

L.M. And then the film is never finished. And people, they say, oh yes, we knew all the time that he was a maker of small films for small audiences. So give him small money.

M.S. But his fantasy is big.

L.M. But his money is small. So, in the studio, they no longer try to sell him.

M.S.   And that, my friend, is what happened after *Unity*. It was
       not just one film that was lost. He was broken. He could no
       longer go back to where he was before. Where he was before
       is no longer there.

L.M.   If you cut off an artist's fantasy, you cut off his arm ... his leg.
And to think that everything sprang from a chance visit on a rainy
evening in Edinburgh. Were you at the Festival?

L.M.   No, for a little while, we were strangers. We had – how do
       you say in English? – a lover's quarrelling.

M.S.   But between friends.

L.M.   We looked after our childrens. Wolfram was not happy. He
       said that childrens were the enemies of art.

M.S.   He was so much a child himself.

L.M.   Then, one day, the telephone rang. It was Wolfram. There
       was no voice which meant it was only Wolfram.

M.S.   He always smoked on his cigarette before he spoke.

L.M.   He wanted us to play Joseph and Magda Goebbels. For the
       first time we were husband and wife.

M.S.   Perhaps it is not the husband and wife we chose. Goebbels
       is not at the tip of an actor's list. A dwarf. A cripple. But he
       is also the intellectual among the Nazis. An artist who
       wrote a novel and a drama. Evidently, Wolfram saw those
       qualities in me. Anyway, the Joseph of your friend's script
       was the private man, the bon vivant, interesting for every
       woman. If he planned to show the cruel demagogue, I do
       not believe that Wolfram would ask me.

L.M.   Wolfram told me directly. Magda is a surface woman: an
       elegant, pleasure-loving woman. But she is also a mother
       who, later, killed six of her childrens in Hitler's bunker.
       Wolfram saw her as the model for the Greek tragedies that
       he wanted me to play.

M.S.   *Medea* would have become Wolfram's masterwork. And
       yours.

So you were both present throughout the filming. You watched events unfold. Can you give me your impressions of what happened to Felicity?

L.S.   Only a person who does not know Germany has done what she has done. It was the action of someone who laughs at a joke that she does not understand.

From a reading of Luke's letters, the key factor seems to be that she fell in love with Wolfram.

M.S.   There speaks a man! And a young man. I admit that there was a time many, many years ago, when I thought that there were attractions between Liesl and Wolfram. But there was nothing.

L.M.   He had so much spirit. Everyone fell in love with Wolfram. Women. Men. Everyone.

M.S.   Naturally, I also fell in love with his spirit. But not his person. Our friend here speaks about his person.

L.M.   It was a long time ago.

So Luke was alone in rebuffing his advances?

L.M.   He was very young.

M.S.   We were very young.

L.M.   Yes, but he was still younger.

Do you have any abiding memories of him?

L.M   He was very British: very good-mannered; very 'fair play'.

M.S.   I think most of all he was sad.

About life in general or the film in particular?

M.S.   Maybe both. He had Wolfram always hanging on his shoulder. He had Felicity who was not the right lover for him.

What makes you say that?

M.S.   They were night and day. He wanted one Felicity. She wanted many Lukes. That is all I must tell you. He was interesting for Wolfram – too interesting. He was not interesting for me.

I'm afraid of tiring you when there's still so much ground to cover. So perhaps we should move on. I've told you about Geraldine Mortimer's diary. It suggests that Felicity plunged into a crash course of German radical politics.

M.S.   This makes no sense. Did you ever take part in making a film?

Sadly not. Two of my novels have been optioned for films, but neither has made it into production.

M.S.   It is so exhausting. Some days not a thing happens. You sit in the van and, at the end, you feel like you walked up the Alps. You have no energy to read and certainly not to study politics.

There I must disagree. Geraldine writes that she ordered some books to be sent from England, which Felicity devoured.

M.S.   Then you must look for your solutions in England. Think for a moment. You – you, Michael – you go on holiday with your friend. You have a happy time: beautiful girls, or, if you prefer it, beautiful boys. But he lies in bed all week with a bad stomach. Why? You eat the same food: you drink the same water; but you are strong in the stomach and he is weak. And why are you strong? It is because of how you lived before, in England.

L.M.   Manfred speaks correctly. If you want to find the truth about Felicity, you have to go to England. We went. We were surprised by what we saw.

When was this?

L.M.   With Wolfram. For the film. Naturally, we did not play. It was the past – the childhood. But Wolfram asked for us . . . he needed us and Dieter and even Renate. He never made a shooting outside Germany and he was nervous. He was nervous because of the English and their contempt: their contempt against foreigners and their contempt against cinema. In all other European countries, he was Wolfram

Meier. But, in England, the only Germans you knew were Franz Beckenbauer and Gert Mueller.[100]

M.S.   He was never sure if your contempt against cinema was because it was popular or because it was new. It was so . . . how do you say when you must have spectacles?

Short-sighted?

M.S.   That is true. You are full of pride that you win the War, he said, but then you throw away the victory. You despise the Americans but you must bend the knees to them. They were once your colony; now, you are theirs.

L.M.   Everything in England begins with language. What about pictures? They are the world's language. But no, you give your money to Sir Bamforth and the classics, as if perfect vowels bring with them perfect morals.

I wouldn't deny that we prize our literary tradition.

M.S.   My friend, you speak as if the past is the only measure of judgement. But what about excitement? What about experiment? Where was the English *nouvelle vague*? Where was the English *nouveau roman*?

We tend to admire narrative as in the great nineteenth-century novels.

M.S.   I feel sure that you admire other nineteenth-century things like 'Britannia rules the waves', but you can no longer have them. So Britannia tries to push back the waves. 'We are an island,' she says. 'Keep out your filthy foreign ideas along with your filthy foreign dogs.'

L.M.   I never felt so hated for being a German as in England. In France and in Belgium, there is more reason and less reminder. In England, I felt as if I was all the time wearing a sign. It was not even as if you hated us for what we did in the War. It was for what we did afterwards. You wanted us

100   The two stars of the 1966 German World Cup team.

to stay the same so that you too could stay the same. Like small childrens, you demand applause not once, not twice, but again and again for the same trick.

That's a little harsh.

L.M.   Wolfram said that British virtue was an illusion. Like a girl who is locked in a convent all her life who is proud that she is a virgin. It is an accident of geography.

You accuse us of living in the past but, if you don't mind my saying, you constantly cite a man who has been dead for the best part of twenty years.

L.M.   Excuse me? I think that is why you are here. I think that is why you wrote me a letter and asked – begged – me to discuss what happened with your friend. I think that is why you send me your books: your books that have not even been made into films.

I'm sorry. At heart, I'm the least nationalistic of men. I suppose that it's human nature to hit back when under attack.

L.M.   But it is just this sort of – how do you say in English? – superiorness that made Wolfram (I suppose you will not object if I name him again) so angry. One evening in the country, Luke made arrangements for us all to see a play that came from London. It was about one of the Channel Islands in the War, where an old duchess stood up against the German invaders. It was a demonstration of your British belief that, deep inside, all foreigners want to be treated like servants. I think it was written by one of your prime ministers.[101] But my question to you is: what happened on the other islands? What happened in

[101]   This is clearly *The Dame of Sark* by William Douglas Home, not a prime minister himself but the brother of one. It opened in London in 1974, with the title role played by Celia Johnson, the pre-eminent exponent of one brand of British courage. It was later played in the West End and on tour by Anna Neagle, the pre-eminent exponent of another.

> Guernsey where the British made collaborations with as much freedom as in any French village? I have not seen any plays about that.[102]

M.S.   Felicity was not fighting against politics in Germany but in Great Britain. You say that there was still fascism in Germany.

I'm simply repeating what I've read. I didn't visit Germany myself until shortly after the collapse of the Wall.

M.S.   We saw that there was still fascism in England. And it was not only your football hooligans. With Wolfram and Mahmoud, we went to the East End. We looked at the sites of the battles between your Left and your Right during the 1930s. There was a strike of the dustbins. Heaps of rubbish were all over the streets (I still have the smell in my nose). Wolfram said that it was surreal – like a painting of Dali. We went into a pub.

L.M.   Not Liesl. Liesl went back to the hotel.

M.S.   Women were forbidden. It was a place for your gay machos. I found it very amusing.

L.M.   You were pleased for once to say 'nein' and to mean it.

M.S.   It was early in the night but it was full like a sardine-box. An old room with lots of wood and a big mirror with advertisements for beer.

I know the sort. It's as though the masculinity of the image were designed to offset the effeminacy of gazing at it.

---

[102] *Theresa* by Julia Pascal (1990) explores the betrayal of the Jews in occupied Guernsey. In the course of her research, Pascal interviewed the grandson of the wartime Bailiff who told her that, after the War, the British authorities could not decide whether to hang his grandfather as a traitor or to honour him as a hero. So, in the end, the Queen knighted him.

M.S. I am remembering now. The name was something German.[103] We told ourselves when we walked in that we were welcome. But we were not. Not at all. At the bar stood three or four men who dressed like the *Wehrmacht* and wore swastikas. We were shocked. In Germany, this is completely illegal.

L.M. Two years ago, a friend of us, Dieter – naturally, you spoke with him! – he was arrested in Munich when he came out of a gay disco and called for a taxi. He lifted his right arm like this and the police said that he made the Hitler greeting. It was a joke, but not for Dieter. The police would like to arrest Dieter because he is Dieter: because he goes to a disco where men can be like Dieter. But they cannot. So they arrest him because he makes a greeting that he did not make. That is how seriously we consider it here.

M.S. But, in England, you have the freedom of speech and the freedom of fascism. Wolfram wanted to talk to the men. He wanted to ask them if they knew that, under the Nazis, they wore a very different badge. But we showed him that it was not so clever. I said that we should now leave, but Wolfram said that it was like leaving the world to the fascists. So they stayed and I came home to Liesl. The next thing we heard was that Wolfram and Mahmoud were attacked as they went to the subway. I wonder still if it was the men from the pub because they hit only Mahmoud. Wolfram said later that he can walk with his boyfriend down any street in Germany but in England he is spitted on and kicked. But, wait, it becomes worse. After he left the hospital, Mahmoud visited the police to make a complaint.

103 The name and the location suggest that this was The Princess of Prussia, a notorious gay pub.

They did not say sorry. Instead, they asked him many questions about why he was here, about his passport, about his friendship with Wolfram. They stripped off all his clothes and made jokes about his penis.

Why? Was it a peculiar shape?

L.M.   It was big. It was brown. That was enough.

I'd like to apologise on the policemen's behalf. Though it doesn't carry the weight of the President apologising for the fate of the Indians or the Pope for that of the Jews, I still want to put it on record. I'm not suggesting that the British are blameless. I know my history. But, while we may have founded concentration camps in the Boer War, we didn't gas the inmates.

M.S.   All we say to you is that Felicity realised what Germans of my age realised when we were very young: we are all cut from the same wood. I have a memory of your great actor, Sir Bamforth, who spoke to us of the three signs that shamed him through his life: 'Closed to Chinese and dogs' in the 1920s Shanghai; 'Beware of Jews and pickpockets' in the 1930s Berlin; 'No blacks or Irish' in the 1950s London.

But Felicity wouldn't have been allowed into an East End leather bar.

M.S.   No, my friend, you do not understand me. It was not necessary. She could see for herself in her own home. You come to Munich to meet us and, to tell the truth, we are very glad. But did you visit her house? Did you speak to her parents?

I stayed with them several times when I was a student and, since then, I've come across them once or twice. I did write to them about this inquiry but I've received no reply.

(At this point, there is a gap in the transcript where the cassette needed to be replaced. To the best of my recollection, nothing of import was said. Manfred and Liesl talked about the journey to

Leicestershire and complained about the inn where they stayed.
They attacked the backwardness of England based largely on the
lack of mixer taps: a subject unlikely to have exercised Felicity.)

M.S.   We made Unity's house in the house of Felicity's uncle –
       not the uncle who was killed but another one.

L.M.   And her mother and her father. They lived all together like
       they were childrens. It was a very beautiful house. Perfect
       for the 1930s. For the 1830s too. So few changes happened.

M.S.   Heike said 'I must do nothing. It is all done for me.' And do
       you remember the old lady?

L.M.   The *Grossmutter*?

M.S.   The *Haushälterin*.[104] She was very nervous next to Mah-
       moud. She saw only one black man before in her life. An
       American in the War.

L.M.   No, you make mistakes. She went to London only one time
       in her life during the War.

M.S.   No, no. She went to London only one time in her life before
       the War. She saw only one black man in her life during the
       War.

L.M.   Perhaps yes. Mahmoud stayed with Wolfram in the house.
       They did not let him pack his own bag when he left. I never
       saw him so angry. 'Why don't they just ask me what I
       steal?' he cried.

No. You – he – have it all wrong. It's old-style country house
hospitality.

L.M.   It was such a crazy house. I also would throw a bomb if I
       lived there.

(There follows a rapid exchange in German which is unintelligible
on the tape).

104   Housekeeper.

203

L.M.   Tell him about the uncle. The baron. The one who showed
you his sex toys.

M.S.   He had a room where women were not allowed. It was full
with sculptures and objects and drawings. And each time he
picked something up, he said 'This is very rare. This is even
more rare. This is the only one of its kind.' Like everything
else in this house, the porno was only good because it was
old.

*Perversity authenticated by history: that would make a fair defini-
tion of the British upper class.*

L.M.   Every meal that we ate there, he had the same white
pudding in the same bowl. We have a phrase about masters
who start to look like their dogs. I think that he looked like
his pudding. It is no wonder that his wife was mad.

M.S.   It is no wonder that his niece became mad.

L.M.   She was the whole day with her horses, making their shoes
and singing her G & S. All of us asked: what is this G & S?

*Gilbert and Sullivan. Another nineteenth-century tradition, I'm
afraid. They don't travel.*

L.M.   They make the perfect English music: big tunes and little
passion.

M.S.   And they must not be mixed up with G & T.

L.M.   Tart's drink!

M.S.   Naturally! Each time she was asked if she wanted a drink,
she answered 'I think I'll have a G & T.' And the other one,
Felicity's father, said each time 'Tart's drink.' 'Tart's drink,'
not into his beard but out loud.

L.M.   And do you remember the mother? Always in the garden.
Always cutting the bushes as if she tries to hold back
Nature.

M.S.   It was very deceiving how someone could be so polite and
also so rude. You told her your name and, right now, she

tried to put you in place. 'Are you one of the Frankfurt von Stückls?' she asked.

L.M.   For me it was worse. 'I met a Martins in Venice once. A steel-maker but still a gentleman. Are you any relation of him?'

It's as though, ever since Queen Victoria placed her children on all the thrones of Europe, the whole world could be found inside an English address book.

M.S.   Or else you do not exist.

She terrified Luke, not to mention me.

M.S.   The most terrifying one was Felicity's father. If you want to find Felicity, you must look first at him. I wrote down some of the things he said. *(He picks up an old exercise book.)* I was asked to write an article about the shooting in England for *Der Spiegel*. But, when the film was stopped, the article was also. These are just small notes, but they are good notes. He liked to talk about Europe.

L.M.   He liked to talk about England, but he thought that it was more accepted the other way round.

M.S.   He hated Europe. He hated the EU or what it was then, the EWG.[105] Great Britain was not long a member. 'It is a sell-out to big business,' he said. 'Has the nation which civilised the world – the nation of Shakespeare and Churchill and Conan Doyle – been reduced to competition?'

L.M.   That is the father who speaks – not Manfred.

Yes, I realise. And, if I may say so, it's an excellent imitation. You've captured him to a T.

M.S.   Excuse me?

Perfectly.

M.S.   'The Europeans are asking us to sacrifice our history. Where does the heart . . . the soul of a nation lie if not in its

[105] The *Europäische Wirtschaftsgemeinschaft* (European Economic Community).

history? You Germans don't have a history so you substitute race. The Americans don't have a history so they substitute money. The French and Italians have a history but it's so ignorant . . .' No. *Moment. Kannst Du dieses Wort entziffern?*

L.M.   Ignominious.

M.S.   Naturally. 'The French and Italians have a history but it's so ignominious that they substitute art. But we British have a history and it's one of which we can be proud.' When somebody said that the country voted to belong to Europe, he stared at him as if he was mad. 'Take a look across the Atlantic. Voting only elects the leader who tells the loudest lies.' He wanted to push back the clock and not to your nineteenth but to your thirteenth and fourteenth century, when all the persons were as one. He spoke to us of his grandfather dancing around a May-tree with his workers. But it was too hard to understand because, as I wrote here, he began to cry.

Too many memories.

L.M.   Too much whiskies.

I really don't think we should overemphasise the role of Felicity's family. They were throwbacks. She used to treat them as jokes.

L.M.   No. She suffered from him. It was clear for us to see. He talked to us because we were Germans, so he thought we must feel the same.

M.S.   He said that the worst thing about the Nazis was what they did to the Jews. Naturally, we thought. We can agree to that. The whole world can agree to that. So why does he mention it? But he didn't mean the camps. Listen, I have found it here. 'The thing for which I can never forgive Hitler is that he made it quite impossible to express one's dislike of the Chosen People. Not as individuals but for what they stand.

Everything is international now. Everything is money. A cheque book is the only passport anybody needs.'

L.M. He never spoke of the Jews but always 'the Chosen People'.

M.S. When someone – I have it in my mind that it was your friend Luke – said that Hitler did far worse things against the Jews, against six million of them to be exact, he shook the head as if it was vulgar to mention figures.

L.M. As if he took a chair before a woman.

M.S. As if he passed around the wine after dinner in the wrong way.

L.M. And they had many friends with similar thinking. We discovered them when they came to the ball. Felicity told Wolfram that he could use them as extras. Wolfram was pleased. He thought that the scene would have more truth. But it had too much truth. The friends of Felicity had the same politics as the friends of Unity before the War. Their heads had not changed any more than their houses.

M.S. And they were happy to speak out loud words that, in Germany, we would not even whisper. Why? Was it because they believed that our heads – our thirty-year-old heads – were also forty years older? Or was it because they did not care what any other persons thought?

It's odd. Although I met quite a lot of people when I stayed with Felicity, I don't remember anyone expressing remotely contentious views.

L.M. There was one man – do you remember, darling? – who wanted to keep silent and who was very angry when Felicity made fun of him. He belonged to a secret party who swore an oath to an ancient king, oh hundreds of years before, because he threw the Jews out from England. [106] She asked

106 Edward I.

him to tell us about it and he shouted back at her and suddenly everything became cold. Later, she tried to make a joke of it. She said that they were a group of stiff old men who wanted to be back in the Boy Scouts. So they dressed in clothes half way between your Yeomen of the Guards and the Ku-Klux Klan. They stood in a circle and carried swords and sang prayers and pretended they were in the Middle Ages.

I've never heard of it.

M.S. It is a secret. That is why he was so angry when she talked of it to us.

Yes, but most secret societies are exposed at some stage. There's always a defector ready to spill the beans.

M.S. Felicity was speaking as if it was some harmless old institute like your Queen Mother. But it was much more. When we asked her how she could stay close to someone who thought like this, she looked at us with big eyes. 'But I knew him all my life,' she said. 'I grew up with his daughters.' We began to understand at last. This is England where to believe in anything – even in God – is bad manners. Fascism is just a bit more extreme. Anyway, you must never condemn a person because he has disrespectful politics. Sure he is still a perfect gentleman where it counts: he is a good shoot; he sits good on a horse; he owns a good cellar. This is why I say to you that, if you want to know what she did in Munich, you must know what she did in England. After all, who was the first one who was killed by her bomb? Her uncle.

4

Geraldine Mortimer's Journal

Given Geraldine Mortimer's resentment of people who regarded
her as a female Peter Pan, I am loath to admit that she looms as
large in my memories of childhood as in Luke's. Unlike many of
her fans – or, perhaps more significantly, their parents – I felt no
sense of betrayal when she joined the International Workers Party.
On the contrary, it affirmed my association of politicians and
actors. She added a rare dash of colour to a national scene as grey
as its image on the television screen. What's more, her placard
politics appealed to my adolescent mind.

It was opening Geraldine's journal – or Pandora's Box, as I came
to think of it – that revived my interest in the Unity saga. I first
had to make sense of the script. The elegant yet strangely dislo-
cated writing would no doubt intrigue a graphologist, but it tried
the patience of the amateur sleuth. Several letters (g, p, q, y and z)
were cut off from their tails. Names were regularly reduced to
initials. The overall impression was of deciphering an arcane,
ancient screed.

I am extracting the journal – the term that Geraldine herself
favoured – in its entirety for the months of September and October
1977. Its record of events differs substantially from Luke's.
Together, they not only provide a more rounded portrait of Felicity
but confirm that the only rounded portrait is one that is true to her
contradictions. Geraldine, who is, of course, writing for her own
convenience rather than mine, makes fewer allusions to Felicity
than I might have wished. Her most significant contribution is to
chart her emerging political consciousness, for which she herself
takes much of the credit. Luke, who made light of Felicity's new-
found commitment, viewed it as an attempt to curry favour with
the Germans. My own knowledge of Felicity would lead me to

211

endorse his conclusion, were it not for the lingering doubt raised by his remark after Ralf Heyn's arrest that we can never know the truth about anyone – not even our best friend. If that is so – and it certainly was in the case of my feelings for him – then I have to admit that Felicity's stance may have been sincere.

A reading of Geraldine's journal adds contrast to my portrait of Felicity but confusion to my portrait of Luke. Most of the references to him are hostile. Given my innate bias, I prefer to leave it to the reader to determine how far these might spring from suppressed attraction. I have particular difficulty in reconciling Geraldine's report on 17 October of the evening when Meier first offered Luke drugs and then seduced him with Luke's in his letter of 2 October which stops short at the drugs. My customary faith in Luke is undermined both by the intensity of his despair and by my reading of Meier's character. While I feel wounded that, having stated his intention to 'tell you everything', Luke should have omitted any mention of his seduction, I can identify with his shame.

My picture of Luke is framed by an even deeper mystery. In January 2001, having completed my appraisal of Geraldine's journal, I sent him a copy for comment. Three months later, he committed suicide. In keeping with so much else in this story, he left no note. I, however, cannot afford such reticence. It may be that the receipt of the journal had no bearing on his state of mind. Logic, however, dictates otherwise. He must have been horrified to discover that, rather than the innocent dupe he had always maintained, Felicity was a cold-blooded murderess. He must have been humiliated to learn that he had been manipulated as much by her as by Meier. He must have dreaded the prospect of his credulity being made public. In which case why, when he mounted the pulpit on the morning of his death, was it not Felicity or Meier or Samif that he denounced but his own church?

If Luke's motives are in doubt, then so, I am obliged to admit, are my own. I told myself – and the Coroner – that I sent him the journal to elicit his views. That was true, but was it the whole truth, let alone the nothing but the truth of my court-room oath? I must have realised that it would revive his most painful memories. So, was I deliberately trying to hurt him: to punish him twenty years on for his failure to recognise – let alone, reciprocate – my love? Or is my guilt mere self-importance: an attempt to play the central role in his death that I was denied in his life?

THURSDAY, 1 SEPTEMBER

a.m.: Arrive Munich. Nerves jangling enough to set off alarm. Customs frosty. Libyan visa = criminal record. Welcome to Germany.

One-man reception committee (Bad skin, teeth and manners). Placard with G[eraldine] M[ortimer] writ large. Rush to push it aside. Thank G., no one sees and escape unrecognised. Relief after Heathrow and woman in VIP lounge: 'Excuse me, but weren't you Geraldine Mortimer . . .? Oops!' Expects me to laugh at her slip.

Hotel quiet, central, moneyed. Crocodile handbags on display in foyer. Welcome to Economic Miracle.

Dark suite. Solid furniture. Alpine prints (breath of fresh air?). One bowl of fruit. Management's compliments to Mr Gerald Mortimer. 1st instinct: raise hell. 2nd instinct: leave it to rot and place it in paternal suite next week. Both over-ruled by 3rd instinct: hunger.

No presents, not even bottle of perfume. Heidi, you're not in Hollywood any more. Maybe producers don't give presents to stars in Germany? Maybe I'm no longer a star? Big sister roles already. Who cares? Acting for Wolfram Meier, one of Europe's finest. It's the work – the work – that counts.

Long soak. Lavender. Good towels. Change into new silk underwear (twinge of guilt at thought of Dermot. Does he really understand? Happy to dress down in public but crave a touch of luxury next to skin).

Tea with producer, Werner (thinning hair, thickset figure, cast in left eye), and Luke, writer (cute, queer, puppyish charm). L. overdoes the 'pinch me' act. Claims he 'grew up on' me. 'Really?' reply in tone as dry as the cake. 'Like free school milk?' Puppy dog's tail droops between legs.

Truth is that he didn't grow up on me; none of them did. Aged, yes, but didn't grow up. Hence reluctance to let me grow up in turn.

Child star = cleft stick. As child, required to be adult (all those dollars resting on shoulders). As adult, expected to remain as fresh/trusting/innocent as child.

G. forbid the English rose should turn red!

FRIDAY, 2 SEPTEMBER

Costumes and make-up. Clothes horse.

Beate (make-up) dripping compliments about my complexion (dyke?) and attitude. Admits fear that I would come on all Hollywood and dictate my own look. Claims that reason English stars so much more effective than Americans in period dramas isn't classical training (all that RADA/RSC shit) but flexibility. Too much Elizabeth Arden the ruin of Elizabethan England.

Beate gives great gossip. A tonic after Hoxton Square.[107] Forgotten how much I missed it. Wardrobe and make-up the hub of every film.

D[iana] M[osley], a beauty. Such a burden – on her and on me. Not beautiful (an adjunct to something else) but a beauty (an unqualified fact). Emphasis on looks so destructive. To be singled out by Nature. Must have thought the whole world revolved around her. No wonder she became a fascist.

To be the constant centre of attention and yet to have no real power. A paradox? Not to a child actress.

Must stop harping on the past. That little girl no longer exists – except in flashes of light on the screen. Am a new person. Serious actress. Proof is I can play a character quite unlike myself: a woman who connived at evil; a woman so unrepentant that she can claim the reason for Blackshirts was simply that they were too poor to keep white ones clean!

Tea with Felicity. A cat – as in feline, not catty (not yet). Complex mixture of owning-class confidence and new-girl-in-class insecu-

---

107 Headquarters of the International Workers Party.

rities. As nervous about working on film as G[eraldine] M[ortimer] about joining Party. Same reason. Will comrades respect commitment or resent privilege?

Benefit of doubt.

Problem parents. After she won place at Cambridge, mother: 'Oh what a pity, darling! Now no one will want to marry you.'

Corrects me on one point. L[uke] not queer at all but her boyfriend. She thinks it v. funny. Promises not to tell him, but know she will. Shaken. Even Dermot in awe of my intuition. What do I have if it's gone?

SATURDAY, 3 SEPTEMBER

Bad night. Double brandy at 2 a.m. Room service (Blond. Sleek. Striped waistcoat. V. tight trousers. ½ moment's hesitation. 'Is that a *bratwurst* in your pocket or are you a vegetarian?' Come to senses. Send him away with tip).

Nightmare: ultimatum from Wolfram that wedding scene cut unless I agree to play it nude. Pressure from Werner and Father. Werner on Nuremberg decree that all marriage-ceremonies between foreigners in 3rd Reich have to be conducted naked. Floods of tears as I unbutton blouse. Father: it's only pre-wedding nerves.

Wake up drenched. Head pounding. Depression made worse by continuing limbo. Recall Werner's advice to use these few days to acclimatise myself to city. But I want to acclimatise myself to set.

Only 2 more days to go. Everyone bound to have formed into cliques. Not just Wolfram's group but the rest. All already worked together in England, whereas my Eng interiors to be shot here in studio (German labour costs apparently less than ½). No doubt waiting to see me take a tumble. Convinced my sensibilities blunted by politics. Or else that I had none to begin with.

Oh really? Critics are vermin, but some exceptions. Pauline Kael[108] on *The June Bridesmaid* where G.M. 'expertly negotiates the transition from the self-containment of the child to the self-consciousness of the adolescent.'
How about the self-awareness of the adult? Watch this space!

Prepare for Wolfram's party. Fret like sociology student over semiotics of clothes. Is smart a mark of respect or an assertion of status? Ditto, casual: relaxation or indifference? In event, no one seemed to notice. Several wearing next to nothing. Were they equally exercised by semiotics of flesh?

Long talk with Rolf/Ralf (smudged cast-list no excuse). Playing Hitler. Met Dermot at the Frankfurt conference. A comrade! Urged me to attend protest-meeting against treatment of Leftist prisoners. Resisted temptation, explaining cost of struggle at home. Slurs. Slanders. Imperative for sanity and standing that I return to work. Not a come-back. Loathe the term. Far too *What Ever Happened to Baby Jane?* More a second chance. Determined to permit no distractions. I'm G.M. the actress not G.M. the activist. He clasped my arm and asked if they mightn't be the same.

1st real chat with Wolfram. Frustratingly one-sided. His hesitancy in English exacerbated by snuffly cold. Broached subject of establishing shot. Explained Gerald's theory that first sight of one's character should be full-length to place it for audience. Assured him that I didn't wish to encroach on his preserve but, unless he had strong objections, I'd like to follow the advice (only worthwhile piece Father ever gave). W. smiled and sniffed.

---

108   Pauline Kael (1919–2001), highly respected film critic of the *New Yorker*.

Interrupted tête-à-tête between Felicity and Luke. F. insisted I join them ('The more the merrier'). F. enchanted with Serpent's Nest set-up. Eager to preserve the memory. Told her she should keep a diary. Overwhelmed by sense of betrayal (of what? this journal? myself?). She probed. Explained that, for me, it was an essential discipline: the life not just lived but recorded. And, in a capitalist society, one way of taking control.

Luke: 'Or it may just be to have something sensational to read on the train.'

Stared at him icily. Why not just come out with it and call me a tart?

SUNDAY, 4 SEPTEMBER

First time before cameras, tho not on set. With Wolfram, Werner, Felicity, Luke etc. to airport to welcome Gerald. Very different from my own arrival (holding big guns in reserve). In lobby, ugly German (sloe-eyed, slope-shouldered) runs up with newspaper for me to sign. F. impressed, L. offended, I oblige. Ugly German looks at paper: 'I was expecting Julie Christie.'

Is there no end to my humiliation?

Short answer: no. Wait by gate. Gerald disgorged. Living rebuff to 'Small is beautiful'. Kisses me as tho by right rather than custom. Introduces Haroko. Can there be any less propitious place for first meeting than airport, surrounded by phalanx of photographers jostling to capture historic moment on film?

Photographs (previous) don't do her justice. Elegant woman. Face concave but attractive. Hair and personality carefully lacquered. And so young (twenty-six). Am I alone in feeling distaste?

All too clear what's in it for him. But what about her? Japanese not Thai or Filipino. Doctorate, not desperate. I suspect something sinister. Embarrassed even to confide it to paper. But have no choice. Certain she must be CIA. Married him in order to gain access to me.

How she'd laugh if she read it! More ammunition for the 'Left = paranoia' brigade. But what other explanation can there be? I scare them. Permanent affront to their pigeon-hole minds. File 'actress' under beauty parlour and sun lamp, not picket-line and public meeting. They need to patrol all their boundaries: national, economic, psychological.

(NB: must keep journal under lock and key).

What more do they want from me? Fined for travelling to Cuba. Deported for protesting against Vietnam. Refused a new visa in spite of offers of work. Is one young actress really such a threat?

MONDAY, 5 SEPTEMBER

D-day. Car 6 a.m. Set 6.15. Hurled into make-up chair and then to wardrobe. Emerge 7. F[elicity]: 'All dressed up with nowhere to go.' Too true! Sit around until noon. Problems with lighting. Then, just as Gerhard, the D[irector of] P[hotography], finally satisfied, the heavens open. Troop indoors for weather cover.[109] But sky so grey, study also needs to be relit.

At least, as a child, given lessons to pass time.

Simple scene. Everyday life with the Mitfords: taking parents to tea with the Dictator. Hard enough with my father playing my father (if he pulls it off, truly deserves an Oscar) without Dora Manners playing my mother as well. Everything I despise in a woman. Professional siren on-stage and off. Gerald claims that in her day she was known as 'ever-open Dora'. From tone, can tell that it was shut tight on him. He proposes taking bets on who'll be her first victim. My money on one of the grips (thighs like tree-trunks), if it weren't so appallingly sexist.

Resolved to play happy families. Little choice since there is ONLY ONE TRAILER. Couldn't care 2p for myself. Burj-el-Brajneh[110]

---

109 An interior scene prepared as a contingency.
110 Palestinian refugee camp in Beirut.

knocked out any concern for creature comforts. But Gerald and Dora are older: they need privacy. Ring Elaine in London[111] (Fobbed off with Melody. Useless!). Appeal to Werner, who doesn't hold out much hope. Same selective language lapses as Wolfram. Chatting away 19 to 12 in London last June. Now requires an interpreter. Most odd.

Father does not help matters by invoking Dunkirk spirit.

Gerhard gives go-ahead around 2 p.m. W[olfram]'s methods unnerving. Talks a lot about rehearsing but doesn't do any. Blocks scene and then runs a bit of it, discusses next bit and then calls for it to be shot (as if his conscious intention were to create a mystery). One take. At end, shouts something (in German) which turns out to be 'Print.' Horrified. Tell him I was just limbering up. He says it's fine. I ask for chance to run it again. He says it would lack freshness. Envelops me in musty hug and assures me it was perfect. I say that it's not what I am used to. He says that is also good.

TUESDAY, 6 SEPTEMBER

1st interview. Publicist (proud of her hair) cites interest from papers across Europe but promises to restrict access to a few select journalists. Urge her to relax restraint. No one with more reason to mistrust press than me ('Geraldine's Goons' – *Sunday Express*. 'From Disney to Trotsky' – *Sunday Times*) but prepared to submit for sake of film. Refused to give interviews in Eng unless politics declared off-limits. Result: no interviews. Lesson.

Interviewer arrives on dot of 11. Brings large bunch of roses. Tactic maybe, but it works! Steer conversation away from Hollywood ('You might as well question someone abducted by aliens') to matter at hand. He asks if it's hard to play second violin.

111 Geraldine Mortimer's agent. See entry for 26 October.

Bemused until substitute second fiddle. Explain that what matters to me is film not part. Besides, Diana is integral. Unity the headstrong romantic but Diana the committed fascist. Rented flat in Munich for most of the 30s. Hobnobbed with leading Nazis. Film might almost be titled *Diana*.

Int: 'Are you afraid audiences might not accept you in the role? After all, very few actresses are so well-known for their left-wing beliefs.'

G.M.: 'That's an advantage. Wolfram hopes it will prevent easy identification. My job is not to justify Diana Mosley (a woman who allowed class interests to override basic humanity) nor even, according to Wolfram, to portray her in the conventional sense but to present her within the context of the film.'

(Trust it will sound as good in German).

Asks why it's so long since I made a film. Remind him that I was eighteen when *Downtown* released. Was I to graduate solely on screen? Was my entire life to take place in parallel universe? No. Defied Father and studios and went to Berkeley. Discovered the chasm between reality of America and sanitised image that it chose to present to world (and to itself).

Always intended to return to screen, but much harder in England where industry so small. Besides, banned by BBC. Nothing official but leaked memo. Not even honest enough to admit it to my face. All decided behind closed doors. Classic strategy of fascist organisation.

He shocked. Germans understandably sensitive about word, but they don't own a monopoly on it. Assure him that a British memo can be just as brutal as a German jackboot. Same determination to stamp out freedom and dissent.

Ten years of struggle have exhausted me. Will never abandon it but need to draw back. Time for new faces to come forward. Very grateful to W. for taking risk on me. Others have tried but yielded to powerful financial pressure (no names but implication clear).

Tape-recorder off; notebook shut: journalist asks for my thoughts on Schleyer kidnap. Look blank. He elaborates. Last night, group of urban guerrillas in Cologne intercepted car containing Head of West German Industries Federation. Exchange of fire left 4 dead. Kidnappers escaped with captive. Phone calls to media claiming that S. will be eliminated at 5.15 tomorrow (= today) if Andreas Baader and several imprisoned revolutionaries not released.

Strove to conceal elation. Made suitably anodyne comment about loss of life. On other hand, freedom of comrades would certainly offer cause for celebration. My sympathies, as always, lay with victims of state violence.

WEDNESDAY, 7 SEPTEMBER

a.m.: Sir Hallam Bamforth arrived. Delayed by 3 days of tests at Middlesex Hospital. 'I'm still feeling a mite fragile. They wanted to perform an exploratory op. They planned to rip me open from belly to chest and examine my entrails before inserting a tube up my private parts. "Awfully kind of you," I said, "but pass." Never trust the London teaching hospitals. At my age, they regard you as raw material for their students.'

In theory, everything I despise. Grandson of Lord Chancellor. Son of bishop. Plays same roles on stage as they did in life. Hands dirty only as Othello. English eccentricity at its most insidious – and marketable. Even his nose shows contempt for conventional proportions. Yet can't help admiring his spirit: totally – and gloriously – himself.

Paid courtesy call with Gerald. All he could do to remain civil. Reason clear on leaving: Sir H.'s suite bigger than his. Incredible! Grown men but still little boys in playground. Competitive instinct never dies. Proof = Byron's sex-change friends in Venice swapping boasts of who has biggest prick for who has biggest

tits.[112] Furious with feminists who refuse to accept them as women. But why? Hormones may transform their bodies, but their minds remain depressingly male.
Worst offender is my father.

THURSDAY, 8 SEPTEMBER

p.m.: Führerbau. Hitler, Unity and I flip through old copies of *Tatler*, listing people who'd support him if he invaded.
1st thought: Why should Hitler whose power-base lower-middle class have such an 'anyone who's anyone' view of England?
2nd thought: Was he merely humouring Mitfords?
3rd thought: Would names be any different if similar trio plotting today?
Struck by technical cock-ups. 5 takes (record!). Take 4: alarm goes off on Werner's watch. W[olfram] volcanic.
Increasingly dismayed by Wolfram's silence. Finally roused to ask why he never says 'Well done' at end of take. W.: 'It is always well done.'
Gee thanks!
Especially odd given Wolfram also an actor who must know that there are dozens of ways of playing scene. Told him, 'I can do it any way you want, but I have to know what you want. Right now I'm constantly trying to second guess.'
W.: 'It is perfect.'
Feel doubly worthless. If everything I do is equally good, then nothing I do matters.

Long talk with Felicity (surprisingly mature). 100% trust in W. Regards him as genius and herself as mere colour on his palette. But then easy for her: not a professional.

---

112 Earlier entries make it clear that Byron was a friend from Berkeley and Venice is Venice Beach.

Could resent her, plucked out of nowhere and thrust into leading role. But disarming: funny, unspoiled and not at all self-obsessed. What's more, not too proud to seek advice. Such a change from H[ollywood?] where questions seen as sign of weakness.

Talked about family. Minor aristocracy. One uncle owns large chunks of Leicestershire. Another, ambassador here in Bonn. But not at all wedded to class. Dismissive of royal link. Tells childhood story of Duke of Edinburgh opening fête in uncle's grounds. He taken aback by sign: Ride on Prince Philip, 6d. It was her pony.

Unexpectedly political. Fascinated by Schleyer case. Buys wide range of German papers which L[uke] translates. Reports that today's lead with trivial story about mass meeting of Schmidts – like Smith, the country's most common surname – postponed while Chancellor (guest of honour) deals with crisis. Meanwhile real news suppressed when government refuses to allow taped message from kidnappers to be broadcast on TV (so-called mechanical fault!).

Interrupted by L. As usual, flushes crimson the moment he sees me. Awe-struck? Attracted? Unnerving.

Feel sorry for him. In an invidious position. Devoted to F. (touching), while pursued by W. (embarrassing), who insists on placing him in many more scenes than scripted. W. much more hands-on with L. than with rest of us. Constantly complains that he is too stiff. To remedy it, strides on to set and tickles him. Result: L. more tense than ever. Strange thing is F. encourages it. At first, thought she was naive but increasingly reminded (try not to be reminded) of Father when Mission[113] was directing me.

---

[113] Christopher Mission directed Geraldine in three films: *The Wanderers*, *Heidi* and *The Great Lakes*. For a detailed account of his career and, in particular, the conflicting theories surrounding his death, see C. Randall Hart, *The Honorary American*, Knopf 1994.

FRIDAY, 9 SEPTEMBER

Any hope that Father might have changed spots dashed by treatment of Sir Hallam.

a.m.: Shooting consulate tea party. Five retakes while Sir H. fumbles for words. Tells W[olfram] with excessive relish that he should spank him. Grip laughs. G[erald] rounds on him: 'Mock all you like, but it's nothing short of heroic. At an age when he could – some might say, should – be sitting back dusting his scrapbooks, he's still out here, taking on every bit part that's offered. So if the rest of us are left kicking our heels while the old brain cranks into gear, it's a small price to pay.'

Result: Sir H. more flustered than before.

Sir H. rallies when we gather for Friday night dinner. Declaims panegyric to G.'s courage in making career in America (as if he'd gone over on Mayflower rather than Boeing). Purports to regard the country as wild and uncivilised where parents, desperate for distinction, christen sons Duke and Earl.

Expresses gratitude for US popularity. 'I've outlived my obsolescence. Of course it helps to have won an Oscar. Such a to-do about nothing. But there's no need to tell you, Gerald. You know how little it's worth.' He smiles innocently, knowing that it's worth as much as G.'s entire career.

Can scarcely restrain cheer at seeing bully bettered. G. berated me for interview in *Die Welt*. Claims I promised to keep off politics. When? Might as well promise to keep off food.

Not prepared to fight him any more, but won't sit back and watch him rewrite history. Pretends my activism has killed his career: that Jews in H[ollywood] refuse to hire him. Fact: his career was dying twenty years ago. I revived it. Even now, only cast because W. thought it neat to have my real father play my fictional one.

Real father: no! Just man who has acquired the patina of parenthood.

And what was this great career I'm supposed to have destroyed? Sure, it began well enough. Gerald Mortimer, clean-cut, straight-batting English actor hits Hollywood in the 30s. Never out of uniform: drumming civilisation into fuzzie-wuzzies or taking pot-shots at the Hun.

Then fight against Hitler. Civilisation under greater threat. At the end of it, everything changed. Interest in imperial themes declined as fast as Empire. Brits no longer given leading roles. G. slid below title: the token Englishman; the white Sidney Poitier. When Errol Flynn won the War, my father stood two steps behind for verisimilitude.

Stroke of luck when he heard about the casting for *The Wanderers*. His career relaunched on back of mine. Played my father and grandfather, my guardian (man & angel). S[heila][114] took fright. Tried to take me back to England, but I stuck with G. Believed S. was one who was jealous! So she returned alone to her Surrey potting-shed life. NB: last week's phone call and her 'exhausting afternoon spent freshening my pot pourris'.

Meanwhile, Father grew greedy. 'Why should the producers and agents get a piece of you and not your own flesh and blood?' (Unlike Sir H., I can remember lines). Said no to the Studio and *Middleton High*. Directed me himself in remake of *The Secret Garden*. Difficult to know which was worse: his direction or my performance. At 17, even with boobs strapped and face scrubbed, made risible 12-year-old.

Audiences duly roared.

And he blames me for destroying his career!

---

[114] Sheila Mortimer née Lane (1913–82). The daughter, wife and mother of actors (her mother, Mrs Ronnie Lane, played Madame Arkadina opposite Sir Hallam Bamforth's Konstantin in a 1924 production of Chekhov's *The Seagull*).

SATURDAY, 10 SEPTEMBER

Not called. Went with Ralf, Werner & Heike to watch the dailies. Huge relief. The visuals are stunning. Only a handful of scenes but already a clear aesthetic. Wolfram sets up an intricate filmic commentary. Diana and Unity in a series of mirror shots. Hitler framed by images of violence: greeting Redesdales in front of *The Flaying of Marsyas*; reading *Tatler* against *The Rape of the Sabine Women*.

Heightened acting and formal compositions preclude easy emotional response. Characters shown not as individuals but as part of a wider picture. Hats off to W. Amazing how, with so little theory, he creates such a clear perspective. Genuinely political film. Relief about F[elicity]. Inexperience on set becomes spontaneity on screen. Plays every moment. Not afraid of inconsistencies that might worry a more seasoned actress.

G.M. not half bad either!

Post-screening drink with Ralf. Perfect rapport. Have completely misread his attitude. Far from scorn, reveals deep admiration for my political stand. Pays ultimate compliment: 'You are so un-English.'

R.'s aloofness = preoccupation. Very worried about current kidnapping. Explains that the Right are out for blood. Police Federation demanding more resources for war against terrorism. Helmut Kohl, Leader of Opposition, insisting on tougher penalties and clampdown on universities. R.: These are troubled times for Germany. Doubly important to make uncompromising film.

Must find out from Beate whether married, single or queer.

SUNDAY, 11 SEPTEMBER (written on 12th)

No need of Beate!

Works outing to Mad King Ludwig's castle at Neuschwanstein. F[elicity], the prime mover. Supposed to be at memorial service for

Israeli athletes assassinated at Munich Olympics 5 years ago last week (Classic liberal tactic: Honour 'innocent' victims and demonise revolutionaries.) Guest-list = politicians and diplomats from around the globe incl F.'s ambassadorial uncle and aunt. She due to accompany them, but Germans, in thrall to history and desperate to appease Zionists, are determined that everything should go 100% according to plan. So service postponed until Schleyer crisis resolved.

F. grateful. Spends long enough in wardrobe without putting on Sunday clothes. Planned celebratory excursion: invited W[olfram], but he refused to waste time on 'that Bavarian shit', preferring Disney version.[115] Added that he was far too busy to take day off, whatever the attractions. Cue pointed look at L[uke]. F. seemingly oblivious. She displays clear symptoms of First Director syndrome: willing to do anything for him (cf G.M. with Mission).

Motley crew of Ralf, Luke (failing to conceal attraction to me beneath cloak of indifference), Dora (more concerned with seeking out restaurant than castle) and Carole Medhurst (No comment).

4 hour journey. R. drives: L. offers: F. vetoes. Long queue at entrance. Have quiet word with F. about mentioning names. Medhurst, overhearing, makes predictably snide remark – though quick enough to take advantage when supervisor ushers us in.

A truly bizarre building: all corridors and stairs and angles and spikes. A paranoid fantasy dressed up as a fairy-tale. In throne-room, party of schoolgirls recognise me – or rather Heidi. Medhurst says that it's just the result of supervisor repeating my name (as sour as she was five years ago). Sign several guide-books, 2 paper bags and 1 hand.

---

115   The castle in Disney's *Cinderella* was based on Neuschwanstein.

R. in long talk with F. about Schleyer. Later confides impressions (Impressed!). Surprised by level of political sophistication. F. responds by praising German social conscience – though I'm not convinced W. best example to pick. Potential recruit? Will speak to D[ermot] and ask him to send selection of books.

Stimulating day. Even more stimulating night. Sleeping with Hitler!

MONDAY, 12 SEPTEMBER

Ashamed of yesterday's cheap climax. You can take the girl out of Hollywood but can't take Hollywood out of the girl.
Did I think I'd read entry in years to come and applaud?

Definitely applaud R[alf]. A true comrade. Tells of extraordinary childhood: product of project dreamed up by Himmler to create master-race. Farms where blond, blue-eyed mädchens stabled like prize mares and SS men put to stud.[116]
(R. traumatised. But is it that different from London Season where upper-class matrons farm out daughters to carefully selected young men?)
R.: 'I know nothing about my father except for his two favourite initials and nothing about my mother except that she cared more for the Führer than for morality or me.'
No memory of his parents. As a baby, handed to childless Gestapo officer and wife. Father = fun. Favourite game: horses. R. sat on his shoulders whipping him. Now agonises over the men and women (and children) father whipped when not at play.
Mother = Nazi poster girl. All bosom and plaits. R. learnt later that, when visiting husband at Buchenwald, she stood at wire

---

116 Himmler set up twelve Lebensborn homes during the Third Reich, partly as an exercise in eugenics and partly to satisfy the sexual needs of frustrated SS men. 11,000 babies were born between 1935 and 1945.

beside Commandant's wife watching naked prisoners on parade ground. Trouble was weather too cold to enjoy it.

After War, both parents imprisoned. R. placed in custody of nuns, who were as hard as his mother was soft. All love reserved for tortured man in chapel, for whose death they (mankind in general; convent children in particular) were responsible. R. grew up confused: were they responsible because children of murderers or children of Eve?

Rest of youth equally wretched. At 12, nuns sold him to Lutheran minister and wife. 'Sold' no hyperbole, even if cash took the form of a donation towards new convent kitchen. R. treated as servant: cleaning; gardening; chopping wood. Kept in ignorance. Allowed no book but the Bible. Words were dangerous – it was then that he learnt to treasure them. He escaped at 17. Even the Bible was subversive, with its stories of heroes and prophets who broke free of Pharaohs and prisons and lions. He made his way to Berlin, where he found menial work in restaurants. A fellow dishwasher belonged to commune that squatted house abandoned by bourgeois on building of Wall. He invited R. to move in. There, he mixed with writers and artists and found answers to question posed in convent.

1) Children not guilty.
2) Evil not in blood but in system.
3) Human nature neither God-given nor Devil-destroyed but a social construct.
4) Change society and the rest will follow.
5) Love and peace not abstract ideals but practical politics.

Fast forward to mid 60s. Several members of commune plan the first Happening. R. persuaded to take part. Shows real talent and is encouraged to play larger role. 'I began to act and to agitate at the same time, although I can't pretend that both have the same impact. Acting is something I have to do for me. It gives me the strength to do everything else.'

(Wish I'd said that).

Fast forward again to 1967. Shah of Iran's visit to Germany provokes non-violent protests against regime. NON-VIOLENT. State responds with Nazi tactics. Police take up arms on streets of Berlin, protecting the Shah and killing one of R.'s friends.

The death changed him irrevocably. He realised that the capitalist state would never voluntarily cede power & became a revolutionary, in life, work and art.

Keen to return the confidence and tell him about my childhood, on paper so privileged, in practice so abused. Wanted to describe how I too had risen from rubble but preferred to make the connection non-verbally.

Blissful fuck.

TUESDAY, 13 SEPTEMBER

R[alf] vetoed my proposal to watch him on set. Determined that W[olfram] shouldn't have wind of our relationship. Convinced he'd use it against us (malicious, manipulative & worse).

I feigned disappointment but secretly relieved. Spent day in state of guiltless idleness as if working nights.

11 a.m. Massage. Dialogue courtesy of Carry On Stroking. 'Now I shall cream you . . . I feel a stiffness along your thighs.'

Tea with F[elicity] who finished filming early. Reveals growing obsession with Schleyer. Complains that W. refuses to discuss case with her. Why? Does he think her too English and stupid to understand? Blatant nonsense! Look at Unity and Nazis. Precisely because she talked politics that so many of Hitler's entourage distrusted her. Or is W. scared for himself? Renate reports previous support for R[ed] A[rmy] F[action]. And papers full of allusions to well-placed 'terrorist' sympathisers. She wants him to know – even if she can only hint at it – that she is in total sympathy with him.

Ticklish moment alone in lift with Medhurst. Absurd for G.M. to feel intimidated by a woman whose finest hour was playing a Cadbury's *creme egg*.

Never forget her agonising over motivation. From fuss she made, might as well have been Hedda Gabler. Then, after weeks of tortuous experiment, breakthrough came when she remembered friend, chief's daughter from Sierra Leone (completely Westernised – went to school in Cheltenham), who used to complain of feeling a misfit: white inside, black on surface. At that moment, knew that she had found key to role.

Medhurst and lift-boy startled by G.M.'s barely suppressed guffaw.

Evening with Ralf. Bad day on set. Threw minor Crawford[117] when W. told him to take putrid sexual imagery in *Mein Kampf* as key to Hitler's character.

Discuss F.: R. that we shouldn't underestimate her because of class background (makes crude comparison with me!). R. also concerned about Schleyer. Fears that positions are becoming entrenched. Increasing pressure on government not to do a deal. Opinion poll in *Welt am Sontag* (poisonous), found 60% of population opposed release of RAF while even more (70%?) wanted death penalty reintroduced for their crimes.

Meanwhile another deadline set by kidnappers for Schleyer/prisoners exchange has passed.

R. revelatory about Schleyer: A FASCIST! Joined Hitler Youth long before it was necessary. Leader of Nazi student organisation at university. Member of SS working in Industry Association in Occupied Prague. Not an 'eyes closed, no choice' man but a 'head first, no qualms' one. Imprisoned for three years at end of War.

So why hasn't a single paper mentioned his past instead of placing him in forefront of fight for democracy?

---

[117] i.e. tantrum. A private reference that recurs throughout the diaries.

R. replies (obliquely): 'After the War, your country . . . your coun-tries' (granting me dual culpability) 'wanted to de-Nazify ours. But they soon found that if they de-Nazified the judiciary, there would be no judges; if they de-Nazified industry, there would be no bosses; if they de-Nazified the universities, there would be no professors. So who would there be to administer the law, to rebuild the economy, to teach the young? And, more important, who would there be to protect Europe from the Red Menace gathering on its borders? That same Red Menace that led you to appease Hitler before the War led you to legitimise his followers after it.'

That is the background to the martyrdom of Saint Schleyer.

And they call us extremists!

WEDNESDAY, 14 SEPTEMBER

Big day. My first screen wedding – though fact that it was to Sir Oswald Mosley took gilt off the g-bread. Had to stop myself giving chief witness[118] smiles reserved for groom. Liam Finch (square-built, inside and out), a prick. Thinks he's God's Gift (or God Himself?) because he's played a couple of princelings at Stratford. Looks down on those of us who cut our teeth in Hollywood – which, for all the hat-doffing to Sir H., is where he longs to be. See how quickly 'selling out' becomes 'risk-taking' as he convinces himself and millions of viewers of the *Johnny Carson Show* that a car chase is as great a challenge as a Shakespearean soliloquy.

Spend an eternity at the register. W[olfram] intent on a cloud plunging the room into darkness the moment we sign our names. Hours passed synchronising effects: time which might be used more profitably rehearsing actors. Blondi's[119] trainer gives him closer direction than W. ever gives us.

---

118 Hitler.
119 Hitler's dog.

At dinner, Gerald hands me *Daily Mirror* cutting sent by his agent (Elaine's silence shows uncharacteristic sensitivity. Is she planning to ditch me?). Piece confirms all my worst fears. Interviewer links Diana's 'extremism' to mine. Far Left & Far Right two sides of same coin.

Predictable jibe from someone who's taken the Fleet Street shilling.

Feel genuine pity for her. Can't be easy being so cynical. Worming her way into peoples' confidence. My own fault for lowering guard. NEVER AGAIN.

Concerted campaign of misinformation. Should take it as tribute. Bourgeoisie running scared. More urgent than ever that we mobilise. And no, Lynda Tressel,[120] we claim no special privileges for ourselves. We believe in equality for all, not a self-styled elite. On the other hand, activists are crucial to provide a lead when materialism lulls workers out of their revolutionary role. How can ordinary people hold out against the weight of government propaganda?

In America, when Johnson turned whole Vietnamese villages into concentration camps, millions of people swallowed the State Department line ('purification zones'). Anything else like admitting favourite uncle – Sam, of course – a fraud.

In Britain, where colonial troops occupy Northern Ireland, there's a consensus that they provide an essential buffer between rival groups of religious fanatics.

Is it extreme to point this out?

THURSDAY, 15 SEPTEMBER

Not called.

G[erald] urging me to bond with Haroko. Suggested shopping!

---

[120] Author of the article, 'Red Queen in Black Shirt', *Daily Mirror*, 8 September 1977.

Male cliché of sisterhood (Has he ever been to a sale?).
Trudge around store. H.'s smile reflected in every surface. Tries to endear herself by repeating G.'s stories of my childhood. Like a fence dealing in stolen goods.

Lunch. H. opens up (a little). Speaks with hand over mouth as if afraid words will wound. Admits to feeling intimidated by my closeness to Father. G. has told her full story of how he brought me up single-handedly after mother's departure.
Excuse me?
Enlighten her that 'brought up' when used by Father a very loose term. Can be roughly translated as handing me over to chaperones and governesses, ignoring me except for my value at Box Office and in bedroom (to lure prospective girlfriends with evidence of paternal solicitude).
Remember only one shared excursion in entire childhood. Visit to aquarium where he took pleasure in pointing out resemblance between every ugly fish and my mother. Returned home in tears.
Presume that, among anecdotes, he has reported his response to my first period: 'For God's sake, don't breath a word to the Studio.' And the 'no more candies' rule he imposed on set when his greedy little girl was crippled with cramps.
Oh yes. A father in a million.
Think I succeeded in setting her mind at rest.

FRIDAY, 16 SEPTEMBER

7 p.m. Parcel of books from D[ermot] waiting for me at hotel. Deeply touched that, despite all the calls on his time, he sent them by return. Eager to repay his commitment and take them straight to F[elicity].
Phoned flat. Luke answered that F. was with Wolfram. Sounded angry (with her? with me?). He asked whether actors in Hollywood socialised through the night when up at dawn the next day. My reply noncommittal: as a child, I was a special case.

Braved Serpent's Nest. Never at home in communes, even at Berkeley. Remember A[hmet?]'s scorn of students for whom dish-washing-rota a revolutionary act. On the evidence, Wolfram & co. equate liberation with mess.

Pick my way through detritus and see unexpected charms in mother's crumb-free code.

F. in kitchen with remains of cous-cous cooked by W.'s boyfriend (tall, taut, lazy eye, sandalwood skin). Hand over books. Spotted by [Carole] Medhurst who cautions F. against Party, like fortune-teller on Titanic.

F. overrules her (over-politely), claiming right to decide for herself. Mortified that Trotsky only one of the authors she's heard of. Amen!

For Medhurst read Judas. Can never forgive her for damage she inflicted on Party and me. Making me look as cranky as someone who consults the I Ching: a refugee from La La Land, whose politics are all pose.

News for her and whole pack of cynics: Hollywood the dream-<u>factory</u>; its studios as exploitative as any sweatshop. Fly me down the coast to Mexico, stick me behind a sewing machine 12 hours a day and you'd cause an outcry. But because I was on covers of magazines: because I had my own tutor and chaperone and chauffeur: because (above all) I earned rows of noughts, people looked away.

I was the classic victim. And too young/ignorant/terrified to speak out. The most taciturn star since Lassie.

And they wonder why I became a revolutionary!

SATURDAY, 17 SEPTEMBER

Reading through last 2 days' entries, fear that impression too grim. Conflicts yes. Dilemmas yes. But, on whole, surprisingly upbeat. Film ✓. Ralf ✓ (esp between the sheets). Temporary hiccup when I told him he was clearly not typecast as Hitler (reputed to be impotent). R. pulled away, saying that was exactly the sort of shit he expected from Wolfram. I apologised but, ironically, created very condition I'd just denied.

Made up (for it) later.

Bavaria Studios present Geraldine Mortimer in Autumn Rhapsody!

11 p.m. Night shoot. Berchtesgaden. Its authentic 3rd Reich railway station standing in for Berlin (D[iana] and U[nity] on a visit). Werner & Jewish backer toadying to train owner (contrast with perfunctory treatment of actors).

What sort of person lovingly preserves Nazi trains?

Drove up this a.m. with F[elicity] and L[uke] (trouble brewing there unless much mistaken), R[alf] and Dieter. Visited the Obersalzberg. Views spectacular but sites disappointing. A Versailles-like set-up: the entire Nazi leadership built villas around Hitler's Berghof. Heavily bombed 1) by Allies at end of War, 2) by Bavarian Government in 50s. All that remains is the Eagle's Nest, a tea-house for VIPs on top of mountain.

So up we went.

Eagle's Nest originally planned by Martin Bormann as surprise present for Hitler's 50th birthday. Surprise? With 3000 men and truckloads of rubble transported daily under his nose?

Reached it via lift (Gilded mirrors and padded leather, cf the Savoy) hewn out of rock. Thrown in with group of American tourists. When told by guide that Eagle's Nest built by slave labour, middle-aged woman, cushioned by rolls of complacency, asked: 'You mean that they had blacks here too?'

Strange reversal in café. Dieter recognised by group of Austrians (fittingly, for performance in W.'s recent *Magic Mountain*); G.M. just part of scenery. Huge relief.

Sign prominently displayed: It is absolutely forbidden to ask questions of the serving staff.

L. (who else?) asked waitress whether Hitler ever came up here during War.

Waitress: Are you blind?

L.: No.

Waitress: Then are you stupid?

Walking outside, bump into 4 English skinheads wearing Union Jack T-shirts. *I'm backing Britain*[121] in quite the wrong way. They look so sinister with their hair shorn and dressed in pseudo-uniform (deliberately designed to thwart identification parade?).

F.: They've come here on a pilgrimage.

L.: It's nothing so depraved – more likely T-shirts bought for Queen's Jubilee.

L.'s Teddy Bear's Picnic mentality exposed when Dieter tells story of Wolfram in London this summer. Went to some queer pub in East End. Picked up yob and had sex with him in yard.

'Suck my Nazi cock,' yob commanded.

W. turned on (Sick!). Presumed it was some sort of role-play. But no, his penis was tattooed and, as it grew, a swastika unfurled.

SUNDAY, 18 SEPTEMBER

Frustration, like everything else, intensified at night. Waited with F[elicity] for hours in trailer simply to step off train and into crowd of SS men (might as well have used 2 stand-ins in hats).

Endless takes to obtain elusive smoke effect.

Sharp divergence of views:

F.: Genius an infinite capacity for taking pains.

G.M.: In W[olfram]'s case, an infinite capacity for giving them.

---

[121] Patriotic economic slogan adopted by the Labour Government in 1968.

Return to hotel at 6 a.m.

Day of sleep and sex.

Forced to qualify yesterday's enthusiasm for R[alf]'s love-making. His expertise not in doubt but the experience would be much improved if he resisted the urge to describe what he was doing as he did it. Like subtitles when you already follow film.

8 p.m. W. throws party. Phenomenal energy. It can't all be chemical. He mocks my premature (midnight!) departure, claiming that, after no sleep last night, he anticipates being up till early hours storyboarding tomorrow's scenes.

Macho posturing? Someone who can only function under pressure? Or both?

F. & L[uke] equally driven. After morning's rest, they took off for Dachau. Devastated by what they saw. What did they expect?

Far too easy to sentimentalise the past. They should examine conditions inside a Palestinian camp: whole families living in huts smaller than an English shed; crushed petrol cans for walls; the pervasive stink of human and animal excrement; silent children with accusing eyes.

Who's to blame for that? Not the Nazis.

Feel need to seek out Mahmoud. He has always been edgy around me as if wanting to talk but nervous. Presumed it was language barrier but his English turns out to be better than his German.

Find him alone in bedroom, nursing bottle of schnapps. He responds so grudgingly to my questions that I'm on point of giving up when he opens heart (understatement). Pours out all his grievances about W. How he deliberately tries to make him jealous/violent. 'He says he loves me so why does he want to hurt me? Why does he want to make me hurt him?'

The current bone of contention is Luke. W. obsessed with him.

'If I catch them together, I will kill him. I will kill them both. Then I will kill myself as a third.'

Invoke F., assuring him L. has a girlfriend with whom he is v. much in love. Argument weakened by revelation that M. has a wife and son in Chatila camp in Beirut. Annoyed at own surprise. His subjection to W. a classic case of sexual imperialism. And yet what started as economic necessity appears to have grown into genuine affection.

Tells me a little about wife, Nabila. His cousin. They grew up together and married at eighteen. Son a wedding-night baby. No jobs in Beirut, so he left to lay oil-pipes in Saudi. While there, obtained permit to work in Germany. Now expired $\therefore$ doubly dependent on W.

Ask if permit can be renewed.

Should have been renewed a long time ago.

With shy glance, he tells me that we've met before. Feel both intrigued and anxious. Describe my work for his people and how I went to Beirut to see oppression for self. Then bombshell. He confides that family name = Samif; brother = Ahmet.

How can one name unlock so many memories?

Berkeley, 1967. Two students thrown together at anti-Vietnam demo. Asked to hold up opposite ends of banner before even introduced. Best news: not seen a single one of my films. Unlike frat-house boys betting on who'd be first to lay Heidi, interested in G.M. for herself.

Only man I ever knew with scars as deep as mine. Grew up in poverty and squalor under Israeli oppression. So brilliant that given UN scholarship to study on most privileged campus in world.[122]

A. opened my eyes. Before we met, I was content to skim surface of life. Turned me into revolutionary.

Mahmoud smiles. Promises fresh meeting sooner than I think. A.

---

[122] UNRWA (United Nations Relief Works Agency) funded an extensive educational programme for Palestinians.

now working as journalist for *al-Hadaf*.[123] Flying to Munich to cover Schleyer case.

Stunned. Unsteady. 4 years since I last saw him. Will he have changed? No matter, I have. Can't let myself fall back beneath his spell. There's too much at stake. Everything that happened, + and – , happened because of him. I might be Jane Fonda if we'd never met.

Beat rapid retreat from party. Tell R. that I've started period. Couldn't bear to sleep with him tonight (ever again?).

MONDAY, 19 SEPTEMBER

Lunch. Standing behind G[erald] at caterer's van. Cheap jibe re last night's chat with Mahmoud (who told him?). Reply that it was totally U-certificate. Bedroom = setting not substance. G., affecting disbelief, mentions Ahmet. Claims I was 'politicised by Arab cock'. Scorn of his casual sexism empowers me. Counter that, no, satisfied by Arab cock; politicised by Hollywood cock. Strictly kosher. As no one knows better than he.

G. suffers sudden loss of appetite. Tactical withdrawal.

p.m. On set, watch Manfred & Dieter wrestle with Goebbels & Streicher: at loss to comprehend, much less convey, their depravity. Interesting role-reversal. Girl who grew up in lap of luxury knows all about evil. Boys who grew up in ruins of war find it remote.

They should book seats on Geraldine Mortimer's personal tour of Hollywood (Forget all the Homes of Stars shit; this is real thing). Discover the one place comparable to 3rd Reich. A few square miles of realised fantasy in which gods flout laws governing ordinary mortals. A world so corrupt that people fall in love with their

---

123 Weekly Arabic newspaper.

own corruption, where fulfilment becomes commonplace and excitement found only in extremes.

I catch Haroko watching me. Gaze of studied sympathy. What does she see?

TUESDAY, 20 SEPTEMBER

Black Tuesday.

1) Diana/Mosley wedding footage worthless. Flutter in camera due to fault in electricity supply. So much for German efficiency! Any reshooting bad enough but that the worst. Another day next to Liam (don't cramp my ego) Finch. What's more, scene placed right at end of schedule, foiling chance of early escape.

2) Should be 1). But G.M. as me-centred as any Hollywood star. Grim news from Middle East. Picked up Sir H.'s *Times*. Fresh reports of Zionist expansion. Israeli soldiers have crossed into Southern Lebanon to reinforce Right-wing militia under attack from Palestinian guerillas. Israeli gunboats have gathered outside port of Tyre and fighter planes made forays over battle zones.

In age when other countries forced to camouflage imperialist ambitions, Israel flaunts them (chosen people/special case). Meanwhile, world looks on in silence. National myths founded on repelling invaders: blood, toil, sweat etc in Britain; heroes of Resistance in France. So why won't they raise voices on behalf of Palestinian struggle against occupying Israeli state?
Question rhetorical. Zionists and allies who control world media conspire to prevent free discussion, instead devoting airtime/column inches to Jewish claim that Chairman Arafat wants to annihilate entire race. Slander doubly despicable from people who were victims of blood libel.

eve: Condolence visit to Mahmoud. Express disgust at Germans, so obsessed by search for 1 worthless old Nazi that they ignore arrest of 1000s of innocent Palestinians. M. in such deep shock that he appears indifferent. Talks only about W[olfram].

Leave after frustrating hour.

WEDNESDAY, 21 SEPTEMBER

a.m. Führer's private cinema. With Unity, Hitler & Göring watching newsreel of Anschluss. W[olfram] neatly using Hitler's fascination with films of his triumphs to avoid need to stage them.

R[alf] strides on set and makes public announcement. Claims no honour left in Germany (Hitler moustache bristles). Has just heard on radio that government has rejected Italian request for extradition of some war criminal escaped from military hospital in Rome.[124] Demands that unit make formal protest. W. demurs, insisting that Leftwing action merely incites Rightwing backlash. '12,000,000 people read *Bild am Sonntag*. Are they going to back you?'

R. looks to me for support. Offer it psychically. Feel inhibited by our relationship & my reputation. Pressure relieved by F[elicity], who declares that if Right are going to use force, Left has to pre-empt them. Hit them where it hurts: banks; office blocks; department stores.

Henry astonished: 'You can't mean to advocate violence?'

F. defiant: 'Sometimes there's no choice.'

Good on her! Not only stands up to voice of English liberalism (in H.'s case, adopted) but contradicts Wolfram (a first?).

Clear she has been reading the books.

---

124 Herbert Kappler, a former SS colonel held in Italy, was said to be suffering from terminal cancer. The court's decision was based on a clause in West Germany's constitution which banned the extradition of German nationals.

W. taken aback. 'Let's make the film.' R. refuses to give up. 'About what? The relationship between a sexual pervert and a hysteric? Shouldn't it be something more?'

W. & R. hammer & tongs in German. F. persuades interpreter to give us gist. W. says film will be about a lot more if only R. lets it. R. replies that he is deeply disappointed in W. Promised a radical political film only to end up with an anti-romantic melodrama. Charlie Chaplin's Hitler a more valid interpretation. May have been played for laughs but accurate portrait of little man harnessing historical forces. Not freak from pages of Krafft-Ebing.

Argument peters out. Scene shot in single take. Even newsreel synch worked without hitch. Returned to COMMUNAL TRAILER (lost cause!). Discussed dispute with H[enry], who'd been there, and G[erald], who hadn't. [Carole] Medhurst, who was neither in scene nor included in conversation (not, as *Sunday Times* readers can vouch, that that has ever stopped her[125]), opined that problem with making Hitler a freak was that it let rest of us off hook. In her view, it was normal not abnormal cruelty that needed explaining.

H. countered that it was neither humanity nor Hitler that needed explaining but God. The same God whom the rabbis at Auschwitz put on trial and found guilty.

'But didn't they say a prayer to him straight after the verdict?' (Medhurst).

'Perhaps that's the ultimate Jewish joke?' (F.).

'Or God's ultimate joke on the Jews? After all, if mankind was made in God's image, who's to say that Hitler rather than Moses or Jesus isn't his true reflection? So, I repeat, we merely have to play Hitler. We have to explain God.' (H.).

---

[125] Carole Medhurst's article, 'The Party's Over', *Sunday Times*, 9 June 1974, led to a police investigation of the IWP's activities and the closure of its training centre.

At which point G., inevitably excluded from intellectual discussion, put in his 2p'sworth. 'That's all very deep, but, unfortunately, I can't see God on the call-sheet.' Went through pantomime of examining it. 'No. No God. Who's playing him? By rights, it should be my old friend, Sir Hallam Bamforth CH. But that doesn't seem to be the case.'

Broke off in embarrassment as others ignored him.

Medhurst to H.: 'Then you have no explanation for Hitler?'

H.: 'On the contrary. I think he was a man so traumatised by the carnage of the Trenches that he went mad. Only a madman would kill one person, let alone six million. Only a madman would fail to recognise that every human being has an inalienable right to life. There are, however, different degrees of madness. The pitiful delusion of the man who thinks he is Hitler is far removed from the genocidal mania of the Hitler who thinks he is God.'

Vow never to make another film where I don't have my own trailer.

THURSDAY, 22 SEPTEMBER

Bayreuth.

Nazi equivalent of Ascot. Party leaders & fellow travellers (incl Unity & Diana) join Hitler in annual beanfeast. This year (37? 38?), unique production of *Lohengrin* since W[olfram] plans fantasy sequence in which Hitler as L. rescues Unity as Elsa from wicked guardian, played (incongruously) by Sir H[allam].

Entire day shooting scene of arrival: cavalcade of cars; SS guard of honour; crowds waiting for glimpse of Hitler; women fainting (cf *June Bridesmaid* premiere).

100s of onlookers include, disconcertingly, Winifred Wagner, standing just a few foot away from her past. Little old lady who might be selling pretzels. Spoke only once, when Hitler walked up to the portico and shook the hand of her younger self. 'No!' came an imperious cry 'This will not do. The Führer always kissed my hand. He knew how to show respect.'

W. modified gesture against protests from R[alf] who preferred false note to offering sop to Nazi. R. nevertheless relieved by her accent. English high priestess at Aryan shrine = proof that infamy not confined to a single nation.[126] The burden of guilt could be shared.

A theme that developed throughout the day.

Dieter and Sir H. comparing Bayreuth and Stratford.

D.: 'Is it true that Shylock was one of your most celebrated roles?'

Sir H.: 'So people are kind enough to say. It's the nose, you see. Plus, I didn't play for sympathy.'

D.: 'The Nazis loved *The Merchant of Venice*. In 1933 alone, there were 20 separate productions in Germany.'

Sir H.: 'Really? How splendid! I had no idea. I doubt that we could have matched that in England.'

D.: 'Between 1934 & 1937, there were another 20. Your friend, Mr Auden, regretted that nothing he wrote saved any of the Jews from Auschwitz.[127] Do you think that Shakespeare could have said the same about the words that sent them there?'

Sir H.: 'Shakespeare was resolutely non-aligned. A literary Switzerland. That's his greatest strength. You can't tell from the plays what, if anything, he believes.'

Cue anecdote of Hattie Lanchester fighting losing battle with moustache when disguised as lawyer in trial scene.

Sir H.: 'Take it from me, the quality of mercy was highly strained when she finally caught up with her dresser.'

---

[126] Like Luke in his letter of 23 September 1977, Geraldine mistakes Winifred Wagner's nationality.

[127] 'I know that all the verses I wrote, all the positions I took in the thirties, didn't save a single Jew. These attitudes, these writings, only help oneself.' W. H. Auden to Anne Freemantle, *W. H. Auden: A tribute*, ed. Stephen Spender, Weidenfeld & Nicolson, 1974, page 89.

Story trivial but salutary. British cultural life in a nutshell. Crucial issue of artistic responsibility shrugged off in favour of gossip.

FRIDAY, 23 SEPTEMBER

12 hour shoot.

Up and down staircase like Grand Old Duke of York. Quick greeting from Hitler and Goebbels, then process repeated. Ad nauseam. Literally for F[elicity] who was sickened by fumes from generator. Or it may have been the diet. Unit catering far worse than Munich. Even stars given sausages!

Sir H[allam] caustic about frankfurters. 'Just salt and grease. Only the Germans could have invented them, let alone made them their national dish.'

Henry rebuked him for perpetuating stereotypes.

Sir H.: 'I know. It's naughty of me. But it saves so much time. I remember when I was playing Vanya in Dublin and asked this pungent local character the way to St Patrick's Cathedral. He replied: "From where?"'

New low! In 20 years of keeping journal, never before been reduced to writing about food.

SATURDAY, 24 SEPTEMBER

p.m. Dispensed whisky & sympathy to R[alf] who'd stormed off set after big bust-up with Wolfram. Conflict brewing for weeks but immediate cause was Wolfram's insertion of scene in which Hitler's niece Geli shits on him.

Confused about context (Geli = fantasy, ghost or flashback?), but, given R.'s mood, it seemed inappropriate to ask.

Whatever the background, R. refused to play scene. Asked for rationale. W. ran through evidence of Hitler's sexual perversion (impossible for me to assess since R. claimed that it didn't bear repeating). Linked to accounts of his impotence, supposedly confirmed by Eva Braun's home movies in which he places hands protectively over crotch the moment anyone draws near. Even cited the famous salute – keeping arm up for hours in absence of anything else.[128]

R. dismissed it as flimflam. Offered series of ripostes. Unsure whether aimed at me or W. or both.

1) Have we grown so obsessed with sex that we need to play out the whole of human history in the bedroom?

2) Freud has a lot to answer for. At least when people believed in God, they looked outwards. Now they look inwards and backwards – two dead ends.

3) When will people take responsibility for the world they live in: the world they can change: the new world they can bring about?

W. apparently suggested he start by taking responsibility for his role and leave him to take responsibility for film. The shit was non-negotiable. R. declared (to his face!) that W. so warped he took comfort from company of fellow-deviants, even if they included Hitler. Then he quit set and headed straight for 4 Seasons. Filming cancelled for rest of day.

G.M. cautious. Danger of being too closely identified with R. Keeping options open not the same as sitting on the fence.

eve: F[elicity] filled me in on turn of events. Crisis meeting of W., Werner and Thomas (backer). Latter Jewish, so of course sides with W. Suits purposes if Hitler a pervert rather than making considered – if excessive – attack on international finance.*

* Conscious even in journal of need to weigh words. If Nazi criticisms of Jews were intemperate, now have opposite problem in world where forbidden to make any criticisms at all.

---

[128] Hitler himself gave credence to this interpretation. Comparing his arm to that of his more obviously virile henchman, he declared: 'I can keep it up for two hours. Göring can only keep it up for half an hour.'

SUNDAY, 25 SEPTEMBER

Painful confrontation with R[alf].

He insisted he would not back down. Urged me to stand alongside him, demanding right as workers to have some control over production/as actors over interpretation. If I show solidarity, Wolfram & Werner bound to take note. Pair of us in too many scenes.

Tried to explain that, while I supported him 100%, my case different (unique). Returning to screen after 10-year absence. If I walk out now, people will say I'm unable to stand the strain: a gifted child not an actress. I'll never work again.

R. piled on pressure.

1) Appealed to my convictions.

Replied that I'd be in far better position to achieve common goal from position of power.

2) Appealed to our relationship.

Explained (gently) that he'd read too much into it. Two people away from home seeking solace in one another's company. No harm – but no more. Circumstantial intimacy.

R. v. cold & vengeful. Thank G. found out this side of him before serious involvement. Declared me as cheap & corrupt as W. (For so-called revolutionary, depressingly unreconstructed vocab. Even resorted to stock device of storming out & slamming door.)

p.m. On set. Not called but needed company. Grateful for communal trailer (Close up on actress eating hat).

Cast/crew shell-shocked.

W[olfram] to take over as Hitler! Alarm bells ringing. Werner worried about workload: 'Wolfram is *Unity*' (echoes of Göring's 'Hitler is Germany'). Claims that cocaine consumption already sky-high. Must be exaggeration. Seen him sniff nothing more toxic than Vic inhaler.

Everyone in huddles. Renate & Dieter concocting conspiracy theories. Sir H[allam] and D[ora] swapping horror stories of ACTOR-

DIRECTORS I HAVE KNOWN. L[uke] fretting that W. 6" taller than R. ∴ Unity's height-distinction lost. Only F. untroubled. To her, W. can do no wrong, either on screen or off.

2 W.s [Wolfram and Werner] poring over rough assembly. Seems that R.'s scenes less extensive than feared. Werner swears that, if all goes according to plan, switch will add no more than 4 or 5 days.

One scene (rally at Feldherrnhalle) to be ditched. Rest to be reshot. Worst news is that it means return to Bayreuth (principals not extras). What with Diana and Mosley's 2nd marriage, we'll be here into early November. Revised schedule built around Henry, who's committed to cold-war epic in Finland, and Sir H., who's to play Pope in bio-pic on St Francis ('Although with the beard they've proposed, I'll look more like one of his goats').

And journalist last week referred to magic of filming!

MONDAY, 26 SEPTEMBER

Depression.

1) Racked with guilt about Ralf. Was I right to place loyalty to film over loyalty to lover? Is it the betrayal of country/ betrayal of friend dilemma in another guise?

2) Steve Biko buried yesterday.[129] 20,000 people attended Requiem Mass. *The Times* reports with typical understatement that 'Violence later erupted in the town,' i.e. the forces of the apartheid state were unleashed on innocent mourners. *Nikosi Sikelel' iAfrika*. I should have been there.

I should be anywhere but here. For years longed for return to cameras and now can't wait for filming to be over. No wonder actors seen as fickle! Besides, what's the alternative? To spend the

---

[129] Steve Biko (1946–77), South African activist and founder of the Black Consciousness Movement, who died while in police custody.

rest of my life getting up at dawn in order to sell *The Warrior* outside Elephant and Castle tube? To give my all (body, soul & £) to Party, only to be sneered at in Press as a dilettante and by comrades as a dreamer with no experience of shop floor? G.M. on shop floor when rest of them still in playground!

10.30 p.m. Solitude so oppressive that threw on clothes and went down to bar. Mistake no 1. All the usual suspects exchanging idle gossip. L[uke] has a friend who saw Dora in *Camille* at Chichester. So what? It's a big theatre. Talks as if he'd been present at private perf for Princess Grace. Dora launched into discourse on agony of playing 'in full corsets. It was a toss-up as to which would come first: death by constriction or consumption.' Pause for sycophantic laughter (L.). 'Audiences are so suggestible. I've never heard such a cacophony of coughing as at the end of the play.'
Discerning patrons might take a different view. L., needless to say, lapped it up. He's an intelligent man: how can he respect a woman who calls herself spiritual just because she reads her horoscope each morning in the *Daily Mail*?
11.30 p.m. Bar as unbearable as bed. Ventured outside. Mistake no 2. Streets crammed with drunken revellers reeling home from *Oktoberfest*. Tried (without success) to enter into spirit of celebration. Small wonder that Hitler engaged in deadly virility contest when the ability to down quarts of beer is a source of national pride.

1 a.m. Returned to suite. Room service (19-year-old. Straggling moustache. Acne). Mistake no 3, 4 + 5.

TUESDAY, 27 SEPTEMBER (written on 28th)

He's here! Covering Schleyer case for paper. So why Germany? Surely he'd find out more abroad? Schmidt as skilful as Goebbels at manipulating media. Built up wall of silence. Kidnappers only break through by contacting foreign press.

Hence today's *Libération* prints message from guerrillas demanding that government stop playing for time. Front page picture of Schleyer with placard: 'For 20 days a prisoner of the Red Army Group.'

He'd have done better to go to Paris.

And if Germany, why Munich? Why not Bonn to make contacts or Cologne where attack took place? Claims to have come to see Mahmoud but little love lost between them. Plain truth is that he's come to see me.

Me! Me! Me! Me! Me!

Not that he would admit it. Feigned astonishment at finding me, followed by anger at Mahmoud for not warning him. So transparent. But I refrain from challenging him. His male pride is the only pride that has not been crushed.

He's here and G.M. nineteen again!

He's here and as handsome as ever: the slick black hair combed back from the broad forehead; the resolute face with the angular nose and square jaw; the skin pulled tight on the rangy frame – skin as warm & soft as sand. How can a revolutionary have such soft skin? But then how can a Palestinian have such blue eyes?

Question answered at Berkeley: Crusader ancestors.

'The imperialists raped my country six hundred years ago and have been doing so ever since.'

Such bittersweet memories. Lying beside him on a manicured lawn and listening to stories of growing up in Beirut. The only Palestinian in his school. Lebanese children refusing to sit next to him because he stank. Him – the sweetest-smelling man I ever knew! But he got his revenge. Top of the class even though he was out on the streets every night hawking gum. 'The rich Lebanese looked away from us like fat women from a mirror. They spoke

French as if Arabic would burn their tongues like *foul*.'[130]
Lebanon refused to educate Palestinians, but his teachers turned a
blind eye because he was so bright. Then, one day, an official
document-check after a disturbance revealed he had none, just an
identity card with a large X next to nationality. 'A man with no
country has even less of himself than a man with no name.'
Worse, to save his own skin, the Principal accused him of deception, expelling him in front of the entire school. Left to complete
his education in the camp, he was brilliant enough to win a scholarship to Berkeley.

He showed me history with a human face.

Just to know that he's in same city makes me strong. Every street
is a possibility, every stranger a friend. Enough (almost) to bring
out the bourgeois in me & make me believe in the stars.

WEDNESDAY, 28 SEPTEMBER

Notice that last entry didn't name him. Am I being unduly
cautious? If so, I shall make up for it now. Ahmet! Ahmet!
Ahmet![131]
Unsure how much of today happened yesterday & how much of
yesterday today. From now on, I pledge to write this journal every
night. I have no problem reconstructing events – this afternoon,
we went for walk through city – but am confused by emotions (as
tortuous as the streets). Thank G. not recognised! A[hmet]
thought my sunglasses affected but he has no notion of *Heidi*'s
popularity. Wish he could have seen how I was mobbed at
Ludwig's castle – just so that he could have dismissed it. He has
no time for superficial celebrity. Scorned Berkeley students in awe

130 Cheap bean dish popular with Palestinians.
131 Geraldine covers the entire border of the page with Ahmets. The effect,
impossible to reproduce here, is strangely Talmudic.

of G.M.'s stardom. Why should a man who works alongside George Habbash[132] be impressed by a girl who sang duet with Frank Sinatra?[133]

Strolling through *Marienplatz*, spotted Sir H[allam] slumped on bench. Nurse Geraldine to the rescue. But no cause for alarm. He was simply waiting for the glockenspiel. Introduced him to A. Surprised (annoyed!) by nakedness of Sir H.'s glances. As if dark skin removed the need for discretion. Prayed that A. wouldn't notice.

Clock chimes plunged the square into silence. All eyes on *Rathaus* facade as miniature figures sprang to life. Sir H. deeply moved. 'I come here every afternoon that I'm not called. It's like the toy theatre I had as a boy.'

Left him to lachrymose memories and proceeded to tea.

A.'s tourist talk depressed me. Plied him with questions. Wanted to know everything about everything in last 4 years. He, tight-lipped, claimed G.M. a temptress. Passing (joking?) ref to sun-bathing in training camp.

Blamed my watery eyes on scalding tea.

A., finally relaxing, revealed that he was married. Willed my blood to keep flowing. To Lela.

G.M.: Simple name.

A.: But not a simple woman. Three children, one for each year of marriage. The future of Palestine.

---

132 George Habbash, leader of the PFLP (Popular Front for the Liberation of Palestine), a breakaway group from Yasser Arafat's PLO, which it considered insufficiently radical. The PFLP and its various offshoots were responsible for the majority of the terrorist attacks of the 1970s and 80s.

133 At a White House dinner in honour of Prime Minister Ikeda of Japan on 24 June 1961, Gore Vidal, one of the guests, described Geraldine's performance in *We're a couple of swells* as 'tired beyond her years'.

Couldn't help thinking of Ralf, and Himmler's attempt to populate Reich. Didn't know who was to be more pitied: the wife enjoined to be fertile or the children brought up in squalor of camp.

Pressed hand to A.'s chest. He jumped back as if it were rubber bullet. Assured him (with deceptive nonchalance) that I wasn't trying to force myself on him, just wondering whether he still had keys. He drew out chain. 'Of course,' he said. 'I shall have them until the day I die. And then my son will have them. And then my son's son. Until one day, a Samif will go back to Haifa and unlock his own front door.'

That dynastic vision explained everything. Marriage to Lela not a love match but a duty. His affections were less easily constrained. Habbash himself acknowledged as much when A. introduced us. Praised him as one of his finest men who would do great honour to the cause unless betrayed by his weakness for women. His meaning was unambiguous. Nevertheless G.M. more flattered than frightened. It confirmed my power. And A.'s unease showed that it remained undiminished. Recoiling not from me but from himself.

His feelings clear but only ½ the equation. What about mine? Is it him I want to recapture or the past? I can revisit my childhood at regular afternoon screenings, but my youth remains elusive. A. the one person who can bring it back.

Over the course of tea, he grew more expansive, admitting that his trip not simply journalistic but to liaise with various groups on behalf of PFLP. Beirut has considerable interest in the liberation of Baader.

No surprise, except for his moment of panic at having said too much (maybe G.M. a temptress after all?). Assured him that talking to me just like talking to himself – only safer.

He escorted me back to the hotel. Every nerve in my body a nettle.

He shook my hand so formally in the foyer that it would have been undignified to press for more. I went up to my suite. To my horror, found myself casting Sir H.-like glances at lift boy. To my greater horror, found them returned. Escaped post-haste down corridor. Ordered dinner in room. As a precaution, insisted that trolley be left outside door.

THURSDAY, 29 SEPTEMBER

Last 2 days it's been easy to forget I'm working on a film – or, at any rate, this film. More like remake of classic love story. G.M.: Garbo/Claudette Colbert. A[hmet]: Rudolph Valentino in *The Sheik*.

(NB: Ahmet, if you ever read this, ref romantic not racist).

Fraught a.m. on set. W[olfram] punishing me for intimacy with R[alf]? Want to reassure him: ancient history. As things now stand, we're almost related. But respect A.'s wishes & keep mum.

W. playing Hitler to manner born. Hate to be disloyal but it may well be an improvement. R.'s agonies about part coloured the character, whereas W.'s no-nonsense approach perfectly suited to a man without self-doubt. Instructive to watch him slip between roles: one minute setting up complicated reverse shot of study; the next, preparing to annexe Austria. Assisted by attitude of unit. Everyone doubly deferential since he put on moustache & hair-piece.

Interior. Apartment. Diana nursing Unity through tonsillitis contracted from heiling Hitler at Anschluss. H. visits. D. runs down corridor to alert Unity, who is determined to look her best for him even on sickbed.

Point out to W. that Diana would never run. Contrary to her entire personality & training. W. deaf to reason. Complains that

Eng actors always looking for something called Character inside which they can hide. Adds that all camera requires is for person to be truly present in scene. Don't have to act being there.

G.M.: That person called Geraldine not Diana.

W.: Find Geraldine in Diana. Find Diana in Geraldine.

(Very easy when woman a fanatical fascist!)

Gerhard to rescue. Explains to W. that I'll have to walk slowly because camera too close to pan at speed.

Saved by a technicality.

Lunch with F[elicity]. As always full of latest Schleyer developments (proof that her boyfriend not purely decorative). Japanese government today bowed to demands of guerrillas who hijacked plane at Dacca. Agreed to release 9 revolutionaries along with ransom of $6,000,000.

F.: 'So why is Schmidt dragging his heels? He can't win. There are millions of young people ready to take up the cause. Ours is the freedom generation.'

Felt sure she was trying to tell me something. First time she has expressed herself so clearly. Resolved to introduce her to A.

Easier said than done. Where is he? After filming, head straight to Serpent's Nest but no one has seen him all day. M[ahmoud] thinks he may have gone to Berlin to meet contacts. Why didn't he say? He can't just walk in and out of my world like a Hollywood father.

Go up to his room. So little luggage for such a big life. Shirts and pants scattered on floor. Press them to face and drink in clean heat of his body. Caught unawares by M. Too late for subterfuge, so slowly drop hands to sides. Surprised by the compassion of his gaze.

FRIDAY, 30 SEPTEMBER

6 a.m.: Drove to Regensburg (standing in for Nuremberg). Bus

reminiscent of Magnolia's. Broke into the Adventure Song.[134] No chorus.

W[olfram] adopted similar solution to shooting Nuremberg rally as Anschluss. Hitler and Goebbels visit studios and watch Leni Riefenstahl editing sequence from *Triumph of the Will*.[135] W. unperturbed by discrepancy between the two Hitlers. On contrary, sees it as another means to prevent easy identification.

Only 2 scenes to be shot here.

1) Diana and Unity greeted by Putzi Hanfstaengl and taken to hotel.

2) The women strolling through streets on way to stadium.

Last night at dinner, Sir H. described visit to 1936 Rally.

Amazed . . . appalled. Was he a crypto-Fascist?

'Good Lord, no! Whatever can have given you that idea?'

Attending Nuremberg Rally for a start.

'I went courtesy of von Ribbentrop.[136] He was a friend of Emerald Cunard.[137] You met everyone at Emerald's: Wallis Simpson; Noel Coward. She'd changed her name from Maud. And who can blame her? Of course you remember her last words. "Pagne . . . pagne." "Yes, dear," the nurse said. "We know you're in pain." "No, champagne. Champagne." Such spirit. Such style. Happy days.'

He rambles like a drunk.

'I'd started to have a certain – if I may say so – modest success in the West End and I was deluged with invitations. Von Ribben-

134 Oscar-winning song sung by Geraldine, Burl Ives and Shirley Jones in the 1960 film, *Magnolia's Ark*, as they drive a converted bus across a flooded prairie, rescuing stranded animals.

135 Riefenstahl's classic film of the 1935 Nuremberg Rally.

136 Sir Hallam's explanation of his visit to Nuremberg differs substantially from the one he gave elsewhere, namely that he went at the instigation of Brian Howard. See Denny page 138.

137 Lady Emerald Cunard (1872–1948), society hostess and mother of Nancy, the first choice of subject for our May Week play.

trop's was one of many. He can't have imagined that I had any influence. I abhor politics. That's why I've steered clear of Bernard Shaw.'

But Nuremberg?

'I expect it sounds bizarre but it was almost like being in Emerald's salon. Half of London society was there. In the 1930s, an awful lot of people thought that there was something to be said for Hitler. All those clean-limbed young men on the march (such co-ordination!). One rather wished there'd been a leader like him in England. And that wasn't just the view of a ninny like me. I recently narrated a BBC documentary series about the War. I was surprised – shocked even – to discover that, as late as 1937, Churchill himself expressed admiration for Hitler's achieve-ments.[138] I ventured to suggest that it might be better to omit the reference. But that cut no ice with the producer. One of the new breed of debunkers.'

'Why not come clean?' G[erald] said. 'You were led by your cock.' Sir H. contrived to look wounded. 'What was it that old nance, Dempster, used to say: "Come to Berlin, where the boys are cheaper than cucumbers"?'

No danger of running into glamorous friends in present day Regensburg: a dull Danube town, its sole raison d'être its own preservation.

Wandered through centre with F. Both preoccupied. G.M. with A.'s disappearance (still no word!). F. with Schleyer's: Might the Right regain power in Germany? Is backlash a genuine prospect? What would become of W. & co if it were?

---

[138] 'If our country were defeated, I hope we should find a champion so indomitable to restore our courage.' Winston Churchill, quoted by Manfred Weidhorn, *Churchill as Peacemaker*, ed. James W.Muller, Cambridge 1997, page 39.

Pointed out that the Right never lost power. Just exercised it differently. $ and DMs rather than jackboots and guns.

SATURDAY, 1 OCTOBER

eve: British Council tribute to Sir H[allam]. Warm drinks, loyal toasts and forced smiles. Boredom alleviated by G[erald]'s fury at not being guest of honour. Claims Sir H. all reflected glory. Played so many kings that people treat him as one.

100% turn-out of British contingent. Plus trio of Germans (2 Goebbelses & 1 Streicher). At last moment, Japanese contingent cries off sick (diagnosis: diplomatic). Very wise unless she wants to bear blame for Pearl Harbour the way Liesl, Manfred & Dieter do for Dunkirk.

Welcomed by Council chairman. Something deeply unattractive about this brand of Brit. All the cultural superiority of imperialist predecessors but none of the missionary zeal. So, instead of blazing trail through tropics bringing Common Law and King James Bible, they host cocktail parties for Ballet Rambert & novelists who don't say Fuck.

Dinner appallingly twee. Menu a quasi-Shakespearean cast list. Eggs Benedick followed by Steak Diana.

Sir H. proved every plaudit justified as he contrived to look touched.

L[uke] to me. 'Just as long as it's not Titus Andronicus pie.'[139]

Smiled blankly. So typical to refer to Sh's most obscure play. Surprised not wearing academic gown.

G. louder & louder as more & more jealous. Discussing politics with Consul. Exchange gradually silenced room.

---

[139] Titus killed Queen Tamora's sons and served them to their mother, baked in a pie.

(Sequence worthy of detailed record).

G. complaining that modern conflicts lack clear moral lines of 2nd World War. 'All those Algerias and Koreas and Vietnams are open to dispute, but the War against Germany was a just war. Those of us who served can look back with pride.'

Hosts embarrassed at insensitivity. Liesl chokes on mouthful of Blanche-d carrots.

G.M. furious at self-deception. G.'s war service 2nd-hand: printing his image on other men's courage so that millions who've never heard of Wavell or even Montgomery have heard of him.

G. proceeded to list his battle honours until Sir H., provoked beyond endurance, pointed out that they were won on Hollywood backlots. G. a war hero who bombed Jerry from the top of a crane at 20th Century Fox.

Bull's-eye!

G. retaliated with long speech of self-justification. 'I was desperate to come home, but Winston himself insisted that I was doing a more useful job among the Yanks. Of course it provoked some antagonism but that was the price I had to pay for serving my country.

Sir H.: 'Yes. People were so obtuse. I remember one newspaper suggesting that you should only ever be filmed in black and white because Technicolor would reveal the yellow of your skin.'

G. furiously to Sir H.: 'Have you ever been in uniform?'

Sir H.: 'Alas no. Although I once played Macbeth in a kilt.'

The British Council ladies coo their delight.

Sir H. warms to his theme. 'I would have made a pretty feeble soldier. The last act of *Hamlet* was always agony. I'm afraid that my war effort was confined to keeping the home fires burning and then taking the productions overseas.'

G.: 'Oh yes. How it must have warmed our lads' hearts as they emerged from the jungle to watch you and Dame Hattie hamming your way through *A Midsummer Night's Dream*.'

Sir H. fixed G. with his gaze and inclined his head just a little lower than necessary to address him. 'Well actually my dear fellow, it was in Singapore that I had the best notice of my entire career, when a young soldier came up to me after a performance and said, "Now I know what I'm fighting for."'

Sir H. genuinely moved as room burst into applause.

Sight of G.'s face almost enough to reconcile me to Quince Jelly & Vanilla Costard.

SUNDAY, 2 OCTOBER

Red-letter day.

1) Ahmet returned in a cloud of mystery. Did not deny my suggestion that he had met R[ed] A[rmy] F[action] contacts and crossed border into East Berlin but claimed that the less I knew the better. Why so cagey? Surely he knows he can trust me? After Havana. After Beirut.

2) Americans and Soviets issued joint declaration calling for Middle East settlement that recognises 'legitimate rights of the Palestinian people'. Israel up in arms. PLO spokesman positive. Expected similar from A. Instead, outraged that no mention of Israeli withdrawal from Occupied Territories. ½ measures worse than 0.

Dinner at hotel with A. and F[elicity]. L[uke] cried off, citing pressure of rewrites. F., after routine disclaimer, admitted relief. Free to discuss the issues without L.'s stifled yawns. Adores him but not blind to his failings, one of which is schoolboy politics. Schleyer case obsessing the whole country but L. barely notices. Film might as well be shot at Pinewood. So insular.

G.M.: 'No, just English.'

F., on other hand, scouring German papers (though, ironically, dependent on L.'s translation skills). Confused by paradox of rightwing attacks on Jews in 30s and leftwing attacks on them now.

Put her straight. Present attacks not on Jews but on Zionists. Not obliged to support Zionism because of Nazi atrocities against Jews. That would be moral blackmail. Besides, Jews themselves not blameless. Some Zionists collaborated with Hitler: willing to sacrifice fellows in order to save family and friends.[140]

F. said that it was news to her.

G.M. pointed out who owned news media.

Explained that Zionism = racism. Where did first settlers come from? Racist countries like England, America and South Africa. Zionism = fascism. Just as Nazism threat not only to Jews but to all civilised people, so Zionism threat not only to Palestinians. A pernicious doctrine that bred hatred & led to Fortress Israel.

Ahmet nodded approval, taking up theme with passion no Westerner could hope to match. 'Zionism is a branch of US imperialism. The Americans refused to take in Jews fleeing from Hitler. So, after the War, to relieve their guilt and under pressure from powerful businessmen, they handed them our country as compensation. The state of Israel is illegal. The UN had no authority to set it up under its own charter. The Israelis went on to seize more land and ignored all UN resolutions that they withdraw. Yet we remain willing to welcome them into a free and independent Palestine in which all people – Muslims, Jews and Christians – can live side by side. So, you see, we do not fight the Jews. On the contrary, the struggle for Jewish liberation and Palestinian liberation is the same, even when it is the Jews who are the aggressors.'

---

[140] Geraldine may be referring to Rezsö Kasztner (1906–57), a Hungarian Zionist who, in 1944, entered into controversial negotiations with Eichmann to allow 1,684 Hungarian Jews safe passage to Switzerland. Prime among them were his family and friends. Kasztner was subsequently assassinated in Israel.

Logic irrefutable whether hearing him speak for 1st (F.) or 1000th (G.M.) time.

F. fired with the enthusiasm of the convert. Especially grateful for the distinction between people and state. Never suspected that, in signing up for film, she'd be embarking on a crash course in international politics. Despite all demands on her time, has learnt more in 6 weeks than in previous 20 years.

F. left early in readiness for 6 a.m. call. Persuaded A. to stay on. My fears that he'd been bored by F.'s chatter and alienated by her background proved unfounded. Declared himself charmed. Teased that F. more politically mature than G.M. on 1st meeting. Replied that more mature full stop (23 rather than 19). Kissed me (on nose!) & warned me not to be jealous (As if!). Thanked me for nurturing her, convinced she might become real asset. Urged me to find out more about uncle in Bonn.

MONDAY, 3 OCTOBER

Are there no depths to which rightwing press won't sink? *Bild* (aka Bilge) has published W[olfram]'s name in list of 12 so-called terrorist sympathisers.

Charge is that, last June, he responded to letter from Gudrun Ensslin's mother requesting money for urgent medical treatment for her daughter & several other prisoners which State refused to fund.

W. sent 3000 marks and pinned letter on Bavaria Studios noticeboard seeking further contributions.

Pure act of charity. Goes some way towards restoring my respect for him – at all-time low after Saturday. (Unaccountably failed to note incident in journal. Group of Turkish immigrants squatted set. W. called on police to evict them, claiming hands tied/backers breathing down neck/no time to relocate. Truth = shameful betrayal of principles.)

p.m.: scene at Munich carnival (W. placing undue emphasis on Unity pimping boys for Brian Howard – and we know why!). Shooting interrupted by police investigating article. How convenient that they should choose moment when journalist visiting set, thereby ensuring maximum humiliation/publicity! Werner ushers her away – too late.

Manfred (Goebbels), playing servant to both masters, offers to assume direction. W. turns him down flat. Scores of extras (masked) mill around tetchily. Frustration. Flare-ups. Tension taking toll.

F[elicity] dissolved in tears. 1st sign of nerves in entire shoot. A record? G.M. and Medhurst to rescue, while L[uke] looks on feebly.

1st thought: Men! Soon disabused. F. & L. have split up (hence L.'s absence last night). Medhurst all cloying sympathy: 'Sure to sort things out' etc. G.M. more reserved. Regret timing (½way through filming when every oz of emotional energy required for work) but convinced it's for the best. Their priorities very different. L. holding her back.

F. agrees. Will always love him but has outgrown him. Feels like child playing with ancient toy to please parents. Nevertheless, been together 4 years. It hurts like hell.

G.M. (ever the older sister) confirms that there's no worse pain. And then to see director/mentor carted off! No wonder she's shaken.

By time W. returned (no surprise: no charges!), light so altered that p.m.'s shooting abandoned. Group of us went back to Serpent's Nest. F. solicitous for W., who closeted himself with L. (symmetry neater than emotions), so took her up to see Ahmet. Found him reading trashy detective novel! (Devising code?).

F. now fully recovered. Amazed us both by force of anger over Wolfram's arrest. Oozing contempt for police state and fascists (using word advisedly) who ran it. Declared that, in Auschwitz, Nazi doctors conducted horrific experiments on prisoners, but Schmidt's government more subtle. Deprived them of essential treatment so as to increase suffering. And when great artist – man of extraordinary compassion (Wolfram??!) – attempted to redress injustice, he was pilloried in press and brutalised by latter-day Gestapo.

A. applauded analysis but insisted that Germany could not be viewed in isolation. Merely an American buffer-zone against democracies of East. Real power resided on Washington–Tel Aviv axis.

F. nodding (agreement? politeness?). Declared that, like W., prepared to give money and not just for medical treatment but to build a society where dissidents aren't tortured: where artists are treated with respect.

A. replied that all contributions valuable but more than money required. F. hanging on his every word. G.M. given no chance, since he cited need to talk to her 1 to 1 and showed me door.

Perfectly understood. In a complex argument, 3rd person a distraction. Nevertheless it niggled. A. remains faithful to Lela (tells me so repeatedly), and yet G.M. and F. cast as sisters. Supposed to be some resemblance. Would his resolve hold when left alone with younger, fresher me?

TUESDAY, 4 OCTOBER

6 a.m. Bus to Augsburg (standing in for Munich) to shoot set-piece procession. Nov 1935, transfer of coffins of 8 Nazis killed in Beer Hall Putsch to newly erected Temples of Honour. Appalling kitsch (Hitler not Wolfram): pylons draped blood-red (for purposes of b/w film, magenta) and inscribed with names of fallen 'heroes'. Whole insidious pomp of 3rd Reich. Diana & Unity's presence ahistorical but appropriate. There in spirit if not in fact.

Set crawling with journalists, invited by Werner. With country in current state of hysteria, any hint of terrorist sympathies could fatally damage prospects. To make matters worse, rumours circulating on Left that film a neo-Nazi apologia. W[erner? Wolfram?] deemed it essential to show nothing to hide.

Reaction already under way. Among drama students/SS men surrounding Hitler, 2 official bodyguards. After yesterday's article, Wolfram bombarded with hate mail – accusing him of masterminding Schleyer plot, threatening to burn down studios. Ironic given that not due to film there for another week.

Scary. Old Nazis never die, just fester on fringes. Admit my concern not wholly disinterested. Among all the letters sent to W., some bound to be addressed to me (known across globe for political stand). Beg Werner to tell me worst, but he alleges I'm not involved. Clearly trying to protect me (or, rather, his investment!). When challenged, he insists that correspondence in hands of police.

A likely story! As if police care what happens to a bunch of radical film-makers – esp after yesterday's visit. G.M. the obvious target. Besides, not even densest neo-Nazi could accuse W. of Leftist sympathies given his latest casting coup: Hannelore Kessel, one of 3rd Reich's greatest stars. Actress chosen by Goebbels to play Josephine in epic *Life of Napoleon* (any resemblance to living dictator entirely intentional). Of course, all traces of Creole background expunged. Like J[esus] C[hrist], Emperor Hirohito and anyone else who needed to be drafted into Nazi cause, Josephine carefully Aryanized.

Opposition to Kessel led by Germans (Dieter & Helmuth). Protest that, while she enjoyed favour, Jewish actors were banned – and worse. True, though predictable that they should single out Jews. Perennial victims. What about G.M.? Contracts cancelled because of support for Palestinians: name at top of Zionist blacklist. But say 0. No wish to muddy waters.

W. either wilfully provocative or culpably naive. Insists that Kessel ideal actress for Fräulein Baum: able to spout Baum's pro-Hitler sentiments without irony or reserve. And yet he must know that hiring 3rd Reich actress not the same as using 3rd Reich building. If he truly believes authenticity all-important, why, when casting one of England's most infamous fascists, did he choose me?

WEDNESDAY, 5 OCTOBER

Day dominated by Kessel.

Scene where Unity given lesson in language & ideology by Fräulein Baum. G.M. not called but on set to watch debut. Joined by Medhurst and several W[olfram] stalwarts.

Kessel: white bun; full lips; limpid blue eyes; disturbingly unlined complexion. Pencil-thin eyebrows sole reminder of starlet past.

No sign of nerves. Single take. Word (& sentiment) perfect. Slight lack of spontaneity, which may be W.'s attempt to highlight robot-like Nazi mind.

Set struck. Returned to trailer. All doubts about K.'s acting abilities scotched. Oscar-worthy perf as 1st meeting with colleagues turned into investigation of wartime conduct. Brits characteristically reticent, so left to Helmuth and Erich to probe Nazi allegiance. K. adopted carefully studied pose of humility tinged with defiance (propagandist past offered invaluable training). G.M. sickened by how easily company duped. Woman a practised manipulator. After all, how did she learn such flawless English?

'I married an American officer at the end of the War. He took me to live in Vermont. I tried to resume my career but as we all know — ' (pout) 'there are so few roles for women of a certain age.' True. Even women-with-a-past parts denied to women with some pasts. For once, Zionist blacklist justified. 'So I returned to Germany, but I found that my fellow countrymen were not as understanding as the Americans . . . I do not say "forgiving" because they ruled at my tribunal that there was nothing to forgive.'

Several of those fellow countrymen began to speak.

(Key exchanges set down to best of my ability. Not only vital historical record but object lesson in performance technique).

Q: 'Are you ashamed of having joined the Party?'

A: 'I'm not ashamed that I became a National Socialist in 1932. I'm deeply ashamed of what the National Socialists went on to do. Try to appreciate what it was like more than 40 years ago. Our lives had no more value than our currency. Then along came this man who said, "Believe in me and I can give you back your self-respect." And he believed in himself so much that he inspired us to do the same.'

Q: 'But didn't you read his policies?'

A: 'He didn't offer any policies. Nothing specific. Just order; discipline; renewal. You were swept up by his rhetoric even before you were swept up by the crowd.'

Horrified to see fellow actors similarly swept up by her subterfuge. Honorable exception: Helmuth, desperate to reassert the truth that had always sustained him.

Q: 'But what about the Jews? Long before the camps, there were the restrictions and the boycotts.'

A: 'You know the old saying, but perhaps our English colleagues (it is too early yet to call them friends) do not. "You can't plane wood without shavings." The treatment of the Jews was worrying, but it seemed so localised, so minor, and so remote. Don't forget that the Jews liked to keep to their own communities. Very few people had close Jewish neighbours. They heard rumours but nothing at first hand.'

G.M. aware of audience being swayed. Determined to cut through the guff.

Q: 'So you yourself never knew any Jews? You were among those who only heard of their fate from afar?'

A: 'That is correct, yes.'

Q: 'Yet you were working in the theatre?'

A: 'Of course I knew some in the theatre. There were so many in the theatre. Too many we used to complain. I'm aware how that must sound. But, in England, don't you complain about the Freemasons among the police and the judges?'

Q: 'Maybe, but we don't murder them.'

A: 'But we knew nothing about the murders. Nothing at all. This was the theatre. People are always on the move. Sometimes they barely have time to pack their bags. Off at a moment's notice to Hamburg or Bremen.'

Q: 'Or Auschwitz?'

A: 'That was during the War. Everything is turned on its head in wartime. People were disappearing every day. Killed in raids or sent to the Front. And, yes, we knew about the camps but only as prisons for dissidents. Didn't you intern people in England too?'

Q: 'So you knew nothing about the deaths?'

A: 'Once again there may have been rumours. But they came so late in the War. There was so little food . . . so much hopelessness. We presumed that people were dying from disease and malnutrition.'

Helmuth poured scorn on her explanation. Kessel turned on him. For a moment, her facade slipped.

'Why should the truth be acceptable to us but unthinkable to you? You with your car bombs and arson attacks and kidnappings. Are your sensibilities really so superior? Believe me, hindsight has never been sharper than it was in 1945. When the Americans released those pictures, it wasn't just the Jews who died.'

Little woman triumphant, turning the set into a sentimental melodrama, tugging at heartstrings as shamelessly as in her films. G.M. rarely felt so alienated from fellow actors. They, at least, should have been wise to her repertoire of tricks. No doubt they would have exonerated Hitler if he'd turned up in dirndl and plaits.

THURSDAY, 6 OCTOBER

Damp page. Clammy skin. Bath so hot that every pore seeping moisture. Small price to pay for feeling purged.

Day of contamination.

Good news is that A[hmet] still trusts me.

My suspicions about his visit to Germany ✓. Planning an action. Waiting to hear whether it's to reinforce kidnap or to challenge settlement. Last week, arranged for Semtex supplies from E. Berlin. Today, drove me to Cologne to order arms. Felt usual queasiness at prospect of casualties.

A. divulged nothing about dealer, so I assumed a comrade. Appalled when ushered into nondescript suburban house crammed with 3rd Reich regalia. Turned to A., but face a 0. As prelude, taken on tour of shrine. Racks of uniforms, flags & emblems, displays of portraits and relics of Party leaders. In pride of place, vast mock-medieval painting of Hitler in character of Parsifal, originally shown in 1937 exhibition of German art.[141] Meanwhile, Stormtrooper songs playing like *Moon River* at Heathrow Airport.

Stifling repugnance, asked how he had built up collection.

Son of woman who fled Czechoslovakia in 1949 while pregnant. As boy, became fascinated by the unmentionable and spent all spare cash on *Wehrmacht* uniforms and Nazi memorabilia (period when SS items obtainable for few pfennigs). Over years, developed hobby into thriving business, supplying companies making films.

---

[141] The inaugural exhibition at the House of German Art, opened by Hitler on 27 June 1937, contained several paintings of the Führer.

My sickening suspicion that one such was *Unity* confirmed when, without prompting, he mentioned current production (fortunately, G.M. incognito). Declared (nudge nudge) that he preferred to handle personal requests. And did just that. G.M. left to explore wardrobe while 2 men disappeared into armoury.

A. returned carrying pistol – spit of ones used by soldiers in film. Took it with him after arranging for rest to be dispatched at later date. Resisted inducements to seal deal by watching secret footage of Führer's triumphant return to Linz.

Challenged A. on journey back about tainted weapons. He doubted that dealer overjoyed about selling to filthy *Türke* but insisted that neither could afford scruples. 'My enemy's enemy is my friend.'

G.M. unconvinced. Felt squalid. Not only buying from rabid neo-fascist but using authentic Nazi guns. A. displayed no such qualms. Guns highly efficient, readily available and hard to trace. Besides, in late capitalist society, there can be no untarnished transactions. Last year, PFLP delegates guests at both communist and fascist rallies in Italy during same week.

Gloom deepened when A. queried my own position on grounds that chief backer for *Unity* a Jew. Forced to examine how far a film discredited by its finance. Take Nazi wartime hit, *The Good Earth*, in which Kessel plays Irish colleen during Famine. She joins Fenians and blows up squad of British soldiers, is captured and tortured by sadistic sergeant but reveals nothing, speaking only to utter scathing denunciation of Britain's so-called Christian values as she mounts the scaffold. In spite of ludicrous last-minute rescue, immensely persuasive presentation of 19thc Republicanism. Saw it with Dermot during NFT's Forbidden Cinema season. Both profoundly moved. Recognised powerful recruiting tool for IRA. And yet nagging question remains: can we accept support (money, guns, images) wherever offered? Or is cause compromised by source?

Sometimes envy Shirley Temple growing up to become ambassador.[142] No urge to remake the world. Just fly the flag and toe the line.

FRIDAY, 7 OCTOBER

A[hmet]'s problems compounded by Mahmoud. Near-biblical contrast between 2 brothers: one a warrior, fighting for rights of his people; other a sybarite, caring for nothing but self.

A. asked M. for help in concealing weapons when they arrived. Perfect hiding place among props to which M. has unlimited access. He not only refused but unleashed storm of resentment against A. Accused him of ruining life, wanting to draft him into struggle that was no longer his.

A. ignored abuse and took out photo he'd kept for just such a moment – photo calculated to fill any father's heart with pride: 6-year-old Rashad in uniform, training for part in driving imperialists from land.

'Look at him,' A. said, 'trying to wipe out the shame of his father.' M. made to grab photo but A. too quick. 'Your whole life says you are no man. You turn your back on your country, your father, your brother. Will you even do nothing for your son? See – ' He rips up the picture. 'He is no longer your son. And you are no longer al Samif. You are no one. I should kill you but there is nothing to kill. Your blood would sully my hands.'

M. hit back with a series of cruel and cynical accusations designed to justify his own betrayal. Quite unworthy of recording here.

eve: Locked into family drama of my own – less violent, equally vile. Dinner at Chinese restaurant which G[erald] with typical

---

142 Shirley Temple (1928–), American child star whose subsequent involvement in politics proved to be happier than Geraldine Mortimer's when she served, first, as American representative to the United Nations and, then, as Ambassador to Ghana.

insensitivity has chosen to 'remind Haroko of home'. She is pregnant. I stare at them blankly, trying to assimilate their 'good
news'. I am 29 years old. Any addition to the family should be
mine not theirs. Is he trying to take that away from me too?

The full indignity of the situation sinks in. Japanese women are
known to be fastidious. How can she endure that old man
labouring sweatily on top of her, his hairy stomach bearing down
on her, all that moral and emotional flabbiness made flesh? Feel
sick but refuse to show it. Offer casual congratulations and beg
them to keep news secret until we have occasion for proper celebration. G. replies that it is too late. Although I am, of course – of
course! – the first to be told, the reason they insisted on taking me
out tonight is exclusive story in tomorrow's *Daily Mail*.

SATURDAY, 8 OCTOBER

Nightmare in which new half-sister thrust into movies by
G[erald]. Throws major Crawford. Wolfram – now in Hollywood –
sacks her and declares that, unless immediate replacement found,
film will be abandoned. G., over-ruling my objections, insists that
I step in & save day for sake of fellow workers. Bosom bound, hair
curled, I am the consummate ten-year-old. Only problem is my
legs which tower over co-stars. So G. fetches saw and prepares to
amputate below knee. At which point I awake.

Sleep impossible and suite oppressive so to dining room for early
breakfast. Empty except for 2 sleek businessmen and Sir H[allam],
who beckons me to table. Find him in elegiac mood. Declares
that, contrary to popular belief, hardest time for old people not
last thing at night when they contemplate death, but first thing in
morning when they've been back among friends only to wake and
find it all an illusion.

½ mind to tell him that lucky not to have my dreams, but
unwilling to add to pain.

p.m.: Filming at one-time Nazi administration building, restored to former infamy with 2 vast swastikas on facade.

F[elicity], whose research borders on neurosis, tells me that Unity born in a Canadian town called Swastika. Can this be true? If so, what does it signify? G.M. born in Maidenhead.

Shooting scene at official reception. Many of the students who frequent the building in its present incarnation employed as extras. Flattered by their familiarity with my work (and inured to inevitable questions about Hollywood) but, when positions reversed, horrified by their lack of political awareness. My enquiries about Schleyer case and what it reveals about government founder on their indifference. Any social concern is reserved for the environment. One young man (Malibu smile) asks: 'What does it matter whether we're Left or Right when, if we continue to destroy the planet, in fifty years time we'll have no future?'

Yes, save the whales. Far more compliant than people.

SUNDAY, 9 OCTOBER

Dynamite interview in *Christ und Welt* in which F[elicity] expresses sympathy with R[ed] A[rmy] F[action] & condones use of violence against repressive, intransigent state. Declares it disingenuous to say direct action does not work. Egs: Castro; suffragettes; even Stern gang. RAF latest in honourable line.

Front page news not arts page ghetto. Printed alongside editorial claiming comments show that sickness of young not confined to Germany.

F.'s approval rating from G.M. ★★★★★, from rest of cast 0. Ring her room (moved to hotel after break-up with L[uke]) to convey support. She invites me round. No regrets about interview, except that the remarks about politics completely overshadow those about film (still has a lot to learn!), but furious that paper failed to print statements about Schleyer's SS past. Advise her against writing letter of complaint.

She relates events of morning. Early visit from 2 W.s: Werner, apoplectic, kept hitting himself over head with rolled-up paper like character in farce; Wolfram, emollient, convinced that all would be forgotten by time film released next year. Forced by Werner to read riot act, but F. swears he winked at her in covert endorsement of her position. W[olfram] himself subject to constraints, so she must speak out on his behalf.

Our conversation interrupted by phone call from F.'s uncle. Rap over knuckles combined with lesson in diplomacy. Surprised by F.'s gymkhana voice: Yes, Uncle; no, Uncle; 3 bags full, Uncle. Even more surprised by unannounced arrival of A[hmet] (Why no call from reception? Is he a regular visitor?). Congratulates her on stand: challenging consensus; provoking debate etc. His (over-) enthusiasm causes mine to wane. Later, when 2 of us alone, he insists that it's a deliberate tactic. Grooming F. for a mission. 'What about me?'

Replies that it might be dangerous. G.M.'s face & politics too well-known. Refuses to say more.

Other front-page news: first confirmation for 10 days that Schleyer still alive. Sent letter appealing to government to negotiate with kidnappers accompanied by photograph holding placard: 'Prisoner for 31 days.'

Nevertheless, looks decently fed. More than his Nazi friends allowed their captives . . . and more than his Zionist allies allowed A. when rounded up during Israeli raid into Lebanon. For 2 days, given no food, made to squat in cell wearing sack over head in which previous victim had vomited.

Think on that Prime Minister Begin. Think on that Herr Schleyer.

MONDAY, 10 OCTOBER

More drama on set.

Henry rounds on W[olfram] for giving him line-readings. Ironic, when some of us yearn for clearer direction. But Henry old school, jealously guards own preserve.

Still, fond of him. Far more incentive to join nightly revelry in bar now that he and Mathilda arrived. As Heidi's grandfather, he was one of my kinder honorary relatives. Treated G.M. with rare respect.

H. making first visit back to homeland for 40 years. Appalled by resurgence of political violence – espousal of 'fascist tactics' by Left. Surprised us all (and frightened Mathilda) by revealing he'd been member of Communist Party in youth.

G.M.: 'You've never mentioned it before.'

H.: 'It's hardly something you discuss with a child, let alone in Hollywood. But we believed in peaceful persuasion . . . in changing society by changing minds.'

G.M.: 'And look where it led you. Straight into the hands of the Nazis.'

H.: 'I think we should change the subject, my dear. I like you far too much to want us to fall out over politics.'

A true ~~citizen~~ subject of his adopted country.

eve: Misery. A[hmet] stood me up for dinner. Rang Mahmoud: no news. Rang F[elicity]: no answer. Early to bed, unable to sleep. Room service (twice).

TUESDAY, 11 OCTOBER

Not called. Nothing to read and no sign of A[hmet]. Hotel suffocating. Unnerved by lift-boy's knowing grin.

Spend morning sightseeing at Nymphenburg Castle, 1-time summer residence of royal family. Strolling through gardens, come across Dora in tears. Against better judgement, ask what's wrong. Catch her off guard. No time for any grit in eye/contact lens guff. Instead, explains that attendant in Stone Hall gave her mirror to see details of ceiling and, holding it up, she caught full view of neck.

G.M. incredulous. Surrounded by life-and-death problems: Ahmet and occupation of homeland; Helmuth and guilt of father; Baader and friends waiting for government action on Schleyer. And Dora distraught about puckered skin!

Then she confesses. Having affair with L[uke]. ½ her age (⅓ more like!). His flesh drum-skin taut; hers subject to subsidence.

Offer curt reassurance, while struggling to check irritation. Is there something in the air that promotes these spring/autumn romances? G[erald] and Haroko all over again – only worse. Whatever L.'s faults, he's undeniably gorgeous. Why Dora? Is he in therapy?

Lose all enthusiasm for castle. Sit in café, sipping hot chocolate and pondering injustice. Gaped at by woman with goitre, who tells me shyly that *Pollyanna* is her favourite film. Stare at her coldly and, when asked for autograph, sign Hayley Mills.[143]

More Dora this eve (sporting choker!) among disparate group in bar. Sir H[allam] regales us with some legendary production from 30s featuring actors with P. G. Wodehouse names whom he invokes as if our personal friends. Interrupted by mysterious old man, whose drably respectable clothes are at odds with his brazenly hennaed hair. He hovers in front of us, keeping hands in pockets (for good reason). Hotel staff converge protectively. No need. Turns out to have been former dresser of Henry's when he

---

[143] English actress who vied with Geraldine Mortimer as the most popular child star of the 1960s. Plans for the two to appear together in a film of Noel Streatfeild's *Ballet Shoes* came to nothing.

acted for Reinhardt.[144] What's more, met Sir H. during pre-war
visit to Germany. Read article about film and travelled to Munich
from Berlin. Persuaded assistant at studios to slip him address of
hotel. And here he is.

Much auld lang syne-ing. Henry draws him out on subsequent
life. Terrifying story of incarceration in Sachsenhausen. Salutary
reminder that, despite compensation camp culture, Jews not only
victims.

Nazi policies never more insane. In theory possible that, had he
achieved world domination, Hitler could have destroyed every
single Jew: confined entire race to museum of anthropology. But
impossible to eliminate homosexuals. Even in Ralf's Lebensborn
homes, 1 in 10 or 20 (or whatever the current statistic) would
have emerged to thwart him. He could wipe out history, culture
and morality, but not nature.

Man (Per) encouraged to join group. Offer of drinks a grotesquely
inadequate response to such suffering. Nevertheless, Per grateful for
any chance to talk. Recites litany of friends from past with Henry,
but refrain of 'dead' spreads gloom. Tries to include Sir H. in recollections, but latter in familiar 'so sorry, my dear boy' vein. Admits
to forgetting everything, even script (rest of us can vouch for that!).
'The only thing I have no trouble with is cast lists. I can tell you
who played the gardeners in a fifty-year-old production of *Richard
II*, whereas I couldn't name the ones who work for me now.'
Per appears hurt. Reading between lines, wonder if they flung.
Face pitted & puffy (plus that hair!) but must have been good-
looking in youth.

---

144   Max Reinhardt (1873–1943), legendary director of the Deutsches Theater
in Berlin from 1904 until the ascendancy of the Nazis in 1933. Unity Mitford
attended his production of *A Midsummer Night's Dream* in Oxford in June
1933. Pryce-Jones page 71.

Poodle in next bay yaps. Per jumps. Knocks over L.'s glass. Profuse apologies. Automatic reflex. Thing for which he hates Nazis most – even above murder and torture – is that they've left him with horror of dogs.

Then he asks Sir H. if he remembers Rolf. Sir H. increasingly wretched at constant 'no's. Per: 'But you must. We took him to Grunewald together. That's when I knew I could trust you because it was so rare for Rolf to warm to someone straightaway.'

Sir H.: 'Yes, of course. Rolf was that charming a.s.m. The one with the sleepy eye.'

Response well-meant but unfortunate. Rolf, it turns out, was a dog.

First thought is to condemn Sir H.'s self-obsession. Then wonder, were I to meet wardrobe staff from Disney now, how many would I recognise?

WEDNESDAY, 12 OCTOBER

In absence of any progress on Schleyer front, Right resorts to ever blacker propaganda. Might expect Schmidt to strive for agreement with kidnappers for that reason alone. Truth = his priorities little different from those of opponents.

Christian Democrats have published 33-page pamphlet designed to show that Left soft on 'terrorism'. It mixes statements – wrenched out of context – from writers (among them, Heinrich Böll, a Nobel prize-winner), academics and theologians. It even includes comments by Schmidt and former Chancellor, Willy Brandt, in section entitled Appeasement. F[elicity] irate that W[olfram] quoted twice. What it fails to mention is that both remarks taken from *The Judge*! Might as well include speech from *Macbeth* and charge Sh with incitement to murder.

Sombre mood on set when Werner brings news that Ralf arrested. Accused of hiding a suspected terrorist in house. Faces jail sentence if convicted.

Story fleshed out later by Liesl (courtesy of mutual friends). Not his Berlin flat but a holiday cottage in Black Forest. Apparently, he hasn't set foot there for 3 years. Lent it to friends, including woman he had an affair with at peace camp. Swears that he had no idea of her R[ed] A[rmy] F[ront] credentials.

Feel so helpless. F. immediately suggests that we send letter, signed by everyone in Unit, demanding Ralf's immediate release and an end to witch-hunts. ✓✓✓ But no response – not even from Germans. Start to despair of fellow actors. Working on film about Hitler, but it might as well be *Peter Pan*.

All they do is sit around in trailer, indulging in idle chit-chat about own responses if faced with friend on run (Teach Yourself Moral Dilemmas). Gerald's contribution a reactionary diatribe about living in a decadent society that distrusts absolutes and places loyalty to individuals above that to country or ideal. G.M. replies that it's no wonder, since placing concepts above people precisely what led to fascism.

L[uke] claims that it's lucky Ralf walked out of film when he did or else even tougher reshooting schedule.

Sick remark, typical of his self-obsession. Dora welcome to him. F. had a narrow escape.

THURSDAY, 13 OCTOBER

Outrage!

Not content with bully-boy tactics on set (3 visits), police search Serpent's Nest. Given anonymous tip-off (probably disgruntled actor) connecting W[olfram] to terrorists. Sweep through house, passing prurient remarks about bedrooms. Unable to grasp alternatives to their own X begat Y lives.

Gun found on top of A[hmet]'s wardrobe. Deeply alarming. He would never have been so careless in past. F[elicity] saves day when, with remarkable presence of mind, she declares that she has pinched it from set for sex games. Police so preoccupied with racist fantasies of Arab A. and Aryan F. that they fail to look for bullets (hidden in bedhead).

Narrowest escape. Thank G that, despite previous cavils: i) A. used same dealer as film and ii) M[ahmoud] refused to assist with storing weapons. 1 extra gun a props department oversight, but not 6. Invite A. and F. for celebration dinner but A. feels that, in circs, he should take her alone. Disappointed but understand.

Another day's shooting lost. Film now seriously behind schedule. Rumours of uncertain cash flow and plan to move us to cheaper hotel. Both given credence on meeting W[erner? Wolfram?] in foyer who claims to have just discovered (oh yes?) that 4 Seasons once the venue for secret fascist society frequented by Hess.[145] Puts whole new complexion on stay. Reply breezily that I never feel oppressed by history. If I did, wouldn't have come to Munich at all.

Shall fight to the last any attempt to downgrade us. Not for self but for Sir H[allam] & G[erald] & D[ora]. Older actors in smaller parts: less clout.

Share lift with Sir H. Explain that I am returning to room to catch up with latest on Schleyer. He comments that 'there is altogether too much news these days' (as if events accumulated to fill slots). Recalls occasions pre-war when BBC announced 'There is no news today.' Wondering whether to link with the ignorance behind his own visit to Nuremberg when reach my floor. Besides, what would be point?

FRIDAY, 14 OCTOBER

Relief that not called. Spend day glued to TV. Last night, Luft-hansa Boeing with 86 passengers on board hijacked on flight from Majorca to Frankfurt.

---

[145] The Thule Society, founded in 1918, devoted to extreme nationalism, race mysticism and anti-Semitism.

According to reports, a previously unknown group claimed responsibility, announcing in Beirut that hijack an extension of Schleyer kidnap, designed to 'secure the release of our comrades detained in the prisons of the imperialist-reactionary Zionist alliance'.

Authorities playing shuttlecock with plane. Allowed brief stops to refuel in Rome and Larnaca, but succession of pusillanimous Middle Eastern governments refused it permission to land. Finally, with fuel running dangerously low, touched down in Bahrain. Statement released in Paris and Geneva by Struggle Against World Imperialism Organisation that Schleyer and all passengers aboard jet will be killed if 11 jailed West Germans and 2 Palestinians held in Turkey not freed by 8 a.m. Sun.

Consensus of opinion that, after playing for time for 5 weeks, government has no choice but to agree to guerrillas' demands. The Nazi will be released but so will Baader and companions.

SATURDAY, 15 OCTOBER

Harder than ever to focus on events 40 years in past. Trailer a cacophony of radio broadcasts. No news. Passengers sweltering on tarmac in Dubai. Government sweating it out in Bonn.

Shooting Goebbels' Olympics party (day for night) at backer's country house outside Munich. ½ cost or 2 x profit? Driveway lined with barebreasted young women holding torches. 1 of them v. distressed. Her aunt (diabetic) and uncle on plane, having won late holiday in church raffle. Assure her that hijackers not monsters. Item on last night's news of their accepting delivery of insulin. Am preparing to discuss broader picture when called to wardrobe.

Wardrobe trailer plastered with photos and sketches of actual party as reference. G.M. and F[elicity] inspect them closely. All at once, pinched shriek (F.). She rips down picture and hands it to me. Hannelore Kessel, instantly identifiable. Not only a guest but deep in conversation with Goebbels.

Stunned.

Interminable takes. Constant battle with noise. Every plane in Germany seems to be flying overhead. Werner: 'Pity they couldn't hijack some of those as well.' Strain tells on worried niece who faints (scorching hair with torch).

10 p.m. Return to hotel in low spirits. Nip to bar for quick pick-me-up to find Kessel holding court to group including Dora, Sir H[allam] and Per (fawning like spaniel). Pathetic how such men seduced by tawdry glamour. Other side of coin from ones who dress up as SS and worship jackboots. No acknowledgement that, while he was being brutalised in camp, she was hobnobbing with murderers.

Determine to ignore her – brain too frazzled for confrontation – but comments on hijack force issue.

H.K.: 'We must fight violence with violence. For every hostage killed, one of the terrorist prisoners should be shot.'

G.M.: 'That's precisely the sort of remark I'd expect from a friend of Goebbels.'

H.K.: 'What friend? I never met him.'

G.M.: (Taking photograph from bag) 'Who's this then? His double?'

H.K.: (On defensive) 'You must excuse my English. When I said that I never met him, I meant that I never met him privately. I couldn't avoid meeting him publicly. He was in charge of the film industry. He could make or break an actress.'

G.M.: 'Sometimes literally.'

H.K.: 'Everyone knew that Dr Goebbels had an eye for the ladies. One day, it turned my way. He invited me to visit his country house. Needless to say, Frau Goebbels was not at home. We walked in the park, at the end of which he made his advances. They were neither subtle nor crude but matter-of-fact. He explained that, if I were to resist, it would spell the end of my career. It was then that I realised I also had power, not much but enough to help my friend, Rachel, a half-Jewish actress who was in hiding in Berlin. I said that I would agree to all his demands – and no matter about my career – as long as Rachel was provided with a safe passage to Switzerland. And she was.'

My need for corroboration forestalled by Kessel's tears. Expressions of regret rise above the sobs: only an actress; knew nothing of politics etc (no wonder G.M.'s own commitment is mocked!). Admits that it may have been a mistake to return to the screen. But so many years have passed. Trusted her fellow actors to appreciate her dilemma.

Dora and Per comfort her. Dora asserts that, if Nazis had invaded, she would have been 1st to play Schiller at Old Vic. Per glares at me as if my accusations were the real crime. Meanwhile, Sir H. ashen. Says he has no right to condemn Kessel. At least she helped her friend. When did he raise finger to save anyone? Reassure him that, on other side of Channel, there was nothing he could do.

Sir H.: 'Oh, but there was.'

SUNDAY, 16 OCTOBER

G.M. the party animal. Straight from Goebbels's to Wolfram's. Amazed that he can find the energy 2 months into filming. What's more, no regular weekend get-together but his annual birthday bash.

Presentation of gifts. My bottle of champagne looks embarrassingly modest beside F[elicity]'s Nancy Mitford 1st edition (appropriated from uncle's library). F. unduly apprehensive. Fears that the author's name not enough to outweigh W.'s well-known antipathy to reading. Pondering last-minute substitution. At which, L[uke] volunteers his head on a plate.

Renate in charge of catering (by default). M[ahmoud] has made cous-cous. Hands bowl (peace-offering?) to A[hmet], who declines it, preferring to share salad with F. Glad to see them so chummy. Know that, despite L.'s predictable inability to conceive of friend-ship between sexes that doesn't involve sex, there's nothing between them. Lela. Lela. Lela. Although for once A. is being equally obtuse with his repeated protestations of fidelity. Why won't he realise that it's not his body I want but his mind? Hard to have both when proximity to his body leaves me utterly inca-pable of thought.

Guests cover spectrum from black tie to tye-n-dye. Not much fraternisation between groups. ½ way through evening, W. ropes *Unity* contingent into game. Players each given scrap of paper on which to write fact about themselves that no one else knows. These then placed in bowl, from which 1 picked out and everyone has to discover who wrote it.

Low-key opening: I'm not wearing any underwear (Renate!); I'm not a natural blonde (Liesl). Game grows increasingly vicious. 3 rounds essential to record.

1) I betrayed a friend. Various wild suggestions. Medhurst even proposes me. Bitch! Then G[erald] claims it must be Sir Hallam. Sir H. protests vigorously, demanding to compare writing. W. declares it against rules and calls on G. to state case.

G. reads it as reference to Sir H. having failed to help Per to escape Nazis. He wanted to come to England (had all necessary papers), but government insisted on sponsor. So he wrote to Sir H., only person he knew (intimately!) asking him to fulfil requirement. But Sir H. refused: v. protective of reputation. Scared to be associated with obvious fairy. Replied, expressing regret but leaving London for lengthy tour. Enclosed copy of *Barchester Towers* as keepsake. Silence broken by W., who asks Sir H. if true. Sir H.: 'Yes. Gerald is always so perceptive. I'm the Judas.' Then walks away.

G. triumphant. Clear that must have prised story out of Per and written words himself. Triumph short-lived as balance of sympathy tilts towards Sir H. for courage of admission.

2) I'm in love with Felicity. Narrow field considering no overt lesbians and so many fags. Obvious from start that it's L. but no one willing to allow him satisfaction of correct guess. He left increasingly disconcerted by bogus candidates, most notably Dieter who delights in being taken for stud. Finally, F. herself proposes W. who responds with one of his most cryptic smiles and asks her to give reasons. Flushing beetroot, she complies:

i: His having cast her in spite of inexperience.

ii: Recent interview in which he deemed it essential for director to be a little in love with leading lady.

iii: Intensity she feels in relationship between Unity and Hitler that she never felt with Ralf.

L., provoked beyond endurance, confesses that paper his. F. furious: 'You're supposed to write something that nobody knows – like the fact that you pick your teeth or you call your penis Billy.'

3) I have killed somebody which I loved. Silence. Admission so shocking that no one dares to suggest attribution. Eventually, L. takes up challenge, naming Wolfram. Repeats open secret that Ernst, W.'s last boyfriend but 1, committed suicide when dumped. General embarrassment. L. defensive: 'No one said it had to be literal.' W. laughs – all teeth. Clear that game over even before Renate summons him to cut (heavily laced) cake.

Speculation on writer continues in private. Misused pronoun points to German, but G.M. suspects double bluff. 100% sure of identity. And, when I look at him standing beside F., he smiles.

MONDAY, 17 OCTOBER

11 a.m.: Coffee with A[hmet]. High drama at Serpent's Nest after I left last night. M[ahmoud] finally roused to action – though typically trivial cause. Attacked L[uke] with fists and cous-cous. Accused him of trying to worm his way into W[olfram]'s bed. Seems that W. took L. to some club, got him smashed and fucked him. Weeks ago. Why rake it up after so long? Sad but on the cards since day 1. Maybe we can now have a little peace.

L. racked with shame. Goes into full 'Lord, was I drunk last night!' routine. Kept trying to justify himself to F[elicity] who, according to A., displayed total indifference. No concern of hers and only hoped it was pleasurable for W.

Surely she can't be that cool? They broke up barely 2 weeks ago. On other hand, never forget our opposing reactions to Dieter's story of Renate stealing from church to pay for W.'s hustlers. G.M.'s disgust v. F.'s admiration.

Is she slightly unhinged?

Revelation confirms suspicions about L.:
1) No one that good-looking can fail to have streak of narcissism.
2) Small step from narcissism to homosexuality.

Reaction confirms suspicions about men:
1) M. absurdly pleased with himself. Violence = virility.
2) Even A. seems to have recovered measure of respect for him – though sorely tested by noises emerging from master-bedroom later that night.

G forbid that I should ever become one of those brittle actresses surrounded by fags, all supposing their lives are unique because different from their parents!

p.m.: After Luke's non-appearance on set this a.m., W. summons him. Inspects black eye and decides that tomorrow, when bruising fully developed, will film scene in which Brian Howard visits Unity after being beaten up by boy she has pimped for him at *Fasching*. L. against it both as actor & writer: 'There are no lines.' W.: 'We don't need them. Your eye and Felicity's face will be enough.'

Meanwhile, back in real world, hijacked plane flown out of Aden and landed in Mogadishu. Schmidt steadfastly refuses to release prisoners. The hostages' blood will be on his hands.

TUESDAY, 18 OCTOBER

Black Tuesday (mark 2).
Personal concerns insignificant in the face of unfolding disasters.

West German commando unit stormed hijacked plane at Mogadishu, killing all 4 guerrillas and freeing passengers. Mixed emotions. Gratitude for safety of hostages tempered by disgust at triumphalism of brass band/brass hat reception at Cologne Airport. Everyone hailing conquering heroes. Not a single expression of regret for 4 fallen revolutionaries. No matter, their names will never be forgotten.[146]

One tragedy follows fast on another. After news of the failed mission reached the 4 comrades imprisoned in Stammheim, they gave up the struggle. 3 of them found dead in their cells: Andreas Baader and Jan-Carl Raspe of gunshot wounds; Gudrun Ensslin from noose tied to window.[147] The 4th, Irmgard Moller, found with stab wounds, although her life not believed to be in danger.

---

[146] Apart from that of Captain Walter Mohammed, the mentally unstable leader of the operation, their names were unknown even at the time.
[147] Raspe did not, in fact, die in prison, but shortly after his arrival in hospital.

Who needs *Oktoberfest*? Whole country in carnival mood. Radio and television given over to constant news broadcasts (poor Sir H[allam]). Telegrams of congratulation pouring in from world leaders, including Begin and Dayan who are keen that tactics should set an international precedent.

All too neat. Suspect subterfuge – although it's as yet too obscure to make out. Might whole stunt have been staged by CIA and Mossad to divert attention from Schleyer and rally support behind their puppet, Schmidt?

WEDNESDAY, 19 OCTOBER

Go through motions on set and off.

F[elicity] commiserates with W[olfram] on Baader's death. W. counters that he barely knew him. He attended productions at Bettlertheater in order to heckle. At first, good publicity but rapidly became an irritant. Story of his life: disrupting the spectacle, but to what end?

F. detects the emotion behind his words. W. a consummate actor, his show of indifference masking deep grief.

A[hmet]'s pain and anger more overt. Mogadishu a serious setback. Western Imperialists, for all their talk of the sacredness of human life, ready to sacrifice a planeload of passengers rather than threaten their interests in Middle East.

Widespread incredulity at official line on Andreas's and Gudrun's 'suicides'. One failed operation no cause for despair; even now the next wave of freedom fighters training in Tripoli & Beirut.

Lawyers who've examined Baader's body fear foul play. How can a bullet wound in the back of the neck be self-inflicted? What's more, how did the most closely watched prisoners in Europe obtain guns?

The authorities respond with scorn. Interior Minister Maihofer tells press conference that people may be sufficiently treacherous to try to pass off suicide as murder. Oh yes? Like South Africans throwing themselves from windows during interrogation?

News this eve that Schleyer found, with throat slit, in car boot in Eastern France. Fitting end to wretched life.

THURSDAY, 20 OCTOBER

a.m.: Eggshell mood on set. 2 line scene where Diana and Unity, window-shopping in *Marstallplatz*, spot large portrait of Hitler haloed by pictures of Christ. W[olfram] demands complex series of reflections despite Gerhard's insistence that it's impossible. Eventually throws himself on ground, raving about conspiracy against him. Everyone unnerved. F[elicity] tearful. Werner calls ½ hour break. Return to find W. in powwow with G. as if nothing had happened. Only trace of outburst the odd sniff.

Tantrum effective: G. rejigs lighting; scene (+ reflections) in single take.

p.m.: Not called but prefer set to solitude.

Scene where Julius Streicher plays host to Unity and, as after-dinner entertainment, orders Jews to cut lawn with teeth. Seems far-fetched to me but F. produces well-thumbed Unity biog and points out ref.[148]

Paper one thing, celluloid another. W. increasingly impatient with Dieter's qualms about character. Gives his usual 'Find Streicher in Dieter' spiel, which must make more sense in German for, as cameras roll, Dieter springs into action, kicking Jews to ground, stamping on fingers, pulling hair and spitting in faces.

Howls of rage from extras. One forcibly restrained from punching Dieter on nose. Yet another scene abandoned (although Wolfram later assured F. that enough footage in can).

148 Pryce-Jones page 112.

Dieter in lightning transformation from raging bully to gibbering wreck. Apologises abjectly to victims before retreating to trailer where he sits, head in hands, alternately berating and justifying self. Lays blame squarely on W., who worms out weakness in order to exploit it. The darker the secret, the greater his power. Answers F.'s protests by asking why else he cast him as Streicher. No looka-like like Henry or Ralf. Warns us all to be on our guard.

Falteringly explains that W. aware of his interest in sado-masochism (German accent makes it sound reassuringly acade-mic). After years of analysis, traced it back to his father, a onetime SS officer, who beat him for the least transgression. Lengthy ritual in which D. made to fetch cane, kiss it, bare buttocks and then, after x many strokes, kiss father's hand. At which point, in spite of pain, always felt an intense sense of peace. The only intimacy they ever shared.

All his adult life, he has defined himself by contrast to the Nazis. Convinced that a refusal to acknowledge the shadow side (in selves as well as society) was what led to Auschwitz, he was deter-mined to confront it. Now fears, however, that, far from neutral-ising murderous instincts, he has indulged them (aggression still aggression however codified). What else can explain the excite-ment of playing Streicher: the brow-beating; the horse-whip; the intimate examination of young girls? So (and, here, he drains voice of all but compulsion) is his freedom from guilt a historical accident? On what side of fence – or wire – would he have stood if 20 years older?

G.M. no help. As a rule, little patience with those who over-emphasise role of sex in human behaviour. Bourgeois attempt to put history on couch. But, in this case, have to admit a perverse logic. Silence broken only when Sir H[allam], seemingly lost in crossword, lowers paper and announces that, if D. having trouble with part, happy to explore it with him.

Typical generosity! Such a celebrated actor that it's easy to forget he's also a distinguished director. Hard to imagine G[erald] offering helping hand to younger colleague. D. gratefully accepts and leaves after arranging session with him for tonight.

FRIDAY, 21 OCTOBER

Sir Hallam: last word in yesterday's entry & first in today's. In hospital, recovering from stroke. G.M. privy to whole story. Sworn to secrecy by Dora, who was in turn sworn to secrecy by Dieter. Big mistake. But then some explanation required by Nazi uniform and prostrate knight in adjoining room.

Sir H.'s offer of assistance less altruistic than it appeared. Boils down to reconciling Dieter to violence in character by offering himself as willing (and worthy) victim. So undignified. So squalid. A man of Sir H.'s age and status. D. (at least according to self) initially reluctant but Sir H. very persuasive. Lay on floor and directed D. to stand astride him in costume, doling out blows and insults ('You dirty queer' etc), which, in spite of D.'s tastes – and, adding to his confusion – he enjoyed. This triggered moment of ecstasy in Sir H., after which he collapsed. Dieter tidied him up as best he could and ran next door.

Long discussion with Dora. Shock short cut to intimacy. Agree that nothing more perverse than someone willingly submitting to jackboot, parodying fate that might have been his.

Ponder attraction of fascism to fags.

1) Is it search for perfect man? If so, does it help to picture him in uniform, all complexities ironed out?
2) Is it militarism: the all-boys-together ethos?
3) Is it exaggerated pose of masculinity? Only ambiguity the cocked pistol in pants?
4) Is it essence of everything unwomanly? Worshipping the leather, steel and sweat?

Dora contends after years of experience, 'even more than you my dear', that most men homosexual but refuse to acknowledge it, taking refuge in homoeroticism: all-male environments of sports-field & army & club. Fascist thuggery just impulse at its most extreme.

Amazed to find her capable of such analysis – even if, tellingly, it's confined to private sphere. Repeat promise not to breathe word (and mean it!). Feel strangely protective towards Sir H. as towards crumbling village church. Make donation in spite of it standing for everything I despise.

Are my contradictions showing too?

Frustrating evening trying to catch up with A[hmet] and F[elicity]. Both nowhere to be found.

SATURDAY, 22 OCTOBER

SUNDAY, 23 OCTOBER

Why do I write this journal? Certainly not for posterity. Mother and Dermot[149] given strict instructions. So is it egotism? The girl who grew up confusing people's readiness to listen to her with having something to say? No! No, the answer is simply to preserve a record. With childhood taken away from me, determined to keep control of what remains.

So painful events must be noted for sake of coherence.

AHMET AND FELICITY ARE SLEEPING TOGETHER.

Not lovers. They made that quite clear. He loyal to Lela and her heart fixed on Wolfram. Such nonsense! If trying to spare my feelings, couldn't they have dreamt up a more plausible story? Besides, if he is not in love with her, why isn't he sleeping with me? If it's comfort he's after, then G.M. the obvious candidate. Or am I past it? Must I step straight from child to older-sister roles both on & off screen?

A. hints once again that he's grooming her for mission (secrecy safest all round). My own fault for training her too well. I'm left with the trudge work while she shares in the glory.

Feel as if a wet towel has been stuffed inside my head and slowly squeezed.

MONDAY, 24 OCTOBER

Backlash already evident. One of the grips, spending day off cycling in countryside, stopped to ask directions in a village. Pulled from bike by 2 men. Mob gathered, brandishing sticks. Serious injury averted only by arrival of priest. What was his crime? To judge by taunts, simply having long hair.

---

[149] Geraldine Mortimer's executors at time of writing.

Welcome to Federal Republic of Germany: a miracle of post-war plastic surgery.

Walking through part. Ironically – no, inevitably – W[olfram] claims to love what I do. Finally getting his blank-page Diana. At least it makes sense of theories that link fascism and automation.

Suffering from delayed shock: nothing else can explain my behaviour. Propositioned by man in street (incongruously fluent English). Accept. Drive to estate on outskirts of city. All breeze blocks and billowing washing. On entering flat, hit by dank smell of boiled cabbage. Bedroom/sitting room off-limits (no explanation offered). I perch on kitchen stool and study railway posters on walls.

Man (remains anonymous) disappears. Returns stripped to grey vest and mottled pants, from which giant belly protrudes like tumour. Moves to stove and, without uttering a single word, begins to cook.

Bracing self to say that not hungry and anxious to leave when pre-empted by banging on wall.

Man sheepishly admits to presence of wife. Lost use of legs – and denied him rest of body. Bed-bound so nothing to fear.

Express regret but insist that I must go. Pleads with me to change mind. Explains that he's been with no one but whores for years and is behind on rent. Begs me to take off bra while he cooks wife's meal.

Unable to decide whether stupefied by request or dangerously attached to own despair; nevertheless I agree. Clutching on to clothes (cleanliness not guaranteed), I stand shivering, while he keeps one hand on pan, intermittently flipping sausage, and other down pants.

With short gasp – and spreading stain – he removes hand, switches off gas, and picks up tray. Barely looks at me as I fumble with dress and depart.

Aching to escape. Even England's grey and murky land preferable to this. Return by proxy tomorrow when we shoot 1st Swinbrook[150] interior in studio. At least end is in sight. Memorise revised shooting schedule. 8th November: flying home.

TUESDAY, 25 OCTOBER

Schleyer given state funeral in Stuttgart. Honour hitherto reserved for former Presidents and Chancellors. Authorities determined to imbue him in death with dignity lacking in life.

Friction on set over whether to observe 3 min silence being held nationwide at start of service. Majority of cast & crew opt for business as usual. Bavaria bosses and B[ücher?] worry about bad press should story slip out. Werner proposes compromise 90 secs. Argument academic since W[olfram] decides to shoot wordless scene. Long (3 min+) pan over drawing room as family vegetates after dinner.

Know he won't use more than 10 secs (if that!) in final edit, nevertheless, can't help admiring tactic.

F[elicity] keeping distance. Guarded over non-love affair with non-lover (currently in E. Berlin). Confides that unforeseen problem of break-up with L[uke] is loss of tame translator. Dependent on Dieter for radio report that surviving R[ed] A[rmy] F[action] member, Irmgard Moller, categorically denies attempt to kill herself or existence of suicide pact in Stammheim. Insists that she was reading until around 3 a.m. when she heard sounds of banging & screeching. Next thing she knew, she was lying on stretcher covered in blood.

Government story exposed as tissue of lies!

---

150 The Mitford family house in Oxfordshire.

WEDNESDAY, 26 OCTOBER

Second marriage. Only this time no cloud over ceremony. Symbolism lost in reshoot.

L[iam] F[inch] flew out on day-release from filming *David Copperfield* for BBC. Taking part in Britain's favourite pastime: pastiching the past. Strides about set as if he'd been appointed Director General not villain in tea-time serial.[151]

Everything proceeds according to plan. Only blip W[olfram]'s distribution of new dialogue ½ hour before scene. Claims it's to pre-empt fake emotions.

Nerve-racking but true.

Fake emotions saved for A[hmet] and F[elicity]. Smile, smile, smile. A. hints that time for action approaching. He has been consulting with various interested parties (hence yesterday's visit). Mocks my suspicion that he may have been planning to disrupt Schleyer funeral. Stuttgart a city under siege. No desire to undertake suicide mission: Palestine needs its warriors alive.

Urgent message at hotel to ring Elaine. Extraordinary news. Seems that word of dailies has reached Truffaut who's interested in me for next film – a French Resistance saga with G.M. in plum role of Englishwoman parachuted behind enemy lines. Maybe *Unity* not a one-off after all?

THURSDAY, 27 OCTOBER

5 a.m.: F[elicity] and I creep out of hotel and take train to Stuttgart (what with Schleyer on Tues and Andreas, Gudrun and Jan-Carl today, fast becoming funeral city). Tell no one – not even A[hmet], who we suspect (rightly) would try to dissuade us. Resolve not to think about disruption on set. Our first responsibility is to fallen comrades.

---

151 Finch played Steerforth.

Impetus came from F. Eager to go both for own sake and for W[olfram] who can't risk such a public gesture. Plus, need to boost numbers. Fear that people will be too intimidated by trigger-happy police to attend, leaving authorities to make mileage out of lack of mourners. In the event, we needn't have worried. Over 5000 supporters brave army of pigs.[152]

Eerie, nervy atmosphere. Police helicopter overhead, drowning out much of eulogy. Police marksmen dotted among gravestones like resurrection of the damned. Most of the mourners wear scarves or wide-brimmed hats to frustrate police photographers who snap away, creating next generation of martyrs. Some carry placards, accusing authorities of torture. As coffins are lowered, a small group, dressed from head to toe in black, unfurl banner stating baldly *They were murdered*. At end of ceremony, when Pastor Ensslin raises fist in solidarity, I feel confident that struggle is entering its final stage.

Surprised by degree of personal recognition: intrusive from reporters, with TV cameras trained on me from cemetery gates to grave; inspiring from mourners, as constant stream of comrades walk up to shake my hand. To them, not child star striving to make comeback but serious actress who sacrificed career to work for Revolution. Several with tears in eyes as they thank me for just being there. F. a mere extra. G.M. (apart from coffins) in leading role.

Clashes inevitable. Police, who kept low profile prior to ceremony, make presence felt at end, setting up road blocks and inspecting papers. Anyone who objects is immediately arrested. Woman behind me desperate. Confides that she's a teacher and, if her identity is discovered, may be dismissed under neo-Fascist laws as

---

[152] Official sources estimated the crowd at between five and seven hundred with a further two hundred reporters and photographers. They were heavily outnumbered by the police.

Enemy of Constitution. Remonstrate with officers on her behalf and, after refusing to back down, am hauled off to police station. Subjected to full force of state oppression. Porcine policemen – all guns and paunches – insist that I am stripped and searched for weapons. Hand me over to bull-dyke colleagues with hard, invasive fingers, while they ogle behind two-way mirrors. Constant clicking of cameras as they capture each humiliation for their locker-room enjoyment. F. meanwhile alerts Studios and, after due representation, I am released. No apologies, just sly, knowing smiles.

Keen to join protesters gathering outside station for march through city – 2 or 300 heroes defying massed ranks of police – but F. explains that she has given word we will go straight back to Munich. To her surprise even W. hostile, his only concern the wasted day.

Return to universal censure. No sympathy for ordeal – not even from A. who accuses me of jeopardising everything (it might help if I knew what!) for sake of side-show. Barely manage to mollify him when forced to contend with Luke, who turns up unannounced in F.'s suite. Baffled how anyone over six can have such a sanitised view of life. A. and I escape, only to part like chambermaids in the corridor.

New message from Truffaut. Can I fly to Paris one day next week for talks?

Yes, yes & yes.

Strange mixture of elation and emptiness. Listen to stomach (literally) and ring Room Service (for meal!).

FRIDAY, 28 OCTOBER

a.m.: Not called. Black looks at breakfast. Attempt damage limitation with Henry and Dora.

Sir H[allam] flown home (frightening how soon he has been

forgotten!). Bump into agent's assistant collecting luggage. Sharp suit. Sweaty palms. 'Quick cuppa?' Hands me his card.

Dinner with F[elicity] in suite.

Discloses details of A[hmet]'s plan. Swears me to secrecy. A. would be murderous if he knew she'd breathed a word – even to me.

Their visit to Olympic Stadium last week not idle tourism.

Memorial Service on Sun for Israeli athletes liquidated by Black September 5 years ago. Imperialists flying in from across globe. Schmidt and his lot. Dayan and ½ Israeli cabinet. Representatives of all governments incl Our Man – her uncle – in Bonn.

(Now I understand why A. so incensed by Stuttgart trip – and so much more concerned about F.'s presence than mine).

Uncle asked F. to accompany him. Neat mix of private reunion and public relations. Chance for HMG to invest stuffed-shirt image with film-star glamour. Quandary over whether to withdraw invitation but decided to proceed as planned. Typically English resolve to keep up a front.

Rigorous security. Having bungled events so badly 5 years ago, the authorities are determined that everything should proceed without a hitch. Nevertheless diplomatic pass = free access. F. sitting in VIP compound, two rows behind Germans and Israelis. Instructed to have device primed before she enters ('Keep it under your hat' – Ha!). A few minutes into service, she will complain of sickness, remove hat, place it under seat and make swift exit to washroom.

A. has warned her that she has 2 minutes to escape blast.

G.M. surprised at time lag. Used to be a matter of seconds.

Fear that F. so committed to mission that blind to consequences. Plan is for her to rush back in hysterics on hearing explosion (an actress after all!). G.M.: 'But, surely, the device will be easily traced?' F. adamant that all eventualities have been covered. Hat made for her by Studio. She takes it to hotel where, unknown to her, A. inserts device. In all the excitement, no time to check whether slightly – ever so slightly (weighs a mere ½ lb) – heavy. A. and F. spotted passionately kissing on steps as embassy car comes to collect her. Another foolish English girl seduced by wily Arab (an actress after all!). Ahmet leaves immediately for E. Germany. Later that day, statement will be issued in Beirut claiming responsibility for attack and exonerating F.

Only trust that it will be so straightforward. F., supremely confident, declares that it's the perfect action. Quotes A. on killing single Jew in street more effective than killing 100 on battlefield.[153] She feels immensely proud to have been chosen. For years, a victim of Zionist propaganda that Munich deaths a Jewish tragedy. Now that she has understood plight of Palestinians, she knows the truth. 11 Israeli athletes revered as martyrs, but what of the 400 Palestinians slaughtered 3 days later in reprisal? Where is the memorial to them?

'It's time to strike a blow against the whole panoply of imperialzionism and Western governments that are complicit in its crimes. The Fascists must be defeated. Remember the British agent who had a chance to assassinate Hitler before the War but turned it down because the Foreign Office thought that it wasn't cricket? Well I shan't make that mistake. I'm a woman. I don't even know the rules of the game.'

SATURDAY, 29 OCTOBER

a.m.: Not called. Shadow F[elicity] around studios. Worried she may let slip remark, incriminating herself, incriminating A[hmet] or, even worse, incriminating innocent party.

---

153 The sentiment is adapted from Ahmet Samif's mentor, George Habbash: 'We think that killing one Jew far from the field of battle is more effective than killing a hundred Jews on the field of battle because it attracts more attention.'

'Her story sounded so far-fetched that I paid no attention. I presumed it was a joke . . . a fantasy . . . a tease.'
To Geraldine Mortimer, the Dick Van Dyke[154] award for least convincing performance of the year.

Shoot scene in Swinbrook lavatory. Unity twisting pet snake around chain to intimidate governess. Snake determined to uncoil. Finally, W[olfram] loses patience and orders it to be placed on top of cistern with head dangling over edge.
F. petrified. Dreading scene. Pleads 1) with L[uke] to cut it out, but he too taken with symbolism; 2) with W. to use a double, but he deplores sham. Warns both – warns everyone – that they are courting disaster. Not governess who will faint but her. In the event, her fears unfounded. Holds snake as if hypnotised. Drapes it around neck and then puts it on cistern before withdrawing to wait for scream.

p.m.: Sitting room. Scene between Unity and Jessica as they speculate on ordering each other's execution. Politics as melodrama. Little different from a child's 'You'll all be sorry when I'm dead.' Nevertheless, deeply poignant to one aware of the context. May be sentimental but I detect a new assurance in F.'s acting: clarity of purpose based on an understanding of what lies ahead.

Return to hotel. Filming seems futile when unsure whether it will ever be completed. If only the service could be postponed another week. Despise myself for putting career concerns first. Proof that I am as bourgeois as the rest. Resolve to read Gramsci as corrective. Persuade maid to let me into F.'s suite. Take back book and several others that may be of use.

---

[154] This appears to be a reference to the American actor's phoney Cockney accent in Mary Poppins.

eve: Attend W.'s regular weekend party. Expediency overrides distaste. Already living in retrospect (alibis, explanations, statements to press). Nerves so strained that I share a joint with Liesl, Helmuth & Erich. Vision remains disconcertingly sharp.

2 W.s [Wolfram and Werner] elated after screening of rough assembly. Sure that *Unity* will be triumph. W. already planning next film: liberal newspaper publisher caught between rival demands of radical journalists & reactionary printers. Suspect thinly disguised autobiography even – especially? – given that publisher a woman.

(Huge relief among old guard that subject domestic. Clear that they find current hotchpotch a trial).

Party in full swing. Luke ecstatic to have F. at side – and all over him. Her conduct surprising in view of a) her taboo on displays of public affection and b) passionate love scene she's due to perform with A. tomorrow afternoon.

A. uncharacteristically edgy. Is he afraid she might give game away? Does she talk in sleep? How would he know? No, mustn't go down that road. It's not my life that's about to be put on line.

Tell him he looks tense. Cite skills as masseuse. Feel cheap. To my amazement, he takes up offer. Invites me to his room. We fuck – no way to describe it as making love. Uses me as if oiling his gun. Then rapidly falls asleep. Grunts. Snores. (His breathing used to be so gentle.) Try to mould myself to his body without success. Creep out of bed, pick my way through fag-end of party and leave.

Feel bruised, inside and out. Share taxi to hotel with Dora. She drunk, deserted: 'That's life. We order champagne but have to settle for beer.' Decline to respond to her chatter and try to work out why A. was so brutal. Was he acting like homeopath, treating me with small pain to ease greater pain of separation? Or was he using me like whore to relieve frustration at Felicity spending night with Luke?

SUNDAY, 30 OCTOBER

This has to be final entry. Journal dynamite. Attempt already underway to portray Felicity as lone wolf, but everyone and everything under suspicion. Who knows what police may impound? Shall write today – must write today – and then mail it to Mother's, where everything safe.

Action aborted. Watched events unfold on TV. By chance, saw precise moment of detonation. Camera on Felicity as she and uncle walked through turnstile. Then Felicity on camera as bomb exploded and bits of her (or others) splattered over crowd. Mayoress of Munich's dress like butcher's apron. Picture blurred as though ageing star photographed through gauze.
4 dead: Felicity, her uncle, one of his security men and diplomat from Poland. 2 others critically injured: Deputy Ambassador and 2nd security man.
What went wrong? Was bomb primed? Was pin unstable? Was it dislodged in the crush?
No reliable news, just the lies of TV bulletins and rumour-mill of hotel. In the end, against all practice, ring Serpent's Nest and ask for Mahmoud. Whoever answers sounds as though on other planet. Promises to fetch him. After 10 mins of crackling emptiness, put down phone.
Listen to World Service. PFLP have issued statement, mourning martyr and promising that struggle will continue until victory assured.

Must stop. Frightened every footstep may be a policeman on way to search room. Can I risk handing package to reception or should I wait for a.m. and take it to Post Office myself?

Is Ahmet safe? Will I ever see him again? Will he make contact or must I wait for another strategic location? Why did he reveal nothing about mission? Was he trying to keep me from danger?

Does that mean that he loves me? He placed Felicity in danger. Does that mean that he didn't love her? Why, after all that's happened, should that make me happy? So many conflicting emotions. No wonder we struggle with those of Diana, Unity and Hitler when we can never be sure of our own.

Was Felicity truly committed to Palestine? Did Ahmet use her? Allowing her to die would seem to be an answer. Yet, in his tradition, all who die for a just cause are promised a place in Heaven. What greater gift can you give someone you love?

Did he love her?

Did he?

Did he?

5

Carole Medhurst

in correspondence

Throughout 2001, I sought out the remaining participants in the Unity story. If distrust stood in my way with the German actors, death did so with the British. Sir Hallam Bamforth died in 1984, days before starting work on the one role for which he remained perfect casting, the Abbot in Hugh Hudson's The Trappist. Unlike many of his contemporaries, he has suffered no decline in reputation (witness the £2500 recently fetched at auction by his funeral service-sheet adorned with doodles by Dame Hattie Lanchester). Geraldine Mortimer was killed in Warsaw in 1986, while shooting a car chase for Necropolis, the film she was making with Gérard Depardieu for Andrzej Wajda. In a moment of bravado, and with a nod to her youth, she dispensed with the services of a double. Unlike Unity, the aptly named Necropolis was released in spite of its leading actress's death. Her father survived her by two years. Having finally secured his knighthood, he retired to the country where, according to his widow, the protracted legal wrangling over Geraldine's estate hastened his end. Dora Manners, though living, is no longer lucid, having contracted Alzheimer's just when her appearance in the BBC docusoap, Old Timers, had won her a new generation of fans.

Contacting Carole Medhurst posed problems of a different order. As a leading Hollywood producer, then working with another Unity survivor, Liam Finch, she was shielded by an army of assistants who placed writers on a par with stalkers and the press. Through the good offices of a mutual friend, Marie-Olivier Septier, I was able, however, to obtain Medhurst's private e-mail address, establishing a means of communication whose blend of informality and distance seemed eminently suited to my approach.

Despite dredging her memories, Medhurst came up with little of substance about Felicity. The favourite-sister status of the characters they played had not been reflected in any off-screen intimacy. Her chief concern, then as now, was with Felicity's reverence for Geraldine Mortimer. This helped to redress the balance since, perhaps on account of my gender (which, according to Geraldine's journal for 7 September 1977, outweighs any other consideration), I have explained Felicity's conduct largely by her relationship with men. Notwithstanding the bias, of which she makes no secret, I find Medhurst's theory persuasive. Her animus against Geraldine is informed by a long-held suspicion of political activism, which has hardened in Hollywood. Nevertheless, her depiction of the international terror network in general and of Ahmet Samif in particular destroys any romantic notion with which I might still invest the figure of the terrorist. Samif's cynical denial of the Holocaust has an even deadlier ring twenty-five years on, when a key weapon in the extremists' armoury is Mein Kampf, *which they cite not as a protest or a provocation but an inspiration, displaying a blithe disregard for their own Semitic heritage.*

In her portrait of a privileged young woman engaged in radical politics, Medhurst offers me a further analogy. But, although her doubts about Geraldine's sincerity echo my own about Felicity's, I cling to the hope that, beneath all the sloganizing, Felicity felt a genuine anger about the abuse of power and the condition of the oppressed. Some years ago, a common formula adopted by apologists for militant activists was that 'their hearts are bigger than their heads'. It is my understanding of Felicity and Geraldine – and, for that matter, Unity and Diana – that, in their readiness to ride roughshod over others, their egos were bigger than both.

From: Michael Arditti <michaelarditti@btinternet.com>

Sent: Monday, May 14, 2001 8.04 pm

To: cm2000@sprintmail.com

Subject: Information

Dear Carole,

You don't know me but I am a friend of Marie-Olivier Septier (who sends kisses). I was also a friend of both Luke Dent, who died last month, and Felicity Benthall, and was the third member of the trio who, back in 1976, conceived of a play based on the life of Unity Mitford.

Last year, I was shown a copy of Geraldine Mortimer's journal for the period during which you were filming *Unity*. It forced me to reconsider the whole saga, something that I had resisted (perhaps too emphatically) in the past. I had hoped that Geraldine's account might help me to solve the mystery of Felicity's motives, but it differs so markedly from Luke's that it has merely left me more confused.

It may be the novelist in me but I remain convinced that it is possible to determine the truth behind people's actions. With that in mind, I am trying to make contact with various survivors of the *Unity* debacle (I trust that you see it in that way). Marie-O has often spoken of you and your participation in the film (one that is well documented by Geraldine) and I am hoping that you may be able to share your memories with me, either by mail (e or snail), by phone or in person. I am quite prepared to fly to Los Angeles should you consider it appropriate.

As previously stated, I am a novelist, not a journalist. If – and it's by no means certain – my researches ever appear in print, they will take the form of a sober assessment of both the film and the surrounding furore.

I do hope that you will feel able to assist me in this project.
Yours, with best wishes,
Michael Arditti

Subj:	Re Information
Date:	05/17/01 16: 01: 08 Pacific Daylight Time
From:	cm2000@sprintmail.com (Carole Medhurst)
To:	michaelarditti@btinternet.com (Michael Arditti)

Sensitivity: Confidential

Help!

I was aware somewhere in the back of my mind that Marie-O had
a friend associated with the *Unity* abortion (I use the word clini-
cally), although I must confess that I'd forgotten exactly how. I
remember being struck by the coincidence until I realised that,
since Marie-O knows everyone, it's no surprise that she knows us!
Please give her my love. I owe her an e-mail.

Like you, I've spent the last twenty years or so trying to erase
Unity from my brain. It was without doubt the most miserable
experience of my professional life (and there've been a few!). I
went in with such hopes. It was my first movie role and I was
working for one of Europe's top directors. I had never been enam-
oured of the Mitfords, who seemed to me to represent a nostalgic
ideal to which the British are all too prone – a nursery world of
private codes and arcane nicknames, where perverse behaviour
can be laughed off as eccentricity and ideological conflicts passed
off as sisterly spats. Nevertheless, I felt sure that Meier, with his
continental sensitivity, would cut through the cant. What's more,
as one still wedded to a communal ideal, I was as impressed by his
methods as his skills. His reliance on the same pool of actors
amounted almost to a cottage industry.

I adored the script – incidentally, I'm truly sorry to hear about

Luke. He was such an attractive man. I think half the unit was a little in love with him (no, that would be a confession too far!). Shooting in England went smoothly but, from the moment we arrived in Germany, as I expect you've already discovered, everything began to unravel. I'd like to give you what help I can – not least to balance Geraldine's distortions. I'm amazed to hear that she was keeping a journal and somewhat apprehensive to find that I'm in it. Would you be able to send me the relevant entries? (I suggest that you cut and paste as I'm having trouble with attachments). Time, as ever, is the big problem. Marie-O is always so generous with hers that she assumes all her friends will be the same. My company is on the verge of a major development deal. We're expecting the go-ahead any day. So forgive me if my contribution is rushed. What's more, I'd prefer not to serve up my memories cold but, if you ask specific questions, I'll do my best to answer them.

Cheers!

Carole M.

From:	Michael Arditti <michaelarditti@btinternet.com>
Sent:	Friday, May 18, 2001 9.46 am
To:	cm2000@sprintmail.com
Subject:	Re Information

Dear Carole,

I'm delighted that you can spare the time from your hectic schedule to respond to my queries. You're quite right. I can't expect a twenty-year-old stream of consciousness. So I've compiled a list of questions which I hope will prod your memory in a useful direction, but please don't feel restricted by it should you wish to raise anything else.

I don't have Geraldine's journal on disc, so I'll Fed-Ex the pertinent months to you as soon as I've transmitted this e-mail. That way they should be with you by tomorrow.

Questions:

1) The biggie. Why did Felicity do it? What was she trying to achieve? Did she consciously commit suicide? Did you have any hints from her behaviour as to what she had in mind?

2) Was Felicity's action in any way linked to the subject of the film? At the time, there was much nonsense talked about demonic possession and so forth. That's patently absurd. But might she have over-identified with political extremism in the course of playing the part?

3) Was the atmosphere on set unduly political? In the letters that Luke wrote to me, he barely mentions outside events and yet Geraldine's journal is full of them. Which more accurately reflects the general mood?

4) Did you see any evidence of Felicity's obsession with Meier? Was she, in fact, as obsessed as both Luke and Geraldine suggest? Might it have been to curry favour with the director that she planted the bomb?

5) Would you flesh out your own relationship with Geraldine? There are various caustic references to it in the journal, as you'll see for yourself tomorrow – or as soon as you have some free time.

6) Can you remember anything about Ahmet Samif? He obviously exerted an enormous influence on both Felicity and Geraldine. Was Felicity attracted to the man or to the cause?

7) Any other business. If there is anything – anything at all – that you think I may have omitted, please don't hesitate to put me straight.

Thanking you in anticipation.
Yours, with best wishes,
Michael Arditti

Subj: Re Information
Date: 05/22/01 18: 08: 06 Pacific Daylight Time
From: cm2000@sprintmail.com (Carole Medhurst)
To: michaelarditti@btinternet.com (Michael Arditti)

Sensitivity: Confidential

The journal arrived safely. Many thanks for its prompt dispatch. I've barely had time to turn the pages but already a pattern is starting to emerge: such egotism! Talk about the Me Generation. I know it's a diary but, even so, you'd think she'd be a little more receptive to the wider world.[155]

I've glanced through your list of questions. It's quite a tall order, but I'll see what I can scrape together as soon as I have a spare hour. In the meantime, if you want a better idea of where I'm coming from, you might like to pick up a copy of my autobiography.[156] I wouldn't recommend it but, fortunately, Oprah did!

I'll be in touch,

Carole

From: Michael Arditti <michaelarditti@btinternet.com>
Sent: Thursday, May 31, 2001 11.23 am
To: cm2000@sprintmail.com
Subject: Very Worried

Dear Carole,

Having heard nothing from you for over a week, I've begun to worry that you may have been laid low by an accident or some

---

155 This is a surprising charge, given that so much of the extract is devoted to the ramifications of the Schleyer affair, and may well reflect Medhurst's hurried reading.

156 *Pizzas in Paradise* by Carole Medhurst, Harper Collins 1994.

personal crisis. Call me paranoid but I even wondered whether you might have had second thoughts about helping me. I have, at least, taken advantage of the delay to read *Pizzas . . .*, which I enjoyed immensely. What a story! The one drawback is that it has made me more impatient than ever to read your reminiscences. I'm well aware of the pressures you're under: it's not all Hockneying in Hollywood. This is just to let you know that I'm on the other end of a modem whenever you have a moment.

Yours, with best wishes,

Michael

Subj:	Re Very Worried
Date:	05/31/01 22: 16: 16 Pacific Daylight Time
From:	cm2000@sprintmail.com (Carole Medhurst)
To:	michaelarditti@btinternet.com (Michael Arditti)

Sensitivity: Confidential

Sorry to have been so out of touch but we're in final negotiations with a very big (not least from the neck up!) British star, who's making more and more demands.[157] Would you believe that a multi-million dollar deal could founder on the tax status of his masseur? One way or another, things have to be settled this week. Then I promise I'll put my mind to the past.

Cheers!

Carole

---

[157] When I informed Medhurst that I wished to publish our complete correspondence, she requested a few small cuts, which have been made. One such was this reference to Liam Finch's arrogance. In a later message, however, she relented. 'That guy put me through nine months of hell! Why the hell should I pussyfoot around him now?'

From: Michael Arditti \<michaelarditti@btinternet.com>
Sent: Friday, June 1, 2001 9.34 pm
To: cm2000@sprintmail.com
Subject: Re Very Worried

Dear Carole,
For very worried read very relieved.
Thank you.
Yours, with best wishes,
Michael

Subj: Re Information
Date: 06/03/01 23: 52: 07 Pacific Daylight Time
From: cm2000@sprintmail.com (Carole Medhurst)
To: michaelarditti@btinternet.com (Michael Arditti)

Sensitivity: Confidential

Finally a gap in the schedule!
The big, champagne-cork-popping news this end is that Liam Finch is on board. As the song says 'There may be trouble ahead . . .' But, in the meantime, *The Leningrad Affair* has been given the green light. My life is now mapped out for the next eighteen months. It's with mixed emotions that I've been dipping into the past. My memories of Munich are surprisingly vivid – which is not to say that they're accurate. Feel free to use them in any way that you choose. I would, however, appreciate a copy before anything appears in print.

Here goes!

Questions:

1)   The biggie. Why did Felicity do it? What was she trying to achieve?
     Did you consciously commit suicide? Did you have any hints from
     her behaviour as to what she had in mind?

Of course I had no idea what she was going to do or I'd have tried
to stop her. We weren't however what you would call close. She'd
thrown in her lot with Geraldine, which meant shunning me.
I couldn't say what she was trying to achieve, beyond the obvious:
a recognition of the plight of the Palestinians. But, as we all know,
such attacks do nothing but generate further repression which,
indeed, occurred when Israel launched retaliatory raids on
Southern Lebanon and Gaza.
I did wonder whether she might have been influenced by a particular scene that we played together as Unity and Jessica. I (Jessica)
was in Munich and within arm's reach of Hitler. I had a line to the
effect that 'If only I had a gun, I could kill him.' And it wasn't
wholly fanciful, as Jessica proved the following year when she
signed up for the Spanish Civil War. That a young aristocratic
woman might have changed the course of history struck a deep
chord with Felicity. She kept asking me whether I thought that
such actions could be justified.
Whatever else she intended, I very much doubt that she meant to
commit suicide. She gave no impression of a woman who had
shaken hands with death. On the contrary, only the previous day
we'd been filming a scene set in Swinbrook and she'd been unusually light-hearted. No, I'm convinced that the explosion was an
accident. Have you ever handled a bomb? I have (don't worry, it
was in my BBC, not my IWP, days). You detonate it by pulling out
the pin. But forget the old-fashioned pineapple grenades you've
seen in the movies. Removing the pin is actually quite hard – and
well-nigh impossible without attracting attention. So what you do
– I speak as an actress not a terrorist – is ease it out in advance

while keeping the depression handle firmly locked in your hand. Then you put it back, but only half-way, and with the end bent for easy access. Felicity must either have put it back so carelessly that it snapped or else have failed to put it back securely. So it went off too soon.

2) Was Felicity's action in any way linked to the subject of the film? At the time, there was much nonsense talked about demonic possession and so forth. That's patently absurd. But might she have over-identified with political extremism in the course of playing the part?

My immediate response is an emphatic 'no'. Any correspondence is quite coincidental. But, delving deeper, I feel less sure. The key to both Felicity and Unity can be found in their sister: Geraldine–Diana (I collate the two). Although they stood at opposite ends of the political spectrum, there was little to distinguish them. Just as fascism is contained by fanaticism as a word, so fanaticism is contained by fascism as a concept.

Unity clearly suffered from growing up in such a large family. She felt the need to assert her individuality and not be subsumed in that amorphous mass, the Mitford girls. Ironically, the sister with whom she was most competitive was the one with whose views she was most in sympathy.

Felicity was likewise dominated by her relationship with her screen sister. For all the claims of her devotion to Meier or her attraction to Ahmet Samif, I'm convinced that it was Geraldine who truly fascinated her. And no one knows better than I do how compelling she could be. Felicity began – unconsciously, I've no doubt – both to mimic her mannerisms and to echo her views. I'll give you an example. We were shooting a scene at a Swinbrook party which showed Unity and Jessica playing at politics. They had adopted antithetical positions and expected everyone else to incline towards one or other extreme. They asked a neighbour if he were a fascist or a communist. He replied that he was neither, but a democrat. At which they both expressed contempt – an attitude I remember Felicity sharing, saying that it showed a typically English lack of passion. I replied that a person might have a passion for Parliamentary democracy: a comfortable, companionable passion, as between two people who'd been married for forty years – or, in England's case, seven hundred. She never discussed politics with me again.

3) Was the atmosphere on set unduly political? In the letters that Luke wrote to me, he barely mentions outside events and yet Geraldine's journal is full of them. Which more accurately reflects the general mood?

If the atmosphere during filming was unusually political, I certainly didn't notice it. Reading Geraldine's journal, I feel like one of those women who spent the sixties up to their elbows in the washing-up.

It would be fair to say that the German actors were more politically aware than their British counterparts who were, by and large, older. There'd been links between some of Meier's group and the terrorists (including, if I remember rightly, Baader himself). Don't quote me on this, but I think that someone from the Munich theatre company was implicated in the very first Red Army Faction atrocity. They firebombed a department store in order to give the German public a taste of Hanoi. It was the occasion for Meinhof's notorious claim that it showed more decency to bomb a department store than to work in one.

The terrorists even sounded like actors!

4) Did you see any evidence of Felicity's obsession with Meier? Was she, in fact, as obsessed as both Luke and Geraldine suggest? Might it have been to curry favour with the director that she planted the bomb?

See the answer to 2 above.

5)   Would you flesh out your own relationship with Geraldine? There are various caustic references to it in the journal, as you'll see for yourself tomorrow – or as soon as you have some free time.

We're entering 'how long is a piece of string' territory. I first met – came across would be more accurate, since meeting suggests some interchange – Geraldine, while appearing in a lunchtime play at a little theatre – it may even have been called The Little Theatre. It was her practice to target fringe companies. She would harangue them about the right of every theatre-worker to earn a living wage, which was all to the good except that she wasn't the one who was performing for nothing. Her name ensured that even the most apolitical actor gave her a hearing. One of our cast was so star-struck that she was late back for her day job and given the sack.

In time, I came to see that as a metaphor.

Remember, Britain in the early 1970s was not the bland, watered-down version of the US that it is today. It was an era of great industrial unrest and social upheaval. There was a genuine revolutionary mood in the air. I'd recently left drama school brimming with idealism. It's easy to laugh now when imitation and irony have made the attitude as self-conscious as an aphorism in a Noël Coward play, but we truly believed that art could change the way people thought. Ah, the innocence of youth!

My idealism had survived the three years of my course, during which I was trained for a rigidly backward-looking theatre. The prevailing creed was that acting was about being active. We were taught to play up the objective in every speech, relentlessly pursuing our character's interests. I was appalled. Far from my dream of collective effort, this seemed to reflect the principles of capitalism, promoting selfishness and competition. It was a view of human nature that I rejected. Of course, now that I operate in Hollywood, where that view can be seen at its most unabashed, I realise that it lies behind the kind of acting that the public wants to see.

My professional career was equally compromised. After a season walking on at the Royal Shakespeare Company which, for all its egalitarian principles, proved to be as hierarchical as a hospital (a cat may look at a king but God forbid a courtier should chat to Richard III), I joined the Bed-Pan Company, an agit-prop group which toured anti-government-health-cuts plays throughout the Midlands and North East, until it collapsed from a combination of factionalism and under-funding. I made a couple of lucrative adverts and joined the 90% of my colleagues in weekly rep at the Dole Office. So, like many other over-trained, under-employed actors, I was ripe for Geraldine's recruitment drive. If you asked me now, I'd have to say that my predominant aim had been to create a society where an accomplished actress would not be reduced to playing a piece of confectionery. At the time, we believed that we pursued a more elevated goal, standing in the vanguard, poised to bring about the historic union between the oppressed masses and the revolutionary elite. The trouble was that the oppressed masses treated us with contempt.

Geraldine was the Party's star – in every sense of the word. I myself was totally in awe of her. I may even have been a little in love with her. Which is how I'm able to understand Felicity. She never laughed, as though she saw it as a sign of weakness to acknowledge anyone's jokes but her own. She was forever changing her clothes (I'm told that Dermot Macaulay had to remind her that haute couture did not feature in the Party's programme). She washed her hands as often as Lady Macbeth. In Hoxton Square, she had a private cloakroom which no one – repeat, no one – else was permitted to use. At first, I attributed it to Hollywood. Later, I learnt that it was the Priory.[158] Even then, she couldn't just have a breakdown like anyone else, she had to be suffering from angst.

158 A private psychiatric clinic in South London.

What's angst but depression with an accent?

Her politics were culpably naive. She viewed the world as if it conformed to the rules of a Hollywood thriller. It's ironic that the most anti-American of women should have subscribed to such a frontiersman view of life. She thought that she could make everything good by her dint of her own good faith. We travelled around US bases in Britain circulating leaflets urging the troops to desert. She still felt bitter at having been deported from the States for campaigning against the draft: an offence for which she was lucky not to have been jailed. At the same time she expected to return to Hollywood and resume her career.

I wanted to ask her why she was so keen to go back when she appeared to have hated it so much the first time, let alone when she believed it to be dominated by the Jewish interests that she so abhorred. It was then that I began to take issue with her. She insisted that her position on the Middle East was not anti-Semitic but anti-Zionist. I was increasingly of the view that the one was merely a legitimate form of the other. She declared peremptorily that the Palestinians were the new Jews, which rather begged the question of what had happened to the old ones. With several other Party members, she made regular visits to Tripoli to meet Colonel Gadaffi. I was horrified to discover that the IWP was part of the labyrinthine network of left-wing groups that he bankrolled (alongside the Baader-Meinhof and the IRA). She spent weeks at a terrorist training camp in Lebanon, where she learnt the skills essential to the urban guerrilla, from shooting at a moving target to falling out of a speeding car . . . which was how she later met her death. According to one party member, who came to share my disenchantment, she made no concession to Arab sensibilities. She complained about the quality of the food and the lack of alcohol. She flouted the local dress code, inflaming her young hosts to the point of mutiny by her practice of sunbathing nude. The longer I spent in the Party, the greater my disillusion. I gradually realised that the official line was not the full picture. The Middle East was not just an imperialist exercise any more than Northern Ireland was simply a colonial struggle. But the primary cause of my defection was the treatment of women. The general secretary was a poisonous ex-railwayman, Dermot Macaulay (happily now dead), who had a medieval view of women – and I don't mean courtly love. He believed that his position gave him droit du seigneur over all the female members. When I objected to his harassment, Geraldine accused me of lack of revolutionary fervour. In an allusion which will be clear from a reading of her diary, she called me a 'bad egg' and said that I should be proud to make any contribution to the cause. She declared that exceptional men had exceptional appetites, comparing Macaulay to Mao – the ultimate idol – who also had a penchant for young actresses. I now prefer the comparison with Goebbels.

Resignation proved to be harder than I'd anticipated. The Party operated like a cult. Two days after I sent off my letter, I was abducted on the street by a pair of heavies and taken to a house in South London, where I was locked up and subjected to a variety of threats and torments. I was terrified. Remember that these people had links to the IRA! I escaped by attracting the attention of a milkman. He called the police and the subsequent raid on the house became front-page news. The IWP leadership succeeded in dissociating itself from the activities of its 'rogue element' but, for a while, the movement went very quiet. I, on the other hand, was suddenly in demand. As the BBC made offers – small parts but in smart projects – my agent declared that the kidnapping had raised my profile higher than any victim's since Patty Hearst.[159]

The piece of string is tauter than I thought. Still, now you know the reason for the anti-Medhurst bias in Geraldine's journal. It

159 The American heiress who was kidnapped in February 1974 by the Symbionese Liberation Army.

doesn't surprise me to find that her influence lay behind Felicity's action. She was as morally stunted as a child. I remember her telling me, shortly after I joined the Party, that people would never allow a child actress to grow up since it reminded them of their own failure – a phrase that spoke of years of therapy. But the only person who wouldn't allow Geraldine to grow up was herself.

6) Can you remember anything about Ahmet Samif? He obviously exerted an enormous influence on both Felicity and Geraldine. Was Felicity attracted to the man or to the cause? \

I remember Ahmet very well – too well: the clarity of the images unsettles me. The first time we met, he looked me over as though he were appraising me in a bazaar. He had obviously been warned against me by Geraldine. Then he moved in close – the distance as calculated as a focus-puller's – and said coolly: 'As a child, I was taught that women are like snakes. The more highly coloured, the more harmless. It's the small, plain ones that are dangerous.' Then he smiled, all teeth, and walked away.

The occasion was one of Wolfram's weekend parties. He held open house every Saturday or Sunday, whether or not he was filming (he would never be cleared for insurance out here). Ahmet had arrived from Beirut. I presumed that he'd come to visit his brother, although we now know that he had a very different agenda (albeit not the one that fed Geraldine's hopes). Germany's Leftist cells had provided support for the Palestinian gang that attacked the '72 Olympics and he had come to repay the debt, supplying arms, money and passports, while attempting to make as much mileage as possible out of the hostage crisis.

He talked passionately about his people's struggle. His words made a strong impression on me – which must be why so many come back now. He spoke about the double standards applied to Israel and Palestine: how the Jew's sense of exile was honoured while the Arab's was ignored. He personified the predicament in his father, a fisherman from Haifa. What fish could he hope to catch in a camp outside Beirut? And yet, from the start, he aroused my suspicions. When somebody urged him to stop fighting the battles of the past – there had to come a time to start afresh, he replied with a phrase I still find disturbing. 'Oh yes, and you can tell your sister to sleep with any man she likes and, in the morning, she'll still wake up a virgin.'

He depicted much of the military conflict in terms of sex. He cited the Jewish passion for truth – for recording the name of every man, woman and child who'd been killed – and then asked: 'What of the broader truth? What of the women whose faces their agents steal and stick on pictures of whores? What of the men whom they then persuade to spy for them, through a torture more brutal than any beating? To an Arab there is no dishonour greater than that of an unfaithful wife. The world salutes the brave Israeli soldiers but does it know what they use for weapons? When the Palestinian men were imprisoned and the women marched in protest, the Israelis did not disperse them with guns. No, they stood in front of them and masturbated. They knew that no Arab woman could withstand such shame.'

There was, however, another side to the story, as revealed by his brother. Film-making was such a family affair with Wolfram that the fraternal row spilt over into all our lives. Ahmet was intensely homophobic (you catch a glimpse of it, liberally toned down, in Geraldine's journal). He attacked Mahmoud for being 'less than a man'. The latter responded by charging Islam itself with hypocrisy. It preached abstinence and chastity and then sent hordes of young men to their deaths with the promise of Paradise, where they would find a bevy of beautiful virgins waiting to fulfil their every desire.

During one violent row, Mahmoud told us the story of his cousin (I'm keen to use this in some form, so keep it under wraps). She'd been married off to a friend of her father's: an old man to whom the family was indebted for a piece of land. The village had been flattened; the land seized; but the debt remained. After some months, the girl left her husband to live with her lover. Her brother and Ahmet bided their time before beating her to death during an Israeli raid, making it look like the work of the soldiers. Photographs of the dead girl were flashed around the world. 'And, not long afterwards, my brother went to America to study and became a great man.'

Ahmet made no attempt to deny Mahmoud's claim. On the contrary, he insisted that he had done what he did for his uncle. In a world where everything else had been taken from him, it was imperative that honour survived.

Such barbarism sickened me, but what really made my skin crawl was his attitude to the Holocaust. He was one of those zealots for whom it didn't exist. In his view, it was all a conspiracy by the Jews to get money out of Germany. They demanded reparation for crimes of the past and exemption for those of the present. And, if you put to him the 'little' matter of the camps, he had a ready response. It was wartime and the country was in the grip of malnutrition and disease. Tuberculosis was rife and, to prevent an epidemic, carriers were quarantined. The Jews, being indolent and weak, were particularly prone to infection and so there was, inevitably, a preponderance of them in the camps. The so-called gas chambers were merely crematoria to burn tubercular corpses.[160] Anything else was a myth spread by the Zionists to justify the rape of Palestinian land.

When I proposed that he took the short trip to Dachau in order to see a different picture, he retorted 'Why? In Florida, I went to

[160] It cannot be a coincidence that Unity Mitford gave a very similar explanation for the function of the gas chambers when photographs of the death camps were released in England after the War.

Disneyland. Does that mean that I have to believe in Mickey Mouse?'

You knew Felicity much better than I did. Do you suppose that she would have had any truck with such a stance? Or might she have been like Geraldine who, while she would never have dreamt of denying the Holocaust herself, regarded Ahmet's attitude as if it were a minor foible, permissible under the circumstances.

Sometimes, notions of relativity can be taken too far.

7) Any other business. If there is anything – anything at all – that you think I may have omitted, please don't hesitate to put me straight.

What a responsibility! No, you seem to have covered all the bases. I do remember, however, that there was a mysterious money man forever in the background, who was the subject of much speculation on set. I don't remember his name and I've no idea if he's still alive, let alone if he'd be amenable, but he seemed to be pretty astute – or am I confusing shrewdness with reticence? Maybe one of your German contacts can put you in touch.

I hope that my jottings may be of use. Let me know if you come up with anything spectacular.

Good luck!

Carole

From: Michael Arditti <michaelarditti@btinternet.com>
Sent: Monday, June 4, 2001 11.02 pm
To: cm2000@sprintmail.com
Subject: Gratitude

Dear Carole,

I can't thank you enough for taking such trouble. I'm delighted to read your opinions of the leading players, both cinematic and political, the national backgrounds and, in particular, the connection between acting and activism. If I'm still some way from solving the enigma, it's certainly not for lack of help from you.

I hardly dare ask anything more, but I wonder if you know whether Geraldine was ever implicated in the bombing (she gives no hint in her later journals) or if Ahmet Samif was ever heard of again. Please don't bother to reply unless you have information (but I hope that you have and you will).

Yours, with very best wishes,

Michael

Subj:	Re Gratitude
Date:	06/04/01 15: 37: 08 Pacific Daylight Time
From:	cm2000@sprintmail.com (Carole Medhurst)
To:	michaelarditti@btinternet.com (Michael Arditti)

Sensitivity: Highly Confidential

As for Geraldine, she continued to be regarded as a harmless fanatic. The refusal of people to take her seriously, which had long caused her offence, now worked in her favour. But remember, for the past thirteen years I've been living in Hollywood where she remained an outcast. Things were very different on your side of the pond and, as you know, she built up a substantial career in France, where a whiff of scandal has always been an attraction. The one thing that she proved is that she was a damn good actress. I just wish that she hadn't allowed her talents to be waylaid.

As for Ahmet, he disappeared on the day of the bombing, supposedly to a safe house in East Berlin and, from there, back to Lebanon. It was a well-established route. Schleyer's kidnappers are also said to have turned up in West Beirut shortly after the end of the crisis, living in a hotel near the Arab university, protected by an armed Fatah guard. One footnote: a couple of years ago, while

watching a CNN report on Arafat's visit to Camp David, I was
sure that I saw Ahmet among his aides. It was only a glimpse but
there was no mistaking the smile.

Cheers!

C.

Subj:	Re Felicity
Date:	06/15/01 21: 18: 08 Pacific Daylight Time
From:	cm2000@sprintmail.com (Carole Medhurst)
To:	michaelarditti@btinternet.com (Michael Arditti)

Sensitivity: Confidential

Hi Michael!

I've no idea whether you're still on the Felicity trail or whether it
has gone cold, but a thought recently occurred to me. I remember
our filming a scene as Unity and Jessica in their Swinbrook
sitting-room. One side was decorated with a swastika and assorted
Fascist posters and the other with a Red Flag and a bust of Lenin.
They drew an imaginary line across the centre which neither was
allowed to cross and sat discussing how painful it would be for
each to have to give the order for the other's execution. It struck
me that it was all a game: politics as exhibitionism. For Felicity, as
for Unity, it was a game.

Cheers!

Carole

6

Thomas Bücher

in conversation

If my work on this book has taught me one thing, it is that I would have no future as a crime writer. The aim of the investigation was to discover the truth about Felicity, but I am left with more – and more disturbing – questions than when I began. I have come to suspect, however, that the project was doomed from the start and that, even had Felicity survived the attack and spent the rest of her life giving interviews inside Stammheim prison, her motives would have remained opaque.

My disillusion was increased by my meeting with Thomas Bücher, whom I soon identified as the 'mysterious money man' of Carole Medhurst's account. I had long despaired of making contact. Liesl Martins and Manfred Stückl both claimed to have no recollection of him and Renate Fischer no interest. My approaches to various British officials in Germany likewise yielded nothing. Then, in May 2002, Andreas Forst, whom I had met at the bedside of his friend Dieter Reiss the previous July, paid me a visit in London. In his student days, Forst had made two films for Bücher's company and he volunteered to act as intermediary. Bücher readily agreed to see me and I travelled to Munich later in the month. It seemed to me strangely fitting, given the course of my enquiry, that it should conclude in a pornographer's office.

We arranged to meet at the company's headquarters above its new erotic emporium in Landshuter Allee. As he was busy when I arrived, Bücher dispatched one of his assistants to give me a tour. The man, a clean-cut, fresh-faced twenty-five-year-old, discussed the marketing of 'the product' as though it were margarine. He led me around the ground floor which, dominated by a display of sex aids, resembled a cross between a medical supply store and a morgue. Next, we moved up to the mezzanine where films and

magazines to satisfy every taste were set out in carefully segre-
gated bays. We passed from Pregnant Beauties through Bestiality
to Family Sex, where I struggled to maintain my composure at my
Virgil's assurance that the children were played by midgets. We
then walked down a corridor of viewing booths to a surreal audi-
torium where a tower of competing video screens stretched up like
a sexual Babel.

Finally, we were summoned to the Chairman's office, a room of
ostentatious minimalism, its white walls relieved only by four
Picasso etchings of a maiden being ravaged by the Minotaur.
Bücher greeted me with a formal, firm-for-his-age handshake and
invited me to take a seat. I was somewhat put out to find that,
while I was setting up my cassette recorder, he instructed the
assistant to switch on one of his own. The assistant then left us
and the interview began. It was conducted entirely in English,
which Bücher spoke with idiomatic precision. Although at the
time I felt frustrated at how little he mentioned Felicity, I realised
on playing the tape that he had revealed far more than I thought.

The unease which I shared with Luke in the face of a man who
had endured such horrors was compounded by his response to
them. Nazism, in his view, was not an anomaly but a microcosm
of human nature. Mankind was prone to evil and Hitler's role had
been simply to bring out its full scope. But, rather than rebel
against this or work to change it, he had accommodated himself to
it. While no one would deny that the world of the camps was
pornographic – the men who forced Bücher to urinate stand along-
side Irma Crese, the Auschwitz guard who reached orgasm by
whipping women to death, and the commandant of Flossenbürg
who masturbated openly while prisoners were being beaten – to
devote the rest of one's life to producing pornographic films would
seem to grant the Nazis a posthumous victory.

Bücher is not alone in his dystopian vision. Several leading post-
war film-directors, among them Luchino Visconti, Pier Paolo

*Passolini and Liliana Cavani – not to mention Wolfram Meier –
have placed sexuality at the heart of their discourse on fascism.
My own qualms about this approach resemble Ralf Heyn's about
Meier's coprophiliac interpretation of Hitler. While it undoubtedly
makes for powerful cinema, the lurid imagery precludes a more
measured response. On the evidence gathered here, however, I am
forced to concede that their viewpoint may be justified. Whether it
be in Luke's father's shocking personification of the violence
lurking between our legs or Sir Hallam Bamforth's secret indul-
gence of his SS guard fantasies, the links between sexuality and
fascism are clear. Moreover, they are not limited to men. Unity
Mitford's worship of Hitler was just one manifestation of the
impulse that led thousands of women to offer to bear his children
and thousands more to line the roads, baring their breasts as his
motorcade sped past.*

*It is an irony which he may or may not welcome that the
emphasis Bücher lays on the dominance of sexuality mirrors that
in orthodox Catholic teaching on Original Sin. Furthermore, like
the Church, he appears to be marketing his own despair (a charge
he refutes with his claim of responding to market forces). It was
only after meeting that I was able to make sense of Meier's remark
(quoted in Luke's letter of 2 October 1977) that no one would
understand Hitler who failed to understand the universal human
need to inflict pain. At the time, I read it as an expression of
sadism: Meier's more than Hitler's and, certainly, more than
humanity's. Now, I wonder if inflicting pain may be the way we
choose to transcend it: whether it be on others, as in the Nazi
atrocities; on ourselves, as in the body-piercing practised by
Bücher's actors; or at one remove, as in the concentration camp
pornography which enjoys such a distressing vogue.*

*Bücher's zeal for pornography was shared by Meier who,
according to Renate Fischer, regarded it as the highest form of film-
making. As one whose acquaintance with him was confined to a*

snub in a crowded dressing room, I am ill-equipped to comment on Meier's sincerity. His assertion may simply have reflected his taste for an acting style which, to judge by his films, was painfully raw, but it may also have reflected a belief that it wasn't just the classics (the subject of his spat with the Edinburgh critic) that were suspect in a post-Auschwitz era but art itself. That he persisted in his artistic enterprise was a paradox that both tormented and fired him.

While Bücher felt no such qualms about his medium, he made no claims for it either, laughing – politely but still in my face – when I suggested that he was performing a moral function by providing society with an outlet for its baser instincts. His contempt put me in mind of Luke's college friend, Simon Lister, who objected to the accepted consensus on the Holocaust because it legitimised Jewish suffering in Christian terms. By identifying the victims with a culture whose most sacred image was a man being tortured, Auschwitz had become the ultimate assimilation.

I trust that I will not raise similar objections by reiterating that it is because of my faith that I am unable to regard the Holocaust – or, indeed, anything else – as an expression of pure evil. I appreciate that my claim must appear meaningless – even contradictory – to many churchgoers, but I find it incomprehensible that anyone who believes in an all-loving, all-powerful God can picture Him locked in a cosmic tug-of-war with the Devil while a downtrodden humanity slides back and forth in-between. Nevertheless, I admit that my faith has rarely been subjected to so strong a challenge as it received from Bücher. The impregnable logic of a man who had known the world at its worst forced me to question whether my own beliefs might not simply be the product of privilege – the spiritual equivalent of the insularity that Meier so scorned.

In the Introduction, I argued that a belief in an objective force of evil absolved mankind of responsibility (which surely accounts for the strength of its appeal). I would like, nevertheless, to preserve one element of the traditional story of the Fall – that of wilfulness – as I propose an alternative version, based not on sin but on solipsism. Everything that I have discovered in the course of compiling this book bolsters my conviction not that human nature is evil and needs to be redeemed, nor that it is wild and needs to be tamed, but that it is selfish and needs to be socialised.

After his visit to Dachau, Luke wrote of the imperative to build our morality on the inviolability of every human life: a phrase that came back to me during my conversation with Bücher. I suggested then that we should redefine evil as inhumanity but, on reflection, I opt for dehumanisation: a denial of another person's needs or pain or, even, basic right to exist; whether that denial be systematic, as in the Nuremberg Laws, or maverick, as in a terrorist's bomb. The one link between the otherwise very different figures in this book – Felicity and Meier, Geraldine and Samif, Unity and Hitler – is their absolute confidence in the supremacy of their own cause. To use a metaphor from the world that we have been exploring, they saw their own life in Technicolor and everybody else's in black-and-white.

M.A. I don't know how much you remember about Felicity.

T.B. I remember that she cost me a very great deal of money.

M.A. I meant more in the line of private conversations – hints that her attitudes were hardening.

T.B. I don't think that we ever exchanged more than a *Morgen*.

M.A. I've spent the best part of this year on her track and I'm still no closer to accounting for her action.

T.B. If you don't mind my saying, you're a little old to believe that human nature obeys discernible laws of cause and effect.

M.A. But that's the basis of all practical morality.

T.B. So?

M.A. Not to mention most serious literature. By learning why people behave as they do, we become able to understand one another better and, hence, to prevent another such outrage taking place.

T.B. A laudable aim but a futile one. I read the documents you sent me with care – even with interest – but without, I'm afraid, much understanding. Who can say what led your friend to act as she did: whether it was love for Meier or the Arab; rebellion against her family at home; revulsion with the English actors out here; genuine sympathy for the victims? We can never know, any more than we can know what motivated Hitler. I remember all the disputes that caused on set. Everyone with his own pet theory – or, rather, his own neurosis. The truth doesn't lie in any particular circumstance but in the heart of human nature which inclines us to do evil.

M.A. That sounds like a recipe for despair.

T.B. Not once you've accepted it. Most people never do. But then most people never scratch beneath the surface. You appear to be an exception. Which means that you can't complain when you draw blood . . . I'm sorry. You came to discover some answers not to listen to an old man's prattle.

M.A. Please don't apologise. I'm interested in anything you have to say. I'm relieved to have made contact. You're extremely elusive. I tried Liesl Martins and Manfred Stückl, even Renate Fischer, all of whom have been most amenable to my other requests, but they denied any knowledge of you.

T.B. There are many people who'd prefer that I didn't exist. Some of them tried to shut down this store. They object to its being here on a busy street, squeezed between a music shop and a butcher's.

M.A. Fortunately, I saw a friend of Dieter Reiss.

T.B. Ah yes, Dieter. He was the best of them. How is he?

M.A. Still alive, which is more than anyone could have predicted. To be honest, I've put off visiting him this time. I found it too disturbing last year. And from what Andreas – Andreas Forst: he did some work for you . . .

T.B. So I gather.

M.A. What he told me disturbs me even more. He – that is Dieter – is very weak and very bitter. There's a passage in Geraldine Mortimer's journal that describes how he felt tortured by his sadistic tendencies. Now he appears to be reconciled to them.

T.B. At long last.

M.A. He spends his days on the Internet, making contact with men – uninfected men – who want to have sex with him – unprotected sex – in full knowledge of his status. A Russian roulette for an age with gun laws.

T.B. And you have a problem with that?

M.A. Don't you?

T.B. There's no deception? The men are all aware of his condition?

M.A. As far as I know, yes.

T.B. Then, no. I don't have any problem. On the contrary, I applaud his spirit. By refusing to compromise, he has eroticised death.

M.A. Surely one of the responsibilities of living in a society – that is a civilised society – must be to try to protect your fellow members?

T.B. But if it's what those men want: if it makes them happy.

M.A. Yes. There you have it. We live in a world where the first consideration is happiness rather than decency or virtue. The accepted creed is that people should be allowed to do what they want rather than encouraged to seek for something better, either because no one can agree what that better is or else because they believe that nobody has the right to impose his or her better on anyone else. I'm sorry: I don't mean to harangue you, but I feel very strongly.

T.B. So I see.

M.A. The pursuit of happiness is actually enshrined in the constitution of America – although it has degenerated into the pursuit of pleasure. We, on the other hand, don't even have that excuse.

T.B. Morality changes. We cannot live as we did in a world where we no longer have seasons, we have supermarkets. Politicians and pundits complain that nowadays no one knows the name of their neighbours. What does it matter when, by switching on their computers, they can talk to people on the other side of the globe?

M.A. Please don't misunderstand me. I'm not arguing for a return to a puritanical code. I myself am a prime beneficiary of liberalisation. I just think that there's a serious flaw in a society where the prevailing ethic is that people should be able to do whatever they want as long as it doesn't hurt anybody.

T.B.   And that flaw is?

M.A.   That they're hurting themselves. Often literally. The current fashion for body piercing can be no coincidence. One of the films playing downstairs shows men and women with so much metal embedded in their flesh that traditional distinctions between animal and mineral break down.

T.B.   Don't people have a right to control their own bodies?

M.A.   They should also be protected from the consequences of their desires.

T.B.   I only hope that everyone who holds that view is as well-intentioned as you. I saw what happened the last time it was put into practice. There's no such thing as an absolute morality. All our lives are simply negotiations between our appetites and our ideals: a fact that frightens our masters. Take the supreme example: the Church. In the Middle Ages, people believed that the essence of life was contained in a man's sperm. A woman was simply the receptacle. So it's no wonder that the Church was so hostile to masturbation and contraception. But times change. We're now told that ejaculation is essential to avoid the build-up of poisons in the prostate while condoms save lives. And yet the Church continues to hang on to its antiquated values. So where would you say that morality lies? With the Pope who refuses to accept the evidence or the pornographer who provides release?

M.A.   That reminds me of Dieter's maxim: 'Don't knock masturbation. It's sex with someone to whose viruses you're immune.'

T.B.   I shall bear it in mind.[161]

[161]   Dieter's parody of Woody Allen's celebrated axiom – 'Don't knock masturbation; it's sex with someone you love' – struck no chord with Bücher, who took it purely as a medical fact.

M.A.   And if I may return to Dieter for a moment. In March, I asked him about the incident at the hotel that provoked Sir Hallam Bamforth's collapse.

T.B.   If I learnt anything from *Unity*, it was to stick to what I know. Here, we make a film in four days. Elsewhere, it's nothing but problems.

M.A.   Geraldine was right. Bamforth's offer of coaching came at a price. He aimed to reconcile Dieter to the violence in his character by taking the blows on himself. So far so perverse. But what if there were something else? A few days earlier, a man called Per – another concentration camp victim – had turned up at the hotel.

T.B.   I remember. Meier gave him a small part. He was fascinated by the coincidence.

M.A.   According to Geraldine, Bamforth was racked with guilt at having ignored his appeal for help to flee from the Nazis. So, what if he were doing penance? And Dieter's – or rather, Streicher's – whip became the scourge?

T.B.   Would it comfort you to learn that he was looking for forgiveness rather than pleasure?

M.A.   No. Well, yes, to be honest. I find the image of that distinguished old actor submitting to a Nazi thug extremely distressing.

T.B.   Then go to see Per. Perhaps he can put your mind at rest.

M.A.   I'd no idea he was still around. Do you keep in contact?

T.B.   Not at all. But I know how you can reach him. I read an article about Hannelore Kessel in *Stern* only the other week. It mentioned his name as her secretary.

M.A.   How bizarre!

T.B.   Not really. They became friends during the shooting of *Unity*. For Per it was a dream come true. And Kessel is suddenly in vogue again after fifty years. There's been a revival of interest in her films. With the passage of time, the propaganda purpose has faded. It's possible to see them purely as cinema: full-blooded melodramas and light-hearted musicals.

M.A. But they were made by Nazis.

T.B. They're not being viewed by Nazis. Or are you afraid that they might spark a right-wing revival? Now whose is the recipe for despair?

M.A. I don't think that any work of art can be divorced from the circumstances of its creation.

T.B. Most Third Reich architecture was destroyed by bombs, so you needn't worry about that (although we were very grateful for what remained when we were choosing locations for *Unity*). But what of futurism? Would you damn an entire cultural movement because of its links – very intimate links – with fascism? You'll end up like the Israelis banning Wagner.

M.A. Given Wagner's rabid anti-Semitism, it strikes me as one of the country's saner attempts at self-protection.

T.B. It's just music. You either respond to it or you don't.

M.A. In my view, music – like all art – has to be judged by more objective criteria. But I feel embarrassed talking about such things to you.

T.B. Don't worry. I can stand it.

M.A. When one of the most painful paradoxes of the entire Third Reich is that of the torturers who liked Mozart.

T.B. Why? The idea that art civilises is sentimental nonsense. You need only go to any opera house – not just Bayreuth – to understand how the Nazis could sit through a performance and then the next day commit mass murder. Music doesn't fill us with finer feelings but rather purges us of baser ones. By giving people a glimpse of beauty, it enables them to live with their own ugliness. Far from wondering how Beethoven and Auschwitz and Mozart and Dachau could co-exist, we ought to acknowledge that the one creates the conditions for the other.

M.A. I don't – I can't – agree.

T.B. That's your privilege.

M.A. I still find it disconcerting that a concentration camp victim –

T.B. The accepted term is survivor.

M.A. Yes, of course, *survivor* should be working for one of Goebbels's starlets.

T.B. And mistresses.

M.A. Really?

T.B. Oh yes. It was revealed in Goebbels's diaries, brought to us courtesy of your Mr David Irving.

M.A. That may be but, as Geraldine describes it, she only gave in to Goebbels's demands on condition that her friend was allowed to leave for Switzerland.

T.B. One of the benefits of the current surge of interest in her career is that we now have a chance to examine the sources. Kessel may have been an attractive woman but I wouldn't have rated her bargaining power so high. Her story was taken straight from the plot of *Viktoria*,[162] in which she agreed to become the mistress of a Jewish landlord on condition that he promised not to evict his tenants. In the film, however, she killed him before yielding to his lust – which seems not to have been the case in life.

M.A. How could she have done it?

T.B. Oh I don't suppose it was too painful. He was a man of enormous influence. He may have been dwarfish and cursed with a club foot, but he appears to have been very potent. He had six children with his wife, while maintaining a string of mistresses.

---

[162] Helmut Käutner's 1942 film in which Kessel played the title role.

M.A.   I meant: how could she have done it morally? Shouldn't it be brought to public attention?

T.B.   What purpose would it serve? This is the new Germany. We've drawn a line under the past. If Hitler were discovered tomorrow, alive and well and living in Argentina, the next day he'd be appearing on chat shows, explaining how his ideas had been misrepresented, while his lawyers plea-bargained for him to be allowed to spend a peaceful retirement in the Black Forest.

M.A.   I'm surprised you're able to joke about it.

T.B.   It's no good being solemn about such things. You'll end up like one of those Seventies radicals who had such a damaging effect on your friend Felicity. Their mistake was to suppose that people cared. Which they didn't. Any more than their parents had cared when they watched us being led away. It wasn't that they were especially hostile or anti-Semitic. They just didn't want to become involved. People don't, you see. And they resent anyone who tries to make them. But the radicals refused to acknowledge it. They read the teachings of their pet philosophers and waited for the workers to fulfil their historic role. Except that they were happy enough with the role they already had. So the radicals resorted to extremism, romanticising their despair.

M.A.   But that doesn't invalidate their ideals. The means may have been misguided, but not the goals.

T.B.   I disagree. They wanted to impose a Marxist system. They berated the country for having abandoned ideology in favour of materialism. What they failed to understand was that, for the Germans, materialism is ideology – or, at least, it acts as a corrective to the ideologies of the past. Besides, no one who has been through the camps can have anything but scorn for Marx. You only had to witness our market (Bread for soup: soup for tobacco: tobacco for shirt: shirt for

347

bread) to realise that commerce, not production, is the basic human activity. Meier knew that, which is why he could never make common cause with the extremists. His position was a mark of intelligence not cowardice or self-interest. He wasn't a Furtwängler or a Riefenstahl[163] neatly sidestepping the corpses on the way to work.

M.A. Is that why you backed him?

T.B. I'm a businessman. I backed him because I expected to make money. Bread: soup: tobacco: shirt: I practise what I preach. Besides, it was an excellent tax loophole. We could use the government credits we were given for the *Unity* equipment to write off the debt on our own. The one thing I wasn't looking for – whatever anyone may say – was respectability. I'm proud of what I do. What's more, I take an interest in my medium. Meier agreed to direct a film for me. I was keen to find out what he'd bring to it.

M.A. You mean to see whether pornography could become art?

T.B. No, I mean to show that, like everyone else, the artist has pornography in his soul. And Meier was an artist: perhaps the finest of his generation: the only one who told the truth about what he saw. He taught us to trust nothing outside ourselves. No gods or prophets. No gurus or seers. The irony is that his vision was so powerful that he himself became a seer. Audiences were desperate for authority. It came of living in a century with too many memories and too few myths.

M.A. Do you have any recollections of my other friend, Luke Dent?

T.B. Yes, indeed. Many happy ones. An amiable man. Attractive. Warm. We had several fascinating talks.

---

163 Wilhelm Furtwängler (1886–1954), conductor, and Leni Riefenstahl (1902–2003), film director, who colluded, to differing degrees, with the Nazi regime.

M.A. Really? You surprise me. In none of his letters does he mention what you do.

T.B. Look out of the window.

M.A. I beg your pardon?

T.B. Walk over and tell me what you see.

I do as he asks.

M.A. A busy street. Pedestrians. Cars. Oh, there's an old-fashioned hurdy-gurdy!

T.B. Now close your eyes.

I do as he asks.

So what do you see?

M.A. Why, nothing.

T.B. Neither did he.

I turn back into the room.

M.A. I'm finding it increasingly hard to maintain an optimistic outlook on the world.

T.B. Then why try?

M.A. It's an article of faith. I understand why it must be different for someone like yourself who's seen people at their worst. But I remain convinced that that was an aberration.

T.B. Was it?

M.A. I can't accept that human nature is fundamentally wicked.

T.B. Nature has no moral faculty. It simply is. And human beings are a part of it. Let me tell you a true story. It took place in Munich, a few weeks before my family was rounded up. I was gazing idly out of the window when I saw a cat stranded on a nearby roof. It had somehow clambered up there and was stuck. I continued to watch as a young SS officer fetched a ladder and climbed to the rescue. The ladder was too short and he reached across at his considerable peril. He risked his life to save that cat and yet I knew that, under different circumstances, he would have had no compunction about shooting me.

M.A.   The bastard.

T.B.   No, he wasn't a bastard. That was what confused me. I wanted him to be one, but he'd shown himself to be a kind of hero. So either it was an anomaly, or else goodness and wickedness were more closely entwined than I'd thought.

M.A.   There's a difference between goodness and sentimentality. Hitler was fond of children and animals. He was a vegetarian. His favourite actress was Shirley Temple, for Heaven's sake! Such people have to wear their heart on their sleeve to prove that they have one. Besides, it's easy to warm to 'innocent' (in inverted commas) children, far harder to do so to complicated, compromised adults. Accepting them means accepting ourselves. Which is the one thing that sentimentalists can never do.

T.B.   What about you?

M.A.   I believe that human beings were created by God and that they occupy a unique place in a divinely ordered universe.

T.B.   I've seen a woman with a mastectomy having her other breast cut off by so-called doctors for the sake of balance. I've seen men punctured like targets in a shooting gallery. I've heard the howling of children wrenched from their parents: a howling that never fades away. It seems to lurk under your bunk, waiting for nightfall in order to rise up and overpower you. What place does that occupy in your divinely ordered universe?

I wait for him to fill the silence.

        I'm sorry. I've done the very thing I most despise: claiming authority by dint of an experience that you are too young and too fortunate to have known in order to win an argument that I don't even recognise.

M.A.   No, it's me who should be sorry. I came here to jog your memory, not to pick at a scab.

T.B.   Tell me, what was the saddest moment of your life? Of course, you're young; you're English; you may not have one.

M.A.   The death of friends. The loss of dreams. The acceptance of failure.

T.B.   Do you spend your whole life agonising over them?

M.A.   I hear what you're saying, but surely it's different?

T.B.   Why? If I make Hitler the defining factor of my life, then he'll have won. The camps are closed. I have a business to run.

M.A.   But you must have an opinion about the people who tortured you.

T.B.   Of course.

M.A.   May I ask what it is?

T.B.   That they were men – and some women – who were behaving as all men and women would when relieved of the moral and social constraints that the world had imposed. Have you ever wondered why it is that the Nazis have become such a potent source of fantasy? It's because they dared to do what others only dream of. They acknowledged the paradox at the heart of being human: the violence in the act of making love. And it wasn't just in the camps: the secret experiments in far-off locations with only the all-seeing, all-justifying cameras to bear witness. Remember what happened in Lithuania where commando units clubbed Jews to death in front of cheering crowds, while mothers raised children high on their shoulders to make sure that they didn't miss any of the fun. German soldiers travelled to the massacres the way that their parents had booked for the opera. There were even some couples who chose to spend their honeymoons at these festivals of blood.

M.A.   It's beyond my comprehension.

T.B.   No. That's too easy. There are two things that are always said to be beyond our comprehension: the crimes of the

Nazis and the ways of God. And I make no apology for connecting them since they were dreamt up in the same place.

He taps his index finger against his skull.

Nor does it come as any surprise that it was God's representative on earth, the Pope, who, at the end of the War, authoritatively dubbed Nazi crimes satanic as if absolving humanity of guilt – while conveniently ignoring his own Faustian pact.[164] It might comfort you to consider the Third Reich an anomaly, but it was the norm. Look back across history. From the Incas to the Romans: from the Crusaders to the Inquisition: every page is steeped in blood. Peter the Great even put his own son to torture. There was no benevolent God on hand with a substitute ram. Or look a little closer to home: to the American soldiers in Vietnam who so exercised our seventies friends. You remember the My Lai massacre?[165] Murder innocent civilians if you must, but why scalp them? Why cut out their tongues and disembowel them? Why carve the company name into their chests? I simply ask the questions. I pass no judgement. The truth is that we're all little boys pulling the wings off butterflies. But, when we grow up, butterflies aren't big enough . . . butterflies don't scream loudly enough to assure us that we're alive. What better way can we find to say 'Yes, I'm a man and I'm making my mark' than by causing pain?

---

[164] In a speech to the college of cardinals on 2 June 1945, Pope Pius XII spoke of 'the satanic apparition of National Socialism'. For an analysis of the Pontiff's own record, including his 1933 Concordat with Hitler, see John Cornwell, *Hitler's Pope*, Viking 1999.

[165] On 16 March 1968, Charlie Company, a unit of the US Eleventh Light Infantry Brigade, entered the South Vietnamese village of My Lai. Four hours later, more than five hundred unarmed civilians – women, children and old men – were dead.

That is the truth. And I give it to people packaged in a video cassette.

M.A.   So you make your films as a safety-valve in order that peoples' darkest fantasies be enacted on screen and not in real life?

T.B.   I make my films to make money. I'm a businessman not a therapist nor the Secretary General of the UN. Besides, I don't suppose that even I could ever fathom peoples' darkest fantasies.

M.A.   I've always subscribed to the Socratic view that no one can choose to be wicked. People only do evil when they're deluded into believing that they're doing good.[166] Pure evil is found nowhere but in literature. We didn't hear Stalin or Pol Pot or even Hitler echoing Milton's Satan in a call for evil to be their good, or vowing that to do ill would be their sole delight. The SS guards behaved as they did because they'd been brainwashed into thinking that they were supermen and their victims vermin. That's why I set so much store by the search for motives. If any precept has sustained me through life, it's Madame de Staël's *Tout comprendre, c'est tout pardonner*.

T.B.   Don't you think that they should have resisted the propaganda and realised that what they were doing was wrong?

M.A.   Please don't misunderstand me. I'm not excusing them.

T.B.   Oh, I'm sorry. My French must be rusty. I thought that that was what *pardonner* meant.

M.A.   I'm trying, first, to make a distinction between the criminal and the crime and, second, to point out that evil isn't inevitable. Whereas you, unless I'm much mistaken, believe that people are evil and there's nothing that we can do about it.

[166] 'No man does wrong knowing he's doing wrong but does so only out of ignorance or delusion,' Plato, *Protagoras*.

T.B.   We can adapt to it. If you live on an earthquake fault-line, you adjust to it – you dig deeper foundations or whatever. We must make similar adjustments to the fault-lines in human nature. I'm a professional adjuster.

M.A.   Do you mean in your life or in your work?

T.B.   Both. To be frank, I'm surprised at Socrates. If that was the best he could come up with, he didn't take the hemlock a moment too soon. Judging evil by intent, you end up with a position in which Goebbels is more culpable than Hitler because Hitler was at least sincere in his beliefs whereas Goebbels was a cynic who believed only in the packaging. His wife's stepfather was Jewish. He admired the films of Jewish directors. His main aim was self-promotion, having discovered an arena in which his hitherto unrecognised talents could thrive.

M.A.   I wouldn't care to choose between Hitler and Goebbels.

T.B.   In which case, what about the youth who knowingly and callously robs an old lady of her life-savings? On the scale of intent, he would be more culpable than either of them.

M.A.   Then perhaps we should define evil as inhumanity: a refusal to recognise other peoples' essential rights. Whether or not we base our morality on a transcendental being will always be open to dispute. But we must be able to agree on a moral code based on our common humanity. Its arbiter will be our conscience – that conscience which, whatever Hitler may have thought, is as intrinsic a part of human nature as language or imagination.

T.B.   You're saying that evil is inhumanity. I'm saying that it is our common humanity. Hitler was no different from you or me or Wolfram Meier or Dietrich Bonhoeffer,[167] except in

---

[167]   Dietrich Bonhoeffer (1906–45), Lutheran pastor, theologian and opponent of Hitler, who was hanged in Flossenburg camp.

degree. It was his humanity that drove him on. That is what you must recognise if you wish to understand Felicity – or, indeed, anyone else. I see, after all, that I must tell you about Auschwitz. And don't be alarmed. For me, it is not a nightmare or a trauma; it is simply the past. I suffered, but I am not ennobled by it. I am not running an art gallery or writing poems or working for an organisation that promotes world peace. I am not my sister, Vera, another survivor, who cares about nothing but rescuing battery chickens. 'It's inhumane,' she says, 'to keep animals under such conditions.' And she doesn't appreciate the lack of logic, let alone the historical insult, in her words. I'm not ennobled by suffering but I am strengthened by it, because I know what life is. Hitler wanted to breed a master-race that would be able to withstand anything, and the irony – the deadly irony – is that we did. And why was I one of the chosen ones? Believe me, it wasn't because I was an especially good person or because God thought, 'I have a mission for Thomas that he should set up the most successful pornography business that Germany has ever seen.' No. It was because I was strong: because I reduced myself to an instinct. And, if you want to know which is the most fundamental human instinct, just ask any former Auschwitz inmate. We saw it even in the contortions of the dead: in the father climbing on to the back of his son, or the mother pushing aside her daughter in order to reach to the top of the gas chamber and suck out the last gasp of air. The answer, in case you hadn't guessed, is to survive.

M.A.   But surely that's only half the picture? I've read about the many acts of altruism that took place in the camps.

T.B.   The only altruism came from those who needed concepts of good and evil to sustain them more than bread. Do you know the biblical tale of Jacob and Esau?

M.A.   Of course.

T.B.   Esau's selling his birthright for a mess of pottage was my favourite bedtime story, preferably narrated in my father's oaky tones. In Auschwitz, we sold our birthright – decency, fraternity, humanity – for a cup of broth, a swill of foetid water that created the illusion of warmth in our bellies. And that wasn't all. Do you know which were the hardest blows to endure in the camp? They weren't the body blows – the kicks from the *kapos* or the beatings from the guards – but the blows to our self-esteem. We were the stinking, lice-ridden dregs of creation, tying pieces of string around our trouser legs so that the shit wouldn't ooze into our boots. You may wonder what was gained by treating us that way. I've read books – scholarly books – that said that, if we appeared to be subhuman, it made it easier for the Nazis to mistreat us. But, no, it was to make it easier for us to mistreat one another. So that, when the guards told half of us to lie on the ground and the other half to urinate in their mouths, we didn't hesitate. And the worst of it is that we began to believe that Hitler was right. How could we be human beings when it was only by behaving subhumanly that we managed to survive?

But I'm running ahead of myself. I was fourteen when I was arrested and sent to Auschwitz but, to my great good fortune, I looked older. The worst injustice, to my mind, was that I'd never set much store by being Jewish. It was an accident of birth like the colour of my hair or the other physical features that have become clichés. As a child – years before I'd heard the name of Hitler – I hated the fact that we allowed ourselves to become victims: that we were taught never to draw attention to ourselves. We were Jews as wallpaper long before they turned us into Jews as lamp-shades and other household items . . . I'm sorry. I see that

I've offended you. You mustn't forget that Jewish humour is almost as legendary as our business sense.

He laughs.

On arrival in the camp, we were marched straight on to the parade-ground. The commandant asked for the names of any barbers. My father was a barber. And, to my shame, I despised the profession as much as I despised the man. But, in a spirit of malice, I raised my hand. And I was chosen. Whereas my father kept his pressed against his side. And he was gassed.

M.A. Wasn't that an example of altruism? He kept his hand down in order to give you a better chance.

T.B. This wasn't a vacancy for a stylist in a fashionable salon! Have you any idea how many people they were preparing to murder every day? They needed a large team. No, the truth is that we'd had a blazing row on the morning of our arrest (it wasn't all laying *Tefillin*[168] and lighting the Friday night candles). That I should have stolen his trade after they had stolen everything else was the final insult. There again, it may have been the wind. Even at the best of times, he was half-deaf. Shall I carry on?

M.A. Please.

T.B. I was placed in the category of 'economically useful Jews' and I vowed to remain there for the rest of my life. I cut the hair of the men, women and, yes, children, who were destined for the gas chambers. Everything happened so fast. You ask how the Nazis could have done it morally. At the time, all I could think of was how they could do it practically. Hundreds of people were killed in a matter of

[168] Small black leather boxes containing Old Testament passages, strapped to the forehead and left arm and worn by Orthodox Jewish men during morning prayers.

minutes. It should have taken longer. If nothing else, they deserved that. But I couldn't talk about it to any of my comrades because, providing I kept my concerns to myself, there was still the possibility that it was only me who was losing my mind.

I watched them as they undressed. First the men: the rabbis and teachers and doctors whom I'd been taught to look up to all my life. Without their clothes, they were nothing. Just dry bones squeezed into sacks of old parchment. I knew then that there was nothing sacred about the body. And that was the first lesson that I learnt.

Next came the women. And, as they stripped, I felt a stirring in my loins. Some of them were ancient and some scarcely in their teens, but my body didn't discriminate. Suddenly I felt alive. I was no longer weak; I was hard. And that was the second.

We didn't simply cut the women's hair, we shaved them: under the arms and on the pubis. It was the first time I'd realised that women had body hair. The guards dropped by to enjoy the spectacle. While we set to work, they poked the women with sticks as though they were prodding cattle. That's why I was never able to join in the general expression of outrage at sixties fashions. I knew the value of hair.

Once, they brought in a group of girls from my neighbourhood. Abandoning modesty as well as clothes, they ran up and clung to me, naked. They were so relieved to find me alive. My survival offered hope for theirs. And do you want to know the truth? I scorned them. How could they be so stupid as to suppose that they were simply taking a shower? Or so naive as to believe that they would be put to work? There were feeble old women and helpless young children among them. One woman had had her wooden leg unscrewed. What earthly use would she be? But no, even in extremis, people cling to their illusions –

M.A. Such as?

T.B. That God is good. That their enemies will be merciful.

M.A. Did you give them any warning of their fate?

T.B. What for? Most were half-dead already. Why poison their last few moments? Some of my colleagues did try, at the risk of their own lives. They claimed that people had a right to know. Perhaps they thought that it would restore their dignity and turn an abattoir into a scaffold. The truth is that, like all so-called morality, it eased their own consciences, relieving their guilt at remaining alive. For that was the cruellest irony: we knew that our presence in the Special Detail depended on regular transports. The moment they stopped, we too would be liquidated. Darwin lives! And so do I. For eighteen months, I survived in Hell. From what I recall, Jesus Christ stayed a mere three days. And in that time I learnt that, if the first human instinct was survival, the second was sex. Women stopped menstruating; nursing mothers lost their milk; but the seminal fluid still flowed. Two men who were forced to share a bunk chose to share their bodies, clinging together in a frenzy of desperation, desire and shame. Years later I read that, when they introduced a brothel into one of the camps – I don't remember which; it certainly wasn't Auschwitz[169] – first in

---

[169] In 1943, a brothel was set up in Flossenburg on Himmler's instructions. One of his aims was that homosexuals should be cured of their disposition by regular visits. The prostitutes were Jews and gypsies from the women's camp at Ravensbruck. They were told that they would be released from imprisonment at the end of six months but, after servicing an average of 2000 clients during the period, they were sent to Auschwitz and replaced by another contingent of 'volunteers'. See Heinz Heger, *The Men With The Pink Triangle*, Gay Men's Press 1980.

line weren't the relatively well-fed *kapos* and foremen but the *Muselmanner*, the living skeletons who looked as if the unaccustomed spurt of energy would destroy them. The sexual impulse prevailed.

Meanwhile, we were all actors in a vast pornographic fantasy, one that was played out not on a screen but on a flag. Rape was comparatively rare, even though it wasn't considered *Rassenschande* – I don't know the exact translation: race defilement comes close. But then, if you'd been a healthy young Nazi, would you have chosen to have sex with a putrid, hairless, half-starved woman with bones instead of bumps? Some did, of course, risking the wrath of their superiors and feeding their own disgust. But they were few. Most preferred to excite themselves by regular visits to the shower-room. Occasionally, bored guards would force a group of women to strip and parade through the camp, lashing them so hard that the blood ran down their legs in a parody of their monthly cycle.

M.A. Then how can you bear to propagate such images now?

T.B. Because they're the truth. I can't endorse conventional platitudes of love and romance as though I'd spent the War in Switzerland. I can't endow the sexual act with a spiritual meaning that it is quite unable to sustain. My films show men and women as they truly are. Why don't you address your complaints to producers in Hollywood? There, everything is titillation. The penis must at all times remain hidden – as though the nakedness of an erection would expose the sham of everything else. My films are real. My actors aren't faking.

M.A. I don't want to offend you, but in what way *real*? They occupy a world of total predictability where sex takes place in locker-rooms with the same nod to verisimilitude that saw Thirties musicals set backstage. It's a world where every nurse and secretary, every pizza boy and plumber, is instantly available and utterly insatiable. And people take that image away from the screen and into their everyday lives.

T.B.   People have always led inauthentic lives but, in the past, they did so like Madame Bovary in the context of romantic novels. Now it's in the context of hard-core films. Which is progress of a sort.

M.A.   So, if I understand you right, you're saying that it was in Auschwitz that you discovered your vocation?

T.B.   (*With a laugh*) What I thought I was saying was that it was in Auschwitz that I learnt not to need one. But, of course, it wasn't that simple. After the War, I planned to make my way to Palestine.

M.A.   Then there was at least one ideal that didn't die.

T.B.   I prefer the word illusion. Either way, the British put an end to it when they refused me entry. So I came back to this derelict town and rebuilt my life. I didn't have a *pfennig* to my name, so I turned to the most plentiful of natural resources. Fortunately, it was in high demand. We were an occupied country full of men living a long way from home. So what did they want? Girls. Especially girls who did the things that girls at home never do. Girls without boundaries. And I cornered the market. Very soon I was ready to branch out, first into clubs and then into films. My fellow entrepreneurs were happy to let me blaze a trail. As an Auschwitz survivor, I had greater licence. I can sense your disapproval . . .

M.A.   No, not at all.

T.B.   But, whatever you may think, ours is a reputable business. We're not SS guards in the ghetto forcing old men at gunpoint to rape and sodomise young girls while our comrades capture it on film. We maintain regular hours and clean conditions. Angel was the first company in Europe to insist on the use of condoms. We lost sales, but it was the only way to safeguard the actresses – some of the girls from the East are so desperate, they'll do anything for a few hundred marks.

M.A. You see. We're not so different. You also believe in protecting people from themselves.

T.B. No, merely from the effects of their poverty. Besides, it was sound economics. Not only did we gain prestige but we forced all our rivals to follow suit.

M.A. May I ask you about the actress who died?

T.B. What about her?

M.A. That must have dented your confidence, if nothing else.

T.B. We were cleared of all responsibility. At the post-mortem, they discovered that she'd had an undiagnosed heart condition. She could have died at any time. Now, to return to more agreeable matters, did you have a chance to look at our merchandise? Is there anything you'd care to take home as a souvenir?

M.A. Thank you. That's very kind, but no.

T.B. We cater to every taste. If we'd been in business in the Thirties, Hitler would never have had to keep his sexuality a shameful secret with Geli. He could have subscribed to our caviar line.

M.A. In which case, if you believe Meier, there would never have been a Holocaust at all.

T.B. Maybe . . . there again, maybe not. If we're lucky, the antidote to history will be pornography. Did you know that there's a thriving underground market in concentration camp films in Israel?

M.A. No, I can't say that I did.

T.B. Does it shock you?

M.A. Less than it would have done an hour ago.

T.B.   Then your visit hasn't been entirely wasted.

M.A.   Is there anything that you wouldn't put on film?

There is a prolonged silence. Bücher appears to be struggling with himself.

T.B.   Branding. It takes me back further than I want to go.

M.A.   I'm sorry. How crass of me to remind you.

T.B.   No. Spare me your expressions of concern. Even now, you retain the hope that, in spite of everything I've said, I shall conform to type. You want me to wear the number on my arm like a war wound. You want me to burnish it like a medal. But it's you that gives me the number. Your pity keeps me in the camp. Of course it will always be a part of me, like a bullet-hole in a building that has never been repaired. But I've put it behind me. Except with Ilse. Ilse likes my number. She teases it with her fingers and her tongue. She identifies the pain. It excites her. And, together, we can invest it with any meaning that we choose. We take it out of the history books and make it our own.

Now I'm at your disposal. Is there anything else you wish to ask?

Notes on the Contributors

THOMAS BÜCHER was born in Munich in 1928, the son of a barber, a profession which, as he describes in our interview, was to save his life during his internment in Auschwitz. After the war, he opened a chain of night-clubs which led, in the early 1950s, to his move into hard-core pornography. In the mid 1970s, he was perfectly placed to take advantage of the video revolution and, by the end of the decade, his company, Angel Films, had become established as one of Europe's leading names in 'adult entertainment'. In 1992, its survival was threatened by the death of Charlotte Haffmann during the making of *Virgin's Island*. Although Bücher was cleared of any personal responsibility, his standing was severely impaired. The following year, he sold his controlling interest in the company, while remaining Chairman of its Board.

RENATE FISCHER was born in Düsseldorf in 1948. She was a founding member of the Bettlertheater, remaining a close associate of Wolfram Meier throughout his career. She occupied an anomalous position in Meier's stock company. While unquestionably a member of the inner circle, she was never given the opportunities on screen that such intimacy might have brought. As she herself states in her memoir, her most significant role was the Virgin Mary in Meier's radically reordered *Faust*. Even so, she appeared in every one of Meier's twenty-six films, generally in unflattering guise, an object of derision.

Notwithstanding her lack of romance in his films, Fischer came the closest of any woman to playing the love interest in Meier's life when she married him in April 1978. The marriage was unconventional and Fischer has written vividly of the humiliations of the wedding-day. Nevertheless, they maintained their partnership both on and off screen. In the years since Meier's death, Fischer has worked as a cabaret singer, night-club hostess and agony aunt. She is currently the presenter of the ratings-topping *Cooking For One*[170] on German television.

LIESL MARTINS was born in Bremen in 1939. Her father, Gottlieb Martins, was a writer of the *Blut und Boden* (Blood and Soil) school of mystical romances, which achieved great popularity after the First World War and were highly esteemed by the Nazis. She was orphaned by the Allied bombing and brought up by her grandmother in Oldenburg, a few streets away from Ulrike Meinhof, whom she never met. She studied in Frankfurt where she became active in Leftist politics. After a brief marriage to Konrad Schreider, owner of the Red Dawn publishing house, she met Manfred Stückl and Klaus Bernheim, with whom she founded the Bettlertheater, which rapidly became the most celebrated of the city's alternative troupes. She first worked with Wolfram Meier in 1965 and, apart from three years in the mid 1970s when she adopted her children, continued to do so throughout his career, playing leading roles in several of his films, notably *Rosa Luxemburg* and *Margarite*. After Meier's death, she worked sporadically for other directors and as a presenter for the State radio station, *Bayerischer Rundfunk*, before taking on the direc-

---

170   The German title, *Kochen Für Singles*, implies both Cooking For Oneself and Cooking On One's Own.

torship of the Wolfram Meier Foundation. The Foundation is dedicated to the conservation and distribution of Meier's films and to the management of the Meier archive. Liesl Martins regularly travels the world, lecturing on Meier's work and introducing it to new audiences.

CAROLE MEDHURST was born in Rochdale in 1950. On leaving drama school at the age of twenty, she worked at Stratford, with several small-scale touring companies and on the London Fringe. In 1972, she joined the International Workers Party, with whom she later had a very public breach. Although her allegations of brainwashing techniques and sexual harassment were never proved, they did permanent damage to the Party's reputation.

Unity was the occasion for Medhurst's last appearance as an actress. As she has described elsewhere,[171] the experience so unnerved her that, when she returned to England, she quit the profession and worked in a series of menial jobs, among them the stint in the fish and chip shop that was to inspire her first success as a writer. *Assault and Batter* was the BBC's sleeper hit in the winter of 1985, its blend of comedy and suspense proving to be even more popular when it was transposed from Burnley to Baltimore and from a fish and chip shop to a pizza parlour. Medhurst moved to Los Angeles in 1988, declaring later that year to *The Independent* that 'I am now a corporation. I can buy shares in myself.' Her company, Battery Productions, has been responsible for a succession of highly successful series on American TV. It is currently developing several projects for the cinema as well as *Circus on Ice*, billed as 'a new concept in entertainment', scheduled to open in Las Vegas in July 2005.

[171] *Pizzas in Paradise*, pages 162–67.

GERALDINE MORTIMER was born in Berkshire in 1948. At the age of six months, she was taken by her mother to join her father in Hollywood, where she spent her childhood. She kept a diary throughout her life. The first, dating from 1956, came from Walt Disney, the studio for which, by a neat coincidence, she was to make her debut the following year. The entries, a mere two or three lines at first, stretch to several pages by the time that she reaches adolescence and give some hint of the painful experiences to which the adult Geraldine will later allude. After 1971, when she joined the International Workers Party, a long account of which is included in the entries for June of that year, the auto-biographical material becomes increasingly mixed with politics – nowhere more so than in the two months printed above.

As the diligent reader will note, in the entry for 23 October 1977, Geraldine writes that she has instructed her executors to destroy all her diaries on her death. No such document has survived. Indeed, as was widely reported, she died intestate in Poland in 1986. Two years later, Sir Gerald Mortimer's victory in his bitter legal battle with the IWP ensured that the journals (along with the rest of his daughter's estate) passed to him. Given his own death later that year, it is unlikely that he read them. They remained in the possession of Lady Mortimer until her death, when they were bequeathed to the British Film Institute.

MANFRED STÜCKL was born in Wiesbaden in 1941. His father was an SS officer who, after the war, successfully assumed the identity of his wife's brother, until a casual remark about the couple's sleeping arrangements by the eight-year-old Manfred prompted an investigation by a teacher who suspected incest. His father was tried and imprisoned, his mother committed suicide, and Manfred was placed in a series of children's homes. At the age of eighteen, he won a prestigious scholarship from the Study

Foundation of the German People and entered Berlin University. On graduation, he worked as a teacher and took part in the early peace movement before leaving for Munich, where he co-founded the Bettlertheater with Liesl Martins and Klaus Bernheim and gave Wolfram Meier his chance to direct. He played the title role in Meier's first film, *The Ratcatcher*, and Josef in his last, *The Holy Family*. In the intervening years, he acted in many of Meier's most celebrated films, including *The Passion of Albrecht Dürer*, for which he received several international awards. After Meier's death, he directed an autobiographical feature, *The Shuttlecock*. Having failed to secure the film's distribution, he moved to television, where he now heads the development division of *Westdeutscher Rundfunk* in Cologne, which funds the new generation of German directors.

Index

Also available from
THE MAIA PRESS

THE GLORIOUS FLIGHT OF PERDITA TREE
Olivia Fane

Perdita Tree, the bored and beautiful wife of Tory MP Nicholas Hodgekin, believes that all married women, and perhaps all women everywhere, should have a magic door through which they can walk into a different life – 'utterly, utterly different, not necessarily better, just something other'. So when she is kidnapped in Albania, she takes it in the spirit of one huge adventure. Adored by her kidnapper, who believes all things English are perfect, she is persuaded to rescue the Albanians from their dire history, and is vain enough to imagine that she can. Together they ride across the country on horseback, singing Beatles songs and preaching freedom. The year is 1991, democracy is coming, but are the Albanians ready for it? And are they ready for Perdita? With this beguiling novel, Olivia Fane considers the nature of love, longing and betrayal and, above all, the art of being free.

'This book is a delight . . . I loved it. . . . It races along at a rate of knots, leaving the reader smiling, satisfied and impressed'—Fay Weldon

'A captivating book – original, intelligent and very entertaining'—Isabel Wolff

£8.99 ISBN 1 904559 13 1

UNDERWORDS: THE HIDDEN CITY
The Booktrust London Short Story Competition Anthology

London has always been a chameleon figure, revealing itself in a multitude of different guises, each as individual as the dreams and aspirations of its many inhabitants.The theme of this collection is the hidden city, and each of the fourteen stories vividly expresses a different mood and aspect of the capital, and the undercurrents of emotion that surge through it – the irrepressible mixture of excitement or tension, fear or freedom. This is the sixth anthology to result from the biennial London Short Story Competition, and features the six winning stories by previously unpublished writers, together with new work by some of the finest authors London has to offer. **Including Diran Adebayo, Nicola Barker, Romesh Gunesekera, Sarah Hall, Hanif Kureishi, Andrea Levy, Patrick Neate and Alex Wheatle.** *Published in collaboration with Booktrust and Arts Council England*

£9.99 ISBN 1 904559 14 X

OCEANS OF TIME Merete Morken Andersen

A long-divorced couple face a family tragedy in
the white night of a Norwegian summer. Forced
to confront what went wrong in their relationship,
they plumb the depths of sorrow and despair before
emerging with a new understanding. This profound
novel deals with loss and grief, but also,
transformingly, with hope, recovery and love.
Translated from Norwegian by Barbara J. Haveland
LONGLISTED FOR INDEPENDENT FOREIGN FICTION PRIZE 2005
WINNER OF THE NORWEGIAN CRITICS' AWARD 2003

ESSENTIAL KIT Linda Leatherbarrow

In these varied and exquisite short stories, Linda
Leatherbarrow brings together for the first time her
prize-winning short prose with new and previously
unpublished work. A wide-ranging, rich and surprising
gallery of characters includes a nineteen-year-old girl
leaving home, a talking gorilla in the swinging sixties,
a shoe fetishist and a long-distance walker. The prose
is lyrical, witty and uplifting, funny and moving,
always pertinent – proving that the short story is the
perfect literary form for contemporary urban life.

RUNNING HOT Dreda Say Mitchell

Elijah 'Schoolboy' Campbell is heading out of
London's underworld, a world where bling, ringtones
and petty deaths are accessories of life. He's taking a
great offer to leave it all behind and start a new life,
but the problem is he's got no spare cash. He stumbles
across a mobile phone, but it is marked property, and
the Street won't care that he found it by accident.
And the door to redemption is only open for seven
days ... Schoolboy knows that when you're running
hot, all it takes is one phone call or one text message
to disconnect you from this life – permanently. Dreda
Say Mitchell was born into London's Grenadian
community. This is her first novel.

GOOD CLEAN FUN Michael Arditti

'Witheringly funny,
painfully acute'—
Literary Review
'A simply
outstanding
collection'—
City Life, Manchester
£8.99
ISBN 1 904559 08 5

This dazzling first collection of short stories from an award-winning author employs a host of remarkable characters and a range of original voices to take an uncompromising look at love and loss in the twenty-first century. These twelve stories of contentment and confusion, defiance and desire, are marked by wit, compassion and insight. Michael Arditti was born in Cheshire and lives in London. He is the author of three highly acclaimed novels, *The Celibate*, *Pagan and her Parents* and *Easter*.

A BLADE OF GRASS Lewis DeSoto

'A plangent debut
... an extremely
persuasive bit of
storytelling'
—*Daily Mail*
'Outstanding debut
novel' —*The Times*
£8.99
ISBN 1 904559 07 7

Märit Laurens farms with her husband near the border of South Africa. When guerrilla violence and tragedy visit their lives, Märit finds herself in a tug of war between the local Afrikaaners and the black farmworkers. Lyrical and profound, this exciting novel offers a unique perspective on what it means to be black and white in a country where both live and feel entitlement. DeSoto, born in South Africa, emigrated to Canada in the 1960s. This is his first novel.
LONGLISTED FOR THE MAN BOOKER PRIZE 2004
SHORTLISTED FOR THE ONDAATJE PRIZE 2005

PEPSI AND MARIA Adam Zameenzad

'A beautifully
crafted, multi-
faceted book: a
highly dramatic and
gripping thriller and
a searing indictment
of cruelty and
inhumanity'—*New
Internationalist*
£8.99
ISBN 1 904559 06 9

Pepsi is a smart street kid in an unnamed South American country. His mother is dead and his father, a famous politician, has disowned him. He rescues the kidnapped Maria, but they must both escape the sadistic policeman Caddy whose obsession is to kill them – as personal vendetta and also as part of his crusade to rid the city of the 'filth' of street children. In this penetrating insight into the lives of the dispossessed, the author conveys the children's exhilarating zest for life and beauty, which triumphs over the appalling reality of their lives. Adam Zameenzad was born in Pakistan and lives in London. His previous novels have been published to great acclaim in many languages. This is his sixth novel.

UNCUT DIAMONDS
edited by Maggie Hamand

'The ability to pin down a moment or a mindset breathes from these stories ... They're all stunning, full of wonderful characters'—
The Big Issue
£7.99
ISBN 1 904559 03 4

Vibrant, original stories showcasing the huge diversity of new writing talent in contemporary London. They include an incident in a women's prison; a spiritual experience in a motorway service station; a memory of growing up in sixties Britain and a lyrical West Indian love story. Unusual and sometimes challenging, this collection gives voice to previously unpublished writers from a wide diversity of backgrounds whose experiences – critical to an understanding of contemporary life in the UK – often remain hidden from view.

ANOTHER COUNTRY Hélène du Coudray

'The descriptions of the refugee Russians are agonisingly lifelike' —review of 1st edition, *Times Literary Supplement*
£7.99
ISBN 1 904559 04 2

Ship's officer Charles Wilson arrives in Malta in the early 1920s, leaving his wife and children behind in London. He falls for a Russian émigrée governess, the beautiful Maria Ivanovna, and the passionate intensity of his feelings propels him into a course of action that promises to end in disaster. This prize-winning novel, first published in 1928, was written by an Oxford undergraduate, Hélène Héroys, who was born in Kiev in 1906. She went on to write a biography of Metternich, and three further novels.

THE THOUSAND-PETALLED DAISY
Norman Thomas

'This novel, both rhapsody and lament, is superb'—
Independent on Sunday
£7.99
ISBN 1 904559 05 0

Injured in a riot while travelling in India, 17-year-old Michael Flower is given shelter in a white house on an island. There, accompanied by his alter ego (his glove-puppet Mickey-Mack), he meets Om Prakash and his family, a tribe of holy monkeys, the beautiful Lila and a mysterious holy woman. Jealousy and violence, a death and a funeral, the delights of first love and the beauty of the landscape are woven into a narrative infused with a distinctive, offbeat humour. Norman Thomas was born in Wales in 1926. His first novel was published in 1963. He lives in Auroville, South India.

ON BECOMING A FAIRY GODMOTHER
Sara Maitland

'Funny, surreal tales
. . . magic and
mystery'—*Guardian*
'These tales
insistently fill the
vison'—*Times
Literary Supplement*
£7.99
ISBN 1 904559 00 X

Fifteen 'fairy stories' breathe new life into old
legends and bring the magic of myth back into
modern women's lives. What became of Helen of
Troy, of Guinevere and Maid Marion? And what
happens to today's mature woman when her children
have fled the nest? Here is an encounter with a
mermaid, an erotic adventure with a mysterious
stranger, the story of a woman who learns to fly
and another who transforms herself into a fairy
godmother.

IN DENIAL Anne Redmon

'This is intelligent
writing worthy of
a large audience'—
The Times
'Intricate, thoughtful'
—*Times Literary
Supplement*
£7.99
ISBN 1 904559 01 8

In a London prison a serial offender, Gerry Hythe,
is gloating over the death of his one-time prison
visitor Harriet Washington. He thinks he is in prison
once again because of her. Anne Redmon weaves
evidence from the past and present of Gerry's life
into a chilling mystery. A novel of great intelligence
and subtlety, *In Denial* explores themes which are
usually written about in black and white, but here
are dealt with in all their true complexity.

LEAVING IMPRINTS Henrietta Seredy

'This mesmerising,
poignant novel
creates an intense
atmosphere'—
Publishing News
'Compelling ... full
of powerful events
and emotions'—
Oxford Times
£7.99
ISBN 1 904559 02 6

'At night when I can't sleep I imagine myself
on the island.' But Jessica is alone in a flat by a
park. She doesn't want to be there – she doesn't
have anywhere else to go. As the story moves
between present and past, gradually Jessica reveals
the truth behind the compelling relationship that
has dominated her life. 'With restrained lyricism,
Leaving Imprints explores a destructive, passionate
relationship between two damaged people.
Its quiet intensity does indeed leave imprints.
I shall not forget this novel'—Sue Gee, author
of *The Hours of the Night*